THE
TAKEOVER

JACKIE LADBURY

Love is in the Air Book 3

Previously published as *The Magic of Stars*

Choc Lit

A JOFFE BOOKS COMPANY

Revised edition 2024
Choc Lit
A Joffe Books company
www.choc-lit.com

First published in Great Britain
as *The Magic of Stars* in 2018

Cover art by Jarmila Takač

ISBN: 978-1781897720

CHAPTER ONE

'What exactly are you doing in Florence, darling?' Emerald Montrose's boyfriend, Rick, asked as he pulled open the door to his hotel room, blinking in shock. 'Erm, at my hotel in particular?' he added, looking pained — and horrified, it had to be said. There was no sign of the lustful glee she'd anticipated. No excitement. *Nope, he's not even quietly pleased*, she thought, peering at the face she had missed so much, taking in the generous smile and the cute freckles that dotted his nose. She hoped his reaction was no more than his terribly British restraint kicking in, but the signs weren't promising.

Lowering the proffered bottle of champagne, Emerald's ready smile drooped. 'Surprise!' The voice that came out was a deflated squeak, not the sexy timbre she'd practised earlier. 'Mr Clarke was using the aircraft to come over for a business deal, so I offered to be the hostie to . . . surprise you,' she said, finishing lamely, as Rick clearly did not like surprises — or at least not the surprise of herself and her bottle, which she couldn't seem to stop waving around.

He gripped the fluffy towel around his waist, pulling it tight, which led Emerald's line of sight down to a giveaway bulge.

She peered closer, then balked. A low-grade light-bulb moment glowed in her mind. Why did he have an erection?

'Problem, honey?' a sultry, very female voice drawled from the depths of the bedroom.

Ah. The light bulb blazed bright.

She peered around the door that Rick, too late, tried to close. The towel protrusion was a bit of a clue, but the blonde in his bed, watching their exchange through smoky eyes while sipping from an elegant crystal flute, was enough to convince her that she'd been pipped to the post in the bedroom department. Her gaze fixed on the woman's huge breasts jiggling with a life of their own as she propped herself, languorously, up on one elbow.

Emerald snapped her eyes shut, wishing she could un-see the image now engraved on her brain.

'If it's the maid, just tell her to come back later.' The voice dripped honey — never had a simple command sounded so sexy.

Rick shot Emerald the rueful smile she knew so well as he ran a hand around his neck, his expression almost willing her to be the maid to save any inconvenience.

She should have slugged him there and then, but shock held her rigid and her inherent good manners saved the bottle of champagne from being cracked over his head. Instead, she smoothed down her silk dress repetitively as if the action would somehow erase this distasteful Florentine farce that she found herself party to.

Helpless, she implored the meltingly sincere brown eyes that had once held so much loyalty and love, willing him to tell her it was all a dreadful mistake. But, sadly, the half-naked Goldilocks in Rick's bed wasn't a figment of her imagination and Emerald didn't think she'd turned up for the porridge.

How quickly her rosy world, spinning on its axis of hopeful new beginnings, could spin off-kilter to crash and burn. She looked down forlornly at the silky dress she'd zipped herself into not half an hour ago stowing her airline uniform in her overnight bag. The emerald-green dress her boyfriend Rick had professed to adore looked more acid yellow in the bright lights of the corridor and she wondered why on earth she'd thought it suited her complexion. 'I wore this especially for you.'

Rick's brow creased in confusion. 'Sorry?'

'The colour highlighted the green of my eyes?' she hinted, surprised that he appeared to have forgotten that the dress was his favourite.

'Did I say that?' His bewildered eyes met hers, peering closely as if looking for the said green flecks.

'Yes, you did.' Her voice was flat. She'd already accepted that, once again, happiness had been denied her. Even worse, she'd made a total fool of herself.

They stared wordlessly at each other until Rick broke the silence. 'Well, as you can see . . . ?' He nodded toward the woman in his bed, before pulling the door closer to block her out. 'I'm so sorry,' he hissed, out of earshot.

'No worries. I'm really busy anyway — I just popped by to say hello.' Emerald backed away while uttering the pathetic words that they both knew were lies. 'Oh, and I bought you this, but it looks like you already have some.' She waved the champagne bottle in the air as she retreated. 'So I might as well keep it. Bye then,' she added as she swivelled on her heels.

'Yeah, call me,' Rick whispered, putting his thumb and forefinger to his ear, mimicking a phone.

She might have left then like the good little girl he expected her to be, if he hadn't said *those* words — the final insult. It was simply too much. She swung back around to face him.

'*Call* you? Are you for goddamn real?' She clenched her fist and took a step backwards, raising her arm, gearing up to thump him one. Or two. Or *hell yeah*, three. It would feel so good even if she regretted it later.

But Rick slammed the door quickly, before she'd even taken aim, possibly seeing the fire in the green eyes he'd professed to love so much, or maybe he just couldn't wait to return to those huge boobs, so clearly up for grabs.

'Two-timing tosser!' she shouted, fighting back the urge to throw the champagne bottle at the door. It had cost a fortune in the duty-free shop and, quite frankly, Rick's hotel door wasn't worth the waste.

The bellboy who had taken her up in the lift poked his head into the corridor and Emerald was forced to contain her anger, her nostrils flaring as she bit back more obscenities. She picked up her overnight bag and sashayed back to the lift, acting as if she hadn't just made a complete arse of herself.

She smiled sweetly at the bellboy.

The bellboy smirked. 'Great alliteration, I thought.'

'Sorry? Oh, I just had to remind my boyfriend of something.'

'What, that he was a two-timing tosser?' His Italian accent made the words sound comical and she grinned in spite of her anger. 'Yeah, better make that my ex-boyfriend,' she said, dismally, her face falling.

'Should've got a punch in too — it would have made you feel a lot better,' he added, raising his fists and jabbing at the air.

'I was going to surprise him,' she said, waving the champagne bottle.

'I think you can safely say you managed that,' the bellboy confirmed.

Emerald managed a weak smile as the hotel lift juddered and moaned its way to reception, taking her far away from the low-life, rotten, two-timing scumbag that was her ex-boyfriend.

By the time she hit the pavement her bravado was as tattered as her dreams, the embarrassing scenario of being turned away from Rick's room as if she were an inconvenience scorched painfully on her mind.

The cacophony of noise in the street was unbelievable: Vespas, buses, cars all honking their horns and screeching to a halt or swerving to dodge tourists, dogs and other cars. It made her dizzy and disorientated but eventually she flagged down a taxi by practically throwing herself at it and climbed in, swiping at her eyes and sniffing loudly. The driver looked anxiously in his mirror, probably more worried about his upholstery than her state of mind.

'Take me to a hotel, please. Any hotel.'

His foot hit the floor and he accelerated, pinning her back in her seat before braking sharply and propelling her forward again. She held on protectively to the champagne, like it was some sort of talisman that proved her worth.

After some rapid gear changes and lots of honking he said in heavily accented English, 'You just left a hotel.' He waved his right hand behind him, in the general direction of the De Medici hotel.

'I know — just take me to a *different* hotel . . . Any one, just not that one.' Any hotel that didn't have Rick and Goldilocks in it would do. 'Here, this one!' she cried and the car skidded to a halt. She jumped out of the taxi and handed the driver twenty euros with a quick '*Grazie*'. She then strode into the forbidding looking building — all Gothic windows and unlikely pillars — having no clue where she was or what she was doing.

But inside it was light and airy, with classical cool white Carrara marble fitted from top to bottom. Emerald nodded her approval as she took in statues of nudes against the walls and water-nymphs playing in small fountains that sent water rippling over real plants and well-positioned Grecian urns.

Suddenly, as the reality of her pilot boyfriend's complete betrayal hit her, she thought she might be sick. The cloakroom was well signposted and she rushed into a cubicle, tears threatening. To think that only an hour ago she'd believed her future was laid out before her like a yellow brick road to happiness — that the trip to Florence was fate telling her to take her relationship with Rick that one step further.

Rick — *the arrogant bastard*, she thought savagely — had spent the last month telling her how much he'd missed her while he was stationed in Florence for the summer season. He wrote her long messages and called her on FaceTime, mostly at inappropriate times, it had to be said, but she'd felt treasured and wanted, not for one second imagining the scenario she'd just experienced, playing out as it had. How she regretted her impulsiveness now.

But at least she'd discovered Rick was a rat *before* she'd slept with him. She wondered if he'd meant any of the declarations of love he'd spouted. He probably just wanted to get her into bed, she acknowledged — and he would have achieved his aim if it wasn't for the fact that someone else was already occupying it. The irony of it would have made her laugh if she hadn't been so busy mopping up the tears sliding down her cheeks.

She put her hand to her chest, her heart actually ached, as if someone was trying to twist it tight, but even as it hurt, she knew she would cope, as she had coped with all of the other knock-backs in her life. She was used to disappointment — even expected it. She would swallow this setback and bounce back, just as she always did.

She left the cubicle and splashed cold water on her face, gave her reflection a good talking to, and slicked red lipstick over her lips with determination. Straightening her shoulders, she left the cloakroom, competent as ever at hiding her emotions as she headed for the reception desk. It was then that she realised she was in one of the most upmarket hotels in Florence, well beyond her means.

Emerald gazed at the huge, twinkling chandelier refracting colours across the floor and walls, the serenity and cool opulence of the interior serving to remind guests that they had chosen the best hotel in town. A low babble of rapid Italian gave a vibrancy and charisma to the whole scene and Emerald had to remind herself to stop gaping.

A chic woman glided across the marble floor, studiously ignoring anyone who looked her way, and Emerald wished she could emulate her assured style. She knew the elegance and confidence came from money as much as beauty — the woman's handbag was probably worth more than Emerald's monthly salary.

The woman drifted out of view and Emerald tuned in once more to her own sorry situation. Lacking the energy or interest to go anywhere else, she knew she just needed to wait it out in this hotel until she accompanied Mr Clarke back to England.

'Just one night, *per favore*,' she said with resignation, kissing her credit card before handing it over, knowing the company finance department wouldn't approve the hotel of her choice. She gave a wry smile to the receptionist, who smiled back in sympathy as she passed her a plastic key card — an unfair exchange, Emerald reflected, but she thanked her anyway — and screwed up the receipt with resignation.

She sighed, wondering how she would fill her time now that Goldilocks with Boobs, in all her naked glory, had spoiled her plans and stolen her boyfriend. In all honesty, the woman probably hadn't had to try too hard. Rick's quiet, boy-next-door friendliness belied the ruthlessness of the man who had chatted Emerald up remorselessly, making her believe she was the only woman he had ever wanted. And she'd believed him. *Got that a bit wrong then, didn't I?* she told herself.

But she pushed away her pain. She determined he would be no more than an annoying blip before too long, but right now the betrayal hurt a great deal and she needed to obliterate it.

A sign above her head attracted her like a siren, luring her to her downfall. She'd found her answer and it was going to be in the bottom of a glass — specifically, a glass in the *Crepuscolo* bar. She squared her shoulders. Right, I'm going to that bar to have a drink, and then I'm going to have another drink. A little voice in her head reminded her that, according to the nuns in the convent school where she had spent most of her formative years, it was immoral to drink alcohol. But it was a very small voice and before it had even cleared its throat Emerald had swept through the archway into the *Crepuscolo* bar.

CHAPTER TWO

'*Un vino bianco per favore*,' she requested, squinting at the bar menu. She'd never heard of most of the drinks on there, but as an afterthought added, '*E una grappa*.' She had never tried grappa but it sounded a bit like gripe and she certainly had a few of those, so she figured now was as good a time as any to give it a go.

The bartender placed a glass of white wine in front of her and, with a small frown, added a delicate tulip-shaped glass. He filled it with a clear liquid and she smiled her thanks, cradling them both in her hands possessively. She didn't intend to share — though the odds of her having to were slight.

Lifting the glass of grappa to eye level, she inspected it carefully. It was a very small drink and it didn't smell particularly exciting, but it was icy cold, which was interesting. She inhaled and lifted the drink to her lips. It was now or never. The fumes coming off it were enough to make her giddy and she wished she could hold her nose as she downed it. She threw back her head and swallowed. An involuntary shiver ran through her as she set the glass on the bar with a bit more of a slam than she intended.

The barman watched with interest as he polished glasses with a tea towel. Emerald gave him a look, daring him to comment, as she moved on to the wine, lifting the glass upwards like a chalice before bringing it to her lips and taking a big gulp. It was sour as hell and she grimaced as the taste buds on her tongue shrivelled in complaint. The grappa was just about the better of two evils but only because it was so cold she could hardly taste it. It crossed her mind that if Sister Mary Bennett from the convent had allowed her to taste the chalice wine, she would have sworn off it of her own accord rather than being pressed to take the pledge.

But needs must, she thought, as she ordered another grappa and downed it in one again, thinking that there should be a more pleasant way of obliterating her foolish notions of a future with Rick.

'Give me another one. Make it a double. No, two doubles.' Her hand wobbled slightly as she raised two fingers to the bartender. If she was going to go have a pity party she might as well make it a memorable one.

'Are you a guest here?' the barman asked, sizing her up as he pushed a small bowl towards her and motioned for her to eat. She nodded and peered into the bowl. The hard, brown squares looked like miniature dog biscuits and, uninterested, she slid her eyes away.

He swapped the bowl for one full of plump green olives, little plastic swords piercing their hearts. She knew how that felt and shook her head, muttering, 'Poor olives.'

The bartender half-heartedly pushed a menu towards her — it was obvious she was not here for food.

'*No, grazie.*' She gave him a small smile to let him know she appreciated the gesture — liquid food was all she needed. She took stock of her surroundings, thankful that the lights were dim and no one cared about a solitary female sitting at the bar, knocking back drinks faster than an alcoholic on death row. The lights flickered dimly around the room and a surreal glow filtered downwards from the ceiling. The bar had a domed glass ceiling Emerald hadn't noticed earlier and she tilted her head upwards to get a better view.

'Lady! Hold on there!'

9

The ceiling suddenly spun and then she felt strong arms wrap around her.

'Sorry — sorry!' She pulled away from the man who held her in a steely embrace as she wobbled precariously on her stool. 'I was fascinated by the gorgeous glow from the skylight . . .' She trailed off as charcoal-grey eyes, stern and judgemental, fixed on hers.

'You didn't know this bar is famous for its stained-glass ceiling, did you? The Mapping of the Heavens — all of the constellations are there.' He cut across her mumbling, his voice clipped and precise. His English was faultless, with just a hint of an accent. 'This is the *Crepuscolo* bar — which means twilight, the beginning of night, when the stars come out.'

'Yes, of course I knew that. I came here to appreciate the constellations and, err, log them in my book — my stargazing log, ship, book thingy.' She wrinkled her nose. Was she confusing stargazing with *Star Trek*?

'Right. No other reason?' he asked, adopting a tight non-smile. He looked her up and down, his gaze focusing on her high heels and the silk dress that revealed more cleavage than she would normally show in public. She bristled at his frank stare. Okay, so she *had* dressed to seduce. She didn't know she'd be sitting in solitary splendour, in a bar, paying the price of a small island for foul drinks. 'I came for a drink, too. I assume that is allowed in a bar?'

'As long as you don't intend to drink that.' He nodded towards the champagne bottle she had thoughtlessly placed on the bar. 'This is not a bring-your-own kind of hotel.'

His gaze somehow managed to make her feel cheap. Why was he asking her such brash questions?

'You are a guest at this hotel?'

'Yes, although I don't know what it has to do with you.'

The man looked over at the bartender, who nodded imperceptibly and said something in rapid Italian.

'Your name is, Miss . . . ?'

'Montrose. Emerald Montrose.' She felt her face heat up. Why did this feel like an interrogation? She was in one of the best hotels in Florence and didn't expect to be treated in such a way. His gaze settled on the rounded top of her breasts again and the penny dropped. 'What? You think I'm a prostitute?'

'Not at all.' The tight smile said otherwise.

The bartender spoke again and the dark-haired man nodded, satisfied.

'I apologise. Allow me to introduce myself. I am Marco Cavarelli, the owner of this hotel.'

'Hello, Marco Cavarelli.' Emerald drawled out his name and saluted him, almost toppling off her stool once more.

Mr Cavarelli put out a hand to steady her again. 'We don't normally see beautiful young women on their own at our bar in this most romantic of cities, that is all. I hope you enjoy your drink. Ah — more than one drink.' He nodded towards the empty glasses lined up in front of her. '*Drinks* then. I hope they help you, Miss Montrose, with your problems, but in my experience alcohol tends to make things worse.'

She peered into her glass, squinting slightly. 'I heard that the answer is always at the bottom of the glass. So, I'm looking for it.'

'Do you know what the question is?'

'Heck, no.' She giggled. 'Am I supposed to?'

The — very handsome, she noted — man's smile loosened slightly, but Emerald picked up on his underlying disapproval. She angled her head away from him, wanting to be left alone to continue on her path of self-destruction. But when she peered sideways he was still there. He looked so stern that she gave another nervous giggle.

He raised his forbidding eyebrows, once more.

'Sorry. You reminded me of my old headmistress for a moment. She's a nun. A really scary nun.'

Mr Cavarelli rested his arm on the bar, looking intrigued. 'I don't think I've been compared to a nun before.'

'Yeah, she had a big black habit and a huge hooked nose.' Emerald pulled on her own nose. 'Ow.' She grimaced as she rubbed her nose.

Her new friend looked amused. 'Tell me more. What was her big bad habit?'

Emerald thought this was one of the funniest things she had ever heard and she snorted with laughter. 'Sorry.' She put her hand up to her face to cover the embarrassing sound. 'That's hilarious, though.'

The hotel owner quirked an eyebrow, unmoved by the hilarity of his question.

She composed her face. 'Not a *bad* habit, a *black* habit.'

'Right.' He still looked uncertain.

'Long flowy thing, black and scary.' She ran her hands down her dress for emphasis. 'And she was always giving me detention for dumb reasons.'

'Dumb reasons?' Mr Cavarelli's forehead creased as he turned enquiring eyes her way.

'Yeah, like bringing an injured rabbit to the dormitory or feeding my dinner to the baby foxes. I mean, she's a *nun* — she's supposed to care about God's creatures. Sorry, I'm going on a bit, aren't I?' She hiccupped and gulped. 'Sorry. I really should stop saying sorry, shouldn't I? Sorry. Damn it!'

She detected a twitch at the corner of the man's mouth and giggled again. Tilting her head to scrutinise him, she came to a decision and hoped she wouldn't sound like the desperate woman she was, as she asked in as steady a voice as she could muster, 'Let me buy you a drink?'

'Novel idea.' He gave her another tight smile, but pulled up a bar stool and sat down next to her. 'Are you always this forthright?' He raised a hand to the bartender, who danced attendance immediately. 'Allow me to buy the drinks, Miss Montrose, and maybe you could try something to eat.' He pushed the bowl of olives into the pathway of lined-up drinks.

'That would be very acceptable, thank you.' Her voice was thick to her ears and she pondered how she could be feeling drunk quite so quickly. She picked up an olive by its plastic dagger and it immediately fell off and landed next to her glass, leaving a slimy trail of olive oil in its wake. She chased it around the bar top trying to spear it until it toppled over the edge onto the floor. Looking down at the floor forlornly, she lamented, 'They're buggers to catch, aren't they?' She abandoned her search for the escaped olive when she heard a rumble of laughter from the man whose name she had already forgotten. Pulling herself upright to examine his face, she wondered fleetingly why he had four eyes roaming around his eye sockets. She closed her own eyes and snapped them open again. Yes, her drinking partner was definitely an alien fly. She closed her eyes again and a horrible feeling of nausea washed over her.

Open. The alien fly was peering at her. She widened her eyes to keep them open. *Focus on alien fly and hold that position*, she thought.

The many-eyed fly ordered drinks in smooth Italian, nodding his gratitude to the bartender, who edged a tall glass of ice and a bottle of sparkling water towards her. Her new friend appeared to be amused by her and she didn't know why. Her eyes hurt from trying to keep them open and she blinked rapidly in quick succession. The blinking brought the handsome man back into focus. She was so relieved that the fly had disappeared.

The man nudged the water closer to her elbow and she scowled, pushing it away in disgust. He simply shrugged and picked up his beer, chinking it against Emerald's glass of ice. '*Per osservare le stelle.* Sorry — I mean, here's to your stargazing.'

'My what? Oh, yes, stellar! Thank you, Captain Kirk.' She was struggling to keep up with the conversation and realised that she'd already achieved what she'd set out to do and was now indeed very drunk. She poured water into her glass and drank deeply, concentrating on the man again, sad to see that the fly was back — although, to be fair, its eyes were strikingly dark and fringed by thick lashes. But four of them were just a few too many.

She breathed in deeply, focused very carefully, and slowly her normal vision returned, along with enough sense to know that she shouldn't order any more drinks.

Her companion took a sip of his beer. 'You know, it's very nice to meet you, but I can't help thinking you would be better off in your room. The hotel prides itself on their comfortable bedding.'

Wow — he's a fast mover, she thought, as she gazed into his brooding eyes. She did a quick once over of the man: tall with a mop of dark silky hair, expensive-looking suit, good olive-coloured skin and enviable white teeth. Decision made, she threw back the last of her wine and coughed as it caught in her throat and dribbled down her chin. Wiping her mouth with the back of her hand, she said, 'Now that's an interesting proposition.' She ran the tip of her tongue over her lips and tried to make her eyes smoky, like the blonde in her boyfriend's bed. Sadly, it just sent her vision out of focus once more. She put out a tentative finger and traced it down the man's tie, looping her thumb under it before yanking hard to draw him closer to her irresistible pouting lips. Or was it the woman in her boyfriend's bed who had those lips — not stupid Emerald, with her boring, un-kissable, devoid-of-shiny-pink-lip-gloss lips, and with absolutely no pulling power whatsoever?

The man grabbed her fingers and loosened her hold on him, setting her back on the stool. 'Not a good trick, if you don't mind me saying so.'

'Whoops, sorry. It was supposed to be an enticement, not a garrotting.' She swayed with laughter and almost toppled off her stool again, the effort of staying upright suddenly difficult.

'Lady, it really is time you left my bar.'

'I'm going, Captain — and my name is Emerald.' She saluted him again as she climbed off her stool, fumbling for her bag. As she stood up she caught her heel in the foot rest and felt herself falling. She clutched at the bar top, her nails scraping as her stomach swooped with alarm—

Marco Cavarelli was by her side in a second, his hand under her elbow, helping her to stay upright.

She winced as she righted herself, the room spinning on a different axis to her own. 'Ooh, I didn't think you could get drunk this quickly.'

'You can if you try as hard as you did.' He grabbed her arm as she teetered unsteadily on her heels.

'I really don't drink, you see.'

'Your impression of a teetotaller is way off kilter, if you don't mind me stating the obvious.' He gripped her arm to pull her up and steady her. 'Take a couple of painkillers with a glass of water before you go to bed — it makes all the difference,' he instructed, his lips a tight line of disapproval.

The barman slid the bill over. 'Just to keep the books straight, *Signore*.'

'Of course, no problem.' He let go of Emerald and turned away from her to sign the chitty.

Emerald shook her head. 'Are you leaving?' She couldn't bear to see him go. It was so important that he stayed, that he understood she really, really didn't want to be as drunk as she clearly was. 'No, don't go!' She dashed a tear away as it rolled down her cheek, only for it to be replaced by another one.

Her rescuer sighed. 'I don't need another maiden in distress, you know.' He ran a hand over his face, puffing out his cheeks. He appeared resigned as he looked at her.

'*Si, Signor Cavarelli*, she is trouble.' The bartender waggled his head, weighing up the dilemma. He turned to Emerald with a sigh, pointing at his boss and enunciating clearly. 'He look after you.'

Emerald was confused by the exchange, but her brain cells were firing sufficiently to know she would never find her room unaided. She grabbed the bottle of champagne from the bar counter and waved it at the barman. 'I don't drink, you see.'

'Had me fooled, that's for sure,' the barman said, winking at her.

CHAPTER THREE

'Right, let's do this.' Emerald's reluctant escort grabbed her arm to stop her from toppling over and threw the strap of her bag over his shoulder.

She caught an edge of exasperation in the man's voice and said, 'You don't have to take me to my room — I'll be fine.'

He sighed. 'What is your number?' He sounded weary and slightly pissed off.

'My phone number?' she asked in surprise.

'Your *room* number.' His voice had hardened and she bridled.

'Well *I* didn't know what number you wanted. You don't have to talk to me like I'm an idiot.' She shucked her arm out of his grasp.

'Then stop acting like one.' He gripped her arm again firmly and propelled her out of the bar, his voice low and intimidating. She widened her eyes with what she hoped was a grateful, but seductive look, ignoring the warning tone. She guessed it didn't have the desired effect as his grip on her arm remained pincer tight and his eyes flashed anger.

'Room number?' he demanded again as she stumbled along the corridor, bouncing off the walls.

'Twenty-three,' she said cheerfully. 'I quite like your Neanderthal approach to this,' she added, before tripping up the stairs — which necessitated another arm-grabbing rescue manoeuvre.

'I mean to put you to bed.' He shook his head as she tried to arch an eyebrow at his words, failing badly. He let out a long, impatient sigh and closed his eyes. '*Dammi la forza.* Give me strength.'

Emerald smiled at him reassuringly as they wound their way up the staircase. 'It will be fine, don't worry,' she soothed.

'I wish I had as much faith in your capabilities as you appear to have.' His eyes flashed darkly and she closed her mouth, biting back the quip she was about to make.

She was dragged past portraits of ancient dignitaries looking down their distinguished noses as she tottered in her heels, while her temporary minder cursed in a mixture of English and Italian under his breath as he held on to his charge with a death grip.

When she stumbled once more, he pushed her up against the wall. In her drunken state, she thought he was going to kiss her. She'd seen it in enough movies — that's what they did, push you up against the wall and pin your hands above your head. But he bent down and lifted up her right foot, taking off one spiky shoe and then, as she obediently lifted her left foot, the other one. The lights in the corridor created highlights in his thick black hair as he bowed down in front of her and, without thinking, she stooped down and ran her fingers through it. Her saviour's head whipped up, his eyes once again flashing anger. 'For God's sake, what do you think I am — some kind of gigolo?'

'Well, you thought I was a prostitute.'

His look told her that he was still undecided on that one, and she grabbed her shoes out of his hand and flounced along the corridor. 'I'll take care of these. They are Manolo Blahniks, if you don't mind.'

'If you say so.' He caught up with her easily as she crashed into a marble statue, sending it wobbling precariously.

Grabbing the statue, he held it steady as Emerald righted herself once more.

'Whoops, sorry!' she said to the statue and then laughed, pointing at it. 'Look, it's made of stone and I said sorry to it.'

'So you did.' The man was clearly unimpressed with her wit and Emerald was disappointed. She thought they were having a splendid time.

'I thought it was funny,' she said petulantly as he propped her up against the wall once more. He fed money into a vending machine tucked in an alcove and two bottles of water plopped into the tray. He stuffed one in each pocket and grabbed hold of her again as if she were a rag doll, pulling her along like this until they reached her room. 'Here we are. Give me your key card.'

'Ooh, I like a masterful man.' Emerald fumbled in her bag for her key card.

'So you said.' He grabbed the card out of her hand and slid it into the lock, pushing the door open with his foot. He pulled her into the room and for a heartbeat she stared at him as sobriety momentarily returned. She was acutely aware that they were alone in a darkened room dominated by a huge bed. She stumbled over to the window to open the curtains, yanking at them unsuccessfully before giving up.

Mr Cavarelli set down a bottle of water on each bedside table, frowning at her antics.

She turned away from the window and looked pointedly at the water bottles. 'Taking it all a bit for granted, aren't you?'

'Both bottles are for you. If you wake in the night, you will find water close to you.' He walked over to the window, pressed a button, and the curtains slid away from the windows. 'This is how they work. I'll shut them again, if you wish.'

'Ooh, that's clever,' she said, immediately pressing the button with a grin. The curtains slid over the window once more, shutting out the one source of light, and a rush of fear gripped her. *What the hell was she doing?* She didn't even know this man. 'You're not staying.' She folded her arms over her chest decisively.

'It had not even crossed my mind.'

'Oh.' She felt a bit foolish, but a wave of nausea stopped her thoughts and she sat down heavily on the bed, focusing on her gurgling stomach and spinning head. 'Sorry. I'm so drunk. Won't do it again.' She waggled her finger in the air. 'But it wasn't my fault — it was that stupid Goldilocks and her giant, heaving tits.' She cupped her hands over her own breasts and jiggled them around a bit to ram home the point. It was important he understood that it was all the ginormous-breasted woman's fault. But even as she spoke, she lost the battle to stay upright and sank sideways onto the bed.

CHAPTER FOUR

Marco Cavarelli had no idea what this young woman was talking about, but he heard the wobble in her voice and, when she started touching her breasts, knew it was time to leave. He didn't need to hear her life story. He had enough problems of his own. He moved decisively away from her.

'Don't you want to stay a while?' the woman asked petulantly.

'No.' He really hadn't the energy to argue with a hotel guest and had an important appointment in an hour. He should have let her fall off her chair on her own. But he wouldn't do that to a woman — especially one with such an air of vulnerability about her that made her appear fragile and lost, in spite of the contrary evidence. Or maybe he was just too much of a gentleman and should have known better than to try to rescue a damsel in distress.

'Listen, I don't care in the least if you want to drink yourself silly, but I do have an interest in this hotel and its reputation.' He headed for the door, eager to leave this woman who didn't seem to mind picking up strange men, and who ought to know better than to get drunk in a strange city. But he hesitated, his hand hovering over the doorknob. No, he couldn't leave until he knew she would be safe. He picked up one of the bottles, unscrewed the top, and thrust it under her nose. 'Drink,' he commanded.

She snatched the bottle from him and sipped it, before banging it back on the bedside table defiantly. 'I'm not a child, you know.'

His eyebrows lifted, saying it all, as he towered over her. He was wary of sitting down — didn't want this young woman, beautiful as she was, to misunderstand his motives.

The woman suddenly deflated. 'I don't know how to deal with this. Don't *you* want to sleep with me either?' She grabbed his hand, tears glittering in her eyes. Her dress had shifted around slightly, showing more of her breasts than was decent, and her nipples pushed proudly against the thin silk. His gaze was drawn to them and a glimmer of heat shafted through his groin, surprising him. An ache of desire, which had been missing for quite some time, now coursed through his blood like a shot of adrenaline and he tamped it down, horrified that his body should betray his morals. But, seconds later, the young woman in front of him sniffed like a child, and he plucked a tissue from the box on the bedside table and waved it in front of her, his vaguely lustful thoughts instantly disappearing.

She took it from him, but simply scrunched it up in a ball and swiped at her eyes. 'Thanks.'

He looked down at her dispassionately: the delicacy of her bone structure, her thick hair the colour of maple leaves just turning in the sunshine, her long slim legs, her full lips, trembling with emotion. As he took it all in, he felt another kick of desire. She was enchanting to look at — but also very drunk and defenceless, and he should not even have entered her room.

'I'll have breakfast sent up to you tomorrow morning — somehow I don't think you will feel like making an appearance in the breakfast room. But be assured, if the church bells do not wake you by seven, the street cleaners will.'

As he took a step forward, unsure whether to shake her hand or pat her on the head, she grabbed his jacket lapels and kissed him full on the lips. He tried to pull away, but she deepened the kiss, holding on tight, and suddenly he wanted to kiss her back. A moan escaped her lips and his earlier unwanted surge of attraction leapt into overdrive. He wrapped his arms around her shoulders, enjoying her sweet, soft lips, urgent against his.

Winding her leg around his, she drew him closer still. The movement was enough to catapult him back to reality. What on earth was he playing at? He loosened his grip and set her away from him, drawing his hand roughly across his mouth.

'A beautiful young woman should not behave like this with a stranger. Get some sleep. I'll wait until you are in bed.'

'I'm sorry — I don't know what I was thinking,' she stuttered. 'It's just that I was supposed to do this with my boyfriend for the first time, but he was doing it with someone else — probably not for the first time, to be honest.' Her eyes filled with tears and she swiped at them with the back of her hand. 'I really thought he was ready for a proper relationship. I am so dumb.' She ran her hand over her brow. 'I feel sick.' She shrugged off her dress in one fluid motion and threw it to the floor, turning to face the handsome man. She stood in front of him wearing only white lacy pants and bra, and a confused expression. 'What was your name again and what did I just confess to you?'

'Marco, and you said nothing that I will remember in the morning, you can be assured of that.' She really was a sad case, he decided, settling his mouth into its forbidding line once more as he resolutely tried not to look at her curves.

She unhooked her bra and Marco turned away as a flash of pale breasts, upturned pink nipples and tempting cleavage, assailed him. Emerald dropped onto the bed and crawled under the duvet, murmuring, 'Please ignore whatever I said, my mind is so fuzzy. I just need to sleep.' She closed her eyes, but immediately opened them again, directing her gaze at Marco. 'Did we talk about the stars tonight?'

'Briefly.' Marco wanted to touch her hair, wild as a lion's mane as it fanned over the pillow. Her eyes were trusting, almost pleading and he fought the urge to sit on the edge of her bed and hold her hand, or read her a story — or something — until she was asleep.

'I don't think they're real Blahniks, by the way — the shoes. I bought them on eBay for thirty pounds.' She shook her head sorrowfully, burrowing into the pillow.

'Thank you for clearing that up,' Marco said solemnly. 'I *was* concerned about their authenticity.'

But the young woman already sounded half asleep and he would be glad to leave before the urge to join her became overwhelming — to rest his head for a while on a soft pillow and let the heat of a woman's body warm him, to sleep the innocent sleep of an untroubled mind.

She smiled, a secret smile, and blinked groggily. It was a smile to melt the hardest heart. 'You said I was beautiful.' Her eyes closed and he watched as the pull of sleep and alcohol quickly overtook her. It made him sad to see how vulnerable she looked in sleep. World-weary, he leaned over and kissed her goodnight on her forehead and pulled the door shut behind him.

CHAPTER FIVE

Marco immediately headed for reception where he booked an eight o'clock breakfast delivery for the young lady in number twenty-three. He checked her credentials while he was at it. It seemed that she was indeed a legitimate tourist — although if she was a local hooker, she would have been a pretty bad one. He smiled at her gaucheness and naivety. He'd been played by the very best in the business — women trying to seduce him, all after a rich husband — she was not even close to their league.

A sharp pain cut through his reverie as he thought of his soon-to-be-ex-wife, the only woman he had ever loved. Instead of loving him in return she had almost broken him, emotionally and physically. He'd known her since he was a teenager and had believed that she loved him for who he was, not what he'd achieved. His mouth twisted wryly. How wrong could he have been? *Ah, Simona, why did you do such a thing?* He shook his head to banish the memories of her treachery. No more. He needed to concentrate on the prospective business partner he'd be meeting any minute now in the bar.

A tall, elderly man entered the reception, wandered over to the lounge and hovered uncertainly around the bar area. His cut-glass English accent was clear and strong as he asked for a malt whisky and the whereabouts of Mr Cavarelli. He smoothed down his hair, which stuck out at odd angles, making Marco think he'd just got out of bed. His attire made him look more like a hobo than a man in possession of an airline — the brown, tweed jacket, with patches at the elbows, hanging off his shoulders and clashing with the baggy, green tartan trousers. He looked like a weathered scarecrow that had escaped from a field, Marco thought, watching as the man patted his pockets and pulled out a handful of crumpled euros and a pipe. Marco half expected him to be clutching straw. The man gazed regretfully at the pipe, slid it back into his pocket, and dumped the wad of notes on the bar.

Marco straightened his tie as he headed towards the man, his hand outstretched, clearing his mind of all thoughts of beautiful young women and passionate kisses. 'Ah, Mr Clarke, I trust your journey was uneventful?' He shook the Englishman's hand and led him smoothly to the best table, which had been reserved earlier.

'Yes, it was perfectly fine. We flew over from the UK on my little de Havilland 125, but sadly I dozed off and missed most of the flight. Lovely little aircraft, the de Havilland.' He looked up expectantly, his eyes shining. 'Are you an aircraft enthusiast?'

'No, sir, I'm afraid I am not.'

'Ah.' The momentary light went out of his eyes and Marco was saddened that he couldn't entertain the elderly gentleman with Biggles-like shenanigans of loop-the-loops and dive bombs.

'I have taken the liberty of ordering a good Italian wine,' he said, hoping it might be a small compensation for his lack of flying derring-do. The vintage Barolo had been opened an hour ago to breathe and he hoped his guest would appreciate the gesture. He was going to win this deal at any cost and intended to present his proposals with the aplomb of an accomplished lover.

Marco had always been good at evaluating people, pressing the right buttons and wooing with flattery and encouragement, and his fleeting character assessment of Mr Clarke already gave him a gut feeling that the takeover was a done deal — but he was a fair man and wouldn't take advantage.

They talked pleasantries, which turned into business, until the subject was concluded to their mutual satisfaction. Marco confirmed, 'So, if we shake hands on this deal, you will be happy for me to be a majority shareholder.' It wasn't a question, just an assurance that Mr Clarke knew exactly where he stood.

'Mr Cavarelli, I need to take a back seat because of my wife's health and, as you can see, I'm not the young buck I once was.' He looked down at his body and chuckled wheezily. 'My wife and I wish to spend more time in our country home with our grandchildren. It is with a heavy heart that I am offloading my small airline, but I'm aware that owning a private airline is no longer a viable option for me, although I am hoping to keep my little de Havilland, which has a special place in my heart.' He sighed and his eyes went misty.

Marco made a note to ensure that particular aircraft stayed with Mr Clarke when the deal was done.

'You have the business acumen and finance to keep us afloat,' Mr Clarke continued. 'My airline brings with it an excellent team of staff and I would hate to let them down.'

Marco nodded. While relieved that Mr Clarke was being so affable, he had expected nothing less — the Cavarelli name was usually enough to seal a deal with little more than a gentleman's handshake. He didn't like to tell the benign Mr Clarke that, more than anything, he simply wanted access to the flight slots to enable his new venture to run smoothly. Mr Clarke's other beloved aircraft would be sold, and newer, more efficient ones purchased. He stood up. The deal was as good as done.

'Thank you for your confidence in me, Mr Clarke. I am sure that, with my backing, Hot Air Aviation will become profitable sooner rather than later.' Marco winced as he repeated the name of the airline. Who in God's name would call an airline Hot Air Aviation? 'You do understand, though, there will be changes that not everyone will appreciate — but I have a very hands-on approach, so you can be assured that I will be fully engaged with every aspect of the airline.'

'Of course. We will work together to make it a better business. I am aware that time and money are needed and I no longer have either of those things.' His smile was rueful as he stood up, patting his pockets once again. 'As an aside, my nephew works at Hot Air Aviation. Indeed, it was he who came up with the name of the airline and the catchphrase. Great fun, I thought. I'd hate to see him sidelined in any way.'

'And the catchphrase is?' Marco repeated faintly, already dreading the reply.

'We go all the way.' Mr Clarke's smile was uncertain, as if he was unsure himself of the meaning behind the words.

'Very . . . ah, creative. So, I shall get my solicitor to start on the paperwork immediately.' His smile was stiff. He was aware that Mr Clarke had just slipped in a caveat that his nephew wasn't to be messed with. He didn't like being told what to do — but one nephew would be easy to handle, he was sure.

He shook Mr Clarke's hand as he led him to a waiting car. 'One of my drivers will see you safely to your hotel.'

Marco waited until the car had disappeared from view before sighing in relief. Giving the man good wine was one thing but he was glad he wasn't staying at his hotel when he would be obliged to entertain him on a grand scale. He was too tired for that. He glanced up at the rooms he now called home on the top floor of the hotel. He was loath to return to the silent emptiness, and an image of the drunken woman flickered briefly across his thoughts. Sighing that such a sweet young woman had allowed herself to get into that condition. He swallowed down the memory of the sensations she'd aroused in him. The urge to check on her surfaced, but he pushed that away too. She was none of his business.

He took the private stairs to his suite of rooms, feeling jaded as he unlocked the door. The sense of homecoming tinged with the loneliness of his single status hit him, along with the familiar smell of lavender polish, mingled with Chanel perfume that still lingered and reminded him so much of his wife. He could not think of her as his ex-wife yet, but soon he would have to face up to the fact that she wasn't coming back to him. He could — he *would* — force himself to bear the agony of her betrayal and the physical hurt of missing her so badly.

He prowled around the sitting room, running his hand over the burnished wood of his bureau and absent-mindedly picking up one of his mother's Royal Copenhagen figurines, which made him smile at her sentimentality. He hefted the weight of a crystal tumbler in his hand as he peered inside the antique decanter containing his father's favourite whisky. It reminded him of carefree days when family get-togethers were easy to engineer. Simona was always there to share a private joke, letting him know she was there for him with a gentle touch to his arm or a special smile. His mother, too, was never far away in the winter months, the waft of a delicious focaccia greeting him after his day's work was done, the smell of fresh bread and rosemary seeming to follow her around.

He placed the crystal tumbler back on the table — unlike the lady he'd escorted to her room, he didn't think that the answer was at the bottom of a glass.

Shaking his head to clear his morose thoughts, he headed for the bathroom. He threw his tie and jacket onto a chair with relief, closely followed by the rest of his clothes. He turned the shower on to the pummel setting and stood under it for as long as he could bear, his shoulders and back tingling under the hot needles of water.

Refreshed, he headed for the balcony, tightening the belt of his dressing gown to keep out the chill night air. Still restless, his thoughts turned, once again, to the young woman now presumably sleeping off the effects of too much alcohol. He didn't even know why she was so drunk. She had been wronged — that much was obvious — but was it enough of a reason to be so wasted? Maybe she was an alcoholic? He fought down the urge to send a bellboy to check on her and sighed. No, everyone has a story to tell — he'd found that out in his years of dealing with customers. But it didn't mean he had to listen to them all, or act on them.

He determined to put her out of his mind and focus on his new business venture . . . But she was so damn defenceless — and what if she vomited in her sleep? No. Enough. He wouldn't let her get under his skin. He changed his mind about having a drink and poured out a large whisky, savouring it with pleasure, enjoying the burn in his throat. He took another large gulp as if trying to drown out the image of the woman's slight frame quivering with nerves — or desire — or whatever the hell it was. Her eyes, huge and confused as she fought back tears, seared in to his mind and it seemed that the whisky burn wasn't enough to eradicate the image branded there.

CHAPTER SIX

'Passengers in ten minutes and there's a pre-board following behind me.' George, the despatch guy dealing with the flight, heaved himself up the ramp and clambered onto the ancient Boeing 737 bringing with him a flurry of paperwork and a lingering waft of body odour. 'Alpha Charlie has just landed so I'll have to be really quick as there's a wheelchair passenger and two unaccompanied minors to deal with. Plus, Stephanie's gone off sick again so we're one man down — woman down, in her case. Sorry, being sexist.' He pushed his glasses back onto his nose as moisture beaded his upper lip and a trickle of sweat slid past his ear.

Emerald, in her lightweight summer uniform, felt for him. The day had warmed up, but the overweight man was still wearing the thickly padded high-visibility jacket he'd put on when the dawn sky was clear and chill.

'Here's your passenger list and your catering form for the return trip.' He wiped his brow and passed Emerald a handful of scrunched-up papers.

'Calm down, George. You can't be expected to do two people's work. Here, let me get you some water.' She reached into the bar and passed him a chilled bottle of water.

'Thanks, you're a darling.' He took a large swig of the water and exhaled gratefully. 'Are you ready then? For your passengers?'

'Wait just a sec.' She turned to find her hat and then did a double take as she remembered that their new uniform didn't have one. 'Sod it, I love this new uniform, but I keep looking for my hat. It's like trying to scratch an itch on an amputated arm when I know the bloody thing isn't there.' She turned back around and straightened up, to be met by a pair of forbidding dark eyes.

'Trying to find what bloody thing, exactly?'

'Oh, I thought you were George . . .' She trailed off as she stared at the man, a terrible, nauseating memory dredging up from the depths like bile from her stomach. It hit her and she gasped.

'Do I look like George?' the man asked, narrowing his eyes.

'No . . . no you don't,' she stammered, gazing past him to see George deep in conversation with another passenger.

The warm olive skin, thick wavy hair and the angle of the man's jaw had no resemblance to George whatsoever. A faint scent of aftershave took her back and her hand flew to her mouth. 'It's you, isn't it?'

The man looked her up and down appraisingly. 'And I see now who you are.' His gaze moved up to her face, his smile lazy as he met her eyes. 'The uniform suits you.'

Emerald breathed in. 'Welcome on board.' Her hands clenched into fists behind her back and she could feel the creep of embarrassment staining her cheeks pink.

The man's smile snapped back into a thin line. He held up a half-empty bottle of water. 'Dispose of this, will you?'

Immediately riled by his tone of voice, she snatched it from him. 'Of course, but we don't normally dispose of other people's rubbish.' She knew her voice was tart and she really tried not to sound too sharp, but honestly, some people.

Though he wasn't just some people, was he? He was the stranger who had haunted her dreams for months, causing a mixture of shame and desire to course through her body in the moments before she fell asleep each night.

She took the plastic bottle from his outstretched hand gingerly, determined not to touch his fingers.

'It was left in the doorway. Very shoddy, if I may say so.' He clicked his tongue in disapproval.

'Oh, sorry.' *George, for goodness' sake*, she thought. But then she couldn't blame him — he was always so busy and in a rush. The man was right, though, rubbish by the aircraft entrance looked very slapdash. 'Do take your seat, I'll be with you in a minute.' She tried to stay calm in the presence of this man who had become so dreamlike in her mind that she had almost convinced herself that their encounter was a figment of her imagination.

'Wow, who's the looker?' Finbar, the steward whispered behind his hand, rolling his eyes towards the passenger. He straightened the headrest covers and checked the seat pockets making his way slowly through the aircraft, his eyes focused on the newcomer.

'I don't know his name. George disappeared before I found out why he was pre-boarded.'

'He looks familiar. I wonder if he's famous. Be great, wouldn't it? Haven't had anyone famous since that boy band — who sadly weren't famous when we ferried them up north.' Finbar sighed and Emerald knew he would forever regret not having his picture taken with the lead singer, who was so cute that even she'd fallen a bit in love with him. She dragged her gaze away from the man, who had settled himself into a seat.

'I'll find the manifest and see who he is,' Finbar added, before disappearing to the rear of the aircraft where the paperwork was stashed.

Emerald's cheeks burned as the memory of the night she'd tried to forget flooded back in all its humiliating glory. She still had no idea who the man was, but she remembered meeting him in the extortionately priced hotel in Florence . . . She wished she didn't. Her hands trembled as she poured champagne, the bottle clinking against the crystal glass as she set it down on a tray and placed a Godiva chocolate next to it. She wondered how she was going to deal with him for the next three hours. Really, what were the odds of coming face to face with the man who had seen her at her absolute worst? She dreamed about him but now he was standing in front of her she wished him a million miles away.

Her recollection of that night was hazy at best: a man in her room and a lingering scent of spice and expensive aftershave. A trance-like memory of a sexy encounter, of kissing him and asking him to stay. Or had she begged him? She groaned. She wasn't even sure what they'd done together, but, oh, what must he think of her?

The man was perched on the edge of a seat on row one and she slunk over to him, quiet as a mouse, praying he wouldn't speak to her. She placed the drink and chocolate on the tray table next to him. 'This is for you,' she said, and turned to quickly walk away.

'Excuse me.' His voice was commanding and it stopped her in her tracks.

Her heart sank as she was obliged to face him. She was mute, waiting.

'What is this — and why?'

She blinked. 'What do you mean?'

'Is it usual to give champagne and chocolates to passengers?'

'Yes, sir. If you are boarded before the rest of the passengers — it's just something we do.' She wasn't exactly sure why they served champagne to pre-boards, but Finbar, in his usual extravagant way, had convinced Mr Clarke that it was worth the extra expense. 'Erm, it's part of the service as pre-boards are usually premium.' Emerald and the man stared at each other, Emerald feeling like a rabbit caught in the headlights of those dark pools that were his eyes.

'And you make it your business to acquaint yourself with all of your passengers, yes?' The eyes hardened further and she felt the stirring of unease grow. Was he referring to their time in Florence? No, he couldn't be. She was so confused. But she had faced the eyes of people with far more than disapproval in them, and she would not be thrown by something as simple as his rude interrogation.

'Yes, we always know who our passengers are, sir, when they are sitting in their correct seat, but looking at the passenger manifest you are — let me see.' She picked up the passenger list from the galley worktop and scanned it. 'Yes, here we are. You are apparently a seventy-one-year-old diabetic named Mrs Caruthers.' She couldn't resist the triumph in her voice, mingled with relief that she had redeemed herself.

The man who clearly was not Mrs Caruthers, glanced at her briefly his eyebrows beetling into a frown. 'You asked me to take a seat and I did as you asked. I don't have an allocated seat as I'll be sitting on the jump seat in the flight deck, as soon as you inform the captain that I have arrived. I do not imagine Mrs Caruthers will thank you for champagne and chocolate either, if she is diabetic, so I suggest you remove them immediately.' He stood up and passed her the untouched tray dismissively. She took it automatically, knowing he was being unfair but unable to articulate it.

'Captain Fraser, please? When you have a minute,' he demanded.

Anger rose inside her at his dismissive attitude. She put up her hand and blocked his way. 'Sir, you can't just pop into the flight deck — there are laws in place. You could be a terrorist or a madman.'

'Do I look like a terrorist?' His eyes levelled with hers, unnerving her further.

'Terrorists don't walk around with a hand grenade in each pocket toting an AK-47 you know,' she said tartly, redemption within touching distance, once again.

'But I am not just anyone, am I?' His smile faded. 'And I suggest you keep your voice down unless you want to show yourself up in front of your crew.'

'Excuse me.' Her voice was loaded with indignation. 'You don't need to worry about my crew or my airline.'

'Oh, I think you'll find I do.' He looked over her shoulder. 'And if your ground guy had been doing his job properly, you would not have offered me an alcoholic drink either, knowing that I would be sitting in the flight deck. At least, I hope you would not — but remembering your propensity for alcohol, maybe it's as normal as supplying coffee. Now, please tell Steven Fraser that Marco Cavarelli would like to join him.'

Emerald was desperate to refuse. He was so arrogant she wanted to assert her own authority, but he knew the captain by name and her inner antenna told her not to make a fuss. 'One moment.' She smiled, ignoring the anger in his eyes and the tightness of his lips as she headed towards the flight deck and entered the key code to open the door.

Her confidence slipped slightly as Captain Fraser assured her that Mr Cavarelli was welcome to join them as soon as he was ready. She wanted to ask why he was flying with them, but the pilots were busy with their pre-flight checks so she simply returned to Mr Cavarelli, saying, 'Captain Fraser said to go on in. Do you think you can find your way?'

'I don't think it will be too difficult. There are usually only two ends on a plane to choose from and most people know that the pilots sit at the pointy end.' He smiled thinly. 'Oh, and thanks for your . . .' He frowned, as if trying to grasp the right word, putting his fingers to his brow. 'Assistance?'

Finbar, watching this unlikely war of words elbowed her discreetly out of the way to stand in front of Marco Cavarelli. 'I'll introduce you to the flight deck — I don't suppose you'll have met them before?'

'Thank you, most kind.'

'I'll have to give you the demonstration card so you can flick through the emergency procedures.' He thrust the demonstration card into Mr Cavarelli's hand and drew his attention to the top line, written in bold red letters. 'Our tagline. "We go all the way." That was my idea.' He beamed. 'Isn't it brilliant?'

'Most innovative.' The thin smile was back in place. *So he was the nephew*, he thought, noticing that the steward's tie was done up like a cravat and it looked as if pink lip gloss adorned his lips. He breathed in the overwhelming aroma of aftershave — or was it perfume?

Emerald noted the slight flare of Mr Cavarelli's nostrils and the frown creasing his forehead as she sidestepped into a row of empty seats to let them both pass. An irrational jealousy flared up as she watched them, noting the broad shoulders inside Mr Cavarelli's unmistakably expensive jacket. She felt momentary relief as he disappeared through the flight deck door, but had a feeling that their spat was just the start of something bad. He was on her flight for a reason, and she needed to know why.

She turned to greet the rest of the passengers who were now beginning to board the aircraft. 'Good morning, madam, how are you today?' She exchanged pleasantries, hefted bags into overhead lockers and checked boarding cards, her practised movements on automatic. But her mind was elsewhere, fixed on the man in the flight deck, her gaze flickering towards the closed door more times than was necessary. Who the hell was he, this man confidently issuing orders and interfering in her domain? The stirrings of unease gathered into a knot of worry as fragments of conversation that she'd dismissed as gossip caught in her memory. Was the airline being taken over, or worse, closing down? There was something going on and it meant trouble . . .

Finbar rushed back down the aisle in a state of high excitement. 'Come into the galley, Emms, quick — you have *so* got to hear this.' He grabbed her arm. 'I've found out who he is. He's not on the passenger list because he's on the crew manifest. You will *not* believe it.'

Emerald's stomach flipped. 'He's a crew member? Since when?'

'He's not a crew member, as such.' He paused and drew in a big, important breath. 'He's Marco Cavarelli.'

'So I believe. What of it?' She closed her eyes as the elusive name came back to haunt her, imprinted on her mind in red neon lights.

'Don't you know anything? Mr Gorgeous himself, whose reputation goes before him — has pages devoted to him on the internet and is in all of the glossies. He's barely twenty-eight and has millions of pounds in the bank, billions, maybe. I don't know but he is *minted*. Got a wife somewhere too, I think, or is it an ex-wife? Not sure, but still the dish of the day.' He drew in a breath. 'And he's our new boss.' He clapped his hands like a seal, grinning with delight.

Emerald felt a rush of nausea and leant on the bulkhead of the aircraft as her legs gave way. 'We have a new boss?'

'I *told* you that getting a new uniform meant something. Airlines always get a new uniform when they're about to go bust or be taken over. Don't ask me why.'

'They do?' The nausea got worse. 'And the new boss is . . . ?' She jerked her thumb towards the flight deck.

'Yes, isn't it wonderful?'

'No, Fin, it's really not. Please, tell me this isn't true.'

'It is true. I can't believe it!'

Emerald let out a ragged breath. 'Fin, you don't know what this means to me.'

'Really? I didn't think you were the starstruck type. You never recognize anyone — even when they're splashed on the front cover of *Hello!* magazine. You're the only person I know who is likely to ask Madonna for her surname.'

'It's not that at all! I had no idea he was famous.' She tried to fight the panic that constricted her throat, making her words inaudible.

'Emms, love, are you gonna chuck up on me? You've gone white as a sheet.' Finbar pulled one of the catering boxes out of its stowage and ran his hand over the top to clear the dust. 'Sit down.' He pushed her gently onto the metal box and pressed a bottle of water into her hand. 'What is it? Tell me.'

She took a sip of the water and said, shakily, 'You know what I told you about getting drunk on that stopover in Florence, when you were off in some pink bar and I checked into that ludicrously expensive hotel, 'cos I'd told crewing I didn't need a hotel room?'

'Yeah. You were surprising Rick with an impromptu visit, but the surprise was on you in the form of old jiggly breasts and it took you a month's salary to pay off one night that you don't even remember, cos unless you wanted to indulge in a threesome, there was no room in daddy bear's bed.' Finbar rolled his eyes. 'I met a terribly sweet guy that night, I remember, who—'

'Yes, okay, we don't need to go through that.' She was not overly keen to listen to Finbar's shenanigans in graphic detail, yet again. 'That guy—' she inclined her head towards the flight deck —'is the mystery man who put me to bed.'

It was Finbar's turn to pale as her words sank in. 'You are *not* telling me that you offered your virginal little self to one of the most sought-after men in the world. That's hilarious.'

She glared at his hands as he lifted them, glee written all over his face. 'Don't you dare clap.'

He froze and tensed, the agony of not being able to cheer with excitement clearly tormenting him. 'He could sleep with any one of the people in *Hello!* magazine and you thought he might choose you?' he hissed, his eyes wild and round with astonishment.

'Fin! Stop it. I didn't — don't — know who the hell he is and I was really drunk because of Rick. Take this seriously.'

'Take it seriously?' He lowered his tone, aware that the passengers on the front rows might hear. 'I am, sweetie. It's just so . . . well, it is bloody perfect, when you think about it. You never drink, and you've only ever had one *almost* boy-friend — a crappy pilot, even when I *told* you to steer away from pilots, and then you throw a double whammy in one go and don't even know who it was you pulled.'

'I didn't pull him, Fin.'

'But you tried, right?'

Emerald nodded miserably. 'I think so. I can't really remember.' She chewed her fingernail and closed her eyes in despair. 'Oh, God, what have I done?' She'd put everything she could remember about that awful night into a little box in her head marked, *do not disturb, under any freakin' circumstances*, and now it was all going to come tumbling out, with more than just bad memories attached to it. It could have serious repercussions on her career, and — oh God, she was going to have to see the bloody man again and again.

She bit her lip. Should she say something to clear the air or should she brazen it out? They hadn't got off to a promising start today, and she was *never* rude to passengers — but he was so full of himself. What had got into her? She massaged her forehead, trying to think clearly.

She couldn't think about it now. Her passengers needed her. She pulled her mind back to the present and tried as hard as she could to forget about the problem of Marco Cavarelli as she attended to drinks, meals, duty-free goods and fretful children.

The intercom from the flight deck beeped and she picked up the handset, cursing — she'd forgotten their drinks. 'Sorry, be with you in a minute.'

'Mr Cavarelli will have a black coffee, please, no sugar.'

'Yes, of course.' She slammed down the receiver. 'Of course he'd have black bloody coffee. Mr Macho Man himself, no namby-pamby milk or sugar for him,' she muttered, grabbing porcelain mugs out of the stowage area. She fixed the drinks, put them on a tray and tried to catch Finbar's eye, signalling that she needed him to take the drinks into the flight deck. She sure as hell wasn't going anywhere near it, as long as Marco Cavarelli was ensconced in there. But Finbar shook his head, eyes twinkling as he smirked. *He damn well knew*, she thought, as she grabbed the tray and punched in the code to get into the flight deck. Forgetting how cramped it was when the jump seat was occupied, she almost banged straight into Marco Cavarelli as she opened the door. 'Oops, sorry. Would you mind passing these over?'

'No problem,' her new boss said, breaking into a far sunnier smile than she had been granted earlier.

She caught her breath as she glanced at him. Bright sunlight flooded the flight deck, accentuating his smooth skin and full lips, and although his dark eyes were covered by sunglasses, his cheekbones and jawline were sharpened in profile. He was laughing at something the captain had said through the headphones, and looked like a completely different person from the owner of the judgmental face that he had presented to her earlier.

She steeled herself to be professional, lifting a mug off the tray and saying, 'This is the first officer's.' Mr Cavarelli dutifully passed it over to the man sitting to the right of him, before turning back to take the other mug out of Emerald's hand. Their fingers brushed and she almost dropped the mug as her hand jolted at his touch. She felt her face flame as he looked up at her, his expression impenetrable through the dark shades of his sunglasses. She prayed he hadn't noticed.

To ensure there wasn't a repeat performance, she offered him the tray so he could take his own drink from it.

'Thank you, Miss Montrose,' he said.

Trying not to inhale his unmistakable lemon-scented aftershave, which brought back hazy unwanted memories, she smiled wanly and hurriedly shut the flight deck door.

He remembered her name? She didn't want him to remember her name. It filled her with trepidation and she hated herself for the sensations that engulfed her at his touch. She wished she'd never set eyes on him.

But she managed to forget about him as the flight progressed and they prepared to wind the service down, the aircraft slowing and descending into London Stansted Airport. 'I'll do the bar, Fin, if you can do the landing PA, and check the seat belts and lockers, okay?'

'No problem, just shout if you need a hand.' Finbar picked up the PA system as Emerald began checking the bar sales, soon engrossed in tallying up the figures. She knelt on the floor and pulled out the miniature drawers to count the bottles. A whisky miniature was half empty and she unscrewed it, puzzled, wondering if it had evaporated or if someone actually had drunk out of it. She sniffed it. Does whisky go off once it's opened?

'Back with your best friend? You know drinking on duty is a sackable offence?'

She looked up to see granite eyes, flecked with iron, scrutinising her, and her heart stuttered with an emotion she didn't recognise. She scrambled off her knees and faced him. How could she have forgotten he was on board — his presence was huge? He seemed to fill the galley with his aura. 'Oh no, I don't drink.'

He laughed coldly and glared at her with such obvious disdain, it almost brought her back to her knees. He shook his head, his lips twisting. 'She lies too.'

'I do *not* lie.' She thrust her chin upwards. 'How dare you!'

'I dare because I am now your boss and the truth is staring me in the face.' The forbidding eyes pierced hers as he waited for an answer, his lips compressed into a thin line.

Emerald glared at him and drew herself up, squaring her shoulders in defiance of his words. 'Well since you're the boss you'd obviously know, wouldn't you?'

His gaze didn't waver. 'I hear that you are cabin services manager here, so we shall be working together over the next few months. I'll make an appointment to talk to you about what went wrong today.' He pursed his lips and she half expected the steepled fingers to return.

She didn't like the sound of his words. 'An appointment?' She retained eye contact. She would not be bowed. 'Mr Cavarelli, I work incredibly hard to keep standards and morale high. I love my job and I resent the implication that I'm somehow lacking.' She pressed her lips together to stop more words from spilling out.

He raised an eyebrow. 'Maybe your standards are not as high as mine. We will see, Emerald Montrose.'

She was silenced by the soft, intimidating way he said her name, and hated herself for noticing his long eyelashes and darkly stubbled jawline, when she should be taking in his hard and hostile words.

He made to return to the flight deck, but paused and turned back to face her. 'In fact, Miss Montrose, there is no time like the present. Your shift will be finished, I take it, when we land. I'll meet you at the staff restaurant since I do not yet have an office. We can talk about the future of the airline, and your place in it.'

'But it's nine o'clock at night.'

'Something happens to you after nine?' he asked, the sardonic smile back on his lips.

'No,' she stammered. How did he manage to make her feel silly so easily?

'There are no children or a husband waiting for you to come home, I hope?'

There it was again, a veiled reference to the night she wanted to forget. He would never allow her to forget it — of that she was sure. She tore her gaze away from him as he narrowed his eyes. 'No,' she said, seeing that he was waiting for an answer.

'I can, of course, ask my secretary to make an official appointment if you would rather our little chat is put on the record.' He tilted his head, waiting, and she tried to suppress the anger in her eyes, before he spoke again. '*Si*. We will have coffee.'

She wavered for a brief second. A little chat with him was the last thing she wanted. But she nodded, yes, she would be there — she had no choice. For someone who was so good-looking, he really was a most disagreeable man.

CHAPTER SEVEN

Emerald hovered by the door to the café, unsure whether she should go in or wait outside. Her stomach churned with nerves while she tried to look laid back and poised, to appear an easy match for her new boss. She had learnt to paste on a credible veneer of confidence and to use body language to her best advantage, at the convent school where she spent her hated teenage years, quickly finding out that the spiteful ones targeted any weakness. And, right now, this man made her feel like she was back in her dormitory surrounded by beady-eyed girls waiting to find the chink in her armour, while she wanted only to retreat to the safety of the garden with her sketchbook and solitude.

She pushed the door open, then changed her mind and hovered for a moment, indecisive, in the entrance, before finally taking a seat by the window so she could at least watch the aeroplanes glide by. She hoped that if she ordered, and drank a coffee quickly, he would speed up the infuriating meeting when he found her tapping her fingers on the table, waiting to go home.

She tried to attract the attention of the waitress, who was chatting by the counter, but her gaze swept past Emerald as if she didn't exist and Emerald couldn't be bothered to try harder — she didn't want a coffee anyway. She stared out of the window as she waited, a mixture of worry and the unexpected twinge of excitement churning up her stomach.

The roar of air brakes from a large Russian Antonov blocked out all thoughts as it screeched to a halt outside, smoke pouring from its tyres. She marvelled that such a huge beast could stay in the sky. *The smoke from the burning rubber would be an interesting challenge to draw*, she thought, and reached into her bag for her sketchpad.

'Miss Montrose.' The voice was deep and authoritative, the foreign accent more pronounced. Her new boss had caught her unawares again, and the telltale heat of awkwardness suffused her cheeks as she stuffed the sketchbook back in her bag, guiltily. *Not now, please*. She prayed for her body not to give her away by blushing. She tried an old trick she'd learnt and focused on someone else, zoning in on a huge, muscle-bound engineer in baggy overalls, his blond hair mowed flat on the top like a lawn. He was eating a bagel at the table next to hers and chatting animatedly, despite his mouth being full of food. She stared at his face as hard as she could, watching tiny morsels of food spurt from his mouth as he spoke.

Such a tactic usually enabled her to block out her own emotions and stop the blushing that had dogged her teens — and which appeared to have returned with a vengeance since Marco Cavarelli had re-entered her life.

'You know him?' he asked, his gaze following hers.

'Him? Oh, no, I just . . .'

Mr Cavarelli shrugged, clicked his tongue, and sat down opposite Emerald. His mobile phone buzzed in his pocket and he pulled it out and glanced at it before shoving it back in his pocket, frowning.

She had the feeling that she'd done something wrong again. Maybe he thought she fancied the huge engineer she'd been staring at. She was dragged away from her thoughts as the far more handsome — and dangerous — man lifted out a file from his briefcase and dropped it on the table with a thud.

He rifled through the thick folder and pulled out another folder and with a jolt, she recognised her own name written on the front. 'You have a file on me?' She focused on the buff-coloured folder, wincing as she saw her middle name, written large as life in black marker pen. Wilhelmina, greatly ridiculed by the girls at the convent, had been a curse all her life and she wondered how this man had found it out — she certainly hadn't disclosed it to the airline when she joined.

He opened the folder and rifled through some bits of paper.

This is so much more than a casual chat, she thought, as she wiped her sweating palms down her thighs and edged forward on her seat.

'Okay, so Miss Montrose, this is strictly off the record, but I would like to talk to you about your role in Hot Air Aviation.' He flinched as he uttered the name of her airline and she had to stifle a giggle. Finbar had dreamt it up two years ago when they'd worked with a franchise specialising in adventure holidays. He'd said it was inspirational and showed they had a sense of fun. She still couldn't believe that Mr Clarke, Finbar's uncle, had fallen for it — but at least it made the passengers smile whenever it was uttered.

She managed to remain composed and nodded, widening her eyes slightly to show she was listening to him.

'It's no secret that the airline needs a massive overhaul of its old aircraft and an injection of cash, and I am hoping that with a new budget and the hard work and cooperation of the staff, we will be able to turn this around into a successful first-class airline.'

Emerald nodded enthusiastically, relieved that Mr Cavarelli wasn't singling her out because of their shaky start.

'For example, champagne and chocolates before take-off is fine for an airline with a huge budget, but for one like . . .' He faltered, obviously having trouble uttering the name of his newly acquired airline. 'For Hot Air Aviation it is doubly ridiculous, since I am led to believe that the champagne is taxed — is that correct?'

'Yes, we're only allowed to open the duty-free bar after take-off.' She'd queried it herself, but Finbar normally had the last word and sometimes his flamboyancy and generosity got the better of him.

'And the ground guy leaving the water bottle behind. I am assuming you have filed a report on him?'

'George? No way. He was really busy. They're often understaffed — it really wasn't his fault.'

'Then if it wasn't *his* fault, it was *your* fault.' The eyes grew steelier, if that were possible.

'Oh.' Emerald had no answer to that one. She would have to take the flack as she certainly wasn't going to report George, who was under enough pressure as it was.

Marco Cavarelli's jaw tightened and he clicked a ball-point pen open and closed repeatedly, drawing Emerald's gaze to his hands. The skin was tanned, with a dusting of dark hair by his knuckles, the nails short and well-groomed at the end of long, finely shaped fingers. *They would make an interesting study in charcoal*, she thought idly.

'Are you listening to me, Miss Montrose?'

'Sorry. Yes.' Her head snapped up as she focused on his face, once again.

He continued. 'I was saying that the security on that flight was lax — you should have asked me for identification before allowing me into the flight deck.'

'Yes, sorry.' Emerald nodded dumbly. She was done with arguing her case, and what could he do about it — sack her?

'These are the sort of problems that need addressing, Miss Montrose, but for now I need to focus on you.'

His words set her heart hammering. 'Focus on me?' She prayed that he wouldn't mention the night they'd met — surely he wouldn't.

His nostrils flared slightly and the pen clicking stopped. 'Yes, Miss Montrose, we need to set some ground rules right now regarding your personal weaknesses. That is, if you want to continue working for me.'

She sat up straight. 'Pardon?' Why was he saying such a thing and why did he keep repeating her name, loading it with ominous overtones? She was so taken aback she gawped at him. 'Personal weaknesses — what do you mean?' And what was that about keeping her job? She hadn't known it was on the line. Was he actually going to sack her? She put her hands to her cheeks as they flamed, too shocked to try her usual diversion tactics.

With no more than a nod from Mr Cavarelli, the waitress appeared and minutes later she placed two coffees in front of them, giving her handsome customer a wide smile — while completely ignoring Emerald. She turned away from the table with a coquettish flick of her long ponytail.

Emerald was thankful that her new boss had waited until the waitress disappeared before he continued with his accusations, but she could only watch in disbelief as he began shaking out papers from the wallet and putting them in some sort of order. She couldn't for the life of her imagine how he had enough on her to fill a file — she hadn't exactly set the world on fire with her career so far.

She looked away from the typed pages that might hold her fate in their printed words and stared at the waitress, now blatantly flirting with a young man wearing a baseball cap backwards. She wished she could behave in such a coltish way, but she had proved herself incapable of even the slightest hint of expertise when it came to seduction. The man sitting right opposite her could attest to the fact. He'd seen it first-hand. She groaned, wishing fervently that she could turn back time.

Marco Cavarelli glanced up sharply. 'Miss Montrose, please pay attention.'

Realising that he had heard the groan, she turned it into a cough and wondered if things could possibly get any worse.

She jerked back to the reality of sitting opposite the man whose eyelashes bothered her, whose finely shaped fingers bothered her: the man with whom she'd humiliated herself in the worst possible way, who was now mouthing words she really couldn't afford to miss, but couldn't quite believe she was hearing.

'I need your cooperation in all areas and I will expect you to play your part with dignity and poise. We will not be a two-bit airline anymore, and if you want to come along for the ride—' he smiled slightly at the pun and she smiled back, but her mind was reeling at his words '—then you will have to shape up.'

She watched his mouth move, only half listening, as in her mind she was outlining his full and sensual lips in dark charcoal, filling in the paler fullness, his tanned, olive-skinned face, setting the whole thing off to make a dark, brooding Marco Cavarelli — committing him to paper forever.

'Will you give me those guarantees?'

'Mm . . . Sorry?' She blinked in surprise. 'What guarantees?' She took out a pen and a notepad from her bag, hoping to deflect the focus away from herself, or more particularly, her flaming cheeks.

She didn't need to take notes as she had an excellent memory and although she was never without a notebook in her bag, it was normally used for sketching images that took her fancy, not for writing lists.

Mr Cavarelli's cup chinked back onto his saucer as he repeated his words, his irritation apparent. 'I need you to promise that you will not drink alcohol when you are on duty, and that includes when you are at corporate functions. Also, I need you to keep your lascivious tendencies under wraps. I have a high profile with the media, as you might know, and I do not want one of my staff bringing attention to me via the gutter press.'

Her pencil clattered to the table. 'What?' Her mouth dried as a bolt of adrenaline coursed through her. 'But I don't drink. I also don't have any tendencies — of the sort you're suggesting, or otherwise.' Her voice rose as she took in his accusations.

A muscle twitched in his jaw, but apart from that there was no indication whatsoever of emotion, as he continued in the same vein as if reading out a list of charges. 'Miss Montrose, are you denying that you were drunk in my hotel?'

'*Your* hotel?' Her outrage evaporated as she took in this news.

'Suddenly, she remembers.' His mouth was a thin line. 'Maybe you will also *suddenly* remember that you wanted me to have sex with you. Do you deny that a man you had never met in your life before was in your room when you were drunk?'

'Of course not — that man was you.'

'But you didn't know me — at all.'

She opened her mouth to speak and then closed it again as she couldn't recall what had really happened.

He sighed. 'You were in a vulnerable position and I would like some reassurance that this kind of situation won't arise once I take over the airline. It's not true when they say all publicity is good publicity. Trust me on that one.' His gaze didn't waver and she was totally laid bare by this man as he waited for her reassurances. She took in the look of pity on his face and hated him at that moment for being so convinced that he was right. But his stare remained fixed,

Finbar was right, her situation would be comical if it wasn't so pathetically tragic. The one and only person she'd offered herself to, on a plate, in her whole life, was her new boss, who, if she were to believe Finbar, was rich and famous enough to have bagged any film star, millionairess or top model that took his fancy.

She touched her burning cheeks with the back of her fingers to cool them down, before placing her hands flat on the table to stop them shaking. Sister Mary Bennett was right too. It was a fluke that she had managed to conduct herself sensibly so far, in this world that was so distanced from her sheltered convent school upbringing, surrounded by fields and bogs and very little else. She had let herself down in Italy by getting drunk and behaving like a cheap tart and she deserved his loathing.

This forbidding man had every reason not to trust her, even though all was not as it seemed. Bloody Rick: he was the cause of all this. All she'd done was fallen for his smooth lines — and just look where it had got her. She supposed she should be grateful that Mr Bloody Perfect Cavarelli had come to her rescue, but right now she was finding it hard to even like him, let alone consider thanking him.

Tears of self-pity pricked at the back of her eyes and she kept her head down as a tear plopped onto the table. She tried to dash it discreetly away, but as her hand reached the table, she felt the warmth of another hand on top of hers. For one second she wanted to clutch at it gratefully — human contact in any form was preferable to this desolate feeling that swept through her, but when she looked up into Mr Cavarelli's eyes she saw only the softness of pity. She shucked his hand away. She didn't need anyone's pity. She'd dealt with enough of it at St Teresa's Convent, putting on a brave front against broken promises, lonely Christmases and long, empty summers. Let him think what he wanted. She could do what he asked without even trying. He'd got her so completely wrong that she should really be laughing — so why had her emotions so easily turned to tears?

* * *

Marco removed his hand from hers, oddly hurt by her reaction when he was trying to show that he understood. But what choice did he have? He couldn't risk his new business getting bad press from any quarter — an airline was reliant on customers bringing in revenue and any reports of salacious behaviour from his staff could be a disaster. He knew to his bitter cost that there would always be a low-life journalist on the lookout to sully his reputation.

He looked at the unhappy woman in front of him and wished he could make it better for her. He would probably have just found a way to sack her, if it wasn't for — wasn't for what? He had no loyalty towards her. If it wasn't for her big sad eyes, brimming with tears in her lovely face, or her pink lips quivering with the effort of holding back her emotions?

No, he didn't let that kind of thing get to him anymore. But he was still staring at her lips when she rose gracefully, her face shuttered and inscrutable.

She met his gaze. 'If we're done here, I'd like to go home. It's been a very long day.'

He stood up. 'Of course, but finish your coffee.' He nodded towards her still-full cup just as his mobile rang deep within his jacket pocket. The frown she was already becoming used to, was instantly back in place. He dug into his pocket, looked at the screen and said, 'I have to take this. I look forward to working with you, Miss Montrose.' He walked out of the door, somehow feeling he'd behaved with less decency than he should have, and that somewhere along the line he had missed an opportunity to connect appropriately with his new cabin services manager.

* * *

Emerald was so horrified by their conversation that she just sat, stirring her cooling coffee, unable to think straight. She couldn't believe that her new boss saw her as a woman who slept around. She would have to resign! She couldn't possibly work for such a man. But where would she go? Her thoughts strayed back to the convent. It would have been so much easier if she'd become a nun. She shook her head — no one in the real world became a nun anymore, did they — not even in Ireland?

The anxiety of living in a world she was ill-equipped for washed over her again. She fought against it — introspection just wouldn't do. Marco Cavarelli needed to be exorcized and she knew just the right way to do it.

She picked up her pencil and pulled out her sketchpad from her bag once again. Without thinking, she began to draw. Soon, barely realising she was doing it, the face of Marco Cavarelli began to emerge from the page. Black eyes, glowing like burning coals, and a pair of bushy, brooding eyebrows. A hard, straight mouth when he was angry was the thing she remembered most about him and she quickly drew an exaggerated version of it, adding pointy fangs dripping with blood. Lots of crazy, wild hair curled around his head and she drew puffs of steam coming out of his ears for good measure.

She scribbled quickly, feeling better with every stroke, finishing the caricature off with a pair of horns that an antelope would be proud to sport. There. She felt so much better now that he was reduced to his bare essentials: a sexist man with bad attitude.

Emerald pondered over her position within the airline. In reality she could easily agree to what he demanded of her — since she didn't tend to drink and had no interest in getting into another tangled, heart-breaking mess. Perhaps she wouldn't have to see much of him. In fact, once he'd finished bossing everyone around, he would probably swan off back to Italy to be worshipped by an entourage of beautiful women who no doubt followed him around like adoring handmaidens. *They were sodding well welcome to him*, she thought, glancing once more at the caricature. His jaw was probably slightly more angular than she'd drawn it, and his lips were definitely more sensual. No matter, he was still arrogant and rude.

She left the café and headed for her car, phoning Finbar on the way in her need to talk to someone — although she knew he couldn't keep a secret to save his life.

'How did it go?' he asked immediately, in a voice that sounded hungry for gossip.

'He said I had lascivious tendencies.'

'Wow, I'm impressed. He's Italian and he can say words like that.'

'Ha, ha. That's not the point, Fin, as you well know. I have no such tendencies — you know that. I couldn't even spell it, let alone be it.' She heard a splutter of laughter from Finbar and felt better immediately. Maybe she was taking it all too seriously and needed to chill out.

'Sorry for laughing, Emerald, but how is he supposed to know the real you, when you were sprawled out on the bed offering your cute little bod to him?'

'I wasn't,' she protested again, half-heartedly this time, trying not to conjure up the image of herself on that bed, in that hotel — with *that* man.

Joking about it made it seem less horrific. Maybe her boss would realize the truth when he got to know her better. It still hurt, though, and she burned with shame as she played out the conversation in her head. As she threw her overnight bag in the back seat of her car and turned on the ignition, a buried memory surfaced: of Mr Cavarelli holding her tenderly, of a kiss that had deepened and had been reciprocated, and of a warm hand running down her spine. Had such a thing really happened, or was she now weaving fiction into her memories?

CHAPTER EIGHT

The following Monday, Emerald loaded her boot with a box of sweets — pink and yellow bags bursting with sugary pigs, yellow foamy bananas and rainbow-coloured lollipops — and drove to work to run the annual first aid workshop. Most of the employees at Hot Air Aviation had to attend the course once a year and although it was a long day, with an exam at the end, she tried to make it fun.

Dressing down was part of the deal and Emerald took the opportunity to wear jeans and her favourite blue silk shirt over a spaghetti-strap top. Her hair was, for once, loose and untamed, framing her face and making a welcome change from the scraped-back bun she usually adopted for work. Dangly earrings were her only other concession to extravagance. Having lived among the Dominican nuns in the convent school for most of her teen and adult years, she knew only too well that such outward displays of "peacockery", as Sister Mary Bennett would say, were a precursor to "sins of the flesh". She didn't really believe it, but there was a core part of her that would always be Catholic of mind, if not of religious persuasion. She was also aware that she needed to prove her professionalism in light of her chat with Marco

Cavarelli and, although unwilling to wear a suit, she felt the need for a certain amount of modesty.

The office door was already ajar and she kicked it open wide, manoeuvring her box of goodies through the gap and plonking it on the table by the window. The quiet hum of the air conditioning was the only sound in the room as she headed for the cupboard and dragged Resusci Annie off the shelf, where she lived for most of the year. 'Hello, Annie, how've you been? Are you ready for this?'

She answered her own question in a high-pitched voice since Annie, the first aid doll made of rubber and plastic, couldn't speak for herself. 'I'm okay, just need to get the blood flowing in my legs.'

'You ain't got no legs, Annie,' she replied, in her best Forrest Gump accent.

'I *know* that. I would have legged it years ago, if I had,' she agreed, falsetto, giggling. She spun around at the sound of someone clearing their throat.

Marco Cavarelli sat at his desk in the recess, the light from his laptop throwing shadows over his face, annoyingly illuminating his angular jaw and high cheekbones and making her itch to whip out her sketchbook.

She almost dropped Annie on the floor. 'Mr Cavarelli! I didn't know you were coming in today.'

He covered his mouth, stifling a laugh, and she felt her light mood evaporate. This was supposed to be a good day and yet here he was, threatening to ruin it before it had even started.

'Miss Montrose, you're here bright and early.' He stood up to greet her and she was surprised by him all over again. He smiled, for starters. Yes, she knew he must smile occasionally, but she imagined that his smiles were carefully doled out to only the worthiest of causes, and she was pretty sure she wouldn't be on that list.

And what a smile it was. It changed his whole face from one of dour irritability to a sexy invitation. Not literally, of course, but her hardened heart pumped a little faster for a second and she put her hand to her chest, startled. She could barely believe he was the same man who had given her such icy treatment just a few days ago. The sharp suit had gone, replaced by fitted jeans that emphasized an admirable pair of long legs, and his white cotton shirt drew attention to the smattering of dark hair on his chest and his warm olive-tinted skin. His dark hair curled around his neck and a freshly washed scent lingered under the spicy aftershave.

His flinty eyes fixed on her and she realized she was staring at him. He lifted an eyebrow and she closed her mouth. Ogling your boss was not the way forward. But her whole body sparked as her heart gave a small leap of awareness. It was very much against her better judgement — but she couldn't help it. Had she missed his good looks earlier or was she simply in denial? She dragged her gaze away from him, irked that he looked so in control and so . . . delicious.

He smiled again, but it was a perfunctory smile, thinner and more businesslike. On reflection, she preferred it: it was less threatening to her equilibrium. In fact, it would be better for her altogether if he continued grumping around and being bossy — he was a far easier man to dislike that way.

'So, two compensation claims for the National Tie Cutting day?' Mr Cavarelli sipped from a mug as he glanced up from the letter he was reading and waved it in front of her. She recognized the letter, even knew the contents off by heart — she'd read it so many times, along with four other claims tucked away in a folder awaiting the solicitor's perusal.

The odds on the two claimants dying of old age before any claim was settled were quite high, given that Hot Air Aviation's solicitor seemed to think that his *raison d'être* was to invoice the airline monthly without actually doing any work. It was another area of waste that needed looking into and Emerald had a feeling that Marco Cavarelli would be the man to do it.

'Ah yes, Finbar got a bit carried away, unfortunately. He was heading back from some city in Germany where women can cut off the tie of someone they like on one particular day of the year.'

'And the relevance of that story is . . . ?'

'Erm, I guess that he clocked two fanciable blokes and snipped off their ties, hoping they would take a shine to him.' Emerald remembered the mortified stewardess flying with him that day, rushing in from the flight to recount the story of Finbar fixing his beady eye on two men as he dashed through the cabin, squeaking, 'You're gorgeous' before cutting off their ties with the scissors from the first aid kit.

Her boss steepled his fingers in thought. 'So, he imagined that cutting their ties off might make them fall in love with him. At what level does that make any sense?'

'As I said, Fin gets a bit overexcited sometimes.'

Mr Cavarelli shook his head in disbelief. 'He did this while on duty on our aircraft and he still has a job with Hot Air Aviation? Unbelievable.' He waved the letter at Emerald once more. 'If the claims are to be believed, both passengers were wearing the most expensive ties in the world. I think they must have been woven from pure gold.'

'Yes, they're obviously trying it on — although Fin did save one of the ties as a trophy and it has a royal warrant of appointment from Prince Charles. We googled the name on the label, which was on the bottom of the tie — the bit he saved.' Emerald mimicked a snipping motion with one hand while holding the remnants of an invisible tie with the other, before letting her hands drop to her sides as Marco Cavarelli's face registered total astonishment.

She composed her expression to appear suitably horrified by Finbar's actions, even though when she'd first heard what he'd done, she couldn't stop giggling. 'The other two hundred pounds on the claim is apparently for the inconvenience of them having to purchase new ties for their meeting in London.'

'Right. Where they bought the most expensive ties in the history of tie buying.' Marco let the letter drop back onto the desk with a sigh as he picked up another.

Emerald grimaced. She knew what was coming.

'And this one?' He held up a letter that had been read and returned to its folder so many times that it looked like a well-used bus ticket — grubby and limp.

'Ah, yes. That was not Darcy's fault. She simply tried to push the passenger seat back into the upright position and the tray behind tipped up with the passenger's breakfast on it, and . . .' She cringed.

'The passenger literally ended up with egg on her face,' Marco finished for her, dropping the letter back into the box.

'And beans . . .' Emerald spun around on hearing a commotion in the corridor: the sound of a clanging bucket hitting the door and the door handle rattling simultaneously.

A stout lady wearing a dress covered in large poppies, topped by an apron with daffodils around the edge, dragged a mop and a broom into the office. She beamed at Emerald. 'Morning, my lovely. Oh, who's this?' She peered at Mr Cavarelli myopically, through thick lenses. Then she took off her glasses, polished them and put them back on, inspecting the stranger again, before turning to Emerald and giving her a bug-eyed stare. 'Bit of all right, eh?' she hissed to Emerald, angling her head in Mr Cavarelli's direction before turning back to face him.

She spied the cardboard box sitting on his desk and slid it towards herself. 'Ooh, you've got the compo letters out,' she said, picking up the top one. 'We do like to have a laugh now and then, don't we, love?' She directed her comment to Emerald as she unfolded the letter Mr Cavarelli had just dropped. She scanned it, muttering the words under her breath. 'These two geezers should come and take a look at poor Mr Clarke if they think there's any money in the pot for compensation, eh?' She beamed at her captive audience as if she had just made a profound statement.

'And you would be?' Marco Cavarelli's voice dripped acid as he glared at the newcomer.

'I'm Betty.' She squared her shoulders and tried to stand tall, but at five foot nothing, it made little difference.

Emerald could see that Betty was affronted by Mr Cavarelli's tone and she winced, praying that he wouldn't try to take Betty on — he would lose, big time.

'Don't you knock before you walk into someone's office?' His voice was brusque.

Emerald stiffened. Yep, he decided to go there.

'Someone's office?' Betty looked about her, puzzled. She glanced towards the door as if checking that she was in the right building.

'Betty here is Hot Air's national treasure.' Emerald put her arm around Betty's shoulders, stooping slightly to reach them.

He gave them both a hard stare. 'We do not need a national treasure. We need an influx of hard cash.'

Betty glared at the stranger. 'I'm the cleaner, come tea lady, come . . . anything else that's needed, and I'm always here early on Monday to make sure everything is spick and span for the week ahead.'

'Of course, and I'm your new boss. What are your con-tracted hours?' He piled the letters back in the shoebox and banged the lid down.

'Contracted hours? Well I come in when my Alf has time to drop me off and I go home when everything's clean and tidy. And if you are my new boss, you should have known the answer to that one.' Betty bristled as she strode over to the cupboard where Resusci Annie spent most of her days. Dragging out an ancient-looking vacuum cleaner, she plugged it in, huffing and puffing as she reached down to the socket, and switched it on.

Emerald mentally punched the air in support of Betty and watched on in fascination as she started to vacuum around her supposed boss's feet, the noise deafening.

'Lift,' Betty demanded.

Mr Cavarelli gazed at her, bewildered.

'Lift your feet,' she bellowed over the noise of the vac-uum cleaner.

He lifted his feet with alacrity.

They both stared at Betty scouring the carpet underneath the desk he was sitting at, his feet hovering awkwardly.

He threw Emerald a bemused look and she gave him an unimpressed look back.

That'll teach you, it said.

Betty zoomed around the room like a whirling dervish until, finally, she switched the machine off and smiled brightly at Emerald. 'There we go. That'll do for now. Have time for a cuppa, do you, love?'

'That would be brilliant, Betty. Mr Cavarelli has black coffee, please.'

Betty threw the man a look that told him all he needed to know about her opinion of him and his black coffee, but nevertheless, she wound up the cord of the vacuum cleaner, stowed the machine, and headed for the tiny kitchen.

'Don't tell me.' He held up his hand. 'She's related to Mr Clarke.'

Emerald nodded, trying to hide a grin. 'No one messes with Betty.'

A hint of a smile played around Mr Cavarelli's lips as he said, 'Am I about to discover a dead fly or something equally unpleasant in my coffee?'

'No. Well, probably not. Betty's a sweetheart. Just ask her about her grandchildren and she'll be putty in your hands. Mind you, try not to get her started on the photos or you'll be there all day — she keeps them in her apron pocket.'

'I really don't have time for such things.'

'Quite.' She was beginning to understand what motivated her new boss, and it certainly wasn't people. 'Anyway, moving swiftly on, have you met Annie?' She lifted Resusci Annie up and draped her over her arm like a ventriloquist's dummy, straightening her very yellow hair, which sat lopsidedly on her head like a particularly ill-fitting Donald Trump wig. The doll was surprisingly heavy for someone with only half a body, but Emerald supported her as she attempted to speak in her Annie voice. 'Hi, pleased to meet you.' She pushed out Annie's pink rubber arm in greeting.

Marco threw Emerald a mock withering look, but he shook Annie's hand and peered at her chest. 'That has to be the worst boob job I've ever seen and I have seen some, believe me.'

So, the man had a sense of humour behind that stern exterior. She wondered how many boobs he had seen and immediately wished such a thought hadn't crossed her mind. She covered the mannequin's ears. 'Don't say such things in front of Annie, she only gets out once a year and she's very sensitive.'

'What does she do, when she comes out to play?'

'She lets us practise defibrillation and CPR on her. She's *very* sick, but she loves the craic of it all, don't you, Annie?' She put Annie on a chair and patted her on the head, just managing to refrain from replying in her falsetto Annie voice again.

'Sounds like fun,' he said drily. 'Now, tell me again in English.'

'Oh, it's mouth-to-mouth resuscitation, hence her name — Resusci Annie — and defibrillation is when you get the heart rhythms back in sync if someone's having a heart attack. Although, you probably know that if you've ever watched any *Scrubs* or *Casualty*.'

Marco glanced at her, incomprehension written all over his face. He shook his head imperceptibly.

'No, I don't suppose you have much time for telly. Doesn't matter — you don't need to attend the course anyway. I'm a qualified first-aider, by the way. I can show you my certificates if you want.'

He narrowed his eyes, reminding her that he was the boss and could do with her what he liked, certificates or not. 'I would like to be included. Where do we go?'

'We?'

'Why not?'

'It's hardly relevant for you.' She tried for a dismissive tone, to sound as if she didn't really mind either way, but her heart thumped. She couldn't face him watching her every move to check if she had an intravenous drip of vodka attached to her arm or was behaving lasciviously. The familiar heat rose in her face as she remembered his words. She bit her lip, silently begging for this one wish, as she threw a longing glance over at his laptop, willing him to return to his emails. But he picked up the first aid manual and flicked through it. 'It might come in useful one day — and I do have a private pilot's licence, you know.'

'Of course you do.' She scowled at him: the man who had everything.

He took a step towards her, his gaze unwavering. 'Is that a problem for you?'

She swallowed, trying to get some moisture flowing into her mouth as he took another step in her direction. He was close enough now that she could see the black flecks in his irises and a cute mole just above his top lip — it was an endearing flaw. She swayed slightly as his increasingly familiar scent assailed her senses. He put his hand on her arm and gazed down at her. Was he going to kiss her?

'I said, do you have a problem with that?' A hard edge in his voice negated the hypnotic effect of his whispered words and brought her back to her senses.

She took a step backwards and collected herself as sweat broke out on her forehead. Oh, my God, what had she just imagined? She was mad — certifiably insane — there was no other reason for her thoughts. She had wanted Marco Cavarelli to kiss her, turning her into the very thing he professed to dislike about her. She needed a reality check — and quick.

'Are you okay?'

She flinched as he raised his hand towards her face, grazing her cheek with his fingers. It felt like ice and fire scorching her flesh — all in one hit. His eyes, which only seconds ago were shooting steely shards of displeasure at her, softened.

Her breath hitched and then steadied as he let his hand drop to his side.

'Yes, I'm fine.' She touched her cheek, surprised that it wasn't seared to the bone, quickly running her fingers through her hair to mask the movement. God, he'd nearly had her then. He'd be accusing her of trying to seduce him all over again if she didn't watch it.

Luckily, Betty came trundling in again, bearing a tray loaded with mugs and slices of cake. 'Orange and poppy-seed drizzle cake, one of my best recipes, if I say so myself.' She set down a mug and a plate of cake on Emerald's desk and banged the same down for the new boss, next to his laptop, rolling her eyes in his direction as she did so.

'He's nice really. You'll get used to him,' Emerald whispered. She had no idea why she was defending him. He hadn't exactly won Boss of the Year in her books.

'No cake—' Marco began, before Emerald interrupted him.

'Has ever looked so divine, Betty.' She glared at Marco and he picked up his piece of cake.

'Looks delicious.'

Betty preened as she made herself comfortable in the only easy chair in the room. She sipped at her tea and bit into her cake. She was not a lady in a hurry. 'What's on the agenda today, then?' she asked, looking from Marco to Emerald.

'As you can see, we've brought Annie out for her annual treat,' Emerald began.

'On which note, I think it's time for us to depart for the course,' Marco exclaimed, rising. He closed his laptop decisively.

Emerald looked meaningfully at the cake still sitting on his plate and he took a large sip of his coffee and a small bite of the cake. Emerald stood up, shoving the remainder of her cake into her mouth as she picked up the paraphernalia for the day and slung it into her voluminous bag. 'Delicious as ever, Betty,' she gushed, through a mouthful of crumbs.

'I'll save your cake for later, then,' Betty said pointedly to Marco. 'We have some foil in the kitchen,' she added, as she eased her shoes off.

'Thank you, Betty. Most kind.' Marco looked pointedly down at her stocking feet.

She wiggled her toes, beaming. 'Take the weight off, eh?'

He nodded at her imperceptibly and said, 'Quite.' Then he turned to Emerald. 'Shall we?'

Emerald saw that she wouldn't be able to deflect Marco from joining her, although she had no idea why he wanted to. Didn't he know that's what staff were for — to take care of things, so he could just swan around being important and handsome, showing off his long lashes and kissable lips? Why couldn't he just leave her to do the job she was paid to do?

She wilted internally as she took in his determined features. He wasn't one for changing his mind, that much was clear.

She gave in. It was easier than fighting. With a sigh, she picked Annie up and threw her over her shoulder. 'Come on, then — wouldn't want Annie to miss her yearly snog, would we?'

'Atta girl,' he said cheerfully, sounding totally unlike himself, before striding out the door, leaving Emerald to stare after him in shocked disbelief.

CHAPTER NINE

Marco strode along the corridor, reluctantly readjusting his opinions of Emerald. Maybe she wasn't just a lacklustre member of staff who needed to shape up or ship out. He was struggling to place her all over again — wanting to dislike everything she stood for, but unable to shake off the strange feeling that had assailed him when he touched her cheek. He knew he would have to remain professional throughout, but admitted to himself that he was at a disadvantage to start with. Not every boss would have seen their new employee semi-naked in a hotel room.

Realising he didn't know where they were headed, he stopped to let her pass him and, although he didn't want to look, couldn't miss her shapely legs, sheathed in tight jeans. His gaze drifted to her perfectly rounded bottom, peeping out from under her shirt, which swished tantalisingly as she sashayed along the corridor. It sent his mind into an unwanted train of thought that he quickly brought under control. He was her boss and there was no room for a woman like her in his life.

They reached the boardroom, the only room big enough to hold all the staff at one time. Emerald dumped Annie in a corner and set about moving chairs, sorting out test papers and tip sheets, and piling up her treats in big wooden bowls for the staff to take whenever they wanted.

Marco was intrigued by her enthusiasm. 'Why are you trying so hard over this? What are these sweets for?' He couldn't get that she cared enough to make a tedious day interesting.

She frowned at his question. 'I'm a qualified first-aider and it's part of my job.'

'No, I mean, this.' He pointed at the bowls of sweets and lollipops, bewildered. 'Everyone has to attend today regardless. You don't have to entice them.'

Her brow creased. 'It can also be a fun day that makes us a skilled team, capable of pulling together if the need arises. And actually . . .' She unwrapped a purple lollipop and slipped it into her mouth '. . . sucking lollies is good fun. Very therapeutic — you should try it.'

He shook his head as she held out a lollipop, his eyes fixed on her mouth, watching her pink tongue flick over the sugary confection while his brain tried to understand. Okay, he knew she was messing with him, but he was grudgingly impressed by her work tactics.

He normally thought about his employees as statistics and pay cheques, their productivity and suitability being the deciding factor in whether they stayed or went. This touchy-feely *let's all have fun* idea was alien to him and doubts stirred in his mind that he might have it wrong. He felt her eyes on him and banished his thoughts. Indecision was not a word he acknowledged.

'If you want to help,' she continued, putting the lollipop back in the bowl, 'put Annie on her back and get the wipes out and leave them by her head. People are jittery when it comes to sharing saliva — though you wouldn't know it if you went to a few of the nightclubs I've been dragged to.'

'You don't like nightclubs?'

She twitched her nose. 'Err, no, do I look like a clubber?'

'No, you don't.' He adjusted his opinions again. What about the drinking and the propositioning men in hotels? He narrowed his eyes, as if she had been pulling the wool over them on purpose.

She frowned again. 'You're doing it again. Stop it.'

'Doing what again?'

'Looking like you're trying to work out if I'm vegetable, mineral or animal.'

'I'm not.'

'Yes, you are. It's like you're doing this.' She thrust her face close to his and peered at him fixedly to prove the point.

Marco could almost touch her nose with his. He smiled — it was a cute nose.

She spun away from him. 'And you're always giving me that supercilious smile.'

He nodded acceptance, unwilling to start an argument. He'd been accused of many things, but being supercilious was a new one on him. Fair enough, though, if that's what she thought.

'Morning, Emms.' A high-pitched squeal pierced the room and a flash of pink and black cut across Marco's vision. Finbar waltzed in, wearing a pink cable-knit jumper and purple skinny jeans, surpassing anyone's worst fashion nightmare. His hair was jet black at the roots and peaked to a blond point at the top with a heavy fringe pulled over to one side to reveal a large hoop earring in his right ear. Marco flinched as he took in this antithesis of style in his eyes. The man standing in front of him totally violated his own carefully nurtured fashion sense. And *Emms*? A flash of jealousy went through him. He wanted to have the right to call Emerald *Emms*.

'Fin, hiya, glad you're early.' Emerald looked him up and down approvingly. 'You certainly made the most of dressing down day.'

'That is not dressing down, that is dressing up,' Marco's view was unequivocal as he stared in horrified awe at the man in front of him. He now recognized him as the steward from his earlier flight — although it was hard to be sure with all that garish make-up plastered on his face. He fought back the urge to order the man home until he had learnt how to dress like a grown-up — and Emerald *approved* of his outlandish attire?

Emerald ignored Marco's comment. 'Will you sort out the laptop for me, Fin? I've got a really good clip of an aircraft crash in the Rockies, showing how they coped with the injuries using the limited equipment they had on board. Actually, would you mind working it for me? I'm useless with PowerPoint.' She blew him a kiss. 'Thanks, honey.'

Finbar pouted and returned the air kiss. 'Don't worry, we'll sort it out — we always do.' He threw a look at Marco, who wasn't sure, but thought it was possibly smugness.

Marco didn't like the way Finbar laid claim to Emerald's friendship and he had a ridiculous urge to outmanoeuvre him — which was completely pointless as Marco was already the silly young man's superior. He was his boss and could easily sack him.

He caught an adoring look from Emerald to Finbar and suppressed a childish impulse to declare that he could work a laptop as well as any man. He remembered now. 'You are Mr Clarke's nephew?'

Finbar beamed. 'Yes.'

Marco's heart sank. So, maybe he couldn't sack him with the flick of a wrist, after all. 'Ah, we can credit you with the name of this wonderful airline?'

'Hot Air Aviation? Fab, isn't it?' Finbar grinned from ear to ear as he flicked his fringe out of his kohl-ringed eyes and pursed his pink, dewy lips.

'Fab indeed,' Marco replied, accepting that he would never be able to criticize or reprimand this ridiculous young man who clearly took everything too far. Trying to stay focused he grabbed one of Emerald's circular lollies, tore off the wrapper and sucked at it savagely. Slowly the outrageous sweetness and fruity taste took him back to days he couldn't quite pinpoint, but knew had been blissful. His frayed nerves were soothed and he smiled at the novel idea Emerald had once again been right. A lollipop full of sugar and flavouring had done the job that therapists, charging an extortionate rate, had never managed to achieve. Even if it was transient, the world looked a better place within a few short minutes as he welcomed pilots, engineers and cabin staff into the room.

Emerald rapped on the table for attention. 'Okay, for anyone here who has somehow missed Finbar's monthly newsletter with images of Mr Marco Cavarelli splashed all over it, this is our new MD. He will be joining us today for our annual first aid course and is looking forward to chatting to you all. I hope he will leave this room a more knowledgeable man.' She threw him a glance loaded with meaning.

'Mr Cavarelli, these fine people here are the crème de la crème of the aviation business and I hope that in time you will be as proud of them as I am.'

Marco stood up and bowed slightly, impressed with her introduction. It was beginning to look as if he'd got someone rather special working for him. 'I'm looking forward to getting to know you all and hope you will continue to enjoy being part of the revamped, erm, Hot Air Aviation.' Once again he stalled over the name of the airline, his mouth forming a moue of distaste.

Emerald stifled a giggle and he threw her an amused look, before turning back to his employees. 'And, please, call me Marco.' He threw his hands wide in a welcoming gesture. 'That includes you too, Miss Montrose,' he said as an aside to her.

'Then I suppose you will have to call me Emerald.'

He nodded. 'A very pretty name, if I may say so.'

She smiled tightly and he wasn't sure if he'd done the right thing by being so casual, but it was a small airline and being high-handed wouldn't do him any favours. He perched on a desk and folded his arms, preparing to be entertained. Emerald seemed the epitome of composure and the slight nerves he perceived beneath the surface made this outward appearance even more attractive. He liked her hair loose and a bit wild, he decided, and the ice-blue shirt complemented her auburn colouring beautifully.

She beamed. 'Right then, team . . .' A mobile started to trill and Emerald held up her hand. 'Mobiles off — c'mon, gang, you know the drill.'

Marco took out his phone and glanced at the screen. 'I'll take this outside.' He gave Emerald a sardonic smile and made for the door.

Emerald looked flustered. 'Sorry, I didn't know it was your phone.'

She coloured up and he felt a bit mean, but he wasn't used to being told what to do and wasn't likely to start any time soon.

'I won't be a moment.' He strode to the door and Emerald watched him leave, feeling wrong-footed.

She turned back to the expectant staff. 'Okay then, bandages are as good a place as any to start, I suppose. We'll give ourselves half an hour to tie each other up, yeah?'

'We do like a bit of bondage, don't we?' Finbar said, winking at her. She gave him a grateful smile as she slung a wodge of bandages diagonally across the tables, noticing Marco slide back into the room. 'I know it's a bit boring and we've done it many times, but I have to tick the boxes to prove it, so take a partner and let's get cracking with those Girl Guide knots.'

Marco looked around the room and Emerald felt his gaze settle on her. 'Emerald,' he said, flicking his fingers toward her. 'You can pair with me.'

'I don't need to, Marco, I'm qualified.'

'That may be so. I, however, am not.'

'And we've already established that you don't need to be here.'

'Humour me. Please.' He couldn't help the sarcasm in his voice, but for heaven's sake, he shouldn't have to ask permission from his own staff. He noted her reluctance and wished he had time to analyse it, but he wasn't going to hang about. He opened one of the triangular bandages and snapped it, a persuasive grin on his face. 'Go on, you know you want to.'

She rolled her eyes and tutted as she held out her arm to be bandaged.

He unfolded the large bandage. 'So, it's corner to elbow and keep the arm elevated, yes?'

She nodded slowly. Clearly he already knew how to elevate a broken arm.

'Then come closer — I cannot bandage fresh air.'

She edged towards him. She really didn't want to be so close, didn't want his scent lingering on her body afterwards, didn't want another close-up of his face with the adorable mole gracing the top lip.

She admitted to herself that she liked the way he looked, that was for sure, although she was having difficulty trying to understand why he seemed to gravitate towards her, when he could so easily avoid her. Was he testing her in some bizarre way, or trying to prove that her so-called weaknesses could erupt at any given time.

She saw the determination in his eyes as he unfolded the bandage. He was a man who did nothing by halves and he had more power over her than anyone else in the world right at that moment. She had no choice but to do as he asked.

'So, you put the bandage under your arm, the point to your elbow, like so?' He slid the bandage under her elbow before looking at her for reassurance.

'Yes.' The word came out breathily and she cursed and straightened her spine, determined to get through this ordeal without giving anything away.

He elevated her arm. His touch, soft and warm, unnerving, his fingertips a silken caress on her skin. She tried to speak, but her voice caught in her throat and it came out like a whimper.

'Did I hurt you?'

'No.' She coughed to mask the audible moan. 'I'm just reminding you that I have a broken arm.'

'I'll be gentle,' he whispered, a hint of a smile crossing his face. 'So, the next move is to secure the bandage with a knot by the collarbone, yes?' His breath was warm, close to her ear, his all-too-familiar scent intoxicating, his voice soft and low. 'Just so?'

She shivered as he lifted her hair gently from her neck and whispered, '*Bei capelli.*'

She understood a smattering of Italian and blinked. *I have beautiful hair?* Her senses heightened to full alert as he blew a loose strand away from her neck. A sirocco wind blasting hot, dry sand would have been easier to bear — and if she had been the sort of girl to swoon, she would be flat out.

He ran his finger down the side of her neck, stopping in a natural hollow where her shoulder sloped. His thumb skimmed across the clavicle, setting her senses on red alert. Surely he knew what he was doing to her?

'And you tie a knot . . . just here,' he crooned, his breath tickling her ear, the mundane words sounding like a declaration of love.

'Yes, very good,' she managed, her voice strangling in her throat. His lips twisted with concentration as he examined the sling, tested the strength of the knot. His fingers brushed hers as he slid his hand down the length of the triangular bandage to where her fingers peeped out.

Emerald's nerve endings tingled all the way up her arm and she stiffened, not wanting Marco to see how his touch unnerved her. Their eyes met briefly and she stepped backwards in shock, thinking she saw tenderness in his eyes.

But then he blinked and his expression once again became unfathomable, his eyes the usual immeasurable grey. 'All done,' he said, smiling firmly and then murmured something else in Italian that she didn't understand.

His every move seemed to be larger than life to Emerald and she was glad when he stepped away from her, needing the distance, needing the air space. She breathed freely, relieved, although her chest still felt constricted — as if her lungs were full of concrete rather than air.

Marco casually rested his hip against the desk, his arms once again folded as he surveyed his handiwork. 'How does it feel?'

'Sorry?' Why was he asking that? 'Feel?'

'The arm. Now I have made it secure?'

'Oh. Fine. Lovely.' She flapped her arm in its bandage. He was joking, right? 'Never felt better.' She waggled her fingers in the sling as Marco studied her, his head tilted to one side.

She blew upwards, trying to cool her cheeks down with her breath as heat washed over her. Lurching forwards on her decidedly weak legs, she turned back to face the class. 'I think we all know how to administer bandages now, but there is one last thing to remember. Can anyone tell me what that is?'

Finbar's hand shot up and his suggestion rang out loud and clear. 'Is it kissing it better, miss?' There was no mistaking his insinuation, and Emerald, who was holding on by a thread, felt her body temperature hit meltdown.

She swallowed hard, trying to regain her equilibrium. 'No, Fin, that isn't the answer I wanted, although a bit of TLC never hurt anyone. The last thing is to check that the fingertips don't turn blue.' She held her own burning fingers up to emphasize the point, half expecting sparks to fly out of them. 'If they do, you've tied the bandage too tight.' Her heart was thumping erratically as she glanced over at Marco. If this carried on, she would be the one needing defibrillation.

'We'll have a break now and then we'll split into two groups. One can work on Resusci Annie while the other practises splints and burns.' She gripped the edge of the table, trying to look nonchalant, but her mind was racing as quickly as her heart. Had she really fallen for that man's sex appeal?

A few minutes later she watched Marco as he tried to breathe life into Resusci Annie, his lips pressed firmly over Annie's rubber ones. For one second she imagined those lips on hers — but she cast aside the image quickly. Marco gently put his hands over Annie's breastbone to practise heart compressions and she noticed her own breasts felt oddly tingly under her shirt. She was just too hot, that was all. It meant nothing.

'Right, one last thing to do and then we're finished,' she said, her voice over-bright as she looked down at her notes.

Pressure points. No, she just couldn't practise putting pressure on such intimate parts of the body with Marco. 'Sorry, I was wrong there.' She looked up, folding her notes in half, decisively. 'That's the end of the session. As soon as we've completed the multiple-choice questionnaire, we're finished.' She passed out the exam papers and had started to gather her own paperwork together when an engineer stuck his hand in the air. 'Yes, Billy?'

'Yeah, sorry, Emerald, but there's a question about pressure points — did I miss that bit?'

'Oh, did I forget? Well, the answer is . . .' She looked down at the exam paper to buy some time. 'Erm, your pressure points are areas where you press hard on a major vein to stop blood from a wound pumping out. One is at the top of the arm, like so.' She pressed her right-hand fingers to her left arm. 'Another major pressure point is at the top of the leg by the groin. Okay?' She pressed her fingers to her groin and instinctively flashed a look at Marco, who was watching intently, the annoying half smile on his face once more.

Then his mobile beeped and he frowned as he checked the message. He picked up his jacket and threw it casually over his shoulder, heading towards the door without giving Emerald so much as a glance. He hadn't filled in the answer sheet either, which threw into question his claim about actually wanting the qualification. She shook her head, puzzled. What was that all about, then, and should she assume he would be back to his usual grumpy self the next time they met?

She watched Marco standing in the doorway, speaking into his phone, his normally severe expression relaxed as a smile played around his lips. Emerald resisted the urge to eavesdrop — although why it would matter who he was talking to, she didn't know.

He finished his conversation and glanced over at her. She shot him a smile, but in return he simply nodded, pocketed his mobile and turned on his heel to leave. She felt snubbed and guilty in one hit, her earlier good mood evaporating as he strode off. Staring through the open doorway, she tried not to feel hurt as he marched away from her.

'Earth to Emerald?' Finbar stood beside her, following her line of vision, his lips tight. He held the remnants of the sweets in the basket and Emerald glanced at them as if she'd never seen them before.

'What? Oh, right.' She looked around the room surveying the exam papers now in a pile on the desk, the chairs stacked neatly on top of each other and her laptop back in its case. 'Thanks, Fin, I was miles away.'

'You don't say.' Finbar's sarcasm held a note of concern and Emerald looked up sharply, finally pulling herself back into the room.

Finbar leaned against the desk casually, but Emerald knew him too well. She read the signs correctly. 'Okay, hit me with it — I know you've got something to say.'

He looked down at his nails, painted in shiny black lacquer, then looked back up into her eyes and pouted.

'Well?'

'Just don't shoot the messenger, okay?'

'I can't promise anything,' Emerald said, 'especially if the messenger is wearing a pink jumper.' She knew that Marco would be the topic of conversation and that Finbar would already have dug deep for information about their new boss. A shiver of apprehension ran down her spine.

'You know . . . ?' He shrugged, faltered, and tried again. 'It's just that—'

'Say it, Fin, I know it's not going to be pleasant.'

'It's just that I was doing a bit of chatting on an online forum about Mr Cavarelli. It turns out that he has work tactics.'

'Tactics — as in warfare?'

'Not quite on such a grand scale I hope, but apparently when he acquires a new business he befriends one particular person, mostly a woman. Which makes it easier for him, I imagine.'

'Easier for what?' She paused, adding, 'Are you jealous, Fin, of me working with Marco?'

'Yes, of course I am. He's gorgeous — but that's not what I'm talking about.'

'Aren't you?'

'Well . . .' Finbar wrinkled his nose. 'Anyway, I've heard that he pumps his chosen victim for information, gets them to do his dirty work, then sacks them — sometimes leaving them broken-hearted, if you get my meaning.'

'Oh, Fin, that's a terrible claim to make about someone.'

'I know. I hold my hands up for being the bad guy, but it's because I know how naive you can be in so many ways, especially towards men. You just haven't done the rounds, honey. You're not tough enough to deal with someone like him.'

'Fin, I know you mean well, but please don't worry about me.' She placed her hand over Finbar's. 'That man wouldn't touch me with a bargepole anyway — he thinks I'm a loose woman and might sully his reputation. Apart from his being my boss, which he never tires of reminding me, I am nothing to him. He barely knows me.'

'That's what worries me. He hasn't got a clue what you're really like and maybe he thinks you're game on. I can tell that you like him, Emerald, but remember Icarus, who flew too close to the sun?'

'What?'

'In Greek mythology. He flew too close to the sun, his wings melted and he crashed and burned in the sea.'

She rolled her eyes. 'Right. And your point is?'

'Marco is your sun. You are drawn to him and you will get burned if you're not careful.' He squeezed her hand. 'Okay?'

'I'll be careful, Fin, but honestly, he's just my boss, that's all.' But even as she spoke she relived the whisper of Marco's breath on her neck, his fingers touching hers. She hugged Finbar reassuringly and wished she were as confident as she sounded.

'Come on, let's get out of here and grab a drink. My treat. But it'll have to be apple juice. We don't want you getting drunk again, do we?' He tucked his arm through hers and she bumped him with her hip as they walked out of the crew room and headed for the car park.

'As if!'

'Two drinks and she's anybody's — that's what our new boss tells me.' Finbar bumped her back and threw her a look of caution, even as he teased her.

* * *

Marco watched this exchange from his car as he talked on his mobile, stopping mid-sentence as a fierce, illogical anger rose up inside him, making him catch his breath. 'I'll call you back,' he said into the mobile. His fingers clenched around it, as he watched Emerald laughing up into Finbar's face. Marco couldn't take his eyes off her, following her every move like a voyeur, jealous of her pleasure at being with Finbar.

It had been too long since he'd felt any emotions for a woman and was irritated that the only emotion this young woman had caused him so far was an exquisite kind of pain. The sort of pain that went hand in hand with unrequited love. And he was certainly done with love and all of its complexities so it absolutely couldn't be that.

He acknowledged that he was envious of Finbar having the right to link his arm through Emerald's and laugh with her, through a natural friendship and mutual admiration, whereas he was just her demanding boss who had set himself above her.

Mastering casual friendships with women had never been easy for him, believing that they were mostly eyeing him up for a wedding suit as soon as they met him. He was also aware that he had a certain kind of charm, or was it just his wealth that was splattered all over the internet and celebrity magazines? He wondered if that was why he found himself drawn to Emerald: as far as he could tell, she wasn't the gold-digger sort, and clearly had no clue about his identity when she met him. Both times!

He sighed. He couldn't understand her at all and it frustrated him as he was usually a good judge of character. Emerald Montrose — she was confusing the hell out of him.

It would be nice to make her smile the way Finbar did, he thought, watching her eyes crinkle with laughter. He dragged his gaze away and sighed. Maybe he was a little homesick. Such introspection was not one of his usual afflictions. He couldn't help but think of his siblings and the success they'd made of their lives. Two sisters, happy to be mums to their adorable children, and one brother, also happily married and busy running the nautical side of the business, while his wife made fashion design a career that was beginning to hit the headlines.

Whereas he, Signor Marco Cavarelli, had — or rather didn't have — Simona, his wife, specialist at spending money and screwing him over. He also now owned an airline that was spewing money faster than water in a broken drain, and a penthouse apartment that the paparazzi stalked, imagining it was brim-full of beautiful women desperate to have sex with him, if the fabricated articles were to be believed. In truth, there probably were plenty of women who would happily have sex with him, but sadly the desire was rarely reciprocated.

He watched Emerald and Finbar until they turned a corner and disappeared from sight. Even then he couldn't tear his gaze away, as if hoping she'd come back.

He made a decision. He would speed up his involvement in this new enterprise and go back to Italy sooner than he'd anticipated. Emerald Montrose spelled trouble — he had known it the first time he set eyes on her — and the sooner he left these English shores, the better it would be for his sanity.

He turned the ignition key, the throaty roar of his classic AC Cobra reminding him that he could be back among the hills he loved so much within a couple of days if he chose to. He would focus on that, not think about Emerald Montrose, although his fingers tingled at the memory of his fingertips touching her skin, and the silkiness of her hair as he slid it away from her throat.

He shook his head. Such madness must stop before he started on another path of self-destruction. He slammed the car into top gear as he took to the motorway, enjoying the throb of the engine. Soon Emerald Montrose would be relegated to the position of just another employee, and he would be back in the mountains of Italy where he belonged.

CHAPTER TEN

Emerald flicked on the computer and headed to the tiny kitchen at Hot Air Aviation to fill the kettle, tapping her fingers restlessly on the work surface as she waited for it to boil. Endless admin jobs seem to have been created since Marco had taken over the running of the airline and Emerald was missing the camaraderie of flying.

A small charter plane had just landed and she looked at it with longing, but she dutifully sat down at her desk and opened her emails like the good employee she was determined to be.

She was to accompany Mr Clarke to Aberdeen for a business meeting in a few days' time and was looking forward to getting away from the office, where she was beginning to feel stifled. She often flew with him in her capacity as cabin services manager, but lately she was becoming more like a PA or a carer to the dear man. She wondered how long it would be before he took a back seat completely. And where, a little voice asked, would she be then? Would Marco Cavarelli use the opportunity to fire her?

She sighed. This wasn't helping her to sort out the emails and the sooner she did that, the sooner she could escape. Since Marco had decided to set up his own desk in her office, she was permanently jumpy, reminding herself of the timid ginger cat back at the convent that would leap into the air at the slightest noise. Her head swivelled around, almost of its own accord whenever she heard footsteps in the corridor, and she'd started biting her nails again, something she hadn't done in years. Every time the door creaked open she was fearful that it would be Marco, or even more fearful that it wouldn't be. None of it helped her nerves.

She scanned the messages, and the name of the very man she'd been thinking about leaped out at her in an email, mixed up with the spam and invoice requests.

Emerald, Mr Clarke is not well so have rescheduled the trip. No longer Aberdeen but Edinburgh as it suits me better and the 125 aircraft is being utilized elsewhere.

She scanned the next sentence with a light heart, pleased that he was going to be absent for some time. Then her stomach swooped in foreboding though, as she finished the email.

Report at Luton 06.00 tomorrow. Flight number EDI204 leaving at 7.30 hours. I have attached your boarding card. Please print it out. See you at Luton Airport.

She read it twice, the horror growing as she took in the implications: two days on her own with Marco Cavarelli, the man who possibly mistrusted her, quite probably disliked her and definitely had too much sex appeal for her blood pressure.

No, she couldn't do it.

She hadn't seen him since the first aid day a week ago and had unsuccessfully tried to erase him from her mind to concentrate on more important matters. She was playing a losing hand where Marco was concerned and it hurt to think he held her in such low esteem. She just wanted him to go back to Italy and out of her life.

Her hand strayed to her throat, the memory of his cool fingers on her skin making her sigh. If she hadn't been so messed up when they'd first met, things might have been different. No — she couldn't think that way. He was her boss and her position in the pecking order was as low as his opinion of her. He also had the power to sack her if he chose to, and she really needed to remember that.

She composed a reply to his request, almost knowing she'd lose the battle before it started.

Unfortunately, can't make rescheduled trip as have too many admin duties to complete.

She chewed her lip as she wondered how to sign off. Regards, Emerald? Best wishes, Miss Montrose? Lots of love? She grinned at that one, but in the end just signed her name.

Emerald.

She waited for him to reply with increasing irritation, her eyes fixed on the computer screen. She didn't want to go anywhere with him — she didn't like the emotions he stirred up inside her. She took a sip of her tea and tried to dredge up the enthusiasm for a VIP catering uplift scheduled for a flight next week. She tapped her foot and drummed her fingers, glancing at her inbox every ten seconds.

Nothing.

Minutes passed and she tried to imagine his mood as he read her email. Her mobile phone rang and she picked up, not recognising the number.

'Emerald, it's Marco. Look, I'm not arguing about the trip. Just be there. It's an important meeting.' She started to protest, but he swept on. 'There's no one else. All the pilots are flying and Robert Clarke is poorly. This is not a request, Emerald.' He ended the call abruptly, leaving her wide-eyed and gawping at her mobile.

'Who was that?' Finbar sauntered in with a couple of plastic carrier bags, the contents steaming gently. His hair had a decidedly pink hue to it and he looked as if he had a sparkly powder on his cheekbones. Emerald sighed. She'd almost given up ticking him off about his non-uniform

uniform — he'd only say he was being discriminated against. He would deliver this statement falsetto, and accompany it with a huge theatrical wink that would make her laugh. He was totally incorrigible, as he knew she didn't have the heart to reprimand him.

'Emms? Who was it?' he repeated, as Emerald continued to stare distractedly at her phone.

'It was the man who thinks he owns me,' she answered, throwing her mobile onto the desk. 'How did he get my number, even?'

'Ooh, Mr Handsome Gorgeous himself. I wouldn't mind being owned by him.' Fin raised his eyebrows suggestively.

'He is neither of those things.' Emerald transferred her glare to Finbar.

'Don't take it out on me. I bring you good tidings: airline breakfast, the food of the gods.' He lifted up one of the paper bags and waved it in front of her nose.

Emerald snorted. 'Very poor gods, if that's the best they can do.' She took one of the breakfasts and loosened the lid, peering inside. 'How was the flight?' she asked, more to get her brain back on track for work, than out of genuine interest.

'Oh, the usual, I—'

'That man is so arrogant!'

Finbar pursed his lips and tilted his head to one side. 'My mistake, I thought we were talking about me, for a minute.'

'Sorry, but he is so unreasonable. He's just commanded me to be at Luton Airport tomorrow morning to fly up to Edinburgh for two days for some kind of meeting.'

'To stay in Edinburgh? Darling, rooms to rent are as rare as rocking-horse shit. It's the Edinburgh Fringe Festival and everywhere is booked. Unless you want to share and I can't quite see Mr Cav. slumming it in a makeshift attic con version, sleeping top to tail with a trapeze drag artist called Trixie-Belle, can you?'

'God, you're right. That band we flew up there the other day said it was hell to find accommodation.' The butterflies in her stomach flew away, and with them the unlikely scenario she'd allowed herself, for just a moment, of listening to kilted Scotsmen playing "Amazing Grace" on their bagpipes, while wandering around Edinburgh Castle, and maybe meeting Marco later for drinks and supper. She wasn't quite sure when the last bit had snuck into her daydream, but it had somehow ended up as an inevitable end to the day.

She sighed and took the lid off the hot breakfast tray without enthusiasm. This was more like her average day — eating leftover airline food, not swanning it up in a top-class restaurant in Edinburgh. 'I guess I'll just do as he says and hope we end up getting the late shuttle back at the end of the day.'

'Well, you never know, he might have all angles covered and you'll find yourself eating haggis and chips in the local boozer and washing it down with a pint of heavy.' Finbar was good at impersonations and this was said with a thick Scottish accent, making Emerald laugh. 'You can round off the night singing your favourite Proclaimers songs on karaoke together on a makeshift stage, swigging back Glenmorangie and calling each other *ma wee hen*.'

She giggled at the thought. 'Yeah, 'cos that's really likely to happen, isn't it?'

'Well, you know what you're like after a couple of whisky chasers.' He winked and laughed, before turning serious. 'Actually, he also knows what you're like after a few drinks, unfortunately.'

She groaned. 'I have spent my whole life not drinking, purely because alcohol and me never collided in my sheltered world. I tried it and drank one too many.' She sighed. 'And it seems I will never be allowed to forget it.'

'The results were so spectacular, though, you have to agree.' Finbar grinned, adding slyly. 'Now, eat up, you'll need lots of energy for Edinburgh.' He pulled the lid off his breakfast tray and sighed. 'And if you should happen to bump into that Jamie Fraser from *Outlander*, be sure to give him my phone number.'

She grinned. 'In your dreams.'

'I know.' Finbar rested his chin on his hands, a dreamy smile on his lips. 'Jamie Fraser and Marco Cavarelli. My cup runneth over. I'd certainly teach them a thing or two.'

'Finbar. Please. Do not go there. I'm about to eat.' Emerald speared a mushroom, although her stomach had nose-dived again, something she was becoming used to whenever she had to interact with Marco. 'I know: why don't I see if you can go instead?'

'Something tells me I'm not the sort of glamour he's after, sweetie.' His look was wistful, but he soon rallied. 'Promise you'll tell me all the gory details when you get back.'

'I don't imagine there will be any. The most excitement I'm likely to get is a glimpse of hairy Scottish buttocks under a kilt.'

'Aye, well, that's probably better than nothing,' Finbar agreed, before taking a bite of croissant, showering the desk with pastry flakes.

'Gross,' Emerald said.

'Me or the hairy buttocks?'

Emerald laughed in a preoccupied way as an image of Marco's naked bottom jumped into her mind unbidden: all smooth skin and taut rounded muscles, and all of it totally, totally out of bounds. Not thinking, she snatched up her sketchpad, which was never far away, before pausing and sliding her pencil back into her bag as common sense took over. *Do not start drawing fantasy images of any part of your boss's anatomy, Emerald Montrose*, she told herself. She pushed aside her sausage and eggs. There was no room for food amid the butterflies that filled her stomach.

She wished she could dislike Marco as much as he so richly deserved, but somehow the right emotions didn't sur-face even though she was pissed off that he had put her in an untenable position. She ground her teeth — something else she had not consciously done since childhood. If this carried on, she'd be certifiable.

The only way she could manage to survive the ordeal was to retain an aloof veneer and keep her distance — and that was what she would absolutely, undoubtedly, indefatigably do.

CHAPTER ELEVEN

Marco half expected Emerald not to show, but there she was, looking sweet in a flowery dress, her legs bare and brown, her corkscrew hair slightly wild, giving her the look of a forest sprite. He took it all in approvingly, as a surge of pleasure that he was her travelling companion rose in his chest.

'Emerald, glad you decided to join me,' he said.

'Happy to be here. Love me an early morning flight,' she drawled, and Marco couldn't miss the loaded sarcasm.

'Let me take your bag.' He put his hand out to take her case and she recoiled at his touch as their hands collided. He wouldn't have been any more surprised if she'd slapped his hand away.

She thrust out her chin as if daring him to comment. 'I can manage on my own, thanks.'

'Fine,' Marco said, raising his hands. She was not a woman who took orders easily, that much he already knew, but he couldn't understand this new animosity towards him. 'Is something wrong?' he asked, determined to get her on side, one way or another.

'No, and we need to go this way. I've flown out of Luton loads of times.' Emerald marched ahead of him and stopped at the check-in desk, a resolute frown ruining the overall delightful face.

'Not a morning person, Emerald?' he offered, although it was practically lunchtime by his body clock. His mornings frequently started at 5 a.m. so he knew all about early starts. Surely she could meet him halfway and be polite, even if she couldn't manage friendly and sociable.

But it seemed not.

'I'm fine, really.'

Marco would have liked a smile to go along with her blatant lie. He liked it when she smiled, it warmed his soul, but it seemed that she'd used up her quota of genuine smiles and a surly frown was all she could muster.

He sighed. She was back to behaving like a toddler. So be it. They queued up at the gate in silence, boarded the aircraft in silence until they found their seats. She took her seat next to him and carried the grey cloud hovering over her head with her. She clearly didn't want to be anywhere near him and was making it as obvious as she could. He was starting to wonder why he'd thought it a good idea to get to know her a little better.

It carried on this way into the flight, Emerald pretending to read on her Kindle, although not a page was turned, unless they'd invented some way of turning pages without using fingers. He couldn't concentrate either and stared out of the window at a vast nothingness instead of sorting out business affairs.

'Not hungry?' he ventured a while after the stewardess had set down two breakfast trays and she had left hers untouched.

She didn't raise her eyes from her Kindle as she muttered, 'What, are you in control of my body as well as my financial stability now?'

Marco sighed. She was impossible to deal with sometimes. He watched her surreptitiously, her body held rigid, her jaw tensed, trying to gauge the reason for her bad mood.

Surely it wasn't just because he had demanded that she come with him?

'Why are you looking at me like that?'

'You don't seem yourself.'

'I'm fine. Of course I'm myself, who else would I be?'

He exhaled, exasperated. 'Okay, can you tell me the reason you don't want to be here?'

The question seemed to confuse her and she opened and closed her mouth wordlessly as a faint flush of colour crept over her cheeks.

He pressed home his agenda. 'So, here's the thing. Today I need you focused, not acting like a sulky teenager.'

Emerald turned her head away from him, giving every indication of behaving exactly like a sulky teenager.

'Emerald!' he insisted sharply.

She swivelled around and glared at him. 'Do you ever ask, not demand?'

'What?' Marco was genuinely puzzled. 'Emerald, it is my right to tell my employees what I want them to do. Is that what all this moodiness is about? You do not like to be told, I get it, but, you know, it is the way things work, me boss, you employee.'

She turned her face away again. 'And don't I know it.'

'Okay, if you want to play it this way, as your boss, here are my requests. I expect only positive vibes from you towards Mr Edwards today. Even if it is pouring down and you have to eat haggis, you will comment on the pleasant weather and the delicious food. Do you think you could manage that much, challenging as it will be?'

Her eyes sparked with indignation at the suggestion that she wasn't up to the job and he knew he'd pitched it right.

'Who are we meeting then? And just for the record, I'll eat haggis, like, never. Would you?'

Marco grinned, seeing the ridiculousness of their conversation. 'You'd be surprised at what I have eaten out of good manners. Anyway, we're meeting the director of Hopper, a small Scottish airline that is losing money daily because of the unpredictable weather causing delays. We can rent their aircraft for a percentage of the company profits before we too find ourselves in the same position.'

Emerald blanched. 'I didn't know that was a possibility.'

'Well, you know now. I can throw a certain amount of money at a venture but there comes a point . . .' he trailed off. They both knew what running an airline entailed.

He sighed. If he'd expected a meeting of souls as she pondered on the airline's possible demise, he was sadly mistaken. But she picked at her nails as she stared at the seat back in front of her, showing that she was not wholly unaffected by such news. He silently forgave her. He was beginning to think he had the measure of her. Even though she was prickly and complicated, underneath this exterior she was a decent person. If he could just get her to open up a bit, he might be able to understand her better. He wanted to help her, he really did. He almost squeezed her hand to stop the infernal nail picking, stopping himself just in time to busy himself with a newspaper instead.

In no time at all the aircraft touched down and glided to a standstill. Emerald and Marco emerged from the airport to be greeted by thunderous grey skies and a cold wind whipping around their legs.

'You were right about the weather,' Emerald yelled as the heavens opened and rain fell in a sheet of noise. 'A typical Scottish summer. Chucking it down.' She huddled underneath the roof of a bus stop, while Marco searched in vain for the chauffeured car he'd booked.

'We could get a cab,' Emerald suggested when he returned, unable to find the car. She stared dismally at the snake of people queuing at the taxi rank that increased in volume and size by the second as rain pounded the pavement.

She was shivering within minutes in her summer dress, although she had avoided most of the rain so far by sheltering under a canopy.

'Here, take my jacket.' Marco slid his jacket off in one fluid movement.

'No, really, I'm fine.' She shook her head, ignoring his outstretched arm. 'I have a cardigan in my bag. Put it back on or you'll be frozen too. Scotland is rather different from Italy, you know.' She unhooked her bag from her shoulder to rummage for her cardigan. A bus thundered past her and a spray of dirty rainwater spewed upwards and soaked her legs and the bottom of her dress. She gasped in shock and spun around instinctively, as another car churned up a torrent of water, drenching her again. Her dress dripped icy water onto her bare legs and the shock of it made her catch her breath. 'Oh, my God, that's freezing!' she shrieked, flapping at her dress as the cold water numbed her thighs.

Marco grabbed her elbow and directed her across the road. 'I've just heard from the driver. He's over there, come on.'

The rain slanted across Emerald's face and the wind snatched at her hair whipping it into her eyes, blurring her vision. Water channelled its way down the back of her neck and seeped through her thin dress. Marco's hand on her arm was comforting and solid and she was intensely aware of it warming her skin as nothing else could. They reached the car and the chauffeur jumped out to help them inside, shaking out his newspaper to hold above Emerald's head. She tumbled onto the back seat in a jumble of bags and tangled legs, the rain still biting at her heels.

A bubble of emotion rose up in her chest as she swiped at a strand of hair plastered to her cheeks, rainwater dripping from her chin. 'Oh my God. Oh. My. God.' She didn't know whether to laugh or cry as the cold paralysed her into a catatonic state. She shivered as a blast of air conditioning hit her. 'I think I forgot to pack my cardigan.'

'Turn up the heat, please,' Marco instructed the driver, who immediately obliged. 'Good God, you're soaked.' Marco pushed back his own dripping hair from his face to peer at Emerald.

'Yes, the weather is rather inclement,' she said, deadpan, widening her eyes. 'Although I do so enjoy the rain. And while we're at it, let's hope it's haggis for supper.'

Marco looked puzzled for an instant, before throwing back his head and laughing.

Emerald, seeing no point in being dismayed by her bedraggled state, joined in, enjoying Marco's deep laugh and wishing she heard it more often. The car lurched around a corner and she lost her balance, slamming into Marco. 'Sorry,' she exclaimed, as she tried to right herself, but managed to fall into him again as the driver braked once more. 'I'm so sorry.' She giggled, trying unsuccessfully to push herself upright, her nose touching Marco's chest. Marco's hands closed around her shoulders as he steadied her.

Their eyes locked as she looked up into his face. 'Seat belt?' he asked, his voice unusually husky.

His fingers tightened their grip on her upper arms and she shivered at his touch. Never had *seat belt* sounded so sexy.

'Seat belt,' she repeated, nodding as she dragged her gaze away from Marco's dark and smoky eyes. The words hitched in her throat as if she had run a marathon. 'Right,' she said, staying exactly as she was, pressed into Marco's warm chest. She could smell the freshness of his shirt, his shampoo, his skin.

Her shivering increased, but she was no longer sure if it was because of the cold. The urge to stay snuggled up to Marco was overwhelming, his touch sending vibes of tingling awareness radiating through her body.

Damn it, the breathiness was still there. She cleared her throat, not trusting herself to speak as she pulled away from him and peeked back up at him through her eyelashes, seeing concern and tenderness in his eyes. She tried to look away but she was mesmerised. He gazed down at her and pinned her with his eyes. Something shifted between them, right then. It was no more than a look, but it was enough to set Emerald's heart pitter-pattering.

Marco picked up a lock of wet hair that was sticking to her cheek and held it between his fingers for a second before tucking it behind her ear. Realising that he had behaved slightly inappropriately, he pushed himself forward to address the driver. 'To the Caledonian, please.'

To Emerald he uttered *seat belt* again.

She obliged and buckled up as she asked, 'We have somewhere to stay?'

Marco's frown was back in place, his hands firmly in his lap, leaving Emerald to wonder if she'd imagined the tenderness in his eyes. 'Of course. Why?'

'It's the Fringe Festival. Finbar said rooms are as rare as rocking horse sh . . .' She trailed off. 'Doesn't matter.'

'Rocking horse? Ah, I see. That will be why I'm paying a king's ransom for the only rooms we could find. No matter.' He shrugged, as if something as trivial as securing a room was beneath his consideration. The conversation was closed.

Emerald tried to imagine the day that lay ahead of them, butterflies setting up a slow beating of wings in her stomach. She wished she had thought to bring better night attire than her pyjamas and immediately chided herself for such thoughts. It wasn't as if Marco was likely to see her in her nightclothes.

Was it?

CHAPTER TWELVE

The chill air conditioning in the hotel reception hit Emerald as an affront to her already freezing body. Her dress clung to her thighs and dragged between her legs. 'It's like having a wet fish flapping against me.' She grimaced, pulling at the hem ineffectually as she struggled to keep up with Marco.

Marco started to reply but the words died on his lips as he glanced across at her body. Whipping off his jacket, he demanded, 'Put this on. Now.'

'I'm fine. We're here now.' She shrugged off his concern, but his eyes signalled an urgency she didn't understand. She followed his gaze down to her breasts, clearly visible through her dress, nipples standing out proud. 'Oh, God.' She folded her arms quickly across her chest.

'I'll get your key card and you can go straight to your room. I'll do all the formalities. I'll call you later.' He strode to the reception and spoke rapidly to the girl behind the desk, indicating Emerald. The receptionist passed him a key card and he marched over to the lift, beckoning Emerald with a flick of the wrist in his typical Italian way. 'It's number two on the top floor,' he announced briskly as he handed her the card and indicated the lift.

For once she did as he ordered. Revealing her breasts in the reception area was not the sort of thing that would go down well in a hotel. She called the lift, and as she watched Marco head back to reception she saw the check-in girl give him the once-over through her long fringe. She wasn't surprised — he exuded authority and wealth, not to mention the dark Mediterranean good looks that haunted her dreams.

This is purely business, she reminded herself, pulling his jacket close to her chest as another icy blast of air conditioning hit her. The unmistakable scent of Marco tantalized her senses and she drew the jacket tighter still, enjoying the remnants of his body heat over her shoulders.

She waited for the lift to arrive and admitted to herself that something had indeed passed between herself and Marco to change their status quo. She admitted that she was attracted to him and had been pushing the thought away, as if that would make a difference, but now she sensed a change in his attitude too. The air between them pulsed with something she couldn't quite pin down and it brought about a sense of excitement mixed with panic.

She needed to remember the old Marco, she thought, as she stepped inside the lift. The unforgiving Marco who had considered sacking her. The Marco who was a ruthless businessman and might yet be trying to take advantage of her, as Finbar had suggested. She must stay professionally aloof and work towards gaining his respect as an employee, not let him think she was up for anything. If she could only convince her hormones too, she'd be fine. All of this *stuff* going on and they hadn't even unpacked.

She would have to stay focused and try to keep her distance. She glanced at the mirror in the lift, horrified at what a fright she looked. Her cheeks were blotchy and her hair was full of static: practically touching the roof — sticking her fingers in an electrical socket could not wreak more havoc than the Scottish rain had inflicted on her hair. Worst of all, it wasn't just her boobs on display — her knickers, too, were visible for all to see. She checked her rear in the mirror and more than a hint of her bottom cheeks showed through the material of her dress. VPL had nothing on her: she had the whole caboodle on show.

Emerald needed to change, and quickly, but the lift didn't seem to appreciate her sense of urgency as it didn't move a millimetre despite pressing every button with an up arrow on it — and a few more random ones, just in case. It was a joke, but she wasn't laughing. She peered even more closely at the dials on the lift panel. No floors, just names. The McFlynn and McDuff Superior Suites stood out in red lettering, while McGregor and McDougal seemed to have a whole floor to themselves. What did it mean? Why didn't they just have sodding numbers like normal hotels — and why wasn't the bloody lift moving?

She stamped her foot and considered jumping up and down a little just to give it a nudge in the right direction, but had a horrible vision of a hidden camera with Scottish blokes laughing their hairy arses off as she did a bit of Scottish jigging. This was a top-notch hotel, so why didn't the bloody lift just *move*? She shivered as the air conditioning continued its assault on her skin. *Are you cold enough yet?* it whispered, winding around her legs and bare arms, until her very core was frozen.

She pushed a few random buttons once again in case the lift had seen the error of its ways and was ready to take her to her room. Nothing. She breathed in and exhaled steadily, actually shivering with the cold, ready to kick the door down in frustration when, amazingly and smoothly, it slid open.

Only it wasn't her technological wizardry that had managed it. Marco, surprise registering as he took in the trembling form of Emerald within, furrowed his brow. 'Oh, you're still here.'

'So it seems.'

'Do you need some help?' he asked, his lips twitching.

'No, it's fine. I'm just seeing how long it takes before my blood turns to ice. I thought it would be an interesting experiment.'

Marco gave her a puzzled look, but then his confusion cleared. 'Ah, the English sense of humour.'

'Quite. As you would say. Also, there are no floor numbers, and I couldn't open the door once it had closed to ask what kind of weird-arsed system they used here to make a lift actually *lift*.'

'I see.' His lips twitched again as he slid his key card into a thin slot by the door. The lift started its smooth ascent.

'Ahh.' She nodded. It could have been so easy. She threw Marco a malevolent glare as the twitch on his lips turned into a full-on smirk. 'If you're laughing at me . . .'

He held his hands up to prove his innocence.

She huffed. 'I didn't know you needed a key card to make the lift move, or that everything was called MacDuff or McDoughnut or whatever, did I?'

Marco leaned against the lift wall, taking stock of her. 'Are you okay?' he asked, trying not to laugh.

Aware that he was observing her, Emerald pushed her hair away from her face and crossed her arms again, having forgotten momentarily about her see-through dress. 'I'm just embarrassed — and a bit hungry.' She tried not to glower. 'And don't say a word about me not eating my meal on the plane, okay?'

'I wouldn't dare,' Marco answered, his voice quivering with suppressed laughter.

She gave him a rueful smile, the absurdity of her situation finally hitting her. Chilled and bone-weary, she would have loved to lean against Marco's chest, to lose herself in his warm and comforting arms instead of the cold lift wall. Instead, she leaned her head against it and closed her eyes, pulling Marco's jacket tighter around herself.

* * *

Marco took the opportunity to study Emerald while her eyes were shut, noting the wayward hair tumbling over her shoulders and her cheeks glowing in a bloom of pink. Her neck was creamy against the darkness of his jacket and an unwanted memory of soft skin under his fingers surfaced, unbidden.

His gaze followed the column of her throat to the swell of her breasts and he forced himself to avert his eyes, taking in her face once more. Her lips were soft and pink and looked eminently kissable. He swayed towards her, pulling up short when he took stock of his actions. He cleared his throat and pushed his back against the lift wall, where he intended to stay until the excruciatingly slow lift reached its destination.

Emerald must have sensed the movement as she looked directly at him with those smoky, sultry eyes that suggested she was thinking the same wayward thoughts. He took a deep breath. They needed to move away from this shaky ground, return to a comfortable work status. If only she wasn't so close.

She pushed herself away from the wall, her eyes focused on Marco's. He took a step towards her — the gravitational pull stronger than his common sense — to meet her halfway.

Without warning the lift jolted to a halt, and they both froze as the door opened. A young mother shoved two children inside the lift and pulled a large buggy in behind them. Marco blew out a breath, dragging his fingers through his hair and silently thanking the harassed mother who had stopped him from making a rash move.

He smiled briefly at the woman as she smoothed down a tuft of hair sticking up on her small son's head. 'Terrible weather,' she said conversationally, jiggling the buggy as her baby started grizzling.

Marco agreed. 'For the time of year.' He was perfectly au fait with the English obsession about the weather and even he knew that torrential rain in August was a bad thing, if not wholly unexpected. The woman leaned over the buggy to placate her baby and Marco was forced to edge closer to Emerald. The heady scent of her damp body and the memory of her breasts jutting out of her summery dress sent his thoughts into overdrive once more.

'Stop that!' the mother shouted, and Marco jumped at the command.

'Sorry.' The young woman turned to Emerald and Marco as her son resumed his kicking of the pram wheels, complaining, 'Boring, boring.'

Marco thought that what was playing out between Emerald and himself was not the least bit boring, but sanity was almost restored and he pushed his clenched fists into his pockets to stop them from touching her of their own accord, as he vowed to keep his distance.

CHAPTER THIRTEEN

The lift stopped on their floor and Marco stepped aside to allow Emerald to exit first.

'Apparently, we have the run of the top floor in the presidential suite. I didn't ask for the upgrade, but the whole hotel is full. There are three separate bedrooms so you can choose the one you would like.' He shrugged. 'It was out of my hands.'

'A suite?' Oh, God, no. Too intimate. 'That's lovely,' she lied, aware of a sudden pounding in her chest, as if she'd just run up to the top floor rather than endured a rather damp and infinitesimally slow ride in a lift. A lift in which Marco Cavarelli — her boss, she reminded herself quickly — had gazed at her and stood so close that the all-pervading scent of him filled her with overactive sensations.

She'd seen his eyes full of unspoken desire, although she now wondered if they were just mirroring her own emotions, which she desperately wanted to hide from him. She had thanked God when the lift doors opened, letting fresh air in and pheromones out.

They headed along an endless corridor, her footsteps measured and calm as she mechanically placed one foot in front of the other on the plush carpet. Inside, her emotions whirled as adrenaline and dread pumped through her body. She could have been walking to the scaffold, the way she felt.

Marco slipped the key card in the door and pushed it open for Emerald, but seeing that it was still dark inside, slid his arm around the door frame to find the light switch. Emerald, following closely behind, didn't realize what he was doing and crashed into him. She reeled backwards, almost falling over her suitcase.

'Sorry, I was just trying to put the swipe card . . .' Marco's arm wrapped around her, stopping her from losing her balance. She righted herself, but still he held her tight. 'We need to find the key card slot to make the light work.' His voice was husky, low, and very close to her ear.

She froze as his breath fanned her neck, his touch electrifying her in the dark, making their position appear more intimate than it was.

'Did I stand on your toes?'

'Only a little bit.' She wiggled her foot, trying not to wince. A heartbeat passed as she remained in his arms. She stilled, frozen, convinced he was going to kiss her, then was left blinking in surprise and regret when he drew in a breath and cursed. At least, she imagined the Italian expletive was a curse. It certainly didn't sound like an endearment and the way he shoved her away from him and tutted in exasperation made her totally rethink the kiss thing.

'One moment please,' he said as she heard a click and light finally flooded the room. 'Swipe card for the power,' he said, heaving in another breath as he shot her a warning glance. That confused her even more. Was it her fault he had stood on her toes?

He dumped their bags on the floor, exasperation etched on his brow as he stepped away from her into the main sitting room.

Tuning in to his mood, she stayed silent until her eyes adjusted to the light that streamed in from the window. It was her turn to draw in a breath as she took in the magnificent view through the panoramic bay window. Edinburgh, lit up, but eerily shrouded in mist, opened up to her like a Grimm fairytale. The majestic castle stood proud, high up on the hill, half hidden by the low-lying cloud. It was so close that she felt she could reach out and touch it. 'My God, the castle is wonderful.' She raced over to the window and pressed her face against the glass.

Marco strolled over to join her after searching for the bathroom to hand her a huge fluffy towel. He passed it to her, saying, 'You can always guarantee a giant-sized towel in a hotel such as this.' He stared out at the view. 'It is magnificent, although I confess to feeling slightly let down that the presidential suite doesn't seem to impress you.' He pulled a wry face, mocking himself.

Emerald hugged the towel to her chest gratefully, too engrossed to immediately get changed. She spun around on her heels at Marco's words, taking in the stone fireplace complete with real logs, the flock wallpaper, the thick-piled tartan carpet and heavy drapes. It was a replica of a real Scottish retreat, recreated in a top-class hotel. She almost expected to see a smiling moose head pinned to the wall and hear background music of Amazing Grace played on some invisible bagpipes. But it was the view that stopped her in her tracks. She gazed, mesmerised by Edinburgh castle in all its glory,

Marco coughed pointedly and she turned regretfully back to the décor of the room, knowing instinctively that he wanted her approval. 'It's beautiful,' she said, nodding in approval. But the pull of the view out of the window won out and she turned back to look through the window. The castle sitting on its rugged bed of black rock would make a fantastic subject for one of her larger abstract art pieces and her fingers itched to sketch it out before the soot-coloured clouds either dissipated or totally engulfed the ancient castle.

Instinctively, she checked the angle of shadow to see how long the light would hold out. A shaft of sunlight broke through the clouds and turned the raindrops into magical stars, sparkling through the haze. She picked up her bag and sighed in frustration as her fingers closed around her sketchpad. If she could manage even a sketchy outline it would be better than nothing, then she could fill the rest in later. She turned to check out Marco's whereabouts, almost bumping into him. He was right behind her, watching with interest as she took in the view.

She caught a gentle smile on his lips, his grey eyes, soft and tender for once, distracting her more than they should.

Fighting down an almost unbearable urge to pull out her pastel sticks she toyed with the idea of letting Marco in on her secret passion, just so she didn't miss the wonderful opportunity that was fading away before her eyes.

She glanced at him, considering it. No, she didn't want to tell him. Ever since her school days, when anything she did seemed to be fertile ground for teasing, she had been used to keeping her own counsel. She let her sketchpad drop back into her bag and turned away from him uneasily, hoping her inner thoughts were not transparent.

She sighed as she turned back to the view and formed a furtive square with her thumbs and forefingers, imagining the size and perspective of the picture she could make.

Marco coughed politely and she let out a breath of irritation, her hands falling to her side. She turned away from the view and only half attempted to conceal her frustration.

'That certainly held your attention. For a moment there, you disappeared.'

Emerald turned on him. 'Am I not allowed my own thoughts?' Even as she said the words she knew she was being unfair. It was her problem that she felt as if she'd been caught out misbehaving, not his.

He held his hands up in surrender. 'Of course. I'm just trying to get a handle on what makes you happy — what makes you who you are.'

'You don't need to find out what makes me happy, and anyway, I thought you'd already labelled me as damaged goods.' Her hackles were up, when only seconds ago her mind had been thinking dreamy thoughts of Marco.

'And you are blaming me for that?'

'Here we go again.'

He shrugged. 'You brought the subject up, and since you did, I *was* the focus of your intentions, remember?'

'Actually, I can't — remember, that is. Not much anyway. You appear to remember enough for both of us, though, so feel free to keep judging me and taking the moral high ground. My integrity, or lack of it, against your God-like virtue, yeah?' She knew she should just shut up, knew she was pushing the boundaries of their uneasy relationship, but right at that moment, the emotional see-saw that he constantly forced her to ride with him was reaching tipping point. 'And actually, who are you to judge?' she demanded, warming to her theme. 'I'm sure you've been through God knows how many lovers yourself, if Finbar is to be believed, *and* you've managed to lose a wife along the way.'

Marco's head snapped up as if he'd been punched under the chin. His eyes clouded and his jaw tightened. 'You have no right to bring that up and you know nothing about my circumstances.' He spoke with controlled anger as he glared at her.

She was instantly contrite. She'd said too much. It was just that he unnerved her so much, and she was sick of second-guessing him. 'I'm sorry. I spoke out of turn.'

Marco shook his head. 'It's fine.' His voice was clipped. 'But what's happening here, Emerald? Why are you so angry with me?'

'I'm not . . . I don't know, just stop trying to get inside my head.' She raised her palms to warn him off.

He seemed to get the message and changed the subject. 'Why don't you have a hot bath, get changed and have a rest? You must be tired.'

Ashamed of her outburst, but still feeling affronted, she shucked off his jacket, throwing it on the sofa. 'Good idea,' she said brusquely. She clutched at the towel having once again forgotten about her see-through dress.

He picked up his jacket and draped it carefully over the back of a chair, which irritated her for no good reason and she wondered if, after all, she was a bit overwrought.

'The bedrooms are that way.' He ran his fingers through his hair looking agitated, and all but dismissed her, lifting his chin in the direction of the corridor.

'Thank you.' She picked up her overnight bag and began to walk towards the bedrooms, hating herself for her behaviour. She stopped and turned. 'I'm sorry.'

He smiled weakly. 'I have booked dinner at seven with Tom Edwards, the owner of Hopper. I hope, of course that you will join us.' Marco was back in boss mode. 'Do you have a cocktail dress?'

She shook her head looking down at the dress that clung to her curves, noting Marco's eyes scan her body briefly. He was nothing if not a gentleman though, and she felt a stab of disappointment that he didn't seem to find her body irresistible.

For one mad second, she considered asking him to help her disrobe. She'd seen it played out on films enough times — where the heroine couldn't quite reach the zip at the back of her dress and before you knew it the sultry hero was kissing her neck and helping her with more than just her dress. But she'd probably just have a fit of the giggles and the zip would get stuck, or even worse, Marco would refuse to help her. Oh, how embarrassing would that be?

While she stood there debating, Marco reached for his wallet and pulled out a wad of notes. 'When you've rested, go and buy something suitable for this evening. The shops are minutes away.'

Emerald was surprised and touched by the gesture, until he added, 'Don't forget it needs to be sophisticated — to inspire you to be a lady.'

She eyed Marco and the proffered notes, her momentary gratitude evaporated. He didn't even seem to realize he'd just insulted her — again.

'It will be marked as expenses, so don't think of it as anything else,' he added, misreading her reaction.

She snatched the notes out of his hand. 'What's the real reason for all of this, Marco? Only I'm struggling to understand why you're including me in your business dealings at all, when you clearly don't trust me to behave. Are you hoping I'll be your eyes and ears at work? Grass on my colleagues if you butter me up enough?'

Confusion creased Marco's brow. 'Is that what all this huffiness is about?'

She didn't know why she wanted to hurt him. Perhaps she wanted a reaction that was more than cool disdain. Perhaps she just wanted the truth. 'I've been told it's what you do — get close to one particular person to glean information from them, even try to sleep with them.' Now she'd uttered the words she realized how unwarranted her accusation was, but it was too late to take it back.

Marco's nostrils flared slightly and a flash of the old flintiness returned to his eyes. His smile was scathing as he shook his head, slipping his wallet back into his pocket. 'Priceless, absolutely beyond belief.'

Emerald winced. 'So, you weren't hoping to do — what I just said.' She trailed off, feeling silly.

'Emerald, I have no need to use you in such a way and actually I think you are overstepping the mark to suggest such a thing.'

'Why, what's so wrong with me?' she asked, suddenly defensive.

'For goodness' sake, stop twisting things around,' Marco said in exasperation.

'But you confuse me. One minute you're all officious, "don't forget who is the boss around here," and the next minute you turn on the warmth and charm as if you . . .' She floundered. 'I don't know, you're like a crocodile tenderising me up just to rip me to shreds later.'

His eyebrows raised at this. He bestowed on her a tight smile as he inclined his head. 'A crocodile? You have an interesting imagination, Emerald.' He paused as if weighing up his words carefully. 'For the record, I am inured to temptation, having been enticed by too many sophisticated women hoping to procure a husband.' He smiled thinly, eyes glittering dangerously.

'Don't worry, I promise I won't try to tempt you,' Emerald retorted, stung by his words.

'You are not one of those women,' Marco said, confusing her further. 'And I consider it unprofessional and unethical to have a relationship with someone from work.'

'I'll try to remember that.'

'You will have no need,' he retorted dismissively.

Her cheeks seared with humiliation as his words sank in. She crumpled up the money he'd given her and threw it onto the table before grabbing her bag and marching down the small corridor, burning tears of anger brewing behind her eyes.

She grabbed the nearest door handle, praying it wasn't a broom cupboard or a bathroom, to complete her humiliation as Marco watched her flounce away. She shoved at the door angrily. How dare he? Well she'd show him she was as good as any one of his *sophisticated* women. Although — she began to calm down — why did she want to prove anything to him — they couldn't even manage a civilized conversation?

She sat down on the edge of the bed and looked around the room: the huge spa bath, thick white towels and silk embroidered eiderdown. It made her want to cry. It was a room for sharing, for laughing and being happy, for making love — not for sitting forlornly on the end of the bed, unhappy and unwanted. Not that she knew much about making love or being happy, thanks to the confines of the convent and that creep Rick with his secret woman.

The contrast with her meagre accommodation in the convent suddenly made the opulence of the hotel room seem shameful and brought back the old convent doctrine that humility was the only way to save her soul.

She shrugged off such weighty thoughts, having fought long and hard with her demons and her supposed sinful ways. She would not let her past shape her future. There was one thing she had learned, though: if you couldn't share the good times with someone you cared for, the good times weren't worth having — apart from getting to eat the free food all on your own, she thought sadly, eyeing the overflowing fruit bowl and chocolates. She picked up an apple and then put it back again. She would rather paint it than eat it. The colours were tempting and aesthetically pleasing, but then, really, it was just more damned pictures of fruit.

She sighed, undressed, draped her wet clothes over the radiator and turned on the shower. Feeling more positive after washing her hair and thawing out her body, she pulled on her jeans and jumper and unpacked, arranging her inadequate outfits on the bed, in a slow acceptance that she had nothing vaguely wearable for a five-star restaurant. Even though she was cross with Marco, she didn't want to look dowdy or out of place. She would either have to stay cooped up in her room all night like a naughty girl, or turn up looking underdressed and risk embarrassing her boss.

Mulling over the dilemma, she decided she would, after all, shop for a new outfit, slightly resenting Marco for making her do this, even as a small part of her looked forward to dressing up. She would buy a sophisticated dress and amaze him with her impeccable taste and her good manners. No more tea dresses and flowing locks for her. That would open Marco sodding Cavarelli's eyes.

She grabbed her handbag off the bed and headed for the door. As she passed by Marco, she pretended she hadn't noticed him typing on his laptop, pretended she hadn't seen his strong forearms as he pushed his sleeves up to his elbows, or his feet, now bare and brown as they rested on the thick carpet.

He didn't even glance up as she sauntered past. Dear God, he was infuriating. She slammed the door on her way out.

CHAPTER FOURTEEN

Emerald headed into the first department store she came across and managed to get the attention of a sales assistant, who stuck closer than a limpet on a rock when she realized her customer was going for the whole works: shoes, bag, dress and makeover.

"Call me Gemma" persuaded her to buy a long, fitted red jersey dress that was beautifully fluid, draping around her body as she moved. Emerald couldn't help admiring herself in the mirror, wondering why she'd thought red wasn't her colour. An elegant sparkling necklace and high wedges with contrasting bag was added to the ensemble, and at the last minute she added some diamanté hair jewels to twist into her hair. It was all carefully wrapped by Gemma while Emerald had her make-up done at the beautician's counter.

The make-up artist went a bit overboard with the red lipstick, Emerald thought, although having said she was going for the vampy look, what else should she have expected? She blotted the gash of bright red that was her lips as soon as she left the store, but thought the soft grey eyeshadow and coral blusher suited her colouring.

She was pleased with the look and felt good as she walked back to the hotel, half hoping that Marco would fall immediately in lust with her, just so that she could rebuff him.

Unfortunately, he was asleep on the sofa when she let herself back into the room, which rather diluted the whole, "Oh, my God, how come I didn't realize how beautiful you are?" effect that she'd been hoping for. A newspaper, flat on his chest, fluttered in the breeze from an open window. He had showered, by the looks of his damp hair — and the fact that he only wore a T-shirt and boxers. His features were softened in sleep and she gazed at him, a deep ache filling her chest. He was infinitely more beguiling when he wasn't bellowing down the phone over some misdemeanour or frowning over an inflated invoice.

She smiled to herself, feeling her own features relaxing as she watched him. Quickly she took out her pencil to sketch him, her eyes sweeping over his body. She took in his perfection. From an aesthetic point of view he was an artist's dream. His long legs were firm and his T-shirt showed off his impressive abs. She drew in his face, deftly colouring in his closed eyes and spiky, long lashes and used charcoal to shade in his heavy eyebrows and sharp cheekbones. His lips didn't look severe when he was asleep, they looked soft and generous, and as she sketched them on her drawing pad she felt a tiny pull of something in her gut — a small twisting like a flutter of tenderness.

He stirred in his sleep and she flipped the page on her sketchpad, hiding the charcoal image while backing away from him, in case he woke up and caught her spying on him. He remained asleep and blissfully unaware of her, though, and she watched his chest as it rose and fell in time with his steady breathing. She ached to touch him, but knew she wouldn't — couldn't. Just imagine his reaction if he woke up to find her caressing his face? It didn't bear thinking about. She paced the floor a bit, her earlier tension returning.

Her mouth twisted at the irony of her situation. Here she was, make-up-ready, dress to die for, just waiting to wow Marco with a grand entrance, and instead she was watching him sleep, with no more than the urge to stroke his face.

As Emerald watched over this handsome man who, against all odds, she was beginning to like, she wondered why he had such a deep need to be a perfectionist and what it was that impelled him to be a ruthless businessman. She knew deep down that there was another side to him — a caring side that he didn't often show — but she hadn't exactly tried too hard to find it, had she?

The tug happened again, deep down: a sharp, sweet, aching feeling that almost hurt as she fought the desire to smooth his hair and trace the lines around his eyes. She snuck a few inches closer. His face was so much softer in sleep, the resolute and forbidding Marco banished for the moment.

She needed to stop staring at him, she thought, but she felt incapable of tearing her eyes away. Quickly, to distract herself, she took her parcel into the bedroom and changed into the dress. She looked sophisticated, even she could see that, but did she also look like a wanton hussy who would have sex with any man who crossed her path? Possibly. She sighed and threw a longing gaze at her flowery day dress drying on the radiator. Should she? She glanced in the full length mirror again smiling with approval. Why should she have to adapt herself for Marco? She hadn't even used his money. Deciding she might as well go the whole hog she put on the earrings, threaded the hair jewels through her hair, and slipped into the shoes.

Sashaying back into the sitting room, smiling as she did so — it was so unlike the woman she was — she peered at the still-sleeping figure, willing him to wake. As if on cue he opened his eyes and Emerald almost fell over her feet in her haste to distance herself from him. She expected him to snap at her — she was so conditioned to feeling wrong-footed — but he smiled a lazy, sleepy smile and she returned it, spontaneously.

'Hi, I must have dozed off.' He stretched and pushed himself upright, sending the newspaper scattering to the floor. He blinked and screwed his eyes up, focusing on Emerald. 'Wow. Who stole Emerald and replaced her with a movie star?'

Marco propped himself up on his elbow and looked her up and down approvingly, and this time she didn't find it rude or patronising.

'Very nice — lovely, in fact,' he continued. She couldn't resist doing a twirl, but his nod of approval was short and sharp and she felt slightly disappointed. What did she expect? Did she want him to sweep her off her feet and tell her she was the only one for him? Unfortunately, she rather thought she did.

Marco instead swung his legs off the sofa and walked over to the kettle, flicking on the switch. 'I need a coffee. Would you like a cup of tea as we have some time to kill? You can tell me a bit about yourself so that Mr Edwards doesn't think I'm paying for you by the hour.'

She narrowed her eyes, but he didn't seem to be aware that he was blatantly insulting her again. 'No thanks.'

He laughed in surprise. 'No thanks to which bit, the tea or the talking? Most people cannot say enough about themselves — and most English girls do not refuse tea.'

'Fine. What do you want me to tell you?' She sat, unenthusiastically on the sofa that was still warm from Marco's body. She glanced up at him, her gaze straying to his muscled thighs and then upwards towards the boxer shorts before she snapped her eyes resolutely back to his face. Was she really having a conversation with her boss while he walked around in his pants and a T-shirt? He certainly didn't seem as affected by her new vampy look as she was by his semi-naked state, as he folded his arms and leaned against the wall waiting for the kettle to boil and for Emerald to talk.

'This isn't an interrogation, Emerald, I'm just hoping to get to know you better — so we are comfortable with each other.'

His tone was gentle enough to convince Emerald that he had no sinister motive, so she took a steadying breath and prepared to tell Marco a little about herself, albeit reluctantly. 'I was born in England, but my father is Irish. I see my mum rarely as she lives in Joburg and I can't afford to visit very often. Finbar is a good friend, as you probably know, and I have a cousin in London who I am close to. She rescued me from the Dominican nuns, as she likes to say.' She all but dusted her hands with the finality of summing up her life and friendships. 'That's about it, I guess.'

'You needed rescuing?'

'I suppose I did. I was twenty years old and was doing little more than teaching the children at the convent in Ireland, unofficially, as I had no other income and nowhere to go. I was existing, rather than living. Suzie brought me to England from Ireland. She knew Mr Clarke and got me this job and I finally managed to earn a decent enough wage to rent my tiny flat.'

'I like the sound of this Suzie.'

'Yes, she's the only family I have — that I'm in regular contact with, anyway. Suzie makes gorgeous jewellery and sells it in a gallery in London that also sells art and artefacts. I go over there and help out sometimes when I have a few free days.' She stood up and dusted down her dress. 'Okay?'

'What? We've only just scratched the surface. Sit down.'

She balked, but sat again when he added *please* to his demand. 'Tell me about one of your pets. You must have had a pet when you lived in Africa.'

'You know I lived in Africa? That's not on my CV.'

Marco fixed their drinks, man-handling an intricate looking coffee machine with ease and pouring boiling water into a small teapot along with a couple of teabags, while she watched, warily, as if he was going to try and slip a truth drug into her drink.

'I make it my business to find out about my staff,' he said, as he took milk out of the mini fridge and popped the lid.

'So why have you asked me?' She stared belligerently.

In reply, he simply raised an eyebrow.

Because he can, Emerald decided, her mind racing as she acknowledged that the extent of his efficiency had included background checks on her life. She wasn't pleased. Her past was for her to know and no one else, and she wanted it to stay that way.

Marco, however, didn't appear to notice her reluctance to share. He simply stirred the tea and fished out a teabag from her mug adding milk and gazing morosely into the milky liquid. 'Tea and the English.' He shook his head unable to hide his disdain for it. He set a cup down for her and picked up his coffee mug sipping as he quirked an eyebrow to show he hadn't forgotten their conversation and expected an answer.

She looked at him and sighed heavily and pointedly, knowing she wasn't going to get away with ignoring the question. 'My parents moved to a farm near Zambia when I was three as my dad was — is — a gemmologist and he works at the emerald mines there. That's how I got my name. It seemed quite natural to be called Emerald in Africa, but when I moved here, well, it was something else to be teased about especially as I was the typical gawky teenager, all elbows and knock knees — hardly worthy to be named after a beautiful precious stone.' She pursed her lips remembering times she would rather forget at school. 'Still, my life was idyllic in Zambia. I was given a pony as soon as I could ride, and eventually my own horse.' She smiled at the memory, even as she resented his probing. She looked at the floor as her memories surfaced, before gazing back at Marco. 'He was more than a horse to me — he was my soulmate. I'd ride him for miles and miles to beautiful, secluded places where exotic plants and twisting trees concealed animals you'd never see in Europe. They weren't afraid of me and I felt safe, too — as if we had an understanding, you know? Probably a bit naive of me, but, well — I'm still here.' She checked Marco wasn't laughing at her and huffed into her tea before continuing. 'I would take my stepmother's mastiff, Tubby, to my . . .' She swallowed and bit her lip, finding it inexplicably hard to continue.

Marco sat on the arm of the sofa and waited, his serious eyes fixed on hers, as she struggled to finish the sentence. She couldn't tell him about the shelter she made to escape from the real world, it was too ingrained in her to keep such things to herself. She could, however, glower at him for being so intrusive — then maybe he'd stop quizzing her.

'Do you still have a horse?'

'Yeah, he's parked right out back next to the Porsches and Ferraris, swishing his tail at the ladies and wowing them with his stud history.'

'I don't mean here.' He smiled gently, but she didn't want to smile back, the memories were too painful. She stared into her mug, her mind in a different time, a different place.

'No, my father wouldn't pay for the upkeep once I hit eighteen and refused to go home to visit him and his wife. As far as I know he was given to a neighbour. I never really found out.'

'That's a hell of a story.'

'You think I'm making it up?' Her head shot up and she flashed hurt and angry eyes at him.

'No, that's not what I meant! I'm sorry, that is really not . . .' He raised his hands to placate her. 'What was your horse's name?'

'Star.'

'Star! You're kidding me.'

'What's wrong with Star?' She threw him a warning look. If he carried on the way he was going she'd tell him to shove his dinner date. She'd get straight into her pyjamas and binge-watch Netflix all night. That or she'd start walking home.

'There's nothing wrong with the name Star. Sorry.' He sipped his coffee and prodded the thick pile of the cream carpet with his toes, looking thoughtful.

She glared at him, her chin jutting out. It was bad enough that he'd made her return to a part of her life she wanted to forget, without him laughing about it into the bargain.

'It's just not a very original name.'

She shrugged wearily. 'Ava, our maid, bought me a hamster and I called him Hammy, so I probably didn't think too deeply about such things.'

'I had a duck called Puddleduck, so perhaps I am not much better.' He smiled again, and this time she returned it. 'I was brought up on Beatrix Potter, so I guess that was inevitable. If I'd had a rabbit it would be named Peter.' He smiled encouragingly. 'See how easy a conversation can be?' he said. 'I already know you had two pets and your maid was your only friend.'

'Well, we were a bit short on neighbours to hang out with, so yeah, I suppose Ava was a friend. *She* was kind to me at least.' She looked down at her tea, willing him not to dig deeper, but it seemed he wasn't letting up. 'So, you stayed on the farm for most of your childhood — until you went to senior school? Were you happy at home?'

'I was until Mum left and *she* moved in, then I went a bit wild.' She looked at her nails, trying to tamp down the spark of anger that used to fire her up at the unfairness of how her life changed. She swallowed. 'I didn't really go to school when I was little but then I was sent to boarding school in Ireland where my father grew up. It was a convent school for young ladies. I was twelve — and a bit too out of step with everyone else to make proper friends — and far too young not to care.' She shrugged. 'Not making friends seems to be a habit I've found difficult to break.'

'Was school better than home?'

She shrugged again and Marco raised an eyebrow in encouragement.

She looked at him bleakly, knowing that he expected to hear that maybe life was better away from her stepmother. Finally, she said, 'I was a wild redhead with a dodgy accent and a penchant for keeping stray animals hidden in my room. You tell me.' She sipped her tea, hoping the cross-examination was almost over.

Marco nodded. 'I can understand that being difficult when you are at an awkward age, although I find your accent quite charming.'

She peered at him from under her lashes, trying to work out if he was being sarcastic. She didn't think so. In fact he

115

sounded almost emotional when he spoke. 'I cannot imagine a life so different from my own upbringing, filled with love and nurturing.'

'Yeah, well Italian families are famous for that, but don't brag about it too much, you're not exactly sorted out in the life department, if everything in the society magazines is true.'

He winced but smiled. 'Ouch. I suppose I asked for that.'

'You did. And now it's your turn, if we're going through with this touchy-feely bonding experience.' She settled into the squashy sofa, tucking her legs neatly by her side. 'Pets are optional.'

He looked at his watch. 'Is that the time? I'd better get ready.' He drained his coffee and took Emerald's mug from her hand.

'Nice one,' Emerald said. 'Wish I'd tried that move,' she called after him as he headed towards his bedroom door.

Marco turned and winked at her. 'I've had more prac-tice.' He stopped, his face becoming serious. 'I honestly didn't mean to offend you, Emerald, when I offered to buy you a dress. You really must let me reimburse you.'

'That's okay, I needed one anyway.' She grinned lopsidedly.

'You're such a bad liar,' Marco said, taking a step towards her smiling. 'I'm sorry we seem to rub each other the wrong way, but I am trying.'

'Yeah you are. Very.' She grinned at her weak joke.

Marco raised his hands. 'Walked into that one, didn't I?' His eyes crinkled endearingly as he smiled again, and she felt a warm glow in the pit of her stomach when he said, 'You will outshine everyone tonight, trust me on that one.'

'And I hope you appreciate how much trouble I've gone to, so don't try to upstage me with your glitzy connections and your magazine smile.'

'I will go just as I am.'

'I hope not — boxer shorts tend to be frowned on in posh restaurants, and it would give you an unfair advantage over me. There's bound to be a pap lurking around somewhere, to splash you all over social media.' She grinned and nodded towards his bare legs, his T-shirt only just covering his boxers. If she hoped to embarrass him, she was sadly unsuccessful.

'Ah, I miss being at home in the mountains where everyone wears shorts.'

'I'd like to visit the Italian mountains.' She could have bitten off her tongue as soon as she said it, realising that it sounded as if she was angling for an invitation.

Marco gave her a measured look before saying, 'It's the best place in the world. It is where I intend to live out my days, eventually.' He placed the mugs side by side on the service tray. 'I will be ready to leave in half an hour,' he said before walking into his bedroom.

CHAPTER FIFTEEN

Marco showered quickly, his thoughts returning again and again to Emerald and her lonely teenage years. It fitted in with the woman he was getting to know — prickly, but fiercely loyal and loving if she was given the chance. His heart went out to her as he pictured the frightened young girl, banished to another country on her own, suddenly expected to toe the line after a childhood of freedom and space.

He understood why she was determined that no one would ever get the better of her — she'd had to fight her corner for so much of her life.

Earlier, he had wanted to promise that as long as he was around he would shield her from the world, wanted to smooth away the hurt that was etched on her face, her lips flattening to prevent the tears he saw gathering in her eyes as she recounted her past, fists involuntarily clenched. But such thoughts were alarming and he resolved — yet again — to try and remain the impartial boss he had to be.

As he dressed, he reminded himself that his priority was to the owner of Hopper, not the pale redhead who was in danger of bewitching him with her guiles. He fixed his cufflinks as he walked into the sitting room and picked up his wallet.

'Very nice,' Emerald said approvingly, standing to join him, a tiny clutch bag tucked under her arm.

Marco saw her anew, dazzled by the change in her looks as rays from the sun shone through the large sash window, tinting her hair in a halo of burned bronze. He took in the high cheekbones, wide, green eyes and full lips, newly adorned with red lipstick. She looked every inch the sort of woman he normally dated and it was disconcerting to know that underneath all of the veneer of sophistication was the Emerald he'd mistrusted such a short time ago. He brought up his defence shield, reminding himself once again that she was out of bounds. He gave her a thin smile. 'We need to go.'

Her ready smile faded at his curt words and he felt a pang of guilt for being sharp — but it was necessary for him to mark the gulf between them, and for her to understand that this blurring of lines between boss and employee was only temporary.

* * *

A few heads turned as they entered the restaurant, but Marco was used to being stared at, especially in his home country where the family name was known to all, and himself and his wife were all over social media. It took him a moment to realize it was Emerald they were admiring. She looked striking under the subtle restaurant lighting, her hair piled up into a loose chignon, tendrils curling around her neck to soften the severity of the style. Hair jewels, weaved throughout her curls, sparkled in the light from the chandelier, shooting out tiny rainbows of colour and emphasising her natural auburn highlights. Her red lipstick drew attention to her generous, full lips, which, he was starting to realize, he had studied far too intently. Her dress draped softly over her hips and the split at the front showed her bare legs as she walked with cool confidence and elegance.

The desire to grab her hand, to claim possession, startled him. Getting a grip on himself, he compromised and took her elbow to escort her to their table. It seemed a sad substitute.

Emerald, true to form, threw him a puzzled glance and muttered, 'I can walk unaided, you know,' as she shook off his hand.

His lips tightened. 'I'm just being chivalrous,' he whispered into her ear, adding, 'And I am assuming you will behave like the poised lady you are portraying tonight.' He inhaled her scent as he spoke, suddenly wishing he had the right to catch hold of the curl of hair falling onto her cheek, or plant a proprietorial kiss on the nape of her neck.

Once more he earned a sharp look for his words, but it seemed to him that she responded to his touch, swaying in towards him as he held on to her elbow. He fought the urge to pull her close to his side, just to see how receptive she would be, hoping his feelings were just a simple caveman reaction to a beautiful woman and nothing more. He prayed the aching need that had assailed him from nowhere would disappear when Emerald was back to being — well, the Emerald that he knew, rather than this different species of woman who walked beside him.

But he would appreciate the new Emerald, until the spell, which would return them both to their roles of employer and employee, wore off.

Tom Edwards was hovering by the bar when they arrived. He was younger than Marco had imagined — probably because of a preconceived idea of British airline owners he had, after meeting the frail Robert Clarke. He held out his hand and Tom Edwards shook it warmly.

Marco quickly turned to introduce Emerald who stood unassumingly by his side. Marco recognized the flicker of interest that flashed into the other man's eyes as he took Emerald's hand in his own.

'This is Emerald Montrose,' Marco said briefly. 'The Girl Friday of Hot Air Aviation. She can tell you so much more about our airline if you decide to come on board with us. As you know, we are looking for investors to enable Hot Air Aviation to become the company I envisage.'

His spiel died on his lips as the debonair man's manicured fingers wound around Emerald's with far too much ease and confidence. 'Call me Tom, please,' he said as he raised his lips to Emerald's hand.

Oh, please! Marco thought. He identified one of his own type — wealth and looks giving him an automatic right to be in the top tier of their species, and he resented it.

He tried not to be irritated by the flattering moves Mr Edwards was pulling on Emerald as he willed her to prise her hand away. To Marco's disappointment, she didn't, and Marco's smile of welcome turned into a rictus of mistrust as a long-buried emotion was unearthed. The first time he'd met the man who became his wife's lover, the same instinct had kicked in, and the urge to wipe the perfect smile off Tom Edwards' face surfaced. He prayed that Emerald would be savvy enough to rebuff the man and his obvious charm offensive.

The three sat down companionably enough and the conversation remained light-hearted. Emerald played her part extremely well, Marco had to admit, and he tried to be solicitous and charming. It was strangely satisfying to behave in such a chivalrous way, even though Emerald shot him a look, her eyes widening slightly, when he put his hand on top of hers to drive home a point he made. He wondered if the only real point he wanted to make by the gesture was that Tom Edwards should keep his distance. He was intrigued, though, to find that she didn't pull her hand away from under his, and it was temptingly easy to caress her soft, warm skin underneath his palm.

He was enjoying her company and he knew it would bother him later, but right at that moment he couldn't care less. He was unable to imagine how he had failed to notice quite how enchanting she could be, and a couple of times almost forgot that they weren't on a date.

Emerald's eyes twinkled when the waiter produced menus and Tom Edwards mentioned that haggis was the special of the day. He asked her if she had ever tried it.

'I haven't, although I know Marco is dying to try some,' she purred, throwing Marco a wide smile as she picked up her menu. Then, lowering her voice, 'Look, Marco, you can have it with mash and swede — are you going to go for it?' she asked, patting his arm. Her smile was barbed and Marco knew she was paying him back for his playacting.

'The haggis really is excellent here — do try it,' Tom Edwards pressed, beaming at Marco's apparent enthusiasm. 'I'll be interested to hear what you think.'

'That would be lovely — great idea, Emerald.'

Emerald's grin was wider than the Cheshire Cat's when the waiter reappeared to take their orders and Marco feigned a smile as he ordered the haggis.

'I'll have the salmon, please.' She closed the menu with a decisive snap.

Marco had to smile. He probably deserved the haggis, but he insisted on Emerald trying some when their food arrived and watched closely as her lips puckered around the forkful he offered. He did it to pay her back, and also to let Tom Edwards know that she was not available — just in case he wasn't certain.

All in all, Emerald was rather too attentive to Tom Edwards, Marco felt, and it jarred with him, even though she was of course entitled to flirt with whoever she wanted. He had, indeed, demanded that she act out the role of the perfect hostess, but now that she was doing so, he resented it.

It hadn't crossed his mind until now that she might be actively looking for a boyfriend. She was pally with Finbar but he was clearly of a different persuasion and loved Emerald as a friend. But Tom Edwards was in a different league altogether. For a split second he wished he hadn't invited her along to meet the oily, rich man in front of him, especially when she looked more like a princess than the hustler he had presumed her to be, when he first met back in his hotel.

Marco was still pondering the uncomfortable possibility of Tom Edwards chatting up Emerald when he heard the inevitable words.

'Do you know Edinburgh well, Emerald?'

Instantly he was on high alert.

Emerald tilted her head towards Mr Edwards, giving him all of her attention. 'I have flown into the airport many times, but this is the first time I've had a chance to visit the city.'

Marco groaned inwardly. He knew exactly where this line of conversation was heading and he determined to cut it dead before Tom Edwards offered to show her the sights. He cleared his throat noisily.

Emerald glanced at him, her eyes bright.

'I wonder if you would like to take this opportunity to leave us to our boring financial talk, Emerald? I know you have no interest in number crunching.' Marco knew he'd hit a nerve when a bloom of pink appeared on her cheeks, her eyes narrowed almost to slits and red lips tightened.

However, she inclined her head towards him before turning to Tom. 'I do hope you will forgive me. I have something I need to attend to. It was lovely meeting you.' She bestowed a wide smile on him and Marco waited for the put-down he felt was inevitable.

Tom Edwards scraped his chair back as he stood up to shake Emerald's hand, caressing it as he spoke to her. 'If ever you are in Edinburgh again, be sure to call me.' He slid his business card discreetly into her palm before turning back to Marco, who had seen the exchange and was not amused.

Marco tried to catch Emerald's eye as she picked up her bag. She straightened and paused, before leaning over the table, so close to Marco's ear that he thought she was going to kiss him. Instead, she whispered in his ear, 'I'm going to find a bar, Marco   and drink grappa. Enjoy.' She pressed his arm and sashayed away.

A real sense of fear grabbed him. He wanted to demand that she return immediately or remain in the suite — as if he had the right to send her to her room. Surely she wouldn't go to a pub — especially dressed as she was — on her own — in a city he presumed she didn't know? He stared after her, knowing that he could not demand anything from this independent woman. She had spent her whole life looking out for herself and she wasn't likely to change with a few strong words. As he watched her glide regally out of the restaurant, he noted that once again a few heads turned towards the beautiful woman wearing a slinky red dress.

When there was nothing left to stare at, he turned back to Tom Edwards, whose look was quizzical and penetrating. Marco searched his mind to drum up a neutral conversation to divert the conversation away from Emerald. No way was he going to discuss her with a man who clearly had a vested interest in her status. Both sets of eyes strayed to Emerald's empty chair more than once, and the evening quickly fell flat without her. Marco was suddenly keen to wrap up the business talk and he drained the last of his wine with finality, calling time with an easy handshake and the promise of financial talks later in the month.

CHAPTER SIXTEEN

Marco opened the door quietly and turned on the low lamp by the television as he threw off his jacket and undid his tie, convinced that Emerald would be in her room. He took in the spectacular view of the illuminated castle from the window but soon turning away, anxious to make amends. However, as he looked around the suite he realized there was no sign of her: no kicked-off shoes and no handbag slung on the table. His blood ran cold.

He put his ear to her bedroom door, but couldn't hear anything. Was she asleep? Could he check on her or would that be overstepping the mark? Instinct told him she wasn't in and he suddenly didn't care about overstepping the mark. He rapped on the door, turned the handle and headed inside.

It was empty. Her dress was crumpled up on the bed as if she had undressed in haste, her tiny clutch bag sat on top of the drawers and her heels lay askew on the carpet. He checked the wardrobe, relieved to see her overnight bag at the bottom of it. So, she hadn't checked out, that was something, he supposed, but he would never find her if she was wandering the streets of Edinburgh.

A single woman in a city at night could be asking for trouble, and surely she was joking about the grappa, wasn't she? He wasn't even sure Scottish folk had such a thing. He knew she could hold her own, but still, he needed to find her — he needed to be with her. No other man would look out for her the way he could. His thoughts were running away with him. Damn that woman — or were his own insecurities the real problem?

He picked up her discarded dress, testing the feel of the soft fabric between his thumb and fingertips, trying not to imagine how it would be to run his hands over her body while she wore it. He brought the fabric to his nose and breathed in, before quickly dropping it back on the bed. This would not do. He was not behaving appropriately.

He groaned. For a brief moment, he was back in his hotel in Florence kissing her, caressing her skin, cupping the roundness of her bottom. tapping his fingers impatiently on the metal handrail as the lift creaked its way to the ground floor. His first port of call, the hotel bar, found no more than a gaggle of girls sipping lurid-coloured drinks while a couple of older businessman leered at them. There was no sign of Emerald and he wasn't prepared to wait any longer. He tapped out her number on his mobile phone.

She answered at the third ring. 'Mr Cavarelli?'

He sighed. No *Marco* this time. She was plainly pissed off with him. 'Where are you?'

There was a pause before she answered. 'I'm not sure. Is something wrong?'

'Yes. Where are you?' He tried to contain his anger, convinced that he could hear glasses chinking, and the babble of people in the background.

She blew out a long, drawn-out exaggerated sigh. 'I'm just seeing the sights.'

'I'll come and get you. Stay where you are.'

'Marco, for fuck's sake, I'm fine.'

The silence lengthened. He dragged in a deep breath, trying to remain calm. He listened intently to the background noise. All was silent. 'Can you come back to the hotel, please?'

'I suppose so. I thought you were talking business and I was surplus to requirements.'

He heaved out a breath of relief. 'We'll talk on your return — if that's okay with you,' he added, surprised at his own magnanimous attitude.

There was no answer, but he thought he heard a huff of agreement as he ended the call, relief flooding though him. He knew he had been unreasonable, practically demanding that she leave the restaurant and now insisting that she return, but he didn't seem to have control over his emotions, right then. He headed back to the reception area and paced the foyer, waiting. And then she was there, pushing through the doors, looking like a teenager in her jeans and ugly boots that reminded him of Victorian hob-nailed boots. Her hair was falling all over her face, a belligerent expression taking the place of the earlier beatific smile she gave to the slimy Tom. He was even pleased to see the annoying oversized satchel she took almost everywhere with her, banging against her hip.

He rushed up to her and gripped her arm. 'Where have you been. Did you really go out drinking?'

'What?' Emerald's chin went up. 'Where are we right now, Mr Cavarelli — in some kind of Regency time warp? There is nothing wrong in taking in the sights. Am I supposed to have a chaperone or something?'

'Don't you know what can happen in a big city at night?'

She raised an eyebrow at him. 'What, worse things than spending a week in the outback on my own?'

Marco hardly listened as he propelled her out of the foyer and towards the lift, back up to their suite.

She twisted out of his grasp as he pressed his palm to the small of her back and continued the steady march along the length of the marble floor.

'I was enjoying the street shows — it's an art festival out there. No one should be stuck indoors.'

'You didn't go to a pub?'

'No, I just said that to wind you up.'

'Oh.' His facial muscles relaxed. 'Bene.' He knew he had overreacted at her disappearance, but he was still too annoyed to concede that he was in the wrong.

Emerald narrowed her eyes. 'What's good about me not going into a pub? Are you jealous, Mr Cavarelli, worried that I might, heaven forbid, meet a *man*?'

'Of course not. Don't be ridiculous. You can do as you please.'

'I know that, but do you know that?' She was not prepared to let up. 'So, tell me, what *did* you think would happen to me?' Her voice rose to match his. 'Did you think the zombie apocalypse would finally kick off tonight, drawn by the magnitude of tasty, arty luvvies — was that it? Or maybe the Vikings are back, 'cos it's been some time — they must be missing all that haggis and porridge. Nice bit of rape and pillage to see them right for the evening.'

Marco had no idea what she was going on about and didn't care. He was just relieved that she was safe and back with him. Safely tucked away in the hotel suite, where he called the shots.

She pushed him away and flung her hands up in the air. 'Will you just let go of me, *please*?' She stormed on ahead, her bag weighing her down as she walked.

What could she have in that stupid bag that was so important? Marco thought, realising for the first time that she was seldom without it. 'You are technically at work. I thought you were in your room,' Marco hissed, catching up with her.

She turned around and glared at him taking him by surprise. 'For fuck's sake, Marco, what do you want from me? I am not your bloody puppet to manipulate — to fit into some weird mould that suits you.' She tried to bat him away as she turned to him, her eyes flashing, lips pale. He noticed she'd removed her lipstick.

He stopped, paused for a bit. This was heavy stuff she was spouting and he didn't feel able to dissect it right then, but still she wasn't finished.

She clenched her fists. 'Are you seriously expecting me to do exactly as you say because I'm being *paid* for this? You are bloody unbelievable.'

'No, I'm just looking out for you.'

She twisted away from his grasp. 'I don't need you to look out for me,' she hissed into his face. 'I've been doing it perfectly well on my own for the last twenty-three years.' She pushed him in the chest as he tried to catch her arm once more. 'Leave me alone.'

Marco knew perfectly well that she didn't need his hand to guide her into the lift, but he did it anyway, only letting her go when they were shut safely inside.

He stood rigidly by the door, his fists clenched, trying to work out how to explain that he had been worried about her — though he was pretty sure she was past caring what he thought.

The lift soared to the top of the hotel and Emerald stared ahead, apparently thinking the emergency information panel was more interesting than he was. He toyed with the idea of quipping that Health and Safety had neglected to include zombie invasions to their checklist, wondering if this might defuse the atmosphere, but he didn't think Emerald would see the funny side.

She marched ahead of him until they reached the door of their suite, where she refused to meet his eye as she fumbled with her key card.

Marco followed her in and headed for the drinks tray. Without saying a word, he unscrewed the top of a bottle of malt whisky, poured a generous amount into a glass and tossed it down his throat, hoping the burn would help him rationalize his emotions.

He glanced at Emerald, regret already filling the place where anger had been. Gulping back another mouthful of whisky, he worried at his temples with his fingertips. He knew he should apologize, but she would throw it back in his face. Although, it could perhaps lead to a truce, which might lead to . . . to — God knows what. He sighed. 'It's late. I have work to do.'

Emerald's eyes flashed raw fury. 'What? Is that it? You drag me back here acting as if the devil has possessed you and then . . . and then, you expect me to put myself to bed like a good little girl?' She paced the length of the sitting room with her godawful backpacking boots pounding the deep-pile carpet.

Marco pushed down an image of her draped across his own bed, hair spread out over the pillow, plump lips inviting him. He thumped his glass down. 'No.'

'What then? Why are you being like this, and what exactly do you want from me?' she whispered. Her eyes looked over-large in her face, her expression tremulous.

Dear God, what did he want from her? He closed his eyes, briefly. Everything.

'Nothing,' he said.

Ignoring the hurt in her eyes, he picked up his laptop bag and dragged out his laptop, banging it down onto the table with enough force to make him fear for its safety. 'I have work to do.'

She caught her bottom lip in her teeth and made to move towards him, her eyes fixed on his. 'Mr Cavarelli, I would like to know why you appear to be so upset at the thought that I might be out enjoying myself tonight, on my own — as in, specifically without you.'

He took a step backwards. No way was he going to let her close to him. He turned away from her with a click of his tongue, slid his laptop to the other end of the table and opened the lid.

She strode towards his laptop and slammed the lid shut. 'And why you sent me away when you thought Tom was going to offer to show me the sights.' She took another step towards him. 'I hope to God you didn't think that I would embarrass myself — get drunk and throw myself at him. I'm hoping you know me better than that by now.' She fixed her gaze on his face. 'Or was it something else. Jealousy, maybe?'

She took another step forward. 'Possessiveness, maybe?'

He met her gaze, seeing only honesty in her eyes, as if she was offering him an opportunity. Maybe, if he accepted her unspoken offer he could return to being the Marco he was before: the Marco who loved and laughed and trusted, instead of the Marco whose life was about making money and building empires. For a heartbeat he was tempted, but instead of pulling her into his arms and kissing her, as he thought he should, he raised his hand and drew his knuckles softly down her cheek.

They stared at each other for another heartbeat. Emerald moistened her lips with her tongue and Marco's gaze lingered on her mouth. *Business and pleasure, never mix the two.* He could hear his father's words.

He took a deep breath. 'Goodnight, Emerald, I'll see you in the morning.' He took hold of her shoulders and pushed her very gently away from him.

Her look was pitying as she took a couple of involuntary steps backwards, her hand fluttering to her throat. She shook her head. 'You can't even be true to yourself,' she said, before swivelling on her heel. She stalked across the sitting room towards her bedroom, her back ramrod straight.

Marco swallowed, instantly regretting his decisions to push her away. 'I'll see you at seven for breakfast,' he tried, hoping she might turn around and he could make amends.

'I'll get something at the airport,' she threw over her shoulder with a toss of her hair.

Hating himself for being so mercurial, he exhaled slowly, watching her flounce into her room. He'd managed to resist her and he was thankful for that, even though his hands shook as he pressed fingers to keyboard. He sloshed more whisky into his glass. It was going to be a long night.

CHAPTER SEVENTEEN

Emerald scrubbed at her face with a flannel in the bathroom, holding her thoughts at bay. She wasn't even going to try to work out how much of a fool she had just made of herself in showing her emotions, and she wondered how she could face Marco again.

She leaned against the sink, seeing in her reflection what Marco must have seen. Desire had widened her pupils, heated her cheeks and plumped up her lips. She rubbed harder with her flannel, hoping to eradicate the signs from her face, along with the remnants of her makeup. It didn't work.

She had no idea why Marco had touched her hand and smiled into her eyes, playing with her emotions at the restaurant, but it had unleashed feelings that she had tried to suppress but had foolishly believed that she could level with him — that they could level with each other.

Big mistake.

She closed her eyes against the image of his shocked face when she'd accused him of jealousy, and his confusion as he'd listened to her criticise Italian families. If ever there was a taboo subject when talking to an Italian, that would be the one. The mortification that showed in his eyes would stay with her for a long time.

She pulled her pyjamas on slowly, listening to the monotonous voice of a television presenter through the wall, imagining Marco on the other side, shaking his head with incredulity at her words. Even so, she still wondered what had prompted his outburst and why he was so bothered about her wandering off. She could understand it from a business point of view if he'd thought she was going to go off with Tom Edwards, but was his opinion of her really so low that he thought she would be that unprofessional?

She climbed into bed and turned on the bedside lamp. She would not give him the honour of being analysed by her overwrought mind. Instead she would look over her sketches and see if the evening's efforts were as good as she thought they were. She'd worked quickly with her pastels to capture the light over the castle as the moon rose, and had sketched a rough charcoal of a piper, tall and proud. When she returned to her flat, she would paint the images in oil, which would give greater depth and perspective.

Her camera had taken the place of her drawings when the subject was too transient — the street dancers and acrobats she would work on when she had more free time.

Emerald's cousin had asked her to exhibit some work in her studio, where handmade jewellery jostled with huge sculptures and exquisite miniatures of unknown and upcoming artists, but she'd always said no, convinced she wasn't good enough. Recently, however, she'd noticed something different in her work. There was a new edginess to her pictures that surprised her. She almost believed they were worth exhibiting, even though she didn't think she would be brave enough to do so.

She spread them out on the bed now, inspecting each one in turn, before glancing through her photographs. It calmed her looking through her images and it took her mind off her worries and the thorny problem that was Marco.

Satisfied, she finally tucked them back in her folder which she slid into her bag.

Hesitating, with the knowledge that she was torturing herself, she pulled out the small sketchpad she kept in the zipper compartment of her bag and pored over the charcoal and pastel drawings that she'd doodled when daydreaming. Marco's frown. Marco's generous lips. Marco's eyes — pages of his smoky eyes, drawn in charcoal, over and over again, some from memory — filled up her sketchpad.

She traced her finger over the small drawing of Marco on the sofa, asleep, an indefinable ache settling in her chest once more. She'd managed to compose the angle of his body perfectly, and the lines on his face, softened in sleep. It was faultless. *He* was faultless.

She felt tears well up out of nowhere and swiped them away, terrified that Marco might come in and see her crying, although the sensible part of her mind knew he would never enter her room. She glanced over at the door. There was only a wall between them but it might as well be the Amazon river. One door, so easily opened, one door that closed off her access to the person she wanted to talk to more than anyone else. She put the pictures back in her bag, zipping them away to keep them hidden.

Marco's voice, as she lay in the darkness, was faint and gently cajoling as he talked into his phone, and although she could not make out any words, the intonations of his accent sounded more pronounced, making her think he was speaking in Italian. To an Italian woman? A wash of jealousy flooded her body and she curled her knees into her chest and put the pillow over her head to block out his voice. She could hear her own breath as she lay there, and in the almost complete silence she was more awake than ever.

She checked the time and sighed. Eleven forty-five. She had played this clock-watching game too many times. The later it got, the more anxious she became, and as anxiety piled upon anxiety, the less likely she was to sleep. It was an exhausting bit of nonsense that came with the territory of shift work.

To add to her troubles, she was desperate for a drink of water and the bottles of cold water were in the minibar in the sitting room, which was now completely out of bounds. She turned over, her pyjamas twisting around her legs, as the thought of cool, fresh water sliding down her throat overrode any other thoughts.

She imagined the water in the bathroom tap would be fine to drink but she had become so conditioned not to drink hotel water, as stories of Legionnaires' disease abounded — or that story that did the rounds now and then, that if you swallowed a tapeworm it would grow so big its head would come out of your throat, that she couldn't possibly even take a sip. She shivered and groaned simultaneously. Now she felt slightly sick too.

She knew she wouldn't sleep at all unless she found some water. Climbing out of bed, she pressed her ear to the door. Marco had stopped talking and she could hear nothing so she inched the door open, praying the coast was clear.

Marco was fast asleep on the sofa, the ghostly light from his open laptop illuminating the contours of his face. He must have fallen asleep while working, she thought, glancing at him warily for a moment before tiptoeing over to the fridge, pulling out a bottle of water and downing half of its contents in one go. She couldn't help but look back at Marco. The image was one she would never tire of looking at: his jawline with its dark shadow of stubble, his long eyelashes flickering in sleep, his hair curling slightly around his ears.

Then his eyelids fluttered once more and his eyes opened, sleepily.

She blinked in shock and instinctively took a step backwards at his slow, lazy smile which threw her off guard.

'Hey, it's my beautiful guardian angel.' Slowly and drowsily, he murmured, 'Come over here.'

Emerald almost turned around to look for the beautiful guardian angel that lurked in the background waiting for such an invitation. She didn't move an inch, simultaneously fearing and hoping that his words were meant for her.

'Come.' He threw off the blanket and she stumbled towards the sofa, automatically, feeling foolish when he closed his eyes once more. He reached out and she took his hand, allowing him to pull her down next to his warm body as he covered them both with the soft blanket and gathered her into his chest. '*Cara mia*,' he whispered into her hair.

She froze as his hand glided down the length of her body and he nuzzled into her neck. She was not the expected recipient of this attention, of that she was sure. Any second now he would become fully conscious and her embarrassment would be absolute. He dropped a gentle kiss on her ear and his hand slid into her hair as he pulled her around to face him. This was it, she thought, the moment when he would recoil in horror. But he didn't. Instead he kissed her and deepened the kiss further as he whispered her name.

The sensations rippling through her body were too delicious to resist and she melted into his arms, the taste of whisky unfamiliar, but welcome, on his lips. She knew she ought to leave, ought to stir him from the sleepy trance he was in, but as he traced her shoulders with his fingertips, moving lower down her back and to her hips, her resolve disappeared. She returned the kiss with an urgency that was new to her.

His hands drifted down further and she knew it was time to speak up, although she was almost mute with confusion and desire. 'What are we doing, Marco?'

He groaned as he slowly traced up to her midriff with his fingertips and loosened his hold on her. 'I have no idea what we are doing. Tell me to stop.' He sighed into her neck, his breath flaming her skin and setting her body alight as if tongues of fire danced over her. 'Or tell me not to stop, Emerald.'

She stilled at the mention of her name. So she *was* the intended recipient of this unlikely encounter. She relaxed. 'Don't stop,' she agreed, a hitch in her throat making her sound breathy.

His head dropped back to the cushion as he drew in a deep breath, his arm firmly tucked in around her body, despite his words. She lay still in his arms, in case any movement broke the magical spell that had thrown them together, leaving her with nothing more than hollow dreams.

Marco's breath steadied and slowed, his body relaxing as he held her cocooned in his embrace. Unable to resist the unfamiliar solidity of his body next to hers, she settled into his chest, knowing she should leave — and she would — in a few minutes time. Just for now, though she would pretend that lying next to Marco was a normal occurrence. She wiggled her toes in preparation for standing up. She would leave any minute now, she thought, as the pull of sleep dragged at her.

CHAPTER EIGHTEEN

Emerald surfaced from sleep, a sharp spike of pain in her back hurtling her towards consciousness. She lifted her head and rubbed at the base of her neck, trying to work out where she was and why her shoulders ached so much. Her mind whirled as she took stock of her situation. Memories of last night's encounter on the sofa kick-started her train of thought and her panicked eyes darted around the room and settled on Marco, who was facing away from her packing away his laptop.

With a sickening lurch, she knew that she hadn't dreamt it. Eyes still fixed on Marco, she put her fingers to her mouth, as if her lips would confirm that they had indeed been kissed.

Marco's demeanour gave little indication that he recollected anything out of the ordinary as she sat up, acutely aware of her disadvantaged position. She had no idea how long he had stayed with her on the sofa. It could have been minutes, it could have been all night. It would be fine, though, once they'd had a chance to talk it through — as adults, right? Things might be a little difficult, sure, but Marco would reassure her, and—

'You have thirty minutes before the cab arrives.'

And, then again, maybe not. She slumped into the feather cushion that served as a pillow and pulled the blanket up around her neck, peeping over the top of it, as one certainty struck her: Marco was going to pretend last night hadn't happened.

'You now have twenty-eight minutes.' His voice was clipped and he sounded more like an automated alarm than a man.

She was dishevelled, wearing ancient pyjamas, and was tangled up in a blanket while Marco was showered, dressed and edgy, with a note of quiet irritation in his voice.

She groaned quietly. Okay, she could do this. Her brain was finally up to speed on the situation, although she rather wished it wasn't. The reality was that she'd kissed her boss, and with rather more ardour than was sensible — not that anything they'd done last night had been sensible.

She took a deep breath. All would be well.

She would just stay on the sofa until Marco returned to Italy — or took a one-way trip to another planet, maybe. And she'd simply settle for the blanket over the head trick until he did, blocking out everything she didn't want to see. If she couldn't see anyone, then no one would see her. Everyone knew that was a fact.

'Twenty-five minutes,' the speaking clock that was Marco declared.

She groaned, inwardly this time. Although she was not surprised by Marco's clipped tone, she could have done without it. *Wake up darling*, maybe? A gentle brushing of her cheek with his thumb? It would have been kinder, but she almost snorted at such an unlikely scenario. Her more immediate worry was having to climb off the sofa in her pink bunny pyjamas. Marco would see them and be horrified at how gauche they were, and her Medusa bed hair would be frizzing with a life of its own, unless the hair-straightener fairies had worked their magic while she was sleeping.

She raised herself up on her elbow, trying to plot an escape route to her bedroom that afforded her a semblance of dignity. Or, maybe she could just roll off the sofa and hope the momentum took her to her room. She stifled a giggle and

Marco gave her a pointed look and made a show of checking his watch. But still she couldn't get her body to move.

He threw her another glance. 'Twenty-two minutes. I've turned your shower on. Come on, we don't want to miss this flight, I need to get back.'

'Right. Yes, I'm on it,' she said, giving the tartan blanket another tug up to her chin.

'What are you waiting for?' Frustration was clear in his voice, but also he looked at her with something akin to kindness — or maybe it was just pity.

'I'm just wondering why there's never an invisibility cloak around when you need one.' She attempted a smile, hoping humour might be enough to break the barrier of formality that Marco had erected between them. If he had returned her smile, even slightly, it might have done the trick and they could at least have acknowledged last night's foolishness and moved on, but his face was shuttered, accepting no compromise.

She sighed and dragged her fingers pointlessly through her hair. 'I'm going — and just for the record, I never oversleep,' she challenged, thrusting her chin out, waiting for a counter-argument.

'I'm glad to hear it.' Marco fixed her with his unrelenting gaze, not even turning away as she clambered off the sofa in an undignified scramble, almost falling over the blanket as it fell to the floor.

Marco adjusted his tie and smoothed down his dark blue jacket, looking irritatingly gorgeous and totally in control as she shuffled past him, wholeheartedly wishing the zombie apocalypse had been real and she'd been eaten in the night.

Back in the safety of her bathroom, she took a minute to rethink the situation. At least there was no sign at all that they had . . . had they? No, of course they hadn't, but he had kissed her and touched her body. She remembered his heart thudding next to hers and his clean smell, with the underlying aroma of whisky on his breath, the stubble on his chin rasping slightly at her throat as he nuzzled into her neck. She shivered, weak with longing. 'Oh, God, I'm doomed,' she said into the mirror as she ran a hand over her face, blotchy with sleep.

As she showered she tried not to think about Marco lying next to her on the sofa in the deep of the night, and already it seemed a dream-like, unreal scenario. If he wanted to pretend it had never happened then that suited her, even though she would hold the memory close and dust it off from time to time when he was safely out of reach.

For now, though, she would have to face him. She tousle-dried her hair in minutes and fumbled into her clothes, throwing the rest into her airline bag. Giving herself no more time to think, she girded her metaphorical loins and slammed through to the sitting room. 'I'm ready,' she announced, stopping dead as Marco held up his forefinger in a gesture to quieten her as he spoke into his mobile.

He ended the call and pocketed his phone, giving her the once-over. 'Ah, the real Emerald returns. Good.'

'Good? Why's it good?'

'It is good that you are back to being — well — Emerald.'

She nodded. So he was safer with the old Emerald who wasn't a threat to him, was he? Fine, it was easier being the real Emerald anyway, so win-win all around, she thought. Except that Marco seemed to be attracted to the Lady in Red Emerald, the Emerald she wasn't.

The only constant she had amidst all this confusion was that Marco Cavarelli was back to being no more than a boss, and a grumpy one at that. It wasn't fair that he called the shots all the time, and the injustice of it annoyed her too much to remain quiet. 'And just so it's clear in your head, I wasn't the one drinking whisky last night,' she said.

Surprising her, his eyes softened and he smiled gently. 'I know you weren't — I have an excellent memory.' He scooped up her overnight bag and headed for the door.

And that, she thought, was the closest she would get to an acknowledgement of last night's musical beds.

CHAPTER NINETEEN

Emerald had the weekend off work and would normally make the most of it, catching up with her cousin and shopping for frivolous items, but this time she spent most of it stewing in a hot flush of indecision, wondering if she could ever face Marco again.

She'd been tempted to talk her problem through with Finbar, knowing that his ironic spin on it would make it appear amusing and less serious. Much as she adored him, though, she wasn't sure he could keep such a juicy piece of news under wraps and not share it with the entire office. Hot gossip was embedded in Finbar's DNA and Emerald knew it would kill him to keep quiet. So she kept it to herself, her body heating up with humiliation and a touch of lust every time she recalled the romantic interlude she longed to forget.

Her mobile rang, stirring her out of her quandary. She saw Marco's number flash up and stared at her phone hoping it would just stop ringing. It didn't and, sighing, with something close to despair, she answered the call and listened to the unmistakable melodic timbre of his voice.

'Emerald. Good. You are there, then. Took you time answering. Ready for duty, I hope.'

She would have laughed if she wasn't so miserable. So, that's how they were to play this out — he was back to acting all sergeant-majorish and she would be pliant and submissive. Except she had no intention of doing as she was told, and if he didn't like it then he could lump it. 'Yes, of course, but don't make me sound like some sort of commando. I'm not going off to fight in the Congo.'

'I have business to attend to, so I shall be away for a few days. Some of the crew are due a firefighting refresher course. I just wanted to check that you knew about it.'

'Yes, Marco, I've been doing this job perfectly well without your backup for quite some time, so don't worry, I've booked a day at the fire station on Friday.'

'Fine, it's just . . . I wondered if you would be coming in to work before I left.'

'I have the weekend off.' She paused. 'Was there something you needed to discuss?' She fiddled with her hair, hating their stilted conversation.

'I thought it might be pertinent to have a chat.'

'Oh?' Her stomach swooped at his forbidding words. Hadn't she been down this road before? She rested her head against the door frame thinking fast. He was either going to declare his undying love for her, or he was going to dismiss her. If it was the latter, which she rather thought it was, then he could do it in company time, not her own. Besides she was done with second-guessing him and trying to live up to his idea of a perfect employee. 'I'm sorry, I'm very busy.'

'Very busy — sitting at home?'

Bloody cheek. 'Yes, I'm doing housework,' she offered, gazing around at her immaculate flat where even the dust molecules thought twice about being disruptive.

There was silence for a moment until she heard yet another exasperated sigh from Marco.

'Have a good trip away, won't you?' she concluded lamely, hoping their conversation was finished.

There was a longer pause before he said, 'That's fine. I'll see you shortly.'

She smiled into the phone. 'Bye, and don't call me Shortly.' As soon as she said it she knew he wouldn't get it. There was another pause, which she filled. 'Sorry, it's something Finbar says. It doesn't matter.'

'Ah, the ever-present Finbar and his witty banter.'

She caught the hostility in his voice and wondered why Finbar rattled him so much. It wasn't the first time he'd shown his dislike of Finbar and she felt the need to stick up for him.

'Well, he makes *me* smile, which is more than some people around here do.' She ended the call, her heart heavy and her body weary. Her eyes were gritty from lack of sleep and she felt miserable and lost. Not for the first time, she thought about leaving her job to save her sanity. It would be wonderful not to have to deal with Marco and all his ambiguities. Tears filled her eyes. No, it wouldn't be wonderful, it would be horrible. And therein lay the problem. She was beginning to fear that she was in love with Marco, and a more unsuitable man on this planet to fall in love with, did not exist.

She wrapped her arms around her chest as the age-old ache of rejection surfaced once more. It was forever present in her subconscious: in her mother's desertion and her father's remarriage — both of them happy to pack her off to a convent like the inconvenience she obviously was.

She tried to compose herself. Her old life was over and she had been so determined to make a go of her new career back in England, but was aware that it was coming apart at the seams. The tight pain in her chest increased, crushing in its intensity at the thought that she might have to start afresh again.

But no, she wouldn't succumb to this feeling. She'd spent most of her life toughening up and wouldn't allow one man to break down the walls she'd built around herself. Marco was clearly out of reach, and she was less important to him than a squashed frog on the road. She needed to deal with that fact and move on. A tear of self-pity glided down her cheek and she dashed it away determinedly. When another tear plopped onto her arm, she slid down on the sofa, finally giving in to the torrent of emotion she'd been bottling up. She reached for the tissue box, her shoulders heaving, as she accepted that there was not one person in the whole world who loved her as she wanted to be loved.

* * *

Marco didn't for one moment stop to wonder if it was wise to call on Emerald, or even if it was too early in the day. He simply pressed the doorbell and readied his large paper bag containing croissants and coffee: his peace offering.

She opened the door and his eyebrows lifted in surprise at her T-shirt that barely covered her bottom. He averted his eyes politely. 'Thought it would be good to have that chat sooner rather than later.' He offered up the bag, bearing the name of the café around the corner. 'Croissants and coffee?' he added, although the bag was pretty much a dead giveaway.

Emerald's eyes darted from his face to the paper bag and back again, reminding Marco of a trapped rabbit. Maybe it hadn't been such a brilliant notion to visit one of his employees at home on a Sunday morning.

'So, when you said you'd see me shortly, you meant . . . here, in my home?' She pointed down to her doorstep and raised an eyebrow at him.

'Yes,' he replied, his smile frozen in place as he cursed himself silently. What *had* he been thinking?

'There's a problem at work?' she asked, shifting from one bare foot to the other.

'No.' *An uninvited guest at a wedding party bearing an inappropriate gift would be welcomed more willingly than this*, he thought, as various emotions played out over Emerald's face, none of them particularly encouraging. In fact, he was sure it was only her inherent good manners that stopped her from slamming the door in his face.

He deserved it, he knew, but he persisted. 'If you keep me standing here much longer your feet will freeze to the step. Plus,' he gestured to his bag, 'if the coffee gets cold it tends to taste like an old ashtray.'

It occurred to him, far too late, that she might have male company, which would make him the biggest idiot ever. He stepped away from her door, preparing to retreat.

Emerald sighed. 'Oh, God, come in then,' she relented, rubbing at her bare arms.

'Thank you,' he muttered as she led him along the hallway and into her kitchen.

'This is the warmest part of the flat — underfloor heating.' She gestured towards a stool pushed up against the tiny work counter. 'Sit down.'

Marco sat and placed the croissants and coffee on her worktop. He scanned the tiny kitchen trying to focus on something apart from Emerald's breasts, undoubtedly braless under her thin T-shirt. He lowered his eyes, but then all he could see were her legs, long and tanned. He huffed out a breath — he was beginning to feel like a dirty old man. 'I assume you haven't eaten breakfast yet, looking at your attire. You have a penchant for boy bands?'

'Oh, this?' She looked down at her top with a kaleidoscope of young men smiling for all their worth, on the front. 'We flew them to Ibiza a couple of years ago.' She plucked at the hem. 'They were so cute. One of them helped me serve their dinner to them.' She gazed at it for too long, wishing it would turn into something more glamorous than a washed-out T-shirt she slopped around the house in.

'And you have black smudges under your eyes.' He wished he had held his tongue. Not the best of lines, but her eyes looked as if she was on her way to a Halloween party and he thought she would rather know about it.

'Thanks for that.' She scrubbed underneath her eyes with one hand while trying to pull down her T-shirt with the other.

Marco watched in amusement. 'Really, I've seen you in a worse state — I wouldn't worry about it.'

Emerald sighed. 'Are you ever going to let that go?'

'My memory is becoming politely hazy, as time goes by.' He tried out a smile to put her at ease, beginning to wonder if he was the one needing assistance. He was normally in control of situations that he had initiated, but he was making a whole mess of this one. 'Maybe we would both be more comfortable if you put some clothes on, but don't do it on my account,' he said, although he really did feel it would help if he could look at her without having to focus intently on her shoulder or some other innocuous part of her body.

He picked out two croissants from the bag. 'Chocolate or almond? I bought both.'

Emerald stared at him and then down at the bag.

'Question too hard, is it? I'll give you one of each. I happen to know you like cappuccino, so we're on safe territory there.' He lifted out two large, lidded paper cups and set them on the table, next to the plates. Peering into the bag he said, 'We even have preserves.' He picked out two jam sachets and put them on the table.

Finally, Emerald spoke. 'This is all very cosy, if unexpected. Can I ask why you are here?'

'Well, I have a favour to ask.'

'So, this is not about, err, the other night?'

'The other night?'

'Erm, I just wondered if . . .' She trailed off and eyed him warily, waiting for an explanation.

Marco admired her honesty as he was having trouble himself processing what exactly had happened the other night, apart from the notion that he needed to apologize. He caught her eye and got ready to give her the speech he'd prepared.

'I think I will get changed, if you'll excuse me for a minute.' She paused, as if deliberating her next move, before saying, 'Why don't you go into the sitting room? It's a bit more interesting than looking at white walls.' She broke eye contact and ushered Marco out of the kitchen leaving his apology stuck in his throat.

He sipped his coffee and glanced around her flat, taking in the rattan lights, colourful throws and quirky coffee table fashioned from glass and hewn wood. Two large and brightly coloured abstract pictures filled one wall, and smaller charcoals, grouped in squares, decorated another. The abstracts were spectacular and he edged towards them to take a closer look, inadvertently knocking off a haphazardly positioned blanket from the arm of the sofa.

As he bent down to pick it up he spotted an empty box of tissues, along with a pile of soggy tissues tucked in the corner of the sofa. So, that was why her eyes looked so wild — she'd been crying on the sofa. He stared at the snapshot scene that spelled out her unhappiness as he hugged the blanket to his chest, his heart going out to her. No one should be without someone to comfort them when they were in need.

He spun around guiltily as her bedroom door opened, expecting to see a sad Emerald, but she emerged from the bedroom looking fresh and composed.

She shot him a puzzled glance and he reined in his expression, dropping the blanket back on to the sofa. 'Great pictures — who painted them? I can't see a signature.' He waved a hand towards the largest image.

'Oh those,' she said airily, glancing up at the walls briefly. She headed for the kitchen without answering him and pulled up a stool. 'Yummy,' she chimed, tearing into a croissant. She lifted the lid from her coffee and inhaled the aroma.

Marco followed her back into the kitchen, bewildered. Only a few minutes before she'd acted as if breakfast was the last thing on her mind and yet now she was attacking her croissant as if she hadn't eaten in weeks. He nodded slowly as realisation dawned. She was acting a part for some reason — to keep him at arm's length, he would guess.

He glanced at the huge pictures once more as if they would throw up their secret. Maybe her father was an artist, or she had inherited them and didn't want to go there. Whatever it was, it was no concern of his, he was mostly just showing a polite interest.

Emerald seemed noticeably edgy as she watched him look at the paintings and it was only when he turned back to his own breakfast and the topic was forgotten that she relaxed a little. It was a timely reminder of her sensitivity, though, and it made him unaccountably nervous about what he was going to ask. He wanted Emerald on his side and couldn't, at that precise moment, come up with a better plan than the one he had hatched.

'I have to go to the Isles of Scilly to look at a hotel. We're thinking of turning it into an upmarket retreat and I can't find anyone to come with me.'

'And you want me to find someone?'

Marco wondered if she was being deliberately obtuse. He sipped his coffee while he contemplated his next words. 'If that's what you would prefer, although I was hoping you might like to join me.'

'I've never been to the Scillies. I wouldn't be of any use.'

He laughed. 'Neither have I, and I'm not asking you to be a guide. I just want a second opinion on the suitability of the location and the possible packages we could promote to tempt the richer clientele down there. Scilly has several Dark Sky Discovery Sites and you gave me an idea.'

'Oh, what idea was that then?' She pulled off another piece of croissant, her face unreadable.

'I shall tell you that when we get there.' He grinned.

'I might not care either way,' she replied breezily.

'True.' He paused looking at Emerald and then down at her plate. 'Nice to see you do actually eat breakfast, by the way.'

'You have a problem with my eating habits?'

'Not really. Actually, I think you were just sulking when we flew to Edinburgh.' He gave her a shrewd look, catching the surprise in her eyes.

She grinned. 'You are very astute. I used to refuse to eat my step-mother's meals whenever she pissed me off.' She placed the piece of croissant back on her plate.

'A hard habit to break, eh?' He shrugged and put one of the jam sachets beside her plate. 'Eat up. I hate waste.'

He nodded once again towards her plate and half-eaten croissant.

Emerald scoffed. 'What would you know about waste, apart from the fact that you can throw away whatever you want, knowing there will always be more where that came from?'

'Don't assume you know everything about me, Emerald,' Marco said evenly. 'My life was not always as it is now. I was sent to live with Nonna, my grandma on my father's side, in a very poor village for many years, and I learned a thing or two about managing to keep body and soul together.' He pursed his lips and was silent as if remembering his youth.

Finally, he said, 'My father decided it was character building. He made his money through property development; building luxury flats on the first piece of scrubland he purchased. The rest, as they say, is history. My grandparents wanted a simple life and declined to move from their homeland. It wasn't about living in poverty, it was about being self-sufficient.' He picked up his coffee, looked at its contents and put it down again. 'Maybe I have more of a food hang-up than I thought.' He smiled. 'We are united in our hang-ups.' He put his hand over hers as if solidifying their united front and she tensed.

He pulled away. 'Sorry.'

'No, don't be — I'm just a bit jumpy.'

He raised his eyebrows. 'I would never have guessed.' He saw her eyes flash, immediately defensive, and prayed his comment wouldn't start off another spat.

'Sorry,' Emerald said.

'It doesn't matter.' He waited. 'So, what do you say — about coming with me?'

She stuffed a large piece of croissant in her mouth, as if to stop herself from answering, as his eyes lingered on hers. 'I'd rather not, if you don't mind,' she said eventually, her eyes flat and solemn.

Marco felt instantly deflated. He hadn't considered that she might say no, and immediately wished he'd sent her an official itinerary instead, although that would undoubtedly have caused even more trouble, he reasoned. She really was the most contrary person.

'Would it help if I said please? I believe it's a beautiful place to visit with its wild scrubland and stormy seas. There isn't much time to convince you, I'm afraid, as I would like to leave tomorrow.'

Emerald broke off another piece of croissant and stared at her plate, giving no indication that she was reconsidering his offer.

The silence lengthened and he felt even more deflated. Being turned down was new territory for him. 'If we don't change direction, bring in fresh routes, the airline will go down the pan. I need to get a firm contract from a travel agent and this is the only way I can think of doing it.' It was shameless, he knew, but he was pretty sure it would do the trick.

She turned solemn eyes up to him — looking pained, he thought.

'Please?' he asked again.

'I suppose so, then — if we have no choice.' She tried out a smile. 'Okay,' she added, apparently steeling herself to get used to the idea.

It wasn't the most euphoric acceptance he'd ever had, but she had said yes, and he was going to hold her to it before she changed her mind. 'Great. I'll delegate the wonderful Finbar to hold the fort while we're gone.' He tried hard to hide the sarcasm in his voice.

Emerald bit her lip and glanced at the clock on her kitchen wall and Marco felt a kick of disappointment in his chest as he recognized an action that normally would be perpetrated by him. *Another first*, he thought, swallowing down the humiliating realisation that his time was up. Unlike most women, Emerald was clearly desperate to get rid of him. He took a last gulp of his coffee and pushed to his feet. 'I should go.'

'I'll see you out.' Emerald scraped her stool back rather too eagerly and it was all Marco could do to sit down again and refuse to leave. Knowing he had no choice, he followed her back down the hallway, thanking her as she turned the catch on the door. He appreciated how the women he'd been involved with might feel when outstaying their welcome, eternally wondering what they'd done wrong.

Marco eyed Emerald for a moment as a pang of insecurity hit him. She was watching him quietly, her eyes sad, her face wan, and he found he wanted to make her happy. He wanted to see the smile that lit up her face so readily for Finbar.

He hovered at her doorway, longing to tell her that he was sorry about the night in Edinburgh — but the timing wasn't right. He'd left it too late. In the end, he settled for raising a hand towards her face, hating the way she tensed as he brushed her lips with his thumb. 'Piece of croissant,' he said.

'Oh,' she said, throatily, her fingertips tracing over the place Marco had touched. 'Marco?' She sighed and rested her head against the door frame, giving him a level stare.

'Yes?' He knew she didn't want to go away with him but equally he knew that they could enjoy each other's company away from the daily toils of the airline. He wanted to try, at least, even if he hadn't quite yet analysed why.

'Is it wise that we do this?'

'Do what?'

She shrugged. 'You know.'

He did know — and his ego wilted even more. 'It's simply business, Emerald.'

'Yes, I know that.' She sounded doubtful and her gaze wandered in every direction apart from his. 'Just for a couple of days, you say?' Her voice was a quiver of concern. She toyed with a silver necklace at her throat and shifted from foot to foot again.

'Emerald, is there something you'd like to talk through?' It was clear that she was upset and he wanted to help, but he wasn't exactly having an easy time of it himself.

'No. God, no. Everything's fine.' She was worrying at the necklace again, her fingers zinging up and down the chain.

He sighed, wished they could be more open with each other. 'Just bring your normal travel bag and I shall send a car at nine thirty. You'll enjoy it, I promise.'

'Fine.'

'Great,' he replied, still rooted to the spot.

'Cool.' She stared at him. 'Goodbye then.' She made to close the door and it roused him enough to move out of the way.

'Tomorrow, then.' He'd barely finished talking before he found himself face to face with her closed front door.

He let out an unsteady breath as his emotions levelled out, although a strange ache in the back of his throat made him swallow hard. He hadn't wanted to leave her and it was a strange reality for him.

He shook his head as he made for his car, aware that he was behaving irrationally and wasn't entirely sure his impulsiveness was a good idea. All of his instincts told him to run, but, he reasoned, it would be an ideal opportunity to ask her about his inherited airline staff once they were away from the day-to-day routine of work. Yes, taking her with him was a good plan, of that he was almost sure — if only that niggle in the back of his mind would ease off.

* * *

Finbar had rushed over to Emerald's flat at her request and was now sitting in the same spot that Marco had recently vacated. He was at his prime in the role of problem solver and he clutched a mug of tea with suppressed glee, pursing his lips, his frown deepening as he pondered over her predicament.

Emerald watched him anxiously. 'That's what he said, Fin, that he wanted help over a hotel he's going to buy.'

'Yeah, right, and he can't think of *anyone* else to take with him to the bottom end of nowhere. Have you been online recently? I think you'll find there are plenty of women hanging off his arm who would be only too pleased to go with him.'

This was a shock to Emerald. 'He sees other women?'

Finbar was quick on the uptake. '*Other* women?'

'No, I don't mean it like that.' She bit her lip to stop herself from asking more questions, surprised at how much this news upset her.

Finbar scrutinized her expression, his eagle eyes glinting at what he was taking in.

She rearranged her face into a mask of polite interest. 'So, why me, do you think?'

He sipped his tea and shook the hair out of his eyes, enjoying the moment. 'There are three possible scenarios here. One is that he likes you and values your opinion. Two, he just wants to get you into bed, and, three, he wants to pump you for information on the airline and its workers.'

Emerald smiled. 'Which one would you run with?'

'Well, I hate to be the bearer of bad news, my darling Emms, but I don't think it's the second one.' He held a hand up as she tried to talk over the top of him. 'Last month he was photographed skiing down the mountain at Klosters with an Amazonian blonde whose daddy owns a chain of hotels and restaurants — it was all over TikTok. And, let's face it, the closest you get to skiing is eating their yoghurts.'

'Great. Thanks for the honesty.' Emerald laughed bleakly. 'So, the odds on him being desperate for my body are quite slight. Is that what you're trying to say?' She didn't know whether to be happy or sad at Finbar's declaration, but she was certainly regretting saying she would go with Marco on the trip.

A dreamy expression crossed Finbar's face. 'I can picture it now, you and the delicious Marco, miles away from anywhere, on a rough and craggy island, with just the puffins and sheep for company.' He shivered in delight.

Emerald almost spurted out her tea. 'That's supposed to sell it to me, is it, puffins and sheep? I don't know what he's thinking, to be honest. He gives out such mixed messages when he's near me.'

'Just be careful, you know?'

'I know, don't worry.' The revelation that he dated women on a regular basis strengthened her resolve to keep her distance. She didn't have him down as a player, but then again, she only saw the side of him that he wanted her to see. She certainly couldn't imagine that he would want to take her to bed when rich beauties were apparently queueing up for their turn.

In fact when Marco had pulled her down on the sofa with him it was probably an errant moment he regretted — he couldn't even bring himself to mention it, afterwards. She shook her head. 'This is ridiculous,' she said to Finbar in dismay. 'He still thinks I'm not much better than a hooker — and a drunken one at that.'

'Yes, sweetie, you're right, and we all know that no man would ever try to have sex with a prostitute, don't we?' He chinked mugs with her. 'This could be interesting. Keep me up to speed, won't you? It all sounds rather Mills and Boonish and I have to confess to feeling rather jealous.'

'Of which bit — getting up close with puffins and sheep or that Marco might try to have sex with me?'

Finbar fluttered his eyelashes to let her know he wouldn't deign to answer such a question. 'Seriously, though, don't lose your head to this man.'

'I don't intend to,' Emerald replied. The thought of him frolicking with sexy, rich women was enough to bring her back down to earth, even though there was a tiny part of her that thought Marco did actually like her — a bit. Why else would he want to be alone with her?

Or maybe she should add an overactive imagination to her long list of personality defects to deal with. Once Marco had driven off back to Italy in his flashy car, it would be over and she could stop — what — loving him? The thought made her stomach clench and she realized she'd already answered her own question: she was undeniably lost in love, with Marco Cavarelli.

CHAPTER TWENTY

Marco had hired a private aircraft to take them to St Mary's, the largest of the Scilly Isles — for which Emerald was truly grateful, having looked up on Google how long the journey would take by road and then ferry. She was no stranger to private aircraft, but the difference in opulence on this aircraft was staggering. Marco's aircraft smelled of fresh flowers, beeswax and expensive perfume, and everything was shiny and polished — including the flawlessly dressed air stewardess who gave her a red-lipped, Julia-Roberts-sized smile as she ushered them into the cabin.

An arrangement of pink and white roses sat on a squat table next to an impressive array of glossy magazines, fanned out to display their titles. Olives and nuts in pretty porcelain bowls were positioned next to each sofa-style seat, making Emerald wonder if she'd need to grab everything on take-off to save it from sliding to the tail end of the aircraft. In fact, the interior looked more like someone's sitting room than an aeroplane cabin, apart from the discreet seat belts and the fire extinguisher and oxygen bottle attached to the aircraft wall.

She needn't have worried about the nibbles tipping up. The aircraft lifted into the sky so smoothly that she had to peer out of the window to check they were no longer touching the ground. She couldn't quite believe she was already heading down south when she had done nothing more than climb out of a car that pulled right up to the aircraft. It was incredible. She tried not to gape as she sat down and smoothed out her dress, imagining for a moment that she was a rich heiress or a movie star.

The air stewardess appeared with a laden tray to serve them lunch and Emerald sat up straight and folded her ankles neatly over each other, as was befitting for someone of her newly elevated status.

Marco glanced up from his phone as the stewardess placed a delicate looking teapot on the table next to an array of sandwiches, fancy cakes and tiny fruit tarts.

'Shall I pour, or leave you to it?' She directed her question to Emerald, making her feel significantly more important than the spare part she mostly felt like when she was around Marco. People tended to snap to attention when Marco spoke and it was refreshing to be asked to take control, even though it was only pouring the tea.

'Leave it with me, thank you. Looks delicious.' She smiled warmly at the stewardess and unfolded her napkin with a flourish.

'Just press the call button if you need me.' The stewardess retreated, pulling the door behind her, leaving Emerald alone with Marco.

She shot him a grin. 'Now this, I could get used to.'

Marco inclined his head. 'I'm glad it pleases, madam,' he said gravely. 'This is the sort of aircraft I'm hoping to make available if my scheme to buy the hotel and others around Europe comes off. Door-to-door luxury will be part of the package.'

'Wow, you're going in big time, then.'

'There's no point in doing otherwise,' Marco replied in a smooth and assured tone.

Emerald looked at the spread in front of her, lifted up the plate of sandwiches and slid around to where Marco was sitting — there was room for two on the small sofa he'd commandeered. She checked the choice of sandwiches before offering the selection to Marco through demurely lowered lashes. 'Would sir like a sandwich? Smoked salmon and cream cheese or ham salad?' She giggled, ruining the effect she had intended, and was gratified to see a genuine smile on Marco's face.

The whole situation was totally surreal. She didn't know why, but she felt a bit like Alice in Wonderland at the Mad Hatter's tea party.

'If only I had sleek blonde hair, it would be perfect,' she said, half to herself.

Marco glanced over at her. 'The sun is dancing in your hair right now, highlighting the gold and bronze streaks — you have no need for yellow hair.' He took two of the sandwiches, put them on his side plate and reached over for his copy of *The Times*.

Emerald blinked in surprise at his observation, absent-mindedly tugging at a lock of the hair that she had always resolutely thought of as ginger. She nibbled on a ham sandwich, glancing surreptitiously at Marco, whose sunglasses were perched on his head, making him look cooler than ever. She smiled gently as she watched him frown over the newspaper, feeling strangely benevolent towards him, or did she just feel closer to him, ensconced together as they were, in a narrow tube flying through the sky.

The stewardess seemed to think Emerald was Marco's girlfriend and Emerald didn't dissuade her of the idea. She sighed. If only. Thinking in such a way would not do her any good, though, so instead she poured out the tea, earning a nod of thanks from Marco as she added milk. Still he kept his nose in the newspaper and Emerald felt her euphoria dissipate. She tapped her fingers on the arm of the chair and made a pretence of flicking through the magazines, but she really couldn't concentrate.

If Marco wasn't going to talk to her she could use the free time sketching, she thought, if only he knew about her closely guarded hobby. Her pastels were never far from her side and it seemed so wasteful — missing out on this chance to draw the light refracting off the aircraft wing, clearly visible from the small window.

Marco glanced up at her occasionally and she noticed that he hadn't yet turned a page on his newspaper. He was either very engrossed in an article or he wasn't actually reading it.

His left leg began to bounce up and down rapidly, a repetitive tic that she'd noticed before. For some reason the air between them seemed charged, as if a thunderstorm was on its way. Marco glanced across at her and then down again, staring at his newspaper. She would bet a million pounds he wasn't reading it. So, what was he thinking?

'Marco?' She didn't have anything to say, so wasn't sure what had made her say his name out loud.

'Emerald?' He looked up from his newspaper. 'You are sitting extremely close to me and I find it quite unnerving.'

She balked. 'Am I that offensive?'

'No . . . it's not that, at all.' His leg was bouncing away ten to the dozen and she focused on it, rather than concentrating on his eyes which were like lasers, seeking her out, the flintiness like hewn granite, black irises searing into her.

She shifted position, tried to shuffle further down the sofa, but it was a very small sofa and she was soon at the edge, having managed to move no more than a few inches. Marco put his hand on her knee to stop her when she made to rise, intending to sit on one of the single chairs.

'No, don't move.' He swallowed. 'Emerald?'

'Yes, Marco?' Her heart rate picked up speed as she directed her gaze at him.

'I feel that I have not been perfectly honest with you.' He folded the newspaper and set it on the table. Then he took hold of her hand. A breath hitched in her throat at his touch, which caused a current of molten lava to zip through her body and heat up her insides.

'Why is that, then?' She prayed her face wasn't giving her emotions away. Cool, calm and composed was the way forward.

'Because I, err . . . I particularly wanted you to be the person I took on this trip.' Marco, for once, sounded a little sheepish.

'You already told me that,' she said in confusion, realising as soon as the words were out, that they might be talking at cross-purposes.

His words unnerved her almost as much as the fact that he was holding her hand. She glanced down to check she hadn't imagined it. Yes, their fingers were indeed entwined. She waited, feeling totally out of her depth.

He leaned in closer to Emerald, his body radiating heat and pheromones or whatever it was that made her lose all sense of perspective. She could see the cute mole on his upper lip again, which meant that if she was close enough to see it, he was close enough to kiss her. His eyes were gentle as he gazed at her, his irises changing from granite to a softer, smokier colour. He was going to kiss her, she knew it. But he pulled back at the last minute and said, 'You know that I'm separated, don't you?'

'From your wife?' This was not a conversation she'd expected. He heaved out a breath. 'Yes.'

'Yes, I believe Finbar's brought me up to speed on your love life.'

'Ah. Finbar and his quirky slant on things. I fear his observations might not be entirely factual.'

'Won't they?'

He sighed and let go of her hand. 'I was forgetting about Finbar and his love of gossip.' He picked up the newspaper once more, gave it a shake and studied it. 'That man.' Was all he added.

She fell quiet, her hand pressed to her chest while she waited for her heartbeat, which she was sure could be heard over the hum of the aircraft engine, to quieten down. She watched Marco through half-closed eyes, resting her head against the bulkhead, the heat from the sun's rays warming her face and arms. This new agitated Marco confused her as he was normally in perfect control of his emotions. It looked, however, as if the conversation, wherever it had been heading, was now closed.

Watching the sky turn from bright blue to a more thunderous grey as they glided through the air, she felt herself nodding off, when a sudden rumble of thunder jolted her wide awake. The aircraft lurched and shuddered and she clutched at the seat instinctively, swearing softly as the plane righted itself. Within seconds she remembered where she was, but still her heart thudded.

Marco's arm was instantly around her shoulder as he pulled her tight to his chest. 'It's okay, it's just turbulence,' he said.

She impulsively clutched at his hand and he engulfed it in his. 'I know. It's fine — I was just confused.' She allowed him to hold her tight as her heart slowed down, swallowing as she took in this new scenario, of Marco stroking her hair and massaging the back of her hand with his thumb.

'Right — as long as you're not scared.' He peered into her eyes, cupping her cheek in the palm of his hand.

'I'm an air stewardess, Marco, I'm used to it. I was just dozing and disoriented.' She leaned her cheek into his palm, however, enjoying the cool sensation of his skin on hers.

'That's okay then.' His gaze was steady and for a moment their eyes locked. 'Emerald, I—'

'Nothing to worry about,' chimed the stewardess as she strode breezily into the cabin, smiling reassuringly. 'We're just going through the clouds and the weather's a bit sticky — at least that's how Captain Turner described it.' She busied herself with crockery and utensils on the low table. 'Are we all done, here? We'll be landing in about fifteen minutes.'

'Yes, it was lovely, thank you,' Emerald said. She turned to Marco, who had slid away from her as if she was a live firework. 'Landing in fifteen minutes? I must have slept for ages.'

'You did. I hope you didn't mind me not waking you, but I figured you must need the rest.'

'Thank you.' She prayed she hadn't dribbled or snored. 'I'll just nip into the bathroom and freshen up.'

Emerald returned from the bathroom with fresh make-up on and a clean-tasting mouth. 'Even the bathroom is posher than posh,' she said, pointing to the bathroom door. 'There's a freaking shower in there.' Marco laughed and she joined in, enjoying the warm glow it gave her.

She sat down again and fastened her seat belt. The sky was now a block of grey, interspersed with fierce black clouds that buffeted the aircraft, making Emerald feel queasy and slightly apprehensive. Small aircraft were never the most comfortable in a thunderstorm. Marco was quiet and she wondered what he had been about to say earlier, before the stewardess had interrupted him.

'So, would I get to be a hostie on this new aircraft if the deal goes ahead?' she said, blurting out the first thing that popped into her mind to break the silence.

She suddenly wished she hadn't reminded him of her employee status, but Marco put down his newspaper and smiled indulgently. 'Hostie? I've not heard that word before.' The corners of his eyes crinkled as he smiled and she wanted to reach out and trace the tiny lines.

'Why are you smiling?' he asked.

'Because you're smiling and it's a good thing to see.'

'I'm sorry I don't smile enough for you. I confess, I've not had much to smile about this past year.'

Emerald shrugged. 'I thought it was just something about me that made you grumpy.'

Her words hung in the air for a moment and Marco considered her for so long that she felt herself blush. His jaw tightened and a shadow crossed over his face. Finally, he spoke. 'If you want to fly on our new aircraft, I imagine you will stand as much chance as anyone. Are you used to flying on your own?'

Emerald was confused. What had caused his mood to change so rapidly? 'I'm used to *being* on my own,' she replied, more truthfully than she'd intended. 'Does that count?'

The captain's voice rang out over the PA system. 'Five minutes to landing. Please take your seats.' Marco didn't take his eyes off her. His stare was unnerving and made her feel as if he was trying to search her mind for an answer to a question he hadn't asked.

The stewardess popped in to ensure they were buckled up, and he appeared to come back to earth. She realized that he wasn't so much staring at her, as mulling over what she'd said.

'We'll talk about this later,' he said, giving her a tight nod. Emerald wished she hadn't asked the question, which seemed to have taken on an enormity it didn't warrant.

The aircraft landed smoothly despite the storm and the stewardess pushed open the passenger door, inviting them to disembark. A gust of wind and squally rain hit Emerald in the face as she hurried down the steps, making her gasp. She rushed towards a waiting Mercedes, making a grab for her hair as the wind blew it upwards. 'What is it with us and the weather?' she shouted as Marco followed her, shielding his laptop bag from the rain.

'What is it with us, full stop?' she thought she heard him mutter as he tipped the baggage man generously and stowed their bags in the boot of the car.

The hire car was waiting for them at the other side of the airport and Emerald's nerves kicked in as Marco opened the doors and loaded the luggage into the boot.

They were entirely alone, with just the swish of the windscreen wipers and the pattering of rain on the roof. Emerald couldn't think of a thing to say as they drove, her mind on a loop of *what ifs*. What if they had the same set-up as in Edinburgh? What if he realized she was of no use to him at Hot Air Aviation and she found herself out of a job? What if they kissed again? She touched her lips, then glanced guiltily at Marco in case he'd spotted the action and guessed where her thoughts were.

Marco's phone beeped and he glanced at the dashboard. 'Damn, I was forgetting my phone isn't connected to this car. See who it is, will you?'

He pulled his phone out from his inside pocket and passed it to Emerald. She raised her eyebrows in surprise, but took it from him to check the screen. 'Heron Airways?' She sighed in relief, acknowledging that she'd dreaded it being one of the many women Finbar had talked about.

'It's the airline we came over on.'

'Okay, I'll take it, shall I?' She spoke into the phone and clutched at it awkwardly when she finished the call, not knowing where to put it.

Marco gave her a tight smile and took it from her. His fingers brushed hers and she felt the familiar jolt of electricity shoot up her arm and straight to her heart.

'They're closing the airport?' Marco asked unnecessarily, having listened to the telephone conversation.

'So it seems. Temporarily. It will probably blow over before too long. I suppose we should have noticed the low-lying cloud base. At least we managed to get here, though, rather than circling for ages and returning to the mainland, as I've done on too many occasions.'

'That's one of the main reasons for upgrading our aircraft. The Scillies' weather is frequently temperamental and my guests will not appreciate delays.'

'And once you are here, you might not want to leave,' Emerald said, as she looked out of the window, spotting golden sand, trees that had bent to the whims of the wind, and a turbulent, yet clear, rolling sea.

Marco threw her an enigmatic smile. 'That's what I'm hoping.' His eyes twinkled and already he looked like a different man, as if the troubles of his business life had been shucked off. He lifted his hand as though to pat her on the knee, but replaced it on the steering wheel, presumably thinking better of it. Emerald caught the movement and a nervous thrill ran through her body. Were those words meant for her?

* * *

Before too long Marco pulled up outside a cottage covered in white-washed cobblestone and double doors facing the sea. He retrieved the keys from under a stone, hefted open the stiff front door and moved aside for Emerald to enter, picking up their bags as he followed behind.

'We're staying here? Wow, it's gorgeous.' Emerald turned full circle in the kitchen, taking in the inglenook fireplace set with logs and a welcome basket on the granite worktop. The kitchen cupboards were in a traditional oak, and a dark blue Aga sat squat against the wall. Emerald ran her fingers over the enamel lids. 'Ooh, it's hot,' she exclaimed.

'Just as well, given the weather outside. It probably heats the water.' He watched her closely, wanting her to be pleased. She twirled around checking out the sitting room, a puzzled frown on her face. 'It's perfect, but why are we staying here? I thought we'd come to check out a hotel. We're not staying there?'

'We have and we will visit it. I just don't want the owner of the hotel to know I am checking it out, before I meet him. If it is entirely unsuitable, then I won't have to have an opt-out speech,' he explained, as another twinge of self-doubt assailed him. In reality he had seen the cottage advertised online and couldn't resist the idea of a bit of peace, loving the thought of balmy weather, walking along the beach and drinking local beer in rustic pubs. Emerald was casually thrown into the mix, although he could, of course, just as easily have left her out of it . . .

No, she couldn't have been left out of it, he realized, wondering why he'd been kidding himself. It had been too long since he'd wanted to spend time with a woman for her own sake rather than simply to show his face on the social circuit, a stiff smile fixed in place as he posed for the cameras. He was tired of feeling lonely in a crowded room, never knowing who was to be trusted and who just wanted a share of the limelight and maybe his money. Emerald pulled no punches and stood up to him — it was a good feeling.

When she'd accused him, on the aircraft, of being grumpy he had had a moment of clarity. He realized he'd tried to keep her at arm's length, to push her away, because in truth he wanted more than a working relationship. He could finally admit it to himself. The question was, could he admit it to Emerald? He glanced over at her now, appreciating the sunny smile that warmed his heart.

'Let's check out the welcome basket,' Emerald said, her excitement infectious. She lifted the cloth that covered the basket and peered at the contents, pulling out scones and a pot of jam along with some tea bags.

Marco picked up a squidgy damp packet, holding it aloft to read the label. 'Samphire? I don't think I've ever tried that.'

'Hmm, I think it's a bit like asparagus.' She sniffed it. 'Doesn't smell of anything in particular,' she said, before putting it back in the basket where it would stay, if she had her way. 'We don't have to go to the hotel yet, do we?' she asked, opening cupboard doors and nosing inside them. 'We could buy some food and eat here tonight. I'm not sure I'm geared up to play my part as the gushing guest, just yet.'

He nodded. 'Good idea, although I think we might have to Google what to do with the samphire.' He filled the kettle with water and placed it on the hob. 'My grandmother used to have one of these,' he reminisced, patting the huge range oven.

'Great, I'll leave the cooking to you.'

'You might be surprised. In fact, tonight, I'll cook dinner.'

Emerald raised her eyebrows. 'It's a deal. I'll bring the wine.'

Marco lifted a bottle out of the basket and studied the label. 'No need. St Martin's home-grown wine, and you don't drink, remember.' He waved the bottle at her before setting it down on the worktop.

'Actually, I was joking about bringing the wine.' Her scowl was back in place and Marco was annoyed that he'd caused it. He sighed as he opened the fridge and placed the wine in the door, lifting out the milk at the same time. 'I know you're not the drinker I initially thought you were. I was trying to be light-hearted. Did I fail?'

Emerald sighed, didn't answer, but moved over to the bay window to gaze at the sea as it foamed into waves and churned up the pebbles. The rain continued to mist the old bay window and a thin wind whistled between the frames. It was rugged and beautifully secluded. She folded her arms and Marco saw that she was withdrawn and looked vaguely unhappy again.

'I'm sorry, that was crass of me. Let's move forwards, shall we?' He moved to stand next to her on the pretext of looking at the sky. 'Maybe we could go for a walk along the beach in a little while.' He only now acknowledged that he'd fantasized about walking along the seafront with Emerald. It had become his focus and would symbolize that they were comfortable together, although in his fantasy his arm was slung around her shoulders and she was laughing up at him, her eyes full of love as he teased her.

'It is beautiful here, isn't it?' He was already envisioning the idyllic walks and lazy breakfasts they would share and it made him feel alive once more.

'It is,' Emerald agreed, her voice wavering, her folded arms tightening around her chest protectively.

'Something wrong?' he asked, praying that his probing wouldn't start another argument.

'This is all wrong, Marco. We shouldn't be here together and I'm wondering why we are. I am staying in a cottage by the sea with the very man who can control a large part of my life and I am hoping that isn't what he has in mind.'

He frowned at her candid words. 'Are you questioning my motives?'

'I think I might be.' She turned to face him. 'Marco, I need to be straight with you. I spend most of my time worrying that everything I do is wrong when I'm around you. I constantly doubt myself and feel that I'm being judged. I used to have confidence. Yes, it was a brash type of confidence, borne of necessity, but sink or swim became my motto — and when I thought that sinking was the more likely outcome, I'd make a bloody life raft.' She shrugged before meeting his gaze, unblinking. 'I think you would sack me in the blink of an eye if it suited you. Can you imagine how stressful that is for me?'

Marco recoiled, stung at her words. 'If I was going to sack you, you certainly wouldn't be here today.'

'I don't know why I am here, to be honest — for all I know, you're evaluating whether my personality outweighs my usefulness, right now.' She stopped and thought for a second, pursing her lips. 'Are you testing me?'

'Not at all.' He raised his hands, floundering for a decent enough reason as to why they *were* there. 'I can't always do what I want. The slightest whiff of scandal can affect the stock value of my businesses, so I thought somewhere remote like this might be good for us. I have to think of my shareholders at all times.'

'Your poor shareholders. Please forgive me if I don't feel particularly bothered by them.'

'That's not what I mean.' He put his fingers to his forehead and worried at the frown between his eyes. How had the conversation taken this turn when he was just about to declare his good intentions towards her?

'Then, why do you want me near you, when I'm clearly a liability. Imagine the scandal, Signor Cavarelli, if this got out.' She couldn't resist the sting in her voice.

'I'm sure you'll be on your best behaviour, Emerald.'

'I'll contain my urges, if that's what you're worried about. There won't be a re-run of Florence, I promise.'

'Emerald, don't do this. Please don't try to turn this into something it's not.'

'So, why am I here? I get it, okay, you're my boss and I have to do what you ask, I know that — you shove it down my neck all the time — but sometimes . . . sometimes you give out mixed messages and it's so very confusing.'

'I need to be careful in my position, Emerald.'

'What position is that then? Lying horizontally with a rich daddy's girl so that you don't let the side down?' She glared at him, stepping backwards towards the table as if she couldn't bear to be near him.

Marco recoiled from her words, balling his fists to contain his anger. 'That was uncalled for and crass. Is that what you think, that I'm just biding my time until the right social-ite comes along? How can you think I'm that shallow?'

'I don't . . . think about you, at all,' Emerald almost shouted, slamming her hands down on the kitchen table.

'Okay.' Marco was calm and measured as he took the kettle off the boil and pushed the mugs to the back of the counter. This wasn't going quite the way he'd planned, which unsettled him as he was used to being in control. 'Why don't we go for a walk along the beach and enjoy the evening? We can collect a few ingredients from the local shop and I'll cook dinner when we're not so agitated.'

'We?' She almost screeched. '*We* are not bloody agi-tated.' She rounded on him, her voice rising higher. 'Just me, okay? You are my boss and that's fine — just stop with the soft words and kind glances, making me lose track of what the hell I'm thinking, let alone what you are thinking about me — you and your stupid smouldering eyes and your crappy oh-so-sexy accent. I'm sick of it.' She grabbed her coat which she'd taken off only minutes before, pushed her arms into it and grappled with the French windows, heaving them open. 'I'm going for a walk. On my own, if that's allowed — or should I write you a memo and make sure I get it signed off first?' She marched through the door and out onto the shingle, hitting the beach at speed.

Marco watched as she stormed off, her back straight and determined, her long strides revealing her fury with him. A hint of a smile played over his lips despite his dismay that the conversation had deteriorated so quickly. Smouldering eyes and sexy accent, eh?

He stopped smiling as he watched her pick her way over the sand, faltering and zigzagging in places, where he guessed large rock pools stopped her in her tracks. A low lying fog hovered in the distance obscuring the sky and the distant sea. Occasionally she put her hand up to her eyes and he won-dered if she was crying, until eventually her outline blurred into the background, drizzle and mist turning her into an amorphous figure on the horizon.

He should leave her to it until she'd calmed down, but was worried that she wouldn't know how to find the cottage on her return as she had no idea of the address.

He sighed. He had to bring her back even though he didn't know how to deal with her. He grabbed his coat and slammed the French doors behind him.

It was time they had a proper talk.

CHAPTER TWENTY-ONE

It wasn't easy for Marco to walk on the shingle as his soft Italian loafers squelched in the boggy sand and water oozed over the top after a few minutes. He made a note to buy some walking boots when they found the high street.

Once he had Emerald in his sights he slowed down, taking time to think about her words and accepting that she was right. He'd given out way too many conflicting messages as he struggled with his remaining professionalism, while fighting down the attraction he felt towards her.

He would not allow people to gossip about his private life ever again, as they surely would if he was spotted with an employee on a distant shore. He knew to his cost that there was always someone lurking around, who would recognise him. He could of course rectify the problem by asking her to leave the company, leaving them both free to have a relationship if they wanted to — if only life was that simple. He smiled at the thought of how she would react to the idea of being dismissed. She'd probably thump him.

He broke into a jog, not wanting to lose her as she turned away from the beach. He spotted her entering a pub, its weathered sign creaking in the wind on rusty hinges, and made his way towards it, pushing the door open. He waited for a bit in the foyer, hoping she would reappear, having just used the facilities but minutes ticked by and he decided he needed to find her — assuming she hadn't exited through a handy bathroom window and legged it.

With some relief he spotted her instantly, and strode over to where she was seated. 'May I sit here?' He indicated a vacant stool next to her.

Emerald looked up, her bottom lip trembling and her eyes red-rimmed, even as they sparked with defiance and anger. She looked vulnerable in her fury and a tenderness that made him want to fold her into his arms and soothe her rose in his chest. He pulled out the stool and straddled it, to sit opposite her, although she hadn't even acknowledged his presence.

She looked hunted as she nursed a hot drink, both hands hugging it to her chest. 'Come back with me, Emerald, please. We need to talk.'

'I just want to go home, Mr Cavarelli. I don't know why you wanted me here. I know I shouldn't have come.'

'What's with this Mr Cavarelli all of a sudden? Call me Marco, for crying out loud.'

'No, I would rather call you Mr Cavarelli.'

'Emerald. What am I not getting?' He shuffled his stool closer to her and she shrank away from him, holding her mug up to her chest like a shield. He wanted to take the mug away from her and fold her hands into his, but settled for barely tracing his finger over her knee, letting her know that he cared.

'You're after something from me and I don't know what it is.' She flinched and pulled her leg away. He sighed. 'Emerald, I don't *need* anything from you. I'm a successful businessman. I practically own an empire, for God's sake—'

'Whereas I have absolutely nothing — thanks for that,' she interrupted, but her voice caught on the last word and tears filled her eyes. Marco exhaled and ran his fingers through his hair. 'What I am trying to say is that I know how to run multiple businesses and compose myself like a gentleman, but with you . . . I swear to God that I have no idea how to deal with you. And I'm sorry, I don't know what part of me thought it was a good idea to bring you over here.'

Except he did know. He wanted to be alone with her, without anyone judging him or watching them. He swallowed.

She suddenly turned to him. 'Do you know I once fought a hyena?'

He blinked. 'No, I didn't know that. I've read your CV twice and I swear it wasn't in there.'

She smiled grimly at his words. 'It was trying to savage my stepmum's dog. Hated my stepmum — loved her dog.'

'Okay. That's interesting.'

'It was quite a small hyena.' She wrinkled her nose ruefully. Marco laughed. 'A hyena is a hyena in my book.'

'And another time I rode off on Star, determined never to come back, and I survived for five days in the desert until they found me.'

She took a large gulp of her drink. 'Of course, I was quite hungry by then and caved in when I smelled steak cooking. Bastards had lit a barbecue and were smoking me out — figuratively speaking, of course.'

'Of course.' He smiled. 'I don't suppose the smell of samphire would have cut it, if I hadn't found you here?'

Emerald's return smile almost reached her eyes and he braved another question.

'What was Star like?'

She smiled. 'He was quite wild, but I rode him anyway — he didn't mind me.'

'Wow.' He had certainly underestimated Emerald when he'd first met her.

'I was a bit of a tomboy.'

'You don't say.' He rubbed at his forehead. 'And here I was thinking a ginger and lemon facial scrub up at the hotel would be all it took to win you over.'

He was relieved to see the hostility disappear from her eyes, but she was still tense and wary, and it was his fault. She put her mug down and stood up. 'I just wanted you to know that I'm not completely lacking.'

'I never thought you were.' He frowned. 'You think this is a challenge — to prove your worth?'

Emerald's face crumpled once more and she pressed her lips together as she held back tears. 'I don't know anymore. I just know I can't compete with all the beautiful women in your life and I feel as if I should just cave in and call it a day.'

Marco shook his head. How had he given out such a completely wrong message to her? 'What beautiful women?'

'The ones Finbar's told me about. They're everywhere.' Her voice rose a notch as she waved her hand around the pub.

Marco stupidly looked up to gaze at the locals, mostly men, and none of them were the slightest bit beautiful.

'I just can't do this.' Her voice became muffled as she pressed her hand to her mouth and sniffed. 'I'm sure it would be for the best if I caught the next flight home.'

'No, it wouldn't. Emerald — you are more beautiful than any of the socialites I mix with. You must believe me.'

He'd said more than he should and there was no undoing it, but in for a penny in for a pound, he thought, deciding to level with her. It was time for honesty and candour and hopefully a chance to make amends. He held out his hand offering a truce.

She stared at it, ignoring the offer.

His intentions took a nosedive. He tried again. 'We are both strong people, I know that, but our emotions are all tangled up. Let's try to sort this out, shall we?' He reluctantly dropped his arm back to his side, his voice pleading. He paused, trying to frame the words he wanted to say. Leaning forward he took her hand once more, gratified that this time she didn't pull away. 'I said earlier that I need nothing from you, and I am wondering if, maybe that's not true. I think I do need something.' Should he say more? He could not lose her now. He took a deep breath and said the words he couldn't retract. 'You. I *want* you. I want to be with *you*.' He hardly dared to breathe as he gazed at her face trying to gauge her reaction.

She blinked rapidly and looked down at her hand now intertwined with his. Inhaling sharply she widened her eyes as if only now registering what was happening.

Marco hoped he hadn't said too much — to make her bolt.

Slowly she lifted her green eyes up to meet his. They stared at each other for a long beat before she nodded her agreement, a measured smile growing.

He heaved a sigh of relief. It was enough for him — for now, anyway.

She dropped his hand, put her mug on the table and hoisted herself upright before raising her eyebrows, as if to say *come on then, let's do this thing*.

Slightly confused but taking her reaction as a positive one he fell into step with her and they started out back along the beach, towards the cottage. Emerald was soon shivering again. Any heat the sun had bestowed before the fog closed the airport and drizzle cooled the island was now eaten up by a chill wind blowing across the beach and scouring them with grains of sand. 'I don't think I brought the right clothes with me. Remind me again, what season are we supposed to be in?' She wrapped her arms around her chest. 'You have to bring me to two of the most unpredictable places in the country, don't you?'

Marco was bewildered. She was acting as if he hadn't just given the speech of his life. He watched her carefully and played along while his mind whirred. 'I guess I am learning the vagaries of a British summer season rather too late in the day. At least I'll be prepared for winter, having already braved Scotland, and now here.' Marco laughed and threw his arm casually around Emerald's shoulders, drawing her to his side, ostensibly to warm her up. He inhaled the scent of her hair and enjoyed the intimacy of her body next to his. He half expected her to pull away, but she stayed in his embrace although she looked at him warily, as if wondering what was coming next. But he was winging it himself and would let her know his intentions when he had worked them out himself.

They walked along the beach in companionable silence side by side as if they were just a regular couple on a break — albeit a regular couple who had no idea about the clothes to pack for the Isles of Scilly. 'I really need to get some better shoes than these,' he said as they headed for the high street. 'This will do.' Marco ducked into a hiking shop, pulling Emerald inside.

While she wandered around, he spoke to the sales assistant, who glanced at Emerald and then produced a cream woollen jumper, chunky and long. 'Perfect. Don't bother wrapping it, she'll wear it now.'

He turned. 'Emerald, come over here.' He held up the jumper. 'Here you are, put it on.'

Emerald rolled her eyes and he apologized. 'Sorry, don't mean to boss you around — again.' She gave him big eyes as she slipped off her thin cardigan and he nodded his satisfaction. As an afterthought, he picked up a woollen bobble hat and popped it on her head, pulling it down over her ears. 'We'll take this, too.'

She laughed as she looked in the mirror. 'I look as if I'm going on a trek to the North Pole, not a walk along the beach.'

'At least you'll be prepared for every eventuality,' Marco said, adding, 'Pretty as a picture.' She blushed and he felt another tug on his heart, pushing it away, quickly.

He added a pair of boots to the pile of merchandise, merely glancing at the size. 'They'll do nicely,' he said and handed over his credit card, taking off his old shoes and stamping his feet into the boots.

Emerald continued to browse finding interesting knick-knacks that were pretty, but unnecessary. She picked them up, inspected them and put them down again, enjoying the mindless occupation while she waited for Marco to inspect the food, check that she would eat lobster tails, and add vegetables and sundries to the stash of purchases before settling up.

He joined her and when he brushed her hand accidentally as he added a soft scarf that would match her eyes to the pile, he was not surprised to feel the tingling of expectation, of a sexual attraction he no longer tried to dismiss. He looked at her fingers, delicate and long as she pointed out interesting-looking food, her fingertips a perfect shell pink. He was lost to her and there was no point in trying to fight it. He longed to touch her and kiss her — and more.

Cautiously he reached for her fingers, folding them into his hand. Her head shot up and she searched his face, apprehension turning to a question as he held her gaze. He turned her hand over and traced his thumb over her palm, enjoying the moment of deliberate contact. Looking into her eyes once more, he couldn't tell if he saw fear or desire in them. 'Okay?' It was one small word, but it was all that was needed.

Emerald tightened her grip on his hand and nodded. 'Yes.' Her voice was small and tentative but it was enough for Marco.

He let out a breath of relief as he squeezed her hand briefly and towed her out of the shop. 'Come on, let's get back.'

CHAPTER TWENTY-TWO

The clouds had cleared and the sun dipped under the horizon tingeing the whole sea a blood orange colour as the evening drew to a close. Emerald watched the sunset from the kitchen in a haze of uncertainty. She didn't want to turn around and see Marco Cavarelli, her boss, cooking dinner for them both, a tea towel fastened around his waist as he wielded a sharp knife and opened cupboards to find utensils and saucepans. That in itself was surreal, but added to the mix was a hint of anticipation in the air that set her heart thumping.

Marco had put his arm around her shoulders and taken her hand on the walk back to the cottage, burrowing it in his own pocket to keep her warm. He had asked her if she was okay with it. She was more than okay, but she was terribly apprehensive too — wondering what exactly she had signed up for, with the simple *yes* as he had enclosed his warm hand over hers.

She thought about the dinner they'd had with Tom Edwards from Hopper, when Marco appeared to change his persona in no more than a snap of the fingers — being all attentive and charming towards her one minute and then dismissing her the next. Was he doing the same thing again, as if she was a pawn in a game of chess easily dispatched when her time was up?

She'd had little experience of the opposite sex, growing up where she had, and the few forays she'd made into dating had been pretty disastrous: Rick the pilot coming first in that particular race. Falling for Marco could be even more disastrous — she could lose her job and her life that she loved so much. Her situation was fast becoming a ticking bomb that might detonate unless she deactivated it. If that was what she wanted to do.

'Would you like to open the wine, Emerald?' Marco asked as he set plates and cutlery on the table. There was no hint of sarcasm, but still she felt the reproach, imagined or not. She took out the chilled wine and pulled the cork. It looked surprisingly inviting and she trailed her finger down the bottle as a mist of condensation formed on the outside.

Then Marco was suddenly behind her. 'Can we talk freely?'

She continued to stare at the bottle as the condensation turned into water and dripped down the side. 'Are you suggesting a Marco special conversation — you know, the one where I tell you all of my secrets and you tell me nothing?' Her heartbeat quickened as their fingers met, but she turned to him defiantly. She was not going to be fooled again. His face was closer to hers than she realized and her breath rushed out of her lungs in surprise.

He touched her cheek, hesitantly. 'Well? Can we?'

She took a step backwards, although his gentle tone was encouraging. 'It depends.' She poured two glasses of wine and passed one to Marco, giving him a warning look not to comment. She took a hefty swig from her glass, coughed and thumped her chest. 'Wow, that's a bit strong.'

'You're not supposed to knock it back like water, you know.' He looked reproving and she set her glass down.

She took another sip and smiled. 'It's good. A lot better than the wine I had in Florence.'

Marco narrowed his eyes. 'Why single out the wine you drank in Florence?'

'It was the last time I tasted wine. If I'm honest, I thought it was so sharp it would put me off for life, but I am pleasantly surprised.'

Marco sipped at his wine before placing his glass on the kitchen table and sitting down. She sat down opposite him, until he steepled his fingers and leaned forward.

'Just don't, okay.' She made to stand up again, recognising the action.

'I haven't done anything.'

'You're working up to a speech, I can tell.'

He waved for her to sit back down. 'I just wanted to say that I no longer believe you have an alcohol problem — I got it so wrong.'

'Good, so apologise for being a patronising git.'

His smile was spontaneous. 'Sorry. Okay?' He raised his hands and Emerald nodded, forgiving him — almost.

'I don't drink really.' She returned to her seat, sitting on the edge, hesitantly. 'Ask Finbar.' She ignored Marco's eyebrows quirking. 'That night at your hotel — it was all Rick's fault.'

'Rick?' Marco's brows lifted higher, but she ignored him, lost in her unhappy memories. She'd hoped she would never have to think about Rick again. He'd caused her nothing but trouble, but finally she had a chance to explain. 'The day I met you, I turned up to a hotel in Florence to surprise my boyfriend, which is another road I don't want to travel down. Suffice to say, I was the one in for a surprise as he was in bed with another woman.'

Marco winced and lifted his wine glass to his lips, but set it back on the table, saying, 'That's tough.'

'I'd never thought about drinking alcohol before — it was something that never reared its head in the convent. Sex never did either — apart from it being the spawn of the devil kind of thing.' She shook her head slowly remembering all the confusion and guilt she'd felt for no good reason. 'The convent was miles away from anywhere, the nuns didn't drink, and we were all led to believe in a vague way that alcohol was sinful. Some of the Catholics even took the pledge, where you vow not to drink alcohol, which was a bit pointless, 'cos they couldn't have laid their hands on any booze if they'd wanted to.' She smiled at the memories that she mostly pushed away.

'But in Florence I felt the need to purge the pain and didn't exactly know that grappa combined with wine and no food was not the ideal combination for staying upright. I've never had a chance to explain properly as you always caught me on the hop and made me defensive.'

Marco's eyes widened. 'So, all of this time—'

'You've been pissing me off, yes.'

'I do indeed owe you an apology.' He lifted up his glass of wine. 'A large one.'

'Well, don't think I'm going to make you feel better over it — you were the one to jump to conclusions.'

Marco took a large sip of his wine. 'Would you like to try some more wine? I can tell you what to look for in a good bottle, if you want.' He nodded towards the bottle.

'Dunno.' She shrugged. 'I guess. Although I don't suppose it will be something I'll ever put into practice. We pretty much have a choice of cheap red or cheap white on our aircraft, apart from the horrendously overpriced stuff we give to our VIPs and that's locked away.' She picked up the bottle and studied the label. 'Nope, haven't a clue what they're on about. Hints of vanilla and peach. Are they having a laugh?'

'No. Although I agree, it sounds totally pretentious. You just need to take your time and appreciate the flavours.'

Emerald put the bottle back on the table. 'Hang on, we haven't dealt with the other bit yet: the bit where I propositioned you. Wouldn't you like to get that one out of the way, just so we can start afresh with a clean slate?'

Marco chuckled. 'You were very sexy, even when drunk.'

'Yeah, right.'

'You were.' He smiled, topped up their wine glasses and then sighed. 'Can I tell you something that hopefully will explain why I'm being — what I'm being?' He took a gulp of his wine and fixed his gaze on her face. 'My wife, who was my absolute rock and soulmate, had an affair. I was crazy in love with her and forgave her, believing that marriage was for life, but it seems that the other man was a drug she could *not* live without. I was hoping she would return to me, but now . . . I don't want her back.' He sighed. 'When she left, I turned into someone even I could not bear to live with, and I regret wasting too much time being miserable and bitter.'

'Oh, Marco, I'm so sorry for you.' She paused. 'It must be hard to trust anyone after such a terrible betrayal.' She bit her lip, not wanting to turn the conversation to herself but she needed to clear the air. 'And while we're offloading I've never propositioned another man in my life and I have no clue why I did so with you.'

'Three double grappas and two glasses of wine in the space of half an hour, I would suggest.' Marco's eyebrows drew together, giving him a fierce expression, but his eyes were bright.

She nodded slowly. 'Yep. Thanks for that. It certainly wasn't your natural charm that spurred me on, was it?'

Marco winced. 'I guess I deserved that one, but I don't think you have seen anything of the real me, Emerald, although I am hoping that I have turned a difficult corner.'

'Would you mind telling me what we actually did on that night, Marco? I am more than a little vague on the particulars.'

He smiled. 'Well, that's my ego taking another bashing. You can't remember that we kissed?'

'I thought we did, but it's a bit fuzzy around the edges.'

'Can you remember almost strangling me with my tie when you tried to kiss me at the bar?'

Emerald giggled. 'Did I really? God, how embarrassing.'

'Your powers of seduction did improve later, when you took your dress off in your room.'

Emerald put her hand to her brow and closed her eyes. 'Stop. I don't want to hear any more.'

Marco was relieved as he didn't particularly want to have to tell her that his hands had roamed over her and that he had enjoyed the kiss, wanted more. His groin tightened at the memory and he groaned inwardly. He should have known that the fates had already decided his future as soon as he entered her bedroom at his hotel.

'So, we're straight now, no more secrets?' Emerald asked, tentatively.

'Not quite.'

'How do you mean?'

Marco raked his fingers through his hair and took another large gulp of his wine.

'You'd have been appalled if I did that,' she said looking at his glass now almost empty.

'You're right.' He took another swig as Emerald watched, warily. He pushed himself to his feet and walked over to the window staring at the view for a second before turning back to Emerald. 'So, what if I . . . we . . . I don't know, dated or something? What do you think?' Marco pinned his eyes on her face, waiting.

'Please, don't ask me that unless you are deadly serious.'

'I am serious, I've already stated my case earlier. How do you feel about it? We are being honest, aren't we?' His gaze was unrelenting and Emerald fixed her attention on her wine glass. She was hearing what she'd longed to hear, but now — she wasn't so sure. She was unable to meet his eyes as she spoke.

'Then, being honest, I would say it's not a good idea. You should be with someone of your own ilk, someone who knows how to ski and look drop-dead gorgeous draped across the deck of a yacht.'

'I really shouldn't, you know. Don't you think I've tried that?'

'Yes. According to Finbar, you've tried it lots of times, with lots of women.'

He sighed. 'Well, I've already told you the truth about that — and anyway, what does he know? Most of the stuff in the magazines is made up.' He shook his head, as if baffled to know what to say next. 'Emerald, I booked this place with the intention of being alone with you. I had no ulterior motives, but I knew you were good for my soul and I wanted to remind myself of how life used to be.'

She eyed him warily. 'And is it working?'

He took a step forward. 'Yes. So far. There is nothing that I don't like about you, apart from your tendency to sulk and get stroppy of course. Even your hair, when you've just got out of bed, is cute.'

'Back-handed compliment if ever I heard one. And you noticed my bed hair. I was praying you'd be too focused on my dreadful bunny pyjamas to notice my hair.'

'Your hair is beautiful, just like you.' He leaned down to where she was seated, lifted up her chin with his thumb and very gently lowered his lips to hers. This time he wasn't in a befuddled state of sleep and he noticed every sensation she aroused in him, from tenderness to a sweet desire. Her lips were as soft and velvety as he'd imagined and his need hitched up a notch as she reciprocated the kiss, firm and insistent, breathing out on a small moan. He stepped back and surveyed her. 'The rabbit pyjamas, however, are a trifle — odd.'

She laughed. 'Ancient, but so cosy.' She hesitated. 'So, you're not testing me?' Her eyes were trusting and shining with ardour, and suddenly he knew no more explanations were needed.

'No, I'm not testing you.' He pulled her up from her chair and folded her into his arms, gave her a serious look and kissed her again. He released her, saying, 'But what if I were?' His grin was mischievous.

'Then I'll try my hardest not to enjoy what you are doing to me.' She angled herself away from him, pretending to distance herself from his touch.

But he held her tight. 'Don't even bother. You're going nowhere.' He ran his hands down to her waist and murmured something in Italian, his eyes burning in their intensity as he moved to kiss her once more.

Her heart beat faster and a surge of heat shafted through her core and down to her groin as his lips met hers. She had never been kissed the way Marco kissed her, full of longing and care, deepening with the urgency of a man who knew what he wanted. She melted instantly into his arms as he pressed his body into hers.

A ringing set up in the kitchen and Marco pulled away. 'The blasted timer. The Scallops Florentine are cooked.'

'Saved by the bell?' She moved on shaky legs, half hoping that Marco would ignore the timer and continue to kiss her while she still had the courage of her convictions.

But he breathed out, letting her go as suddenly as he'd drawn her to his chest. He ran his fingers through his hair in agitation, glancing over at her, his expression troubled.

She bit her lip, feeling as abandoned as a lost kitten. Had he changed his mind already?

He walked into the kitchen, donned a pair of oven gloves and indicated towards the table. 'We should eat.'

'We should.' She smiled as brightly as she could manage and sat down, glad to relieve her shaking legs. Her mouth had dried from the adrenaline rush and her hands were unsteady as she laid out plates and cutlery. She would try to behave normally, as if she hadn't just been struck dumb with the magnitude of Marco's kisses. Marco, after all, didn't appear to be thunderstruck by her attempt at kissing him.

Although the scallops were clearly cooked to perfection, she had difficulty swallowing, as a lump formed in her throat and she felt she might cry. Marco probably didn't realize she was hurt by his abrupt rebuff, but she felt as if he called all the shots and could pick her up or drop her at will. Her lip curled as she wondered if he behaved that way all of the time. So much for resisting him. She really should have tried harder.

Marco ceremoniously dished up the lobster tails, adding tiny new potatoes and salad, along with the samphire which was surprisingly good fried in butter. But the atmosphere, which was intensified by the music that played softly in the background and the lit candles that added a soft glow of intimacy, was strained.

Emerald couldn't think of a single thing to say, although her mind was full to bursting with questions.

'Everything okay?' Marco asked, as he topped up her wine glass.

'Yes, it's delicious.'

'It's just that you don't look as if you're enjoying it.'

'It's lovely, thank you. You clearly know how to cook, a skill I've never mastered, I hasten to add. Having lived on my own since I left the convent I don't seem to have indulged in buying even one cookbook.' Was she rambling again? She eyed the full wine glass, deciding that she wouldn't drink any more as she wanted to keep a clear head.

'How about we go for that walk now the weather has cleared?'

'Yes. It was rather inclement earlier, wasn't it?' She eyed him, hoping he would join in with her weak joke, but he showed no sign of remembering their Edinburgh conversation about the weather and haggis.

It was ridiculous, only half an hour ago he'd kissed her with a passion she had only dreamt of, and yet now they were discussing the weather as if they were strangers on a bus. She glanced at Marco to see if he was faring better than she was.

He sipped his wine and looked at her over the rim of his glass, his eyes dark and brooding. Then he set down his wine glass and she waited for the backtracking she was totally expecting.

'Emerald, this is proving to be more difficult than I ever imagined. I thought I could enjoy a relaxing few days here with you, as a pleasurable diversion to the problems I face every day, but I am finding it harder than I thought. This,' he waved a hand in the air, indicating the room, the food, their intimacy, 'is exactly how I envisaged us spending our time here, but I wasn't expecting to feel . . .' He shook his head, peered down at his food and picked up his knife and fork again, but showed no inclination to continue eating.

'To feel . . . ?'

'Exactly. To feel.' Marco nodded his head and looked thoughtful.

'Marco, I don't know what you are trying to say.'

He sighed heavily and a dense silence stretched between them.

Emerald felt her cheeks heating up as he stared at her.

She laid her knife and fork down. She couldn't eat another morsel. Her throat closed with anxiety but she met his gaze, level and unswerving.

He placed his knife and fork together decisively on his plate and raised his hands, palms upwards. 'I don't know what to do for the best. My thoughts demand that I do the honourable thing, but my body is telling me otherwise.' He gave a short laugh. 'Should we go for that walk, do you think?' He smiled ruefully, but his eyes pierced hers.

Or should we go to bed? Emerald thought, staring right back at him. It was his call.

He looked at her thoughtfully and slapped the table decisively. 'Come on, then. Waterproofs on.' He stood up, walked over to the porch to collect his coat and picked up the new scarf, winding it around Emerald's neck with a flourish as she stood up to join him.

'I can dress myself, Marco,' Emerald protested, pulling at the scarf.

'Humour me,' he said, as he yanked her new hat firmly down past her eyebrows.

'And now I can't see,' she said, pushing the hat away from her eyes.

'I'm keeping you warm.' His eyes twinkled and her heart jolted at his smile, which was still rare enough for her to want to whip out her sketchpad and ask him to hold the pose.

She breathed out. It was going to be okay.

Unsurprisingly, as they walked she could only focus on the thrilling sensation of Marco's fingers entwined with hers, the texture of his skin, his scent, his masculinity — all the time her mind frantically trying to take in his offer, wondering what was making him so indecisive.

She threw him glances, trying to read his thoughts as they walked along the edge of the shore and wandered back up towards the dunes sitting down on a sandy and damp hillock. There was a chill in the air as the clouds once again crowded into the island and the air smelled of brine and ozone with a scent that somehow heralded the beginning of autumn. The waves whispered their way back to the shoreline rattling the tiny stones in their wake before retreating with a sigh. It made her think how uncomplicated nature was, taking its course without the added bother of emotions, opinions and, in her case, tentative new love to cloud the issue.

Marco bumped her with his shoulder. 'You're on a different planet. Come back.' He nudged her hat upwards and pushed her hair away from her face. 'Lavender and sunshine — that's how you smell.' He lifted a strand of her hair and inhaled. 'With a touch of starlight, maybe.'

Emerald didn't have a chance to reply, as Marco continued. 'You have bewitched me, Emerald Montrose, and I don't know how you did it, because you are mostly a pain in the arse.'

'No one has ever called me bewitching before. Pain in the arse, yes, many times.' She smiled up into his face, unresisting.

He allowed a lock of her hair to filter through his fingers as their eyes met. Instinctively she put her arm around his neck and kissed the corner of his mouth, right next to the dimple that only appeared when he smiled. He looked at her quizzically.

'I'm trying to bring your dimple to life.' She kissed the dimple that appeared as Marco smiled. 'Right there.'

Marco caught her head in his hands and brought his lips down on hers, to deliver a kiss so sweet and gentle that she couldn't help but believe his sincerity.

'This is the real me, Emerald, and I fully intend that you will mend my broken heart.'

'That's a heavy burden to lay on me, Marco, but as far as things are going at the moment, I think I like the real you, just fine.' She pulled him towards her and kissed him right back, tasting and teasing until he pulled away on a groan. 'Don't keep doing this to me. At least not when the dog walking fraternity are out in force.'

Emerald laughed as she pulled away, hearing a distant yap of a dog. She wished she felt less wary about this new Marco, though. She feared his motives, and sometimes his mood swings were alarming. It was as if, with no more than a snap of the fingers, he'd decided she was to be his, and all inhibitions — his and hers — melted away under the force of it. She really wasn't sure she would be up to muster, knowing how exacting his standards were — in or out of the bedroom, but she rather thought she was prepared to give it a try.

Marco slung an arm around her shoulders and said, 'Shall we go back into the warmth of our little cottage?'

'What a perfect idea that is,' she said, for once happy to oblige without argument.

CHAPTER TWENTY-THREE

Emerald and Marco returned to the cottage. The earlier fog that dulled the magic of the skies had dissipated and the clouds had scuttled into oblivion, leaving a royal blue dome as the backdrop for the magnificent display of stars. The evening was still and clear and a sliver of silver moon lit their way up to the cottage. Apart from the shushing of the waves, occasionally punctuated by the hoot of an owl looking for its mate, a deep silence shrouded them.

The sky filled Emerald with awe as they stood outside, gazing upwards. 'It's such a strange colour blue, as if it's illuminated from heaven. I thought I'd never see a sky as magical as the one back home and yet here we are, witnessing another miracle.' She sighed with contentment.

'No air pollution, I guess. The stars are so bright. What's that constellation over there — that one with the huge star at its tip? You're a bit of an expert on stars, aren't you?' Marco was smiling down at her, his tone gently mocking.

'Why do you say that?' She threw him a puzzled glance.

'Because you have a star logbook full of constellations. I remember you telling me that the reason you visited my hotel was because of its huge domed glass ceiling.'

She grinned. 'Well, that was a total fib, but I do know a bit about stars. Ursa Major and Ursa Minor, Cassiopeia, they're dead easy. Find the bright superstar Betelgeuse and you've found Orion. Once you start to look out for constellations, it becomes a bit compulsive.'

Marco laughed. 'You actually do know. I'm impressed.'

'I was taught how to navigate by the Southern Cross if I ever got lost when I was in Africa. Mateo the gardener taught me and I — just started to notice their shapes. Over here, you just have to find the North Star, which is always above the North Pole, to guide you to your destination.'

'Mateo the gardener? This is the first I have heard of him.'

'He was Ava's husband — our maid, remember? He was really kind to Star when my father forbade me to ride him.'

'Why did he forbid you to ride him?'

Emerald shrugged. 'He knew Star was my Achilles heel and thought he could control me through him. Basically, I think I just reminded him too much of my mother, so because he couldn't punish her for leaving, he took it out on me.'

Marco slid his arm around her shoulders. 'I think you are a wounded person, my lovely Emerald Montrose, and I have done you a great disservice.'

She shrugged indifferently. 'You won't be the last one, I don't suppose.'

'I would like to think that no one will ever hurt you again.' He drew her close to him. 'Let's go inside.'

He steered her in through the front door of the cottage, where they were instantly enveloped in fuggy warmth from the heat of the Aga. Once inside, the bubble of intimacy seemed to evaporate and trepidation took the place of Emerald's fuzzy optimism and low-level desire. She swallowed hard as anxiety threatened and glanced surreptitiously at Marco to see how he was faring. He caught her glance and his return smile was so gentle and understanding that her pounding heart stilled, somewhat.

He appeared to be, as ever, in control of his emotions and faculties as he dried up dishes and pulled out wine glasses, setting them on the table.

Taking a deep breath she walked over to the fridge and drew out the wine, pouring them each a glass. She had the feeling she, at least, might need fortifying. She smiled at the irony of finally having convinced Marco that she didn't drink, only to go and acquire a taste for it.

He turned to Emerald, whose hand trembled as she lifted her glass to her lips. He folded a tea towel on the work-top and . . . watching her carefully before running his fingers through his hair and letting out a breath.

'Is this too much for you, Emerald? Have I moved too fast? At the moment, you look more likely to bolt than one of those rabbits out the back if I mentioned the word pie.' He chuckled softly, but his eyes were serious.

Emerald let out a breath she didn't realize she'd been holding. 'I do want to . . . you know, Marco.'

His eyes levelled with hers. He took a step forward. 'Spend the night with me?'

She nodded.

'Then you won't need this.' He unfurled her fingers, which were practically welded to the stem of her glass, and lifted it out of her hand with a gentle smile. 'This is not a test, Emerald. There is no time limit, and there are no winners. We are just here to spend time together and make each other happy.'

She nodded in agreement, but an inner trembling started at the core of her body. She was not ready for this — he was right. Marco was all-pervading, too much of a man, too much . . . her boss. She exhaled once more, ready to tell him that it was all a huge mistake. As she wavered, he traced his fingers over her arm in a small skating zigzag as he questioned her once again, his eyes steady on her face.

'Emerald?'

Fear filled her. She was nowhere near as beautiful as his skiing-at-Klosters woman, his model wife — or any number of the rich women who had, literally, passed through his hands and were plastered on the covers of the glossies. And she knew hardly a thing about successful lovemaking. She hadn't even managed to practice with Rick the Rat as she'd taken to calling him in her head. She blinked and breathed deeply. Too deeply.

Something changed in Marco's demeanour. The delicious circling of his fingertips stopped as he turned her face to look at him. 'Emerald?'

'I'm quite tired, Marco. Is that okay?'

'Of course.' But his eyes were troubled.

Emerald let out a breath. She'd ruined it before they had even started, but it was just too much for her. The only emotion she currently experienced was the urge to burst into tears.

Marco returned his focus to her with eyes full of tenderness. He raised his fingers to her cheek and slowly raised himself and bestowed a chaste kiss on her forehead. 'Tomorrow is another day. We'll see what it brings, yes?'

Emerald nodded, already wondering what she had engineered, and why, as she rose on unsteady legs, heading for her bedroom.

'Have a good night's sleep, Emerald, and don't worry about this. What will be, will be.' He swept the room with a practised eye, took his wine glass over to the kitchen sink and pulled up a fireguard to the crackling fire. She turned once and he nodded in reassurance as he headed for his own bedroom. But she was not reassured; anything but, in fact.

She stared at his bedroom door for a moment before wheeling her small suitcase, still sitting by the door, through to her room. So it seemed, she would not, after all, be passing through the same door as Marco that night. She wanted to explain what she'd meant and that it would be her first time, that she still wanted him, but he was so formidable — fighting off a hyena was probably easier than trying to reason with him.

Dragging out some clothes, she finally found her pyjamas. and undressed wearily, heaving her disenchanted body into them, grateful for the flannelette warmth that didn't quite match the heat of Marco's touch but was a lot less troubling.

The bright moon shone through the fabric of the curtains and her bed seemed vast as she lay there on her own trying to clear her mind of unwanted thoughts. She turned onto her side and turned back again, staring at the ceiling, counting the cracks in the plaster.

The waves crashed against the sea wall and the noise of churning pebbles seemed to increase by the second, the sound anything but soothing. A smattering of rain rattled the window and the distant boom of a particularly strong wave set Emerald's heart thumping. She pulled the pillow up around her ears but it didn't help.

More awake than ever, she gave up trying to sleep and climbed out of bed to peep through the curtains. Her eyes widened in shock as waves lapped at the top of the sea wall, sea foam and spray darkening the cobblestones. Surely that couldn't be normal? Fearfully, she stepped away from the window as if the waves might engulf her there and then.

She rushed through to the sitting room to check the level of the sea from the bay windows, grabbing at a curtain and yanking it out of the way. The moon's pale beams shivered on the glittering sea, the stars above looking like pinpoints of twinkling magic. She stilled and folded her arms as she gazed into the crystal-clear sky once again, caught up in the beauty of it. She scanned the room for her bag, found it and pulled out her sketchpad, drawing furiously — she was used to images disappearing in front of her, and curious eyes observing what she did not want them to see. She snapped the image on her phone so she could embellish the drawing later, when she was safely home.

Marco's bedroom door creaked open and she shoved her sketchpad behind the curtain, tipping her charcoal pencil into a handy vase.

'What's wrong?' he asked softly. Apart from the bare chest, Marco looked exactly as she'd last seen him and

Emerald suspected that he too had been awake the whole time.

'Sorry. Did I wake you?' she whispered. 'I was a bit worried that the waves are lapping over the sea wall. Do you think that's normal?'

Marco peered out of the window, squinting against the reflection on the window. 'Have you ever spent much time by the sea?'

'No, I didn't even see the sea until I was fifteen apart from a bird's-eye view from an aeroplane window when I was being carted around by Dad. Not enough hours in the day for a holiday apparently and heaven forbid that he'd have to spend actual *time* with me. I probably should have been at school, but I was home-schooled. That was before Mum left. Afterwards he sent me away — to the convent.' It all came out in a rush when she'd never actually meant to tell him any of it. Dredging up her early years was not something she was fond of doing and she felt her lip tremble with the sheer emotion of reliving it. She tried to remember the point of the question. 'Why do you ask, anyway?'

He tapped the wall nearest to him. 'This cottage is over two hundred years old and I really don't think tonight will be the night it comes tumbling around our ears.'

'Okay. Good.' She hopped from one numb foot to the other, realising the cold stone floor had taken its toll, now that she was out of her drawing trance. 'If you're sure,' she added, throwing a suspicious look at the creeping tide as if it would sneak up on her the minute she turned her back.

Heat radiated from Marco, who stood so close to her she could smell the special scent that was Marco Cavarelli. His chest looked very inviting too: broad and solid, and just right for resting her head on, if he would only put his arm, reassuringly, around her shoulders. But it seemed that any kind of contact was now out of bounds, brought on by her own earlier decision to call a halt to their lovemaking. Instead of folding her into his arms he just asked, in a loud stage whisper, 'Why are you whispering?'

'I don't know. I didn't mean to wake you.' She stared at the rising tide to stop herself from checking out Marco's naked torso again.

He had no such qualms. 'I get to see the bunny pyjamas again.'

'Yeah.'

His lips quirked as she looked down at her pyjamas. She really should be better equipped for this grown-up world she found herself in. 'At least they're warm.' She couldn't find any other redeeming features to the faded flannelette pyjamas she'd had since she was a teenager, no matter how long they both stared at the gambolling pink and blue rabbits.

'They're cute.'

'Thank you.' She dragged her gaze away from where it had returned — Marco's chest, finally looking at his face. His smile was kind, sincere and warm — which, considering the temperature, was quite a feat.

'This is not my idea of fun, you know, staring out of a window in the cold dead of night.' He didn't take his eyes off her.

'Sorry.' She threw another wary look out of the window and back to Marco, resisting the urge to whip out her pencil from its hiding place, as the moon shafted shards of luminous light on his normally dark eyes. She would happily watch moonbeams dance across his face all night, be even happier to trace their path as they danced over his cheek.

He cut across her thoughts, his voice soft and wistful as he gazed out of the window. 'When I was small, Nonno — my grandfather — would take me out hunting on nights like this. The skies were so clear you felt you could just reach up and pluck out a star. He would point out the bright stars, planets even, and explain what they were called. We had a small telescope.' He looked wistful as he turned to look at Emerald. 'I want everyone to be able to see such magic.' He sighed. 'Unfortunately, when I say everyone, I mean the rich, but that is better than no one seeing them.' He smiled ruefully. 'My business is making money for the shareholders, that's why we are here. But, Emerald, being here with you has made me notice the small things again, joyous things, that make life worth living.'

Emerald didn't know what to say to that, so she asked, 'Is your grandfather still in Sicily?'

'No, sadly. He's one of those bright stars, now.' He looked up into the clear sky. 'Nonna showed me which star and I often look for it and remember my time in Sicily that shaped me as a man.' He nodded as if to himself. 'I think he'd be proud of me. I've come a long way since skinning hares.' He paused and took a deep breath. 'But, Emerald.' He pressed the tips of his fingers to his forehead, tried again. 'Emerald, I have laid myself wide open for you; something I am not known for. But in doing so, I feel I have compromised you.' He smiled tightly, his eyes remaining sad. 'So, I have decided to take a back seat in Hot Air Aviation. That way you will not be embarrassed in the workplace by what we . . .' He made a dismissive gesture with his hand as if the conversation was already over.

It wasn't what she wanted to hear. 'You're going back to Italy?'

He nodded and then immediately shook his head, shrugging. 'Well, maybe, until we sort out our emotions towards each other. And I do find I am rather homesick.' His rueful smile showed the lie for what it was.

Emerald stared out at the sea. Had she done that to him? She might never see him again if he forgot all about her once he was back in Florence. His name would become a signature on the bottom of a letter, mentioned in passing as a faceless manager. Her voice was faint. 'Don't leave. I've only just found you.' She took his hand, holding on tight as she faced him.

'I thought—'

She shook her head. 'We've only just found each other. I don't want you to go, I'm just so new to all of this.' Her words rushed out in a tumble of truths as she fixed her eyes on his, begging him to understand, not to turn her away.

And he didn't. 'Emerald . . .' He folded her hand into his and wrapped his other hand on top of it.

Their eyes locked. She knew hers were brimming with longing, love even, and his own hooded eyes darkened and narrowed as he angled his head, questioning. He lifted his hand up to her face, brushing her cheek lightly. 'You are so beautiful in the moonlight, I don't know how I ever thought you were just a skinny wench.'

'Thank you — I think.' He grinned. She pulled a face. Marco was half naked, clasping her fingers in his hand, an unmistakable heat of desire burning in his eyes, and she was wearing the biggest passion killers in the whole world — but, at that moment, it was as if they had finally found a mutual place to move forward.

As the moonlight lit up their faces, Marco's fingers trailed over her jawline, tilting her face to meet his. 'Shall we leave it to the moon to turn the tide? It's quite proficient, I believe, so we will be safe.' He tugged at her hand. 'The moon will keep us safe from the sea and I'll keep you out of the cold.'

He raised his eyebrows and angled his head towards his bedroom.

She nodded. 'Yes, please.'

She trailed behind him into the bedroom. Marco threw back the duvet cover, climbed in and gently pulled her down next to him. He folded her into his body in one easy motion and murmured into her ear, 'We will both sleep better now, I think.'

Her body fitted effortlessly into his, as if she'd found where she belonged. He was so warm, so *male* . . .

She felt his breath close to her ear, heard him inhale and groan quietly. 'Go to sleep,' he said, loosening his hold on her.

Sleep?

He turned away from her, dragging his pillow with him.

She stiffened. Why had he turned away? Was she so totally out of bounds now? She confronted his bare back and lifted her hand to trace his skin, noting another cute mole. 'Marco?'

He sighed and turned back to face her. They were so close they could almost bump noses. He stilled and his eyes sought out hers in the darkness. He ran a hand down her arm and the length of her body, ending at her thigh. 'Goddammit, Emerald — if we start this thing, I might never want to let you go.'

Her body core notched up several degrees at the throatiness in his voice and there was no mistaking his meaning, although his words were hardly endearing. 'So, do you think it would be better if we didn't . . . err.'

He hitched himself up on his elbow and looked down at her, winding a strand of her hair around his finger as he studied her. She felt strangely calm and trusting.

There were several beats of silence before he spoke. 'We could see where the night takes us . . . ?'

'Yes,' she whispered. And she *so* meant it. She ran her fingertips over the fine dark hairs that covered his chest, hesitant at first, then more confident, tracing the rivulet of hair between his rib cage and down lower to his abdomen.

He drew in a breath and the twinkle in his eyes disappeared, quickly replaced by a spark of something more intense. He wrapped his fingers over hers and caught them in his own.

They simply held hands as they both took in the measure of their position, questioning and answering each other with their eyes.

After a moment of allowing her to trail her fingers lower, he said, 'If you carry on doing what you are doing we won't need any more discussion.' He traced a finger over her lips and she parted them slightly. The pad of his finger traced the fullness of her bottom lip and heat flared from her lips straight to her groin.

His fingers trailed past her neck and down her chest, where her pyjamas were buttoned all the way up to her neck. Very slowly, he undid the top button.

'About the tricky business of you being my employer, does that matter too much, do you think? I know you weren't too keen on the idea.'

Marco kissed her throat, his lips trailing lower to the swell of her breasts, his fingers already undoing the next button of her pyjamas. 'I think you should leave that problem to me, Emerald.'

'Okay.' Her voice was small as she surrendered herself to Marco, a delicious heat flooding her entire body as his fingers brushed her skin in their quest to undo all of the buttons on her pyjama top.

Tentatively, she laced her fingers through his dark hair, realising that she'd wanted to do that since the day she'd spotted the damp curls sitting on his neck at the first aid course.

He raised his head and she met his lips with a sureness she had never felt before. It seemed so right that they fit together, and when he slid her top over her shoulders she settled into the warmth of the bed, prepared to abandon herself to whatever the night brought.

Marco stopped in his tracks. 'You suddenly seem very sure of your decision.'

'I trust you, Marco.'

'Good, you should.' He traced her cheek with his finger and lifted a tendril of hair, kissing it gently. 'And you are sure about this?' He breathed deeply as he trickled her hair through his fingers.

She nodded, the light of the moon picking up her action. He seemed to accept this and pulled her towards him, intertwining his legs with hers and simply holding her. 'Kiss me again, Marco, I need to know this is really happening.'

She felt shy and inexperienced, and prayed it wouldn't show. 'Marco,' her voice sounded panicky to her ears but she suddenly had to unburden her fear. 'This is my first time . . . I thought you should know.' Her breath hitched higher as his fingers trailed lower to her waist — and abruptly stopped.

He sighed, shaking his head slightly as he stilled.

She froze. He was going to turf her out, she knew it. But his eyes were gentle and after a long, long pause he said, 'Well then, Emerald Montrose, I guess our first time of making love together will be in a small white cottage by the edge of the sea, and I can't think of a more perfect place to be.'

She nodded, solemn eyes fixed on his face. Tentatively she reached out for him, feeling him tense and then pull away. Her eyes rounded. What now?

'Wait there, I'm just going to my washbag,' Marco said. Emerald blinked in confusion.

'Condoms,' he grinned.

'Ah.' God, she was so dumb — contraception hadn't even crossed her mind.

'Faster than the speed of light.' Marco kissed her nose and slid out of bed.

CHAPTER TWENTY-FOUR

Emerald awoke to hear rain pattering down on the roof of the glass skylight and shifted onto her side, a vague feeling of incongruity washing over her. The shushing sound of pebbles retreating back into the sea, brought her quickly to her senses as she remembered where she was. Her eyes flew open when she registered the dead weight against her shoulder, an arm thrown casually around her waist.

Marco.

The sleepy contentment she'd felt morphed to a low-level panic and she twisted around quickly, checking that she hadn't dreamed being in Marco's bed.

Marco, large as life, watched her with guarded eyes. 'No, *cara mia*, you did not dream it and I am still here with you.'

She did a quick analysis of her body. Yup, definitely stark staring naked but she didn't need proof — the memory of last night flooded back releasing glorious sensations in her body. She smiled, closed her eyes. Marco. So be it. But still she tensed slightly, wondering what would happen next. Would he still want her? Was she any good at this sex thing?

Marco didn't appear to have the same misgivings as he nuzzled into her hair. 'Mm, you smell deliciously of sleepiness and sex.' He kissed her neck, flipping her to face him in one easy movement as if she were feather light. He breathed in. 'Too wonderful to resist, even though coffee is calling to me.'

With his arm still wrapped around her waist he drew her into the warmth of his body. 'But first, I need you.' He rolled her onto her back. 'I just want to make sure you know you are mine now. Stay still . . .'

Emerald's breath hitched in her throat as Marco, to her great surprise worked his way down her body, kissing every erogenous zone she had until she thought she would melt with the heat he stirred in her. Time seemed to warp as she lost her senses eventually coming back down to earth with a gasp, her head thrown back in abandon.

Eventually Marco returned to her side and cradled her in his arms, stroking her hair as her breathing steadied.

Marco studied her with glittering eyes. 'You are mine now, Emms.'

'Are you mine, too?' She was surprised at him using her nickname, as only Finbar called her Emms, but she let it go.

'Hmm?' He looked surprised at her question.

'It doesn't only work one way, you know?' Her lips quirked.

He gave the question serious consideration but answered simply, 'Just give me time. I am a product of my Italian fore-fathers. We like to be macho — or at least appear to be so.' He smiled at his words.

'You think you can tame me, do you, Mr Cavarelli?' She smiled back, lazily, as he stroked her hair.

His brows rose. 'How am I doing so far?'

She laughed. 'Not too bad, as a matter of fact.' She stretched out languorously, feeling secure in his arms and enjoying her nakedness and their shared intimacy. 'I think you might just have turned me into the wanton hussy you thought I was. We have turned full circle. If I could only wear the silk dress that I so foolishly wore the day I, err, visited your hotel.'

'Why can't you?'

'I cut it up.'

'And fed it to the hyenas?' He stroked her arm, his tone teasing.

'You know more about me than anyone else in the world. I don't know how you managed it, but even Fin doesn't know about the hyena.'

'Even Fin, eh?' His smile faded.

She hoisted herself up on her elbow. 'I don't understand how you can be jealous of him. The mighty Marco who has the world at his feet, resents my best friend, who drives a first-generation Volkswagen Up and shares an apartment with a giant mouse called Mousse that steals his food and leaves insolent mouse droppings on his carpet.'

Marco laughed mirthlessly. 'I'm not sure jealous is the right word. I just don't like the way you two are so tight.'

'That's called jealousy.'

'You may be right. I'd like to sack him. He has too much freedom within the company and he is infuriating.'

'He's lovely and he's the best friend I've ever had. He makes me laugh.'

Marco coughed. 'Yes, because cutting off passengers' ties is hilarious. He should have been shot for that.'

'You would have a mutiny on your hands if you try to sack him. That and the small but very significant fact that he is Robert Clarke's nephew.'

Marco growled again looking unimpressed, but changed the subject, moving on to other members of staff. 'And what is the story with Michelle? She seems to be absent more than she is here.'

'Yes, I really need to have a word with her. Her boy-friend lives in Spain and she cuts it too fine to catch flights home. She's forever missing her connection.' Emerald settled into his chest and Marco trailed his fingers in a circular motion on her back.

'And before I forget,' Marco said, into her hair, 'we need to put a lock on the catering store cupboard. Someone is going in there and helping themselves.'

Emerald tutted. 'That'll be Jack, the engineer. He loves our biscuits — says you can't buy them in any shop he knows. It is a small and friendly airline, Marco. We just all treat it as our own, I guess.'

'Sounds more like Robert Clarke was running a charity than a business, if you ask me.' Marco shook his head in disbelief as Emerald continued to recount tales of the staff, putting an interesting spin on each person to make the stories funny. She loved all her colleagues and hoped that Marco would begin to see them in the same vein as she did — even when, occasionally, their actions were less than admirable. She lifted her head off his chest and sighed happily. 'You're good at making me talk. It's not something that comes easily to me.'

'I have other skills too, you know.' He arched an eyebrow and ran his hand down the length of her body.

She giggled in delight. 'I did notice.'

'I can make a mean pancake too. Want me to show you?'

'If it comes with tea, I'm all yours.'

'That's what I want to hear — though I still need coffee.' He threw his legs over the side of the bed and slung on a shirt.

Emerald drank in the smooth skin, the toned muscles, knowing how horrified the nuns would be by her unrestrained ardour.

She offered up a silent prayer, hoping that God might be more understanding than Sister Mary Bennett. Then she made a decision to stop with the guilt trips, enjoy the present, and stop second-guessing what the future might hold.

CHAPTER TWENTY-FIVE

Marco made tea and flipped pancakes while Emerald show-ered in water that was at best tepid, dashing in and out and making a show of shivering. Marco smiled at her antics as she passed by, running on the spot to stay warm as her towel threatened to pool at her feet.

He felt good. No, he felt great. He was doing the right thing here and it was time that his life moved on. Emerald had purged him of the remnants of love he'd felt for his wife and he hoped he was now done with the self-loathing that overwhelmed him when his needs were met by one of the socialites on the circuit. They had merely been a means to an end, but Emerald brought his soul to life again.

'We could go to the hotel today to check it out. You don't mind coming with me do you?' He turned to Emerald who looked radiant. Sex was good for her, he decided, smil-ing. Then he looked a bit closer. She looked wary all over again and he hoped it wasn't the boss-employee thing.

'Yes, fine. It looks as if the windy weather is back to stay, but it'll be good to blow the cobwebs away.' She twid-dled with a lock of her hair and chewed her lip, glanc-ing repeatedly out of the window as if she wanted to dive through it.

Marco strode over to her. 'Come here.' He pulled her closer to face him, smoothing her hair out of her eyes and holding her face, so that she had no choice but to listen to him. 'Don't go all polite on me, Emms. I don't want banalities and pleasantries. I know the English are fixated on the weather, but I can tell the difference.'

'It's hard for me, Marco.'

'What is?' He could hazard a guess, and in a way, he didn't blame her. 'Is it the being-your-boss thing?'

She nodded. 'I think so. It's fine when we're — you know.' She jerked her thumb in the direction of the bedroom. 'But I seem to forget that bit once we're dressed again.'

Marco sighed. 'I think we need more time together. And luckily for you, we can spend the whole week here.'

Her eyes widened. 'How come?'

'I booked the cottage for a week.'

'Without mentioning it to me?'

He held his hand up. 'Wait. Don't think it was intentional — it was seven days or nothing.' He shrugged. 'We don't have to stay that long, if you don't want to.'

She rolled her eyes, but he could tell that she liked the idea. 'We'll be sick of each other by the time we leave.'

'We will not.' He moved in for a kiss to convince her. 'And if I have to keep taking you to bed to reassure you, then—' he shrugged '—I can do that.'

'You're all heart,' Emerald said as he pulled her towards him and kissed her slowly and languidly, letting her hair tumble through his fingers. He groaned and pulled away. 'Let's go buy you a raincoat before the temptation to undress you again becomes too much.'

As he spoke the sun lit up the kitchen, appearing from behind the heavy clouds like an answered prayer. 'Here we go — even the sun wants us to stay.'

* * *

They ate breakfast and Emerald relaxed a bit more. She plaited her hair to stop it blowing in her face when they

207

went out, and layered the fisherman jumper over her flowery dress. Then they braved the weather once more, heading for the shops on the high street.

Marco bought her a rain mac and some bright red wellingtons just because they were cute, which prompted her to do a little jig of happiness when she put them on.

They strolled along the beach, hand in hand, and Emerald collected a few seashells, popping them into her pocket. She picked up a large periwinkle before realising it had a dead crab inside and Marco snapped a picture of her horrified expression, laughing when she threw it at him, shell and all. He chased her over the fine white sand and, pretending to rugby tackle her, drew her to the ground, where he kissed her and untied her hair with slow determination, fanning it out on the sand. 'You'd make a gorgeous mermaid,' he said, straddling her and stroking her hair away from her face.

'No self-respecting mermaid would have hair this frizzy — imagine what the sea water would do to it.' Emerald laughed up into his eyes, her own eyes brim-full of happiness.

Marco heaved himself off her and lay on the sand, spreading his arms wide. 'Relaxing is so good for the soul.'

'Relaxing? I'm totally knackered.' Emerald lifted herself up on one elbow before leaning into Marco who wrapped her inside his — now decidedly sandy — cashmere coat and they shut out the world for several minutes while they kissed, their bodies responding to each other. Marco finally pulled away, saying, 'Tell me this isn't more delicious than food?'

'Man shall not live on bread alone. Matthew 4,' Emerald parroted, raising herself to a sitting position.

'Ah, I forgot I have a good Catholic girl on my hands.'

'Sadly, I've read the Bible more times than I care to admit, but I'm not Catholic.'

'But you are very good,' Marco waggled his eyebrows.

Emerald blushed. 'I have a very good teacher. Now, let's get some provisions.'

As they meandered along, a huge dog ran up to them, snuffling around in excitement. Its owner, an old man with a walking stick, raised his cap to them, saying, 'A fine day for walking. You're staying at Tideline Cottage, are you not?'

'Yes, I believe we are,' Marco said.

Emerald turned to Marco. 'The name explains the proximity of the sea last night, then.'

Marco squeezed her hand. It was a night he would never forget. 'I will forever be grateful to the high tide,' he muttered out of the corner of his mouth.

'Ah, wonderful cottage for young newlyweds.' The man called his dog to heel with a high-pitched whistle, before continuing. 'Generations of babies have been conceived in Tideline. It's a lucky cottage. You'll be well blessed.'

Emerald gave Marco big, scared eyes. 'Right. Lovely to know, thanks for that,' she replied politely.

'More condoms — we need more condoms,' Marco whispered as Emerald giggled, although for a brief second, she imagined what it would be like to have Marco's children. Grey eyes or green — or one of each, maybe? It was a good fantasy.

Marco saluted the old man and made to move on, but it seemed he wanted to chat.

'You might be interested in visiting the Crown pub tonight as it's Sunday.' He waved a hand vaguely in the direction of the town. 'Everyone comes over to eat and we have a bit of a knees-up afterwards. They're a friendly lot — except for the ones who are not, of course. They're stuck in a time warp and don't like tourists or newcomers.'

'Right. Well, if we do make it, we'll pretend we've lived here for years.' Marco smiled and shook the man's hand and they made a hasty retreat.

Emerald put the conversation from her mind saying, 'We haven't been up to the hotel yet. Are they not expecting you?'

'They don't know I'm coming.'

'What?'

'Actually, the hotel I have in mind is not even up for sale.'

'We came all this way for nothing?'

'Not at all. Everyone has a price. At the very least the owners will agree to reach a compromise, if they want to stay there. I'll make them an offer they can't refuse, throw everything at it and after a while, I'll take a back seat and the profits will roll in for the shareholders. Simple. It's on St Martins so we have to get a boat across.'

'Oh.' She pondered on his words. 'Is that what you're doing with Hot Air?'

'Yes, apart from being more hands-on for Robert Clarke, as he is not a well man and neither is his wife.'

'And I thought you were just enjoying harassing me.'

Marco laughed. 'I assure you, I have too many other problems to sort out than to spend time harassing one of my staff.'

* * *

They wandered across the beach in no hurry to visit the hotel, each other's company being enough for now. Emerald had lost the uncertain edge she'd had with Marco, who showed himself to be funny, solicitous and very loving: a different person from the Marco he'd presented at Hot Air Aviation. He kissed the top of her head. 'I'd be happy to stay here with you forever.'

'That'd be nice, but only if you can guarantee a tiny bit more sunshine at some stage of the game,' she agreed, as they picked their way back to the cottage through rivulets and deep pools of water, caused by the retreating tide.

'Let's go back to the cottage. The hotel can wait another day,' Marco said as more clouds gathered.

They spent the afternoon listening to the rain again as they dozed on the sofa with the television on, in the background. Emerald had become used to having the things she loved taken away from her and she snuck her hand into his for comfort and reassurance, saying a quick prayer that this time she might get Marco for keeps.

He squeezed her hand, before allowing his hand to roam leisurely across her waist, sneaking up to her breast.

'We need to move or else we'll end up in bed again,' he said, letting her go and throwing his legs over the side of the sofa. 'Come on, let's go and see what the pub has to offer.'

Emerald would secretly rather have stayed on the sofa, contentedly using Marco's chest for a pillow, but she roused herself and they headed out in the wind once more as the darkness gathered around them.

They heard the pub before they saw it, drawing closer to see customers spilling out of the door, the heady smell of hops and chips enticing them in. The local band playing folk music was tempting enough to make them push on towards the bar. A fiddle, a Bodhrán and a guitar accompanied two singers who belted out songs with gusto, although they were almost drowned out by the noise of the customers shouting over the top of each other to be heard.

Marco grinned at Emerald, grabbing her hand as they shouldered their way through the noisy crowd of people. He ordered a locally-brewed beer for himself and an apple juice for Emerald, and they fought their way back through the throng of people to find a tiny corner of space to stand together.

'If this beer is any good I'm going to serve it in the hotel — and the wine we have at the cottage is from St Martin's. What more could you ask for — a vineyard and microbrewery on your doorstep?'

They garnered a few looks from the locals, but there were surely many tourists in there.

Emerald found it slightly disconcerting. 'Why are people staring at us — aren't they used to tourists?' she whispered under her breath.

'Because you look like a glorious movie star,' Marco said. He looked at Emerald with her long curls, rosy cheeks and big eyes and wondered how she managed to be so unaware of her beauty. He put it down to years of being teased — but he loved her hair, and it certainly reflected her spirited personality.

'And what are you staring at?' Emerald teased as she narrowed her eyes at Marco.

'A woman who has transformed my view on redheads.' Marco leaned forward and lifted a lock of her hair, allowing it to fan over his fingers.

'For the better, I hope,' Emerald said as she stared at the menu on the board. 'Are you hungry?'

'Only hungry for you.'

Emerald spluttered into the drink she'd just raised to her lips. 'Did you really just say that?'

'Yes, I'm trying to be romantic.' He grinned, as he nudged her leg with his knee.

'Then, thank you.' But her eyes danced with laughter and she stifled a giggle. 'But that was really crap.'

'I won't bother next time.'

'Just stick to being you — it's better for both of us.'

She patted his arm, but her insides curled with pleasure. The stern, severe Marco had all but disappeared and she was delighted that she was the cause of his transformation.

She sipped at her drink, contentedly watching the band and the locals, and wondered if it was worth doing battle at the bar again for some crisps.

A man playing a Spanish guitar started up a sweet confection of chords and a singer joined him, picking out a soulful tune. It all looked very impromptu and haphazard, which added to the charm of the evening. A couple of people started dancing, cheek to cheek, and then another two drifted onto a space in front of the singer that doubled up as a makeshift dance floor.

Marco picked up Emerald's hand and she looked up, ready to smile at his sentiment, but, unexpectedly, he pulled her into his arms. 'I haven't danced with you, yet. Can't be considered a proper relationship until we dance together.'

'Really, why's that?' Emerald eyed the tiny space, wondering if they would even fit in there.

'What if we don't synchronize? It will be the end for us. Being able to dance together is more important than sex.'

'You're joking, right?'

'I never joke about dancing.' He drew her over to the tiny dance floor and pulled her in to him. 'I should have mentioned that when I studied at Cambridge, I learned ballroom dancing. I kid you not — as you English would say.'

'You should have mentioned that you studied at Cambridge,' Emerald said, his almost flawless accent now making complete sense.

'Follow my feet, and you'll be fine — we are basically just shuffling around here,' Marco said.

Emerald put her hand on Marco's shoulder and he placed his arm around her waist. Their free hands met and she was terrified that he would start to prance around the floor, like something out of *Strictly*, doing proper ballroom stuff, but he just tightened his grip on her waist and took the lead.

He pressed up to her body and closed the gap between them. Marco brought his hand up to her shoulder and she leaned in to him as he stroked the back of her neck with his thumb. The singer crooned an Ed Sheeran song about being perfect and Marco started to hum under his breath. It resonated through his chest and Emerald relaxed into the rhythm of their slow dance. It was as if it was just the two of them. No one else mattered as they moved, wrapped up in each other. Emerald was melting with longing for Marco, the sweet ache that always seemed to be there for him, pulsing through her veins. She had found the man of her dreams, unlikely as it was. His heart beat next to hers and she pressed her breasts into his chest, her thigh into his thigh, feeling the strength of his muscles as they moved in unison around the dance floor.

Marco groaned as Emerald pushed her pelvis into the erection she could most definitely feel. 'This is interesting,' she whispered into his ear.

'This is difficult,' he murmured into her hair. 'I don't think I want them to put the lights on any time soon.' His eyes were smouldering with heat when he finally pulled away to gaze down at her.

213

'Did we pass the test?' Emerald's voice was unsteady as she came back down to earth, out of the trance that Marco's humming and manly warmth had put her in.

'I'm not sure. I think we need to get back to the cottage quickly to check out the sex again. We need a proper comparison.' Although his eyes danced, his tone was urgent, his voice unmistakably throaty as he ushered her off the dance floor, hunger burning in his eyes.

Emerald felt the same heat flash through her body and was as desperate as Marco to get back. Who'd have thought that just dancing could do that to a person. She fanned her face. She grabbed her rain coat from the chair as they sailed straight past their drinks and their table and out of the door.

'I kind of want to run.' Emerald laughed, as Marco grabbed her hand. She threw him a challenging look as she broke into a trot. Marco grinned and started running. She upped her pace to keep up with him, jumping over potholes and swivelling around gorse bushes as he sprinted ahead.

They crashed into the cottage, barely taking the time to shut the door, before they were undressing each other, their kisses frantic, hands fumbling and desperate. They made love in a frenzy of passion, until exhausted and heaving in deep breaths, they slowly resurfaced.

'Okay, I think it was a close tie between the dancing and the sex,' Marco said, as he pushed himself upright on the bed. Emerald giggled and he threw an arm across her, drawing her into his chest.

'Just remind me not to dance with you again, unless there is a bed within yards of us.' She snuggled into him and pulled the duvet over them both. 'I'll brush my teeth in a minute,' she said, yawning.

'Boarding-school conditioning?' Marco asked, his own voice sounding sleepy.

'Yes, I guess so. Maybe this can be the start of a new defiant me. Sod it, I'll leave it until the morning.'

'Atta girl. Look forward to the morning breath.' Marco kissed her cheek as he settled into the covers.

She smiled in the darkness, listening to Marco's breathing as it steadied. She was exactly where she wanted to be, she realised.

Rain started up again battering the skylight and thrumming on the windows in a cacophony of noise, which only emphasized their cosy room and the warmth they shared.

Marco threw a leg over Emerald and hooked her into him at the sound of thunder. 'Hmm, this is my idea of a stormy night — someone to keep me safe and warm,' he said against her throat as he trailed kisses over her skin.

'You're the man, Marco — you're supposed to keep me safe.'

'I didn't think you were one for stereotypes, but if it makes you happy, don't worry, I'll keep you safe.' He kissed her hair.

'Promise?'

'Forever, *cara mia*.'

The word *forever* played over in Emerald's mind as she lay in the circle of Marco's arms. For the first time in her life she feared she would be unable to cope without a constant love — Marco's love. She pressed her body into his, as if she could melt into him, to be united forever.

Marco stirred and lifted himself up on his elbow and looked down at her. 'What's wrong?'

'I'm scared, Marco.'

'You don't need to be scared, Emms. I've told you I'll keep you safe.'

'I'm not scared of the storm.' She needed his reassurance. If he kissed away her fears, she would put her absolute faith in him.

He smiled down at her. 'You look so ethereal in this light.'

She nodded slowly, acquiescing. The non-starter of a conversation was already closed, it seemed. A rush of emotion filled her heart and she wished she was brave enough to tell him she loved him, but she stayed silent as Marco's breathing levelled out, and he slept once more without saying the words she longed to hear.

* * *

They didn't make it to the hotel until the last day of their stay and, even then, Marco was loath to leave her alone. 'You must come with me. We'll have lunch and you can read while I sort out my very neglected business emails. Hopefully their internet is actually working, unlike ours. I shall decide whether to take my plans any further when I see how the hotel is located.'

She showered and dressed as Marco phoned up the hotel to book lunch, giving his name in the happy belief that no one would have heard of him.

Happily, the boat trip across to St Martin's was uneventful if a little choppy and the coastline was uplifting, although Emerald was sad she didn't spot any puffins to snap for Finbar. She was assured that there were hundreds of them on the Island of Annet which was protected from humans and she made a note to take a boat trip there when she next visited with Marco. She hugged the thought to herself. She had a future and she was loved — she hoped.

The hotel, after they'd trudged up a steep hill and got lost twice, was a rather run-down affair from the outside, with moss and grime coating the black granite walls. The stone steps leading up to the entrance were broken and worn, and a headless statue reclined next to a large magnolia tree that shook as the wind blew.

Mournful terns cried out overhead and a huge seagull eyed up Emerald and Marco from the top of one of the pillars.

'It's a bit depressing, isn't it,' Emerald said, dolefully. 'But it might just be the weather?'

'It has potential though, don't you think? I'm seeing a helipad over there.' Marco gestured to a large field. 'A swimming pool could go over there. Maybe a maze to inject a little fun. The glass dome would be on that part of the hotel.' He pointed to a long flat extension that looked as if it had been added at a later date. 'I'm guessing that's a ballroom or large dining area, but it would be perfect for my stargazers. I would have to install shutters to keep out the light at night-time so that we don't cause light pollution, but that is a minor tweak.'

'Wow! That's ambitious. Here I was imagining a lick of paint was what you had in mind.'

'My new hotel chain needed a good branding idea and after sifting through lots of ideas we decided on the Midnight Skies as the few I have already earmarked are in remote locations. Wait and see how I turned a fortress of outdated misery into a magical castle.'

A strong gust of wind shook small white petals from a nearby tree and they floated and rotated slowly in the wind. Emerald twirled around, laughing, snapping them between her hands as they fluttered down like confetti, her happiness spilling over.

Marco caught her around the waist and kissed her. 'It will be perfect here. England will become my second home, so I might as well make it a beautiful one, no?'

Emerald, who only hours ago was considering that she would soon be very familiar with the Scilly Isles, was suddenly disillusioned when he didn't include her in his dreams for the future.

But then he added, 'We are making beautiful memories already.' A petal fell on her head and he picked it out of her hair and turned it over in his fingers, his expression serious. He stroked her hair tenderly. 'Your hair haunted me, you know, in my dreams.'

She stood under the tree with the petals drifting down over them both and for one second imagined that it really was confetti.

'I love you, Marco.' Although she hadn't meant to blurt it out quite so readily, she felt light as a feather — as if her burden had been lifted. She pulled at Marco's coat lapels to draw him in for a kiss, the sheer joy of being in love propelling her forward, but something in his bearing stopped her, and it took her a moment to process that he hadn't returned the sentiment.

She stopped in her tracks as his eyes clouded. 'That is a very sobering statement to make,' he said.

Immediately she regretted her words. Her arms dropped to her sides and she turned away as tears blurred her eyes.

'Not quite the reaction I hoped for,' she stammered in humiliation. He didn't love her — of course he didn't — and now she'd embarrassed them both.

Marco let the leaf drop to the ground, his lips set in the severe line she remembered so well from before — well, before they'd fallen in love. She laughed bleakly. Before *she'd* fallen in love.

'It doesn't matter — that, you know, you don't . . .' She backtracked, but could barely get the words out and just shrugged unhappily as her words trailed away.

'It does matter, Emerald.' Marco's voice was thick and his expression sad. It was certainly not the look of love — she knew that much. He should be smiling with her, celebrating the joy of being alive and loving each other.

She shook her head. 'No, really, it doesn't. It was just a silly spur-of-the-moment thing to say.' She tucked her hair behind her ears and straightened her back.

'We'll talk about it later.' His gaze was sorrowful as he touched her cheek with his thumb, wiping away — oh, God, was it a tear?

The burn of shame lit up her cheeks and she pulled away from him, feeling patronized, as he tried to tuck her hand into his. He looked unhappy and slightly lost and she wished she could turn the clock back. She'd ruined the day. She trailed behind him to the restaurant — she couldn't think what else to do than follow him.

Marco was as attentive as ever during their lunch, and Emerald tried to be light-hearted and cheery, although she pushed most of her food around the plate before finally giving up the pretence. She folded her napkin over the top of the food, hoping that the chef wouldn't be offended. She thought she'd pulled off the joviality act reasonably well, until Marco took her hand and considered her for a long moment.

Anxiety shot through her spine and radiated out towards her limbs. Her mouth dried. She was expecting the worst. He was going to tell her that their time together had just been a pleasant interlude — an escape from reality and he belatedly realised that she didn't understand the rules. She decided to pre-empt the knock-back. 'I wonder if the weather is better in London. Be good to get back and see some sunshine, won't it. Although I'm wondering if we've seen the last of summer?' She closed her eyes briefly against the banality of her conversation. *The bloody weather is all I can talk about. At a time like this?*

'Yes, I suppose it will. I shouldn't have spent so long away from my business dealings, really. I'll need to make up for lost time.'

She drew in a sharp breath, unable to help herself. His business came first — she should have known. Had she been totally naïve? Perhaps she deserved her newly-built fantasy world to come crashing down on her. Maybe, in the fast world that Marco inhabited, it was considered totally normal for a man and a woman to spend a week together and then go their separate ways — like a friends-with-benefits holiday. She had assumed they were starting something incredible together, but maybe she was, after all, just a small part of the relaxing break that Marco had professed to need.

She was stunned by the realisation, felt as if she was waking up from a dream. She looked at Marco as if she was seeing a different man.

Marco's smile was natural and warm though. He took her hand, clearly having no qualms about the changing status of their relationship.

'Let's sit over here with our drinks, shall we?' He indicated a secluded area overlooking the garden.

She dutifully rose, clutching her drink with hands she tried so hard to keep steady as she followed him.

Emerald sat down and took in the sitting room which was indeed a bit run down a damp patch above her head causing the old-fashioned flock-wallpaper to peel. The carpet had seen better days and the overall impression was tired and in need of an injection of cash.

Marco left her alone to find the manager and ask to set up an appointment with the owner of the hotel, who lived on the island but not on site. Taking out her Kindle, she thought she would try to relax but soon caught herself staring into the fire, trying to imagine life without Marco. How quickly someone else could shape her world and how dangerous it was to allow love into her life. She could be independent, strong, opinionated but did that mean she also couldn't love? Were such traits mutually exclusive? She should have stuck with animals, she thought ruefully, returning her Kindle into her bag, unable to face reading.

She watched Marco as he talked to the manageress. He was eloquent, handsome, a smart dresser, great physique, rich. She sighed. What did she have to give him in return — apart from her body and her hang-ups? Panic beat at her heart as she wondered, for the first time since they had become lovers, if he was, after all, playing her, as Fin had warned.

She shook her head. No, he wouldn't be capable of such duplicity, not to her, anyway. But the nagging doubt had taken a hold in her head and she feared that he just might have had a hidden agenda when arranging the trip.

She bit her lip determined to be grown up and dispassionate. But inside she was desperate, full of sadness and loss.

Her smile was brittle when he returned bearing two cups of coffee and she continued to play her part. 'So, home tomorrow?'

'Yes.' Marco sipped his coffee, regarding her over the rim, his dark eyes once more serious.

'How was the manager?' She suddenly felt as if she had no right to ask such an impertinent question — she was an employee, not a confidante — or a partner.

'Fine. She has arranged for me to meet the owner tomorrow, before we leave.'

Emerald nodded, reeling that he didn't invite her to join him this time. She felt ridiculously excluded and her smile slipped. 'I'd better get packed soon, then. It's been a lovely break, thank you.'

She rummaged around in her handbag so that Marco couldn't see her face and gauge how hurt she was, certain it must show in her eyes. Wondering what on earth she would produce from the depths of her bag, her fingers touched her small sketchpad, now brimming with clandestine pictures of wildlife and fauna, seascapes and the beautiful night sky, not to mention miniatures of Marco that she'd drawn as he slept.

She had used every moment away from Marco to draw what was in front of her eyes, but it was always the images of him that drew her back, over and over — the back of his head as he slept, showing one ear and a tousle of dark hair — but she burrowed her sketchpad away each time afterwards; it would be her secret.

She picked out a tissue and dabbed at her lips, mostly for something to do, but a sudden flash of bright light from the doorway distracted her.

She and Marco turned simultaneously to see a man looming close, pointing a large camera lens at them. Another bright light flashed in their faces and the man disappeared with a clatter of heels. The barman chased after him, shouting, 'Oi! What are you up to?'

'What was that?' Emerald rose from her seat, panicked, but Marco put his hand on her shoulder.

'It's fine. Just some low-life photographer who, no doubt will try and flog a photo or two of us, I imagine.'

He pulled Emerald back down to her seat, his face a tight mask of irritation as he stared at the doorway.

'Does it happen often?'

'Reasonably often, but I wouldn't have expected it out here.' He sighed. 'It'll be on the internet by sunrise no doubt, if they can sell it to an interested party. At least they won't be able to find out who you are. Thank goodness we didn't check in here.' he sighed heavily. 'I hate such intrusions.'

'Because I'm with you?'

'Yes, damn it. I'm not divorced, so they latch on to any titbit of gossip where a woman is involved, to stir up trouble.' His mouth twisted and his eyes flashed, suddenly reminding Emerald of the man she'd first met, whose forbidding attitude she'd all but forgotten.

His anger appeared to be directed at her and it made her own sense of injustice flare. 'Who I am? Because I'm your employee or because I'm your . . .' She lifted one shoulder, unable to decide what word should be used to describe her relationship with Marco. 'What even am I?'

'I do *not* wish to be seen in a compromising position, *that* is all.'

Emerald blanched. She was a compromising position? She accepted that Marco had had far more dealings with the paparazzi than she ever had but, even so, she felt insulted.

'I think it's time we left.' He offered her his hand but she pushed herself to her feet, ignoring the gesture. She knew it was churlish, but at that moment she couldn't bear him to touch her, didn't want the electricity that passed between them to give her any false expectations. Their bodies were perfectly in tune, but their sentiments it seemed, were not.

That night she lay stiff in Marco's arms, tears coursing silently down her cheeks as he slept. He either had no inkling that she was distraught or he didn't care. Earlier they had discussed their trip home and she wasn't sure if she was imagining it, because of her earlier faux pas, but Marco appeared to be withdrawing from her in front of her very eyes.

His demeanour was becoming more formal with each hour that passed. He slipped on a veneer of politeness as easily as he slipped on his cashmere coat. If it wasn't for the fine grains of sand still glinting on it, she might believe that this wasn't the same man who had lowered her to the ground and said she would make a gorgeous mermaid.

By the time she'd watched the sun rise in the clear blue sky and heard the seagulls caw noisily as if celebrating the change in the weather, she'd already decided that she would wear the same mask as Marco. If polite distance was to be the state of play for them both, then she would win hands down. She'd had a whole lifetime of walking the walk and talking the talk.

Emerald had opened her heart to Marco by telling him the truth and now her heart was bruised — and if she could do nothing about it, then at least she could put on a good show of not caring. Marco Cavarelli would not find her lacking in that department, of that he could be sure.

CHAPTER TWENTY-SIX

Two weeks later Emerald walked into the office, yawning and twisting her head to get rid of the crick she'd developed through sleeping badly again, as lustful dreams took her to forbidden heights, with Marco always in the lead role.

She had barely seen Marco since their trip to the Scillies, just about managed dinner twice and gulped a few hurried coffees before he flew out to Italy again. It was bizarre as he had hung around Hot Air like a damp mist for the last few months and now was nowhere to be seen most of the time. The trip to the Scillies was beginning to feel like a surreal dream she had wanted to happen but had sadly imagined.

She was hoping he would be at work as she pulled up outside the offices and felt decidedly nervous about seeing him, having no idea how their relationship was playing out — or even if they had a relationship anymore. He hadn't tried to tempt her into bed when they met for dinner no matter all they had shared when away. Now, he constantly looking at his watch before draining his coffee mug, snatching up his jacket and disappearing through the nearest door.

She'd had no chance to talk to him as he'd busied himself with his laptop on the flight home from the Scillies and had kissed her perfunctorily as he put her in a cab and took a different one straight into the centre of London. She now wondered if he was staying busy on purpose. In her heart, she couldn't believe that he would have stopped wanting her so quickly — they were perfect together. But a niggling voice kept on repeating Finbar's warning. She should have listened to his words of advice.

But there was nothing she could do about it now. Her fragmented heart could break when she was at home but it would be made of steel while she was at work. She pasted on a smile.

'Morning, Charlotte, morning, bump, hope you both feel better than I do.' She stifled another yawn and glanced around the office as Charlotte, Marco's personal secretary, tapped away at the computer.

'Morning, Emms. I'm fine apart from a million aches and twinges that I can't identify,' Charlotte said. 'Oh, it might be something to do with this,' she said, throwing a surprised look at her huge pregnant belly and giving it a rub.

Emerald threw her a commiserating glance. 'Not long now, eh?'

'I guess, but it's lasting longer than an English winter for me. Never. Bloody. Ending.' Charlotte laughed, but she looked pale and washed out.

'I can imagine,' was all Emerald could say to sympathise.

Roz, the receptionist who dealt with the day to day admin and most jobs filed under *any other business* glanced up. 'Morning, Emerald. Marco left some post on your desk to deliver to the right people when you see them.'

'Okay, I'll check the roster and see who's flying today.' She turned to put the kettle on. 'Anything from crewing? Any delays, weather problems or sickness?'

'Apart from Charlotte's chronic indigestion, no.'

Emerald pulled a sympathetic face. She couldn't imagine what it felt like to have a football-sized baby take over her body. A labour of love, she imagined, thinking fleetingly once again of what her and Marco's babies might look like.

'Yeah. Constant niggling pain in my groin and the little blighter is kicking me like it thinks I'm a tin can.' She paused for a moment to resume typing before looking up. 'Mr Cavarelli has finally made it common knowledge that he's streamlining the base. He wants me to come back after the baby and has offered me a generous maternity package, so I'm pleased to know I'm not being "streamlined".' She put a hand to her belly, a frown crossing her face and what looked like a wince of pain.

'He's streamlining the base? Finally?' Emerald faced Charlotte, trying to keep the shock from her voice. This was the first she'd heard of it, but Charlotte knew of his plans. Marco kept things to himself, but surely he would have mentioned such a huge change? Emerald stared at Charlotte, unable to take this news in. Marco had told Charlotte, his personal secretary and yet he hadn't trusted her with this bombshell, when she was supposed to be . . . what was she supposed to be? His lover, his confidante, his employee?

She opened her mouth to speak but closed it again, needing time to absorb the shock of it. Alarm bells rang, faint but insistent as she wandered over to her desk to check the letters he'd left her to distribute. She picked them up and shuffled through them, not finding any common denominator in the names printed on them.

'Where is Marco, by the way? I'm guessing you know? He keeps us in the dark most of the time.'

'Oh, he's his own man all right. I don't know where he is half the time, but I do know he's gone away again. I booked him a flight to Florence, first thing.'

Emerald balked. This was getting worse. 'Really? He didn't say anything to me.'

'Why would he, you weren't here?' Charlotte asked, not unkindly.

Emerald pulled herself up short, remembering that no one knew about her and Marco so there would be no reason for her to know his movements.

Charlotte, however, didn't appear to notice and went on talking. 'It was genuinely weird. The magazines for the aircraft were delivered and Marco signed for them to save me heaving my huge barge arse out of my chair. Then he went all quiet, put his jacket back on and said he was going away. He'd only taken his jacket off minutes before.'

Emerald went cold at Charlotte's words — there was definitely something going on, then.

'He keeps sending me emails asking me to do things, so he clearly still has a lot to do around here.' Charlotte continued peering at her computer screen.

Emerald edged casually across to the magazines dumped on the floor, still sealed in polybags. The top one was a glossy gossip magazine and she opened it idly, not for one moment imagining that the answer to Marco's erratic behaviour would be found within its pages. immediately a picture of herself and Marco looking very cosy together in the hotel at St Martin's jumped out at her. Shock rendered her speechless as she took in the headline. *MYSTERY WOMAN IN HIDEAWAY HOTEL WITH MAGNATE MARCO CAVARELLI.* Emerald winced at the implication that they were being devious, knowing how much Marco would hate it. She didn't much like it herself — but there was no one in her life who cared very much what she did. Luckily, the female image in the photograph looked nothing like her. She was mostly in shadow and her giveaway hair was tied in a casual ponytail. *That was one good thing*, she thought, throwing a look at Charlotte who didn't look the slightest bit interested in her or the magazines.

Flipping the magazines closed to hide the image, she remembered how cross Marco had been about the intruding photographer. She rubbed at her arms, the earlier niggle about the direction of their relationship now cementing into a concrete fear that the picture was the reason for his hasty departure. Could it be that he was embarrassed to be seen with her, a woman of such lowly status?

Finbar sauntered in at that moment. 'Have you seen this?' He asked as he shoved his phone in front of her face.

'What's up?' He must have caught the stricken look on Emerald's face, even though she was trying to compose her features the best she could.

'Nothing, I hope.' Her fingers trembled as she threw the letters into her in-tray. 'What were you showing me?'

'Oh.' He lifted his phone again and showed her the screen. 'Our boss in a hotel with a woman — who looks strikingly similar to you. But it couldn't be you, could it?' Finbar smiled innocently. 'I've Googled it and it's on a ton of the celebrity gossip sites.'

She sighed. 'I've just seen it in the magazine part of the newspaper. It's just titillation.'

Finbar sighed. 'Come on, the game's up, you can't fool me.' He folded his arms and leaned on the desk. 'Tell me all.' But when she didn't speak he narrowed his eyes, noticing her distraction.

'What've you got there?' He nodded towards the in-tray with the letters sitting in it.

She dragged her mind back to the immediate problem. 'Oh, just letters. Fin. Have you heard rumours that Marco is streamlining the airline?'

'No, but it wouldn't surprise me; the man is ruthless.'

Betty, who was polishing the windows, stepped down from her stool and faced them, hands on hips. 'This is the first I've heard of it and I know *everything*.'

'We know you do, Betty, love, which just shows how cunning the man can be,' Finbar said, putting his phone away, his gaze now fixed on the letters.

Emerald thought *cunning* was a bit harsh — he was just a shrewd businessman — but nevertheless a sliver of unease crawled down her spine. Marco was preoccupied and distant and she was left flailing in a sea of doubt and insecurity.

'I know he was talking about merging with a smaller airline in Scotland or buying them — and updating our aircraft so we could start some kind of upmarket spa place. To watch the stars, in silence and — I dunno, a place for burned-out people to recharge their batteries, maybe? But he didn't say anything about redundancies,' she said, finally.

'Surely what he has in mind would mean expansion, not reduction?'

Emerald picked the letters out of her in-tray and tapped them against her thigh thoughtfully. 'I don't know, I'm afraid. I'm not privy to his plans.' She hoped she didn't sound bitter, but she was beginning to wonder, given his recent behaviour, if she had, after all, been a blabbing fool. The sort of fool Finbar had explicitly warned her against. She scanned the names on the letters once more.

'What are those letters?' Finbar asked squinting to read the names on the envelopes.

'They're from Marco.'

Finbar narrowed his eyes.

'It's nothing, I don't suppose,' she continued breezily.

'Then we have nothing to worry about, do we? Apart from the look on your face that says we might have something to worry about.' He flipped the letters out of Emerald's fingers and flicked through them, reading out the names on the front. 'Hannah, Mason, Connor, Taylor, Maisie, Jack. Hmm.' He looked up from the stack, a quizzical look on his face. 'You didn't? Please, tell me you didn't tell him.'

Emerald rubbed her nose and sucked in a shuddering breath. 'They were throwaway comments really, nothing tangible.'

He lowered his voice so that Charlotte wouldn't hear what he was saying. 'You mean throwaway comments like, "We caught Maisie pilfering cigarettes from the duty-free bar, and Connor was off sick but someone saw him in the departure lounge heading for Ibiza" — those sorts of throwaway comments?'

'It was just chatter, nothing specific.' Emerald put her fingers up to her lips as they started quivering. 'He wouldn't do that — he's not who you think, Fin.' But her stomach contracted with anxiety. 'I need to see the contents of those letters.' She glanced over at Charlotte, wondering how unethical it would be to read one and seal it up again.

She inclined her head over to the adjacent room. 'Let's go into my office,' she mouthed and walked the few short steps into the office she now shared with Marco.

Quick as a flash, Finbar slit the top of one of the envelopes and scanned the page, his mouth compressing into a hard line. He passed the letter to Emerald wordlessly, before printing out a new name label and sticking it onto a fresh envelope. Then he snatched the letter back from a pale-faced Emerald and slipped it in the envelope, shaking his head with disbelief.

'God, what have I done?' Emerald sat down with a thump as the awful truth sank in: that she was the direct cause of her colleagues losing their jobs. Colleagues who should have known better, but still had bills to pay and were on the whole, decent people and good workers.

'What a bastard. Sacking — couched in grander terms, but basically firing them.'

'At least he's paying them off.' Emerald could barely take it in. It couldn't be a coincidence. Careless talk costs lives — isn't that what they said, back in the wartime days? Finbar had told her to be careful but she hadn't listened, being too busy losing her virginity and falling in love.

Finbar turned his attention from the letters to gaze out of the window towards the car park. 'Where is the delectable Mr Cavarelli, anyway?'

Betty appeared from the tiny kitchenette area, yellow rubber gloves adorning her hands. 'Florence. Went this morning, in a hurry.'

Finbar jumped backwards and fanned his face. 'Christ almighty, Betty, don't do that. How do you move from one room to another without us seeing you? You're like a bloody Ninja.'

Emerald laughed. 'Betty's had years of practice, that's how she knows everything.'

'I'm the cleaner, no one notices me,' Betty said, pulling off the gloves with a snap. 'Florence,' she repeated.

The single word sounded like a death knell to Emerald.

Betty went on. 'Might be as long as a week. I heard him on the phone making arrangements.' Polishing her glasses with the same cloth she'd just used to wipe the windows she leaned against the desk. 'I put his tea down on his desk and he almost jumped out of his skin. He was being very shifty indeed.' Her eyes narrowed briefly but then her face turned wistful. 'He is so good-looking though — and he ate all the coffee cake I gave him.'

Finbar's lips pursed waspishly. 'Oh, well, if he ate all of your cake then everything must be hunky-dory.'

'No one is black or white, Finbar — you have to give the man a chance. But a week?' Emerald said, bringing the conversation back to what mattered. He hadn't even mentioned that he was going away.

Charlotte's head popped around the door. 'I'm so sorry to bother you both, but my twinges have turned into rather strong pains. I've phoned my husband and he's picking me up. Might as well visit the hospital just to make sure.'

At this news, all work worries were forgotten. Finbar immediately took Charlotte's arm and half-carried her to the door.

'It's probably a false alarm. I can walk.' She laughed as she disentangled herself from Finbar.

'I'm just trying to get you out of here, quick sharp, before your waters break all over our carpet,' Finbar said tutting. 'Betty, get a bucket, just in case,' he shouted, hamming it up.

Everyone laughed and Charlotte looked pained as she laughed and bent over, clutching her bump.

'Oh Charlotte, I hope you're okay. It's not too soon is it?' Emerald asked.

'No, not at all. I'm not worried.'

'How exciting,' Finbar said helping her down the steps and peering around, looking for her husband's car.

'Isn't it? Looks like I might be starting my maternity leave sooner rather than later.' Charlotte laughed.

'Don't you worry about anything. We'll tell Marco you are indisposed, so don't even think about it.'

Charlotte's husband screeched to a halt in his car and he was out of the door in a flash. 'Darling, let me help you.' He guided his wife into the car solicitously, and everyone breathed a sigh of relief as he thanked them over and over.

'Newspaper on the seat might be helpful,' Finbar shouted and Emerald elbowed him.

'Not appropriate,' she said but she was laughing as they waved off Charlotte with kisses and good luck wishes.

Betty had tears in her eyes. 'It reminds me of when my eldest had her daughter. Did I ever show you the photos?' She dug in her apron pocket and Finbar quickly steered Emerald back inside the building.

'Right, let's get back to the disaster in hand, shall we? Betty are you putting that kettle on? Bit of cake, maybe?' He winked at Emerald.

Betty went off to make the tea and Emerald flung herself in her office chair. 'So, where were we?'

'You were about to tell me all the salacious details about you and Mr Cav, whether you wanted to or not.' Finbar was about to sit down opposite Emerald when he suddenly stilled. 'Emms, I hate to say this, but look.'

Emerald followed Finbar's line of sight to his finger, which wobbled as he pointed. Propped up against Emerald's computer screen sat an envelope, personally addressed to Emerald in Marco's unmistakable flowing handwriting. Emerald's mind couldn't compute what Finbar meant but, as realisation dawned, she picked it up with trembling hands.

Finbar grasped her shoulder. 'Sweetie, it won't be what you think. He wouldn't do that to you.'

But Emerald could hear the uncertainty in his tone and a terrible voice in the back of her head was screaming, *he would, he would, he needs to get rid of me — in case I talk.*

'Love, you've turned quite pale.' Betty walked in carrying a laden tray, her eyes now fixed on the unopened letter and then on Emerald's fearful eyes. 'If he goes around upsetting people, he'll have me to answer to,' she said, gauging that it was Marco causing the upset. She puffed out her chest, determination written all over her face. She took off her already spotless glasses and polished them again, manically, as she eyed up the envelope and Emerald's reaction to it. 'Let's have a look then.' She obviously believed she was as much a party to office politics as anyone.

'I've got this one, Betty.' Finbar put his arm around Emerald's shoulders and steered her toward the door. 'Let's get out of here. Don't open it now,' he hissed to Emerald as he grabbed her arm. He winked at Betty. 'We won't be long and I promise I'll let you know the goss as soon as I get back.'

Betty looked for a moment as if she would follow them out of the building, but good manners prevailed and she settled for huffing on her glasses once more and polishing them vigorously.

Finbar marched Emerald out of the office, not stopping until they came to the same café in which, ironically, Emerald had sat with Marco when he'd threatened her with the sack just after he'd arrived. How far they'd come since that day, and yet it seemed possible that the end result would be the same.

Emerald had begun to believe that Marco might yet be in love with her, but she'd clearly been living in a fantasy world. He thought as much of her as any of his other staff — which, by the looks of it, wasn't very much. Though surely he wouldn't dismiss her? Even Finbar said as much and he didn't trust Marco an inch. But perhaps he now saw her as an inconvenience and wanted her gone. With shaking fingers she held the envelope at arm's length, her eyes fixed on it, as if she could see the contents by sheer willpower.

Finbar placed a cup of tea in front of her and stirred his own coffee, waiting.

'And before you say anything, I don't want to hear one *I told you so*. Not one, okay?' Emerald said weakly as she placed the letter squarely in between them both.

'I wouldn't dream of it, sweetie, but—' he held up his hand '—I did warn you.'

Emerald eyed him as she slid her finger under the envelope. 'Oh, it's not even sealed.' She looked inside it, tipped it up and turned it inside out, shaking it. 'It's empty. There's nothing in there. Oh, hang on.' She waggled her finger inside the envelope and a Hot Air Aviation compliment slip slithered onto the table. She stared at it for a second, before sweeping it up with the envelope.

'Phew. That's bloody weird though.' Finbar sat back in his chair. 'Have you checked your phone, by the way?'

'No, I haven't heard it ring or anything. Hang on.' She fished out her mobile and scanned it. 'Oh, there's a message from him.' Something seemed more than *off* today and getting a text from Marco, who was making himself scarce, made her jittery. She bit her lip as she glanced at Finbar before returning her gaze to her phone. She opened the message,

'What's it say?' Finbar's eyes were bulging.

Reading slowly from the screen, she said, 'Well, Mr Cavarelli says hello.' She looked up and nodded, smiling. 'Good start.' She looked down again. 'He suggests that it would be for the best if—' She squinted as she read the message. '"If I clear my desk and wind down my flights for the foreseeable future."' Her voice, rose, faltered and stuttered as she took in his words. 'He will ensure that I am not financially indisposed.' She looked up. 'He will be in touch soon.' She peered closer. 'There's a kiss on the end.'

She looked up at Finbar, stricken. The gaped back at her phone, blew out a breath and slumped into her chair, leaning her head in her hands. She brushed her hair out of the way as it flopped over her face, and stared blankly at Finbar. 'I don't understand. What is he saying?'

'Wait . . . No!' Finbar's eyes were huge and disbelieving, his mouth wide open. 'The bastard,' he said, letting out a loud breath.

'Is he dismissing me, too?' She was momentarily too puzzled to be upset, too confused to be worried about her job. *No, No*, her mind screamed. Nothing had prepared her for this. She dropped her phone into her lap. 'Why would he do this?' She bit her lip, looked up at Finbar for an explanation, her eyes glistening with unshed tears and panic. 'What am I going to do?'

'What happened between you two?'

Emerald just shook her head and looked down at her lap, cradling her phone.

'You slept with him, didn't you?'

She nodded as she bit her lip to hold back the tears. There was no point in denying it.

'What did I tell you? Don't think he's on your side, don't sleep with him and don't tell him anything about the staff.'

'I thought there were going to be no "*I told you so*'s."'

'For crying out loud, though, Emms!' He snatched her phone up and read the message for himself. 'There's is a bloody kiss at the end. The bastard.'

'Yeah. That means nothing. I've done it myself by mistake, loads of times. Too late to take it back once you've pressed send — and the person on the other end is left wondering if you fancy them.' She smiled weakly.

'You're right. It'll be a mistake — or he needs a good slapping for being so heartless.' Finbar swore again and threw the phone onto the table. He patted Emerald's arm. 'It's not your fault, honey. He knows how to play people and he's ruthless. That's why he's so successful.'

She didn't answer, still couldn't believe that he had made love to her so thoroughly and then betrayed her so totally. Not only was she about to lose her job, but all the delightful fantasies she'd harboured, of a future with the man she loved had proved to be an illusion. How could anyone be so cruel?

'But he wasn't like that, ever,' she asserted.

'Of course he was like that. You just didn't see it because he made you all moonstruck.' Finbar sighed and drummed his fingers on the table. 'I don't know what to suggest, right now.'

She shook her head still in shock. But even as she tried to defend him, a deep humiliation crept up on her, colouring her cheeks. To think of the intimate things she'd done with him — totally abandoning her prudish tendencies, believing that it wasn't so much about sex as discovering each other — falling in love. But it wasn't love, it was calculating sex. One merciless man using her in the most callous way possible. Her big beautiful dream had turned into an appalling nightmare.

'If ever there was a time to put a laxative in someone's coffee, this is it,' Fin said, always on her side.

'I'd beat you to it.'

'I suppose he was fantastic in bed, was he?'

Emerald's eyes widened. 'For God's sake, Finbar, I've just lost my job and you want to know what he's like in bed?'

'Yes.' His grin didn't fade. 'Ultimate fantasies and all that — can't help it. And I think you might want to use the past tense from now on about your sex life with Mr Cavarelli.'

'My *ex* sex life then, if that makes you happier.' She was too shocked to cry, but slowly her predicament hit her. 'He knows I have no family to help me.' She shook her head, helplessly. 'All the other stuff we talked about too. I just can't take it in. Does it mean he's sacked me?' She scanned through the message once more and came to the same sad conclusion.

'Do you want to call him? I assume you feel close enough to do that?'

She considered it. Yelling at him and telling him what a bastard he was sounded like a good option, but what good would it do? 'Maybe he doesn't mean it — or maybe it was a mistake — I don't want to make it worse.'

'Or, maybe he just sees you as an annoyance now.' Finbar looked thoughtful. 'And what kind of mistake would "clear your desk" be? I don't think anyone could make a mistake like that, to be honest.'

Emerald sagged. 'At least he had the grace to text me.'

'Really? You are actually grateful that he personally sacked you by *text*?'

'You're right. What the hell am I thinking?' She shook her head in disbelief. 'And how can he expect me to face him, after what he's done to me, what we did together? Oh, God. I can't see him ever again, Fin, I just can't.'

She looked down sorrowfully into her tea, shaking her head saying over and over. 'I can't believe it.'

They both sat staring out of the window watching the aircraft coming into land, saying nothing. Emerald was remembering another time when she sat watching the aircraft, in that same café, with Marco in front of her, berating her for her behaviour. How long ago that seemed now. And yet hadn't she just gone and proved him one hundred per cent correct? Sleeping with the boss, no less.

Finally she blew out a long breath. 'I have to leave. My job, the company, everything I hold dear. Right now.'

Finbar seemed to wake from a trance as he took her hand. 'Wait, sweetie, you can't afford to walk out — and anyway, he's not even here.'

'He's given me no choice, Fin. Staying is not an option. At least this way I can leave on my own terms.'

'Hang on a minute. Let me make a few phone calls and see who's recruiting. You might be lucky.' He pressed her hand and she held on to it like the lifeline it was.

Finbar quickly started browsing through his phone. 'So many names. I can't even put faces to some of them.'

Emerald glanced over at his phone assuming he was talking about boyfriends, one night stands, acquaintances, even Facebook friends. He seemed to have hundreds of names in his contacts list. 'It could take days,' she said.

'Yes.' He sighed. 'Look, why don't you go home and I'll sort out the rosters and the staff? You're not flying today, are you?'

'No, not until Thursday.'

'I'll change the roster and take you off it. I'll sort it. You go home.'

She nodded gratefully. 'Thanks, Fin. I can't go back in there, not now.'

She pushed to her feet and Finbar followed suit. 'I'll call you later, okay?'

She nodded mutely, dragging her heels as she headed for her car, hoping for a last-minute reprieve, although what shape such a thing would come in, was anyone's guess. Marco skidding to a stop in a Batmobile or sliding down the walls like Spiderman, ready to save the day? She didn't think so.

Climbing into her car, she let herself wilt. Spent of energy, she rested her head on the steering wheel as a pain so deep and penetrating engulfed her. 'Why, why?' she wailed. 'Oh, Marco, how could you?' She clutched at her chest, feeling an almost physical pain from his betrayal.

She had allowed herself to fall in love with her boss so easily, but all the charm and the loving kisses had been a ploy to trick her into divulging Hot Air's secrets, and like the idiot she so clearly was, she'd fallen for it. What a total shit he was and what a traitor she had been, causing colleagues to lose their jobs, their livelihood. What on earth had she been thinking? Over and over it ran in her head.

Finally, she fired up her car, smiling like she always did, to the parking attendant as he waved her through the barrier. The journey home made her see things in a different light and by the time she arrived at her front door her new emotions were murderous. Marco was a duplicitous bastard and she would never see him again.

By the time she put her key in the door, she'd decided on a plan. She immediately phoned Finbar and asked him to remove any details from her physical file and the file on the computer, so determined was she never to cross paths with the man she'd believed would redeem her faith in humankind. Never again.

CHAPTER TWENTY-SEVEN

'What do you mean she's gone? Gone where? I've only been away for four days,' Marco snapped as he paced the floor like an expectant father.

'I'm not sure,' Roz replied. 'I haven't seen her for days.' She had explained to Marco that Charlotte had had a baby girl and Emerald was nowhere to be seen. 'I've been holding the fort,' she added, pointedly, waiting in vain for some kind of recognition.

Betty bustled in as Roz finished speaking. Marco covered his face with his hands and groaned as he headed for his desk. He wasn't sure he could cope with Betty right then. She followed him in and slammed a mug of coffee down on his desk so close to his laptop that he had to shield it with his hand. 'Careful.'

'Careful?' Betty echoed. 'I should be saying that to you. How careful have you been recently?'

For a split-second Marco thought she was referring to his sex life and thoughts of Emerald quickly filled his mind. Surely she wasn't pregnant? He wouldn't be the slightest bit surprised if Betty were to know such a thing before he did — before Emerald did, even. He tried to quash his unease in case Betty might spot it and use it against him.

'Sorry?' He stared at Betty, taking in her flashing eyes and her lips set in a determined line. Even her grey curls bounced with indignation.

'Sacking people left, right and centre as if you're bloody God Almighty.'

'Ah, that.' He breathed out silent thanks. He could handle the employees even though he wouldn't be up for a popularity prize any time soon.

He had almost forgotten about the staff he'd sacked, being too busy attending to other business needs and finalizing his divorce. 'It was necessary,' he said, before tempering his words with an exaggerated smile.

It had no impact whatsoever on Betty, who folded her arms and set her stance to fight mode. 'And what have you done to that poor girl?'

'Poor girl?' The timbre of his voice wasn't entirely steady as he felt his hopes lifting. 'Emerald?' he asked hesitating realising that some people would view her as a lost soul when he knew she was a lioness. But he hadn't heard from her since he'd returned and was starting to become concerned. 'You know where Emerald is?'

Betty looked stubborn. 'Depends.'

'Depends? How can it depend on anything? You either know where she is or you don't.'

'No, it don't depend on that, at all. It depends on if she wants you to know where she is.' Betty planted her feet firmly apart to show she was going nowhere fast.

Marco stopped dead in his tracks, suddenly fearful. Now he thought about it, it had been far too long since he'd heard from her. He'd been too busy chasing up builders, signing contracts, and practically giving his ex-wife the shirt from his back. His blood ran cold, remembering the open-ended tickets to Florence he'd meant to chase up, so that he and Emerald could go back to Florence together. He groaned and ran his fingers through his hair as he swung Charlotte's computer screen around. He clicked through the email and there they sat, the open tickets to the airport, in Charlotte's inbox. 'Roz,' he shouted, 'did you print these tickets off and pop them in an envelope for Emerald?'

Roz sauntered over, a puzzled expression on her face. She peered at the computer screen. 'No, why would I?'

Betty was snapping at his heels. 'What is it?'

Marco had given up on the *me boss you employee* tactic with Betty, it wasn't worth the hassle. His voice was quiet, resigned almost. 'Charlotte didn't put the tickets in the envelope with the letter . . .'

Betty unfolded her arms and put her hands in her apron pocket waiting for more, but he didn't have time to explain.

'Damn it! Has anyone any idea where she's gone?' Marco just about kept his voice level and calm.

'Last time I saw her, she left with Finbar who used a lot of choice words when he returned — on his own.'

He shook his head. 'She's not going to know I intended to spirit her away. Christ, my text message, what must she think? I asked her to clear her desk!'

By the look on Betty's face she most likely knew everything there was to know about Emerald and Marco's liaison — gossip was what cleaners were really employed for, after all. Her eyes widened as she stared at Marco, but she didn't say a word, just took off her glasses getting ready to polish them, tucking her chin into her neck in a knowing manner.

But he didn't care about office gossip. He just wanted to find Emerald. He cursed and headed towards the door, tapping in her phone number on his mobile as he went, his irritation dissolving with the anticipation of speaking to her. But her mobile rang and rang and there was no answer. It didn't even click into voicemail.

He thrust his phone back into his pocket, becoming more alarmed as he headed back into the office, unable to hide his irritation.

Why was she so damned headstrong, and how did she not understand what she meant to him — after everything they'd talked about? She really should know how fiercely loyal he was to anyone he loved. He sighed in frustration as it dawned on him that he really should have told her he loved her. Declaring love was tantamount to declaring marriage in his mind. He'd only ever said it once before and had expected it to be for life, but he now realised he had played it all wrong.

He would rectify that oversight the minute he spoke to her, but still he was concerned. Why had he sent her that text message? Why hadn't he talked to her instead of rushing around focusing on too many things at once and neglecting the most important thing of all?

Finbar strolled into Marco's office and sat down in Emerald's chair, put his feet up on her desk, and began painting his fingernails with purple varnish. He blew on his nails indolently as he looked up at Marco, with eyes rimmed in charcoal eyeliner.

Marco closed his eyes and blew out a calming breath. He was going to have to tread carefully with Finbar if he wanted information on Emerald. Betty threw a wan smile in Marco's direction and shrugged her shoulders, as if the scene that was about to be played out was beyond their control. They both watched wordlessly to see what Finbar would do next.

'Where is Miss Montrose?'

Finbar didn't reply, just shrugged nonchalantly.

Marco had never been so close to punching a man in his life. He balled his hands into fists, controlling his temper by breathing in deeply and slowly. He glared at Finbar's feet resting on Emerald's desk, wanting to knock them off. He almost lost it, especially when Finbar casually asked, 'Emerald Montrose?' He glanced out of the window as if expecting her to magically appear.

When Marco didn't rise to the bait, Finbar said, 'Emerald decided to quit.' He shook his fanned-out fingers and blew on his nails once more while leisurely raising his feet off the desk and planting them on the floor, all the time holding Marco's gaze. 'She's a terribly fragile person behind that tough veneer, you know.'

Marco clenched and unclenched his fists, itching to grab Finbar's collar and shake him until his teeth rattled. 'I know her well enough to realize that, thank you. Get me her file,' he barked out, knowing he shouldn't speak to a member of staff that way, but he couldn't help himself being too agitated for niceties.

'Of course.' Finbar ambled over to the filing cabinet and pulled open a drawer, lifting the file out with a flourish.

Marco knew Finbar was dawdling deliberately to infuriate him. He wished all over again that he'd included him in his list of redundancies and hang the consequences.

'Ooh, it's ever so light, her file.' Finbar held it between his forefinger and thumb and upended it, shaking it slightly. A single piece of paper fell on to the desk. It looked like a photocopy of a Christmas menu, sprigs of holly painted in each corner. Marco glared at it but didn't pick it up. He tapped the computer to find her uploaded CV and social security information. Gone. Passport number — gone. Everything had disappeared. It was as if she'd never been employed by Hot Air Aviation.

He scowled at Finbar. 'You know that tampering with official information is illegal and you can be fined for it.'

'Is that a question, or a statement?'

Marco glared at him.

'Anyway, why are you telling me?' Finbar asked, shrugging one shoulder indifferently.

Marco glared some more, rendered speechless with the urge to shout profanities at the most annoying person he'd ever met.

'It's not me you should be telling that to, it's Emerald.' He examined a newly painted fingernail before pulling a pained face. 'Oh wait, of course, you can't *find* her. That's the problem, isn't it?'

Marco's nostrils flared. He shrugged his jacket back on, having taken it off only minutes before. He was going to find Emerald or kill Finbar and at the moment he rather thought the latter would be more satisfying.

'She's moved out,' Finbar said, anticipating Marco's next move.

'*What?*'

'Her flat. She's gone away, I believe.'

'Why?'

'Err, she has no income to pay for it, maybe?' he suggested. 'Or maybe she's gone to stay with a friend?' He shook his head. 'I don't really know.'

'Silly girl,' Marco muttered.

Finbar shook his hair out of his eyes and gazed out of the window as if nothing Marco Cavarelli had to say was worth taking in. 'Do you still want her file?'

'Will it tell me where she is?' Marco glowered at Finbar. 'I don't believe so.'

'You know where she is, don't you?'

'Me?' Finbar's eyes widened in innocence but Marco wasn't fooled — of course he knew where she was. He narrowed his own eyes but Finbar just raised his eyebrows. 'Can't help you, I'm afraid.'

Marco clenched his teeth. 'No problem.' He ran a hand across his jaw, heaping all the hot coals from hell metaphorically onto Finbar's head.

He sat down at his desk, trying to think straight. He knew he had handled the situation badly, and maybe Emerald was more than a little upset with him, but hopefully she would calm down and phone him up and he could tell her he loved her and she would see that his intentions were honourable.

CHAPTER TWENTY-EIGHT

Weeks had passed since Marco returned to find Emerald had picked up sticks and left, and Marco was no closer to finding her. *Emerald Wilhelmina Montrose, where have you gone?* He whispered to the air. There was nothing anywhere to indicate where she could be — purposely designed, he knew, so he had to conclude that she didn't want to be found. Undaunted at first, he'd driven around to her flat convinced they could sort out the misunderstanding, but she wasn't there and as time passed he became more concerned that she really had disappeared. He'd taken to checking his mobile phone every ten minutes and wracked his brains to think of something, anything, he could pin down to assist him with finding her, but so far he'd come up with nothing.

He flicked through some CVs that had arrived that morning in preparation for his newly restructured airline, but he really didn't have the enthusiasm to sort through them. It was a job for Emerald, he mused, as he had no solid idea of what qualities were needed for such a position. Again he cursed, knowing that he would need Finbar's help.

'Finbar, look through these, will you, and weed out the unsuitable ones.'

Finbar's head shot up from behind the computer screen. 'A please would be nice?' His head disappeared behind the screen again.

Marco felt his temperature rise. The bloody man was infuriating. 'Please. And will you officially take over Emerald's role temporarily, until she returns?'

'Certainly. Lovely, a pay rise.' It wasn't a question.

'I'll sort it out,' Marco growled, and threw the pile of CVs onto the desk that Finbar had already acquired in Emerald's absence.

'I don't think she's planning on coming back, by the way,' Finbar said idly, as he flicked through the pile of CVs. 'In case you wanted to turn temporary into permanent.'

He tossed a CV in the bin after scanning it quickly. 'Too old.' Another one went in the bin with, 'Too pretty — she'll be trouble.' He shuddered as he held one out for Marco to look at. 'Oh, that one's been hit with the ugly stick, for sure.' It followed the other unfortunates into the trash.

Marco glanced at the bin in which the applicants' CVs had just ended up. He was sure it wasn't a politically correct way of sifting through job applications, but he hadn't the heart or the inclination to comment.

He tried to focus on his work but it was no good. He really couldn't concentrate on the job in hand. He considered throttling Finbar as a way of reducing his stress levels, enjoying the idea of pinning him up against the wall. As far as fantasies went it was up there with the best of them, but murder might not sit too well with his future plans. Instead he settled for throwing murderous glances at him whenever he could.

He wiped a sheen of sweat from his forehead. He hardly ever perspired, but these weren't normal times. He stood up impatiently. 'I'm going out.'

'Again? Good luck.' Finbar's face was angelic as he waggled his fingers in a silent goodbye.

Marco scowled and slammed out of the door. As he sat in his car, motionless, contemplating his next move, he was shocked at how fiercely Emerald's disappearance had hit him. He was also surprised at how few options he had to track her down apart from driving to her flat — which he was pretty certain was a futile task. Nevertheless, he found himself pulling up outside her door once again, and knocking in vain, hoping that someone would answer the door and tell him where she was. He just needed to see her. Surely she wouldn't have thrown everything they had away, over one stupid mistake he'd made?

He drove back to work. 'Roz, do you know where Emerald's parents live?'

'Africa?' She suggested before resuming her typing.

'This is stupid. How could we employ a woman and know so little about her background?' He thought he'd done a thorough job of finding out her history, but it was all consequential and unimportant. He knew she'd had a horse called Star that she loved, had once fought off a hyena and could find her way by the stars. Not enough, exactly, to bring her home to him.

He also knew she'd spent most of her teenage years in a convent school, but every single convent school he phoned in Ireland had given him a vague answer, as if they were all in cahoots. "Sure now, we've a lot of young girls called Emerald," and, "Hmm, Emerald, that's a pretty name, now." And "Named after the Emerald Isle, so I'm assuming she'll be Irish, will she not?" No one actually gave him any information that he could latch on to.

He ran his finger over a tiny passport-sized photo of Emerald that he'd found stuck in the corner of Emerald's drawer, looking up guiltily when Betty appeared at his elbow. For someone so small, Betty had a powerful presence. Even he was beginning to quake at the thought that he might step out of line.

But for once his mug of coffee wasn't slammed onto the table with the force of a speeding train.

'So, you're looking for Emerald?'

Stating the bloody obvious, he thought, but he'd never dare utter the words. He looked up at her bleakly. 'I think I've run out of options.'

Betty bit her lip and fluffed up her curly permed hair.

Marco narrowed his eyes. '. . . you know something?' His heart skipped a beat.

'Have I ever shown you the photos of my grandkids?'

He deflated. 'No,' he replied, carefully. There was a nuance here that he hadn't quite grasped and he looked over to Roz for help.

Roz widened her eyes and thrust out her chin, indicating that he should play the game, as Betty cleared a space on his desk.

'No, Betty, but I would love to see them—' He looked at his watch, the words *another time* on his lips, but Roz's loud cough had him clamping his mouth shut as Betty dug into her apron pocket and produced a thick wad of photos.

'Lovely.' Marco bit back a sigh, saying a silent goodbye to a productive half hour of work. He thought he heard a suppressed snort of laughter from Roz but didn't dare glance at her. If Betty knew something — anything — that could help him find Emerald then he would suffer even the photos of her dead pets. He didn't dare to zone out for one second, fearing that she might quiz him later and refuse to offer up her information if he had a memory lapse.

'So this is Lulu, the springer spaniel. She died three years ago.'

'Very sad,' he said, putting as much sincerity into his voice as possible. Yep. She was actually going to go the whole hog. If any of the grandchildren had so much as a stick insect, he'd be seeing photos of it any minute now.

Roz unsuccessfully tried to hide her chuckle with a cough, but Marco maintained a straight face, his hopes soaring as the pile of photos diminished.

'And that's all of them,' Bettie said eventually, gathering the photos up.

Marco gave her a forlorn smile. 'Bertie, Jasmine, Toby and Harrison, am I right?' The names would be etched on his brain forever.

'Aren't they angels?' Betty had a satisfied look on her face as she slipped the photos back into her pocket. Marco had a horrible feeling that she wasn't going to tell him about Emerald and ignore their tacit agreement — or maybe he'd just been duped.

Betty's shoulder was inches away from him and he was about to give in to the urge to take her in his arms and beg her to tell him what she knew about Emerald, when she walked over to Emerald's old desk.

'I'll assume you had your reasons for behaving the way you did, but I can see you want the best for Emerald.' Betty pointed to a small drawer underneath Emerald's desk that Marco hadn't noticed before. 'She keeps stuff in there. It's a hidden compartment. It might be of some help.'

'Thank you.' Marco moistened his lips and stared at the desk. Checking out someone's personal stuff didn't sit well with him. He peered at the drawer and glanced up at Roz for approval.

Roz tilted her head to one side, an amused smile on her lips. 'Go on — you want to find her, don't you?'

'Yes. Very much.' He stood up and flexed his fingers as if he was about to unpick a lock and pulled open the drawer. Inside lay a slim folder. It didn't weigh much and he feared that it was empty, but he pulled it out and studied it. After a moment, he opened the folder and stared in quiet amazement as a small but vivid picture of a vast yellow desert interspersed with scrubby purple trees and menacing lions jumped out at him.

It seemed that the landscape was a cover for the rest of the images tucked underneath it and Marco flicked through the other dozen or so, sitting down as the subject matter floored him. Each picture showed an uncanny likeness of him, mostly in various degrees of brooding anger. His first thought was that he had no idea he was so moody and his next thought was that Emerald was a brilliant artist if she'd drawn these — and he had to assume she had. His memory flitted back to the paintings in her flat and he smiled at the bitter sweet memory. She'd painted them all. Of course she had.

Was he so focused on himself and his business that he had not even noticed that the woman he loved had such a talent? He held out an image of himself lying on a sofa, fast asleep, wearing only a T-shirt and his underwear. His hair was tousled and his legs bare, and the depiction exuded the passion and love that had gone into each stroke. He remembered that he'd fallen asleep on the sofa in Edinburgh and was stunned. She must have cared for him, even back then. But then, he was already there, wasn't he? He'd already felt that way. Almost the minute he'd met her. Hadn't he kissed her in her room at his hotel, uncomfortable in his desire for such a vulnerable woman?

He dismissed the thought from his mind as he scoured the pictures for a signature, but all he could make out was "Will M." He tried to think what it could mean. Surely they could only be the work of Emerald — no one else had seen him in such intimate moments.

'These are Emerald's?' he asked Betty. She leaned over his shoulder and picked up the one of Marco asleep on the sofa, raising it up to the light.

'These are good,' Betty said. 'Bloody good. What's she doing wasting time in a job like this, with such a talent? Sorry — no offence, Marco.'

'Wilhelmina,' Marco said softly, a small smile spreading out across his face. He jumped up, pushing the images back in their folder. He kissed Betty on the cheek. 'I've got it. I know where she'll be.'

'Good, that's good!' Betty beamed as he strode towards the door. 'Make sure you look after her this time!' she called to his retreating back.

He stopped, swivelled on his heel, and directed his words to Roz. 'Book me a hotel in central London — two nights, please. I don't care which one — well as long as it's five star, of course. Just text me when you've done it.'

Roz jumped to it. 'Sure will, don't you worry.' She swung the computer monitor around to face her.

Marco breathed out a sigh of relief as he grabbed a taxi to take him to the centre of London, where he would begin his search.

CHAPTER TWENTY-NINE

Emerald was having a surprisingly interesting time working at her cousin Suzie's gallery, apart from missing her old friends at Hot Air Aviation, and of course Marco. Suzie was happy to let her stay in her spare room and had immediately offered her a job at the gallery, persuading her to frame some of her paintings and sell them.

Suzie hadn't asked any awkward questions, much to Emerald's relief, as she couldn't bear to relate what a gullible fool she'd been. She also couldn't utter Marco's name without her voice cracking. She wanted to hate him for what he'd done, but found it infuriatingly hard to work up the requisite anger.

Suzie had also given Emerald access to her airy loft where she was successfully venting her rage in the medium of oil paints, creating vivid and turbulent seascapes in the dead of night when she couldn't sleep.

It was impossible for Emerald to banish the images of Marco from her mind: the gentle smile that she'd thought was reserved just for her, and his spontaneous laugh when they had chased each other on the beach, Emerald amazed to discover that he wasn't perennially grumpy. But she refused to paint his likeness anymore. At such times pain ate away at her heart, and her wild brushstrokes of the African savannah seemed to dull it somehow. Even though she knew he'd used her for his own means, she still ached to hear his voice and she would often close her eyes in the dark, imagining his voice in her ear as he whispered her name.

She brought her mind back to the present and opened the cabinet on the counter to tidy up the jewellery display. Sparkling diamonds nestled next to pearls in exotically designed brooches, along with Ceylon Emeralds and cabochons. The astronomical price tags were an indicator of the type of clientele Suzie had garnered, although the complicated locking system in the gallery was a bit of a giveaway.

Her cousin was discussing one of Emerald's African scenes with a client who was just out of earshot and she marvelled at her selling persuasion. She was shocked at the high price Suzie had suggested for her paintings, and even more surprised at how quickly they were selling, considering she'd only wanted to top up her wage from the gallery work.

It was the difference between sinking and swimming, so even though her heart was starved of love, at least her body had sustenance. The large African scenes were the best sellers, but she had also sold two pictures of Edinburgh Castle and one of the Highland Guard playing the bagpipes, although she had felt as if she was losing a piece of her soul when she'd bubble-wrapped it for the customer, never to see it again.

Working in the gallery was not the same as her old job though. She missed flying and she craved Finbar's daily bitchiness and humour and the camaraderie that was Hot Air Aviation.

So Emerald couldn't help herself but wonder if her daydreaming had taken on a surreal edge when she heard an all too familiar call her name, with an inflection that could only be Italian. Her eyes widened in panic when she heard her name called again.

'Emerald?'

Marco?

The air whooshed out from her lungs on his name, stunned as she was to see him. 'Mr Cavarelli?'

She was gratified to see his brow furrow at her use of his title. She would never again call him Marco. He didn't deserve it. She hated the way that her breath hitched, though, when she spoke his name.

'Emerald, how have you been?'

'Unemployed.'

He shook his head slightly, as if accepting that she wasn't going to make it easy for him.

'We need to talk, I think.'

'I don't think we do.' Her heart rate quickened and her skin prickled with heat and she resented that he could do that to her body, when he had been so obviously absent from touching it. She also hated him for looking so casually gorgeous and unflappable, while she was flustered and fractious from sleepless nights. She wanted to yell at him and throw things to make him see what he had done to her, while he just stood there, the epitome of reasonableness and composure.

'Do you know how hard it has been to find you?'

'Is the answer *very*?' She needed to be cooler than cool, even though her legs were trembling behind the counter.

Marco walked towards her, then stopped and just stared at her, as if drinking her in. He breathed in, paused and then spoke. 'I didn't come here to fight. It was all a misunderstanding — I didn't dismiss you.'

'No, what you did was worse. You betrayed me — and duped me into betraying my colleagues.'

'If we are being pedantic, I already knew everything about my staff, you just confirmed it.' Then he flinched at his words as if realising too late that he wasn't helping his cause.

Emerald's eyes widened. 'Don't you dare turn this around on me. Just leave, please.'

'Please, Emerald, talk to me.'

'There is nothing to say.'

Marco took a step forward, his hands held out, imploring. 'I think there is. And if I have to do all the talking, then so be it. Just hear me out.'

'I've done enough *listening*. What I didn't do was enough thinking, to realize how false your words were — along with your shallow emotions.'

Marco recoiled at her words. 'I never lied to you, Emerald, please believe me and—'

Emerald cut him off. 'This is not the place to be having this discussion, Mr Cavarelli.'

'Will you stop with the *Mr Cavarelli*, for God's sake—'

Emerald turned towards her cousin whose eyes were on stalks as she looked at Emerald and then Marco, and back again to Emerald. '*Mr* Cavarelli is just leaving.'

'Oh, stop being childish, for heaven's sake,' Marco butted in. 'This is the real world. Hot Air is just a two-bit airline that needed shaking up. We need to move on from it and discuss our relationship.' He compressed his lips, realising once again that he was handling the situation badly. He should have prepared better for it.

'How *dare* you be so casual with people's lives — with my life. How dare you think it's fine to call in and speak to me as if what happened between us was a simple business trade-off! If you don't leave now, I will not be responsible for my actions.' Her eyes darted around the counter and she picked up a heavy bronze statue.

Suzie was by her side in seconds. 'No, please don't throw that one.' She prized it out of Emerald's fingers and picked up a china figurine. 'This one's much less valuable — I think it might even be a fake Davenport.' She pushed the figurine into Emerald's hand.

'If it helps, throw the bronze. I'll pick up the bill,' Marco said, eyeing the statue warily.

'You can't buy your way out of everything.' Emerald slammed the figurine back on the counter, her breath heaving in her chest. 'You make me so angry.'

'You don't say?' Marco's eyebrows rose slightly. 'I'm sorry, I'm so sorry that I've upset you. Please meet me when you've finished work. I really want to put this right.'

'Why would I want to meet you, Mr Cavarelli, when I've spent every waking moment trying to erase you from my mind?'

Marco wiped a hand over his face and huffed out an exasperated breath. He stared at Emerald, who stared back, unblinking.

'Okay, you win,' he said eventually, as he shook his head and placed a business card on the table. 'Just in case you have mislaid my number.' His smile was strained and Emerald noted the lines around his eyes. *Good*, she thought. *He deserves to suffer.*

Marco's hand hovered over the card. He looked into Emerald's eyes, and for a moment their eyes locked and it was just the two of them, their eyes full of pain and longing.

But Emerald could not forgive so easily. She pulled her gaze away, focusing on the wall behind him. 'Goodbye,' she said.

Marco gave her a last pleading look but when she didn't respond, turned his back on her and walked out of the gallery.

'Good. Very good. I'm glad he's gone. Very glad,' Emerald reiterated to no one in particular. Her fingers itched to pick up the figurine and hurl it anyway, but instead she simply watched the love of her life disappear down the street, the fight draining out of her.

He had come looking for her — that meant something, surely? But she was so angry with him still and couldn't stand to talk to him. She wanted to forgive him — but could never forgive him.

'So, that was the man who screwed you over so badly?' Suzie asked.

'Yes,' Emerald answered limply, spent of energy. She should have realized Suzie would guess her troubles were because of a man.

'Looks to me like a guy worth fighting for.'

'He's not.'

'Your call.' She shrugged and picked up the business card, reading the front of it. 'Isles of Scilly, eh?'

Emerald grabbed the card from Suzie's hand and studied it. 'He bought the hotel, then. He's a fast mover.' She took a deep breath. Crying was not an option. 'And I don't care.' For a moment, she wanted to clamp the card close to her chest, but she instead traced a finger over the embossed writing before ripping it into shreds, watching as the pieces drifted towards the bin.

* * *

Emerald was surprised and, frankly, quite put out when six weeks passed and Marco hadn't been in touch. She'd thought he might bombard her with messages now he knew where she was, or laughably, thought he might send tokens of love — the occasional bunch of roses wouldn't have gone amiss. She'd even taken to opening the post, fingers trembling when anything that looked like a card arrived. It was usually an invitation to a gallery opening and she now steeled herself to be disappointed. Maybe trying to brain him with a bronze statue was enough to turn him off the idea of sharing his life with her, she thought. She smiled for a brief moment, although her heart was breaking.

She tried to put him out of her mind and even managed it occasionally, although the nights were bad, when her memories assailed her. She did very little apart from go to work at Suzie's gallery and come home again, wondering how long it would take before she felt a stirring of happiness, or a semblance of peace. She hoped what she was feeling was a form of grief and it would be just a matter of time before she could live and breathe without the shadow of Marco darkening her every move.

Another month passed and, with a view to moving forward — or so she told herself — she finally arranged to meet Finbar in Covent Garden, a mixture of happiness and trepidation making her stomach roil. She wanted to hear all of the gossip but dreaded hearing that Marco, too might have moved forward — specifically, with another woman.

If anyone knew anything about him it would be Finbar, who no doubt had his every move recorded. She hoped that he wouldn't include juicy details of bronzed Amazonian women, or any women at all, although the odds were slight that Marco would not have found someone else: someone better and more suited to his lifestyle.

But Finbar was mostly full of the news of his promotion to Cabin Services Manager of the newly formed airline Midnight Skies — the new title that he claimed as his own brilliance, of course, and was excited to relate the story of how the two aircraft had arrived on a foggy Scilly Isles day and were the only ones that had managed to land.

Moreover, Finbar seemed to have been turned by Mr Cavarelli too, and was positively gushing about his unbounded business acumen. 'He got a fabulous deal with a travel agent and we are now specialising in stargazing packages. He's put a domed roof on the hotel, and although it's not even finished, people are booking it for next year. It's attracting the sort of rich people who love the outdoors, but would rather see it from the confines of a sumptuous hotel, and of course they can show off their knowledge to their partners without the inconvenience of actually going outside.'

A pensive look came over Finbar's face as he glanced upwards, as if he could see the heavenly skies as he spoke. 'You should see it, Emerald. You wouldn't believe how gorgeous the stars are on a clear night out there.'

Emerald didn't need to imagine it. She would never forget the evening of the high tide when she was in the Scilly Isles, looking out at the turbulent sea with the navy sky dotted with crystal stars above it. Marco was by her side then, warm and responsive. She wondered if Marco occasionally remembered their magical night together. It would stay etched on her mind forever. She thought she'd found her soulmate that evening, only for it all to come crashing down like the waves outside the window.

She put such intimate thoughts out of her mind as Finbar continued. 'I just can't understand why he didn't use my suggestions though — what an opportunity he missed there.'

'Which were?' Emerald prepared herself.

'Well, we had a promo flight and invited loads of journalists and influencers, with fabulous food and champagne. I suggested bow ties that squirted water, magicians, a clown or two, jugglers — you know as in-flight entertainment in the aisles and a brilliant play on the name — *Scilly* Isles. Dismissed the lot of it, miserable git.' Finbar sighed. 'I would have loved it.'

Emerald could picture Finbar in his element with a red and yellow bow tie that squirted out water as he juggled brightly coloured balls in the aisles. She smiled at the thought. 'It would have been brilliant,' she said, knowing that Marco would have hated it.

'Hmm, I guess. Oh, Emms, we miss you so much — why don't you come back? Mr Cav. — Mr Cavarelli to you, hasn't been seen for a month or so — you wouldn't even have to bump into him.'

Emerald experienced another kick to her heart on hearing that Marco had finally taken a back seat. He always said he would. It was the acquisition and the fight he loved the most, and turning it around until it was profitable. And now she was sure he had hot-footed it back to his home town, so he could whizz around the mountain roads he loved so much in his rich man's car impressing some gorgeous blonde in the passenger seat. She wanted to weep.

Suddenly the light had gone from the day. 'He didn't exactly try very hard to win me back, did he?' Marco had hardly ever been absent from Hot Air Aviation, always interfering and fussing, and now he had gone for good. She tried to feel relieved that she could put an end to that part of her life, but her smile drooped.

'I have to confess that I'm a bit puzzled by his inaction to get you back . . . He acted as if he'd move heaven and earth and then pfft.' Finbar snapped his fingers. 'You didn't actually throw that priceless bronze at him, did you?'

She laughed. 'No. Trust you to remember that bit. I wish I had flattened him with it, to be honest, at least I'd know why he's not been in touch again. Probably wouldn't have even dented the bronze with his thick head.'

'But anyway, I thought you'd be pleased to hear that he'd gone? You said you hated him.' Finbar's eyebrows lifted, his two silver-stud piercings moving in unison on his left eyebrow. Finbar knew how to play the game and he was completely playing her now.

'I *am* — I did hate him, but I can't seem to forget him. It's so annoying!' She glanced at Finbar and did a double take. 'I hope you don't try to get away with wearing that hardware on your face at work, especially now there's no one to stop you,' she added, hoping to change the conversation.

He smiled ruefully. 'It's no fun now, trying to be a nonconformist when I'm practically the manager — the naughtiness has gone out of it. It'd be like trying to wind myself up. You should ask for your job back, you know, I'm sure Mr Cav. would consider it. I could even re-appoint you — probably.'

Emerald shook her head. 'I couldn't work anywhere near him now.'

'Because you're still in love with him.' It was a declaration, not a question.

'I'm trying hard not to be.' She rested her chin on her hand, her thoughts far away on the Isles of Scilly. 'Marco's moved on. He's finished what he came to do and will be back to annoying the natives in Florence — might already have founded another small empire and . . .' Her voice cracked. 'Broken another heart.'

Finbar offered her his hand and she took it, holding on tight. She looked him in the eye for a moment before continuing. 'It was an easy conquest, wasn't it? I don't suppose he had a clue that I had no idea what I was supposed to do when it came to love. Think Marco might be my last attempt at it, too. I'm obviously no good at it.'

'Don't say that. I'll always love you.'

She tutted but gave a small smile. 'Fat lot of good that will do me. But let's not focus on my disastrous love life. I have some good news. I've been selling my art at Suzie's gallery. Actually *selling* paintings, not just putting price tags on for people to laugh at the absurdity of it. It could even become my new career.'

Finbar's forehead creased. 'What paintings? Hang on, those scary pictures on your walls are your own?'

'Yep.' Emerald looked abashed. 'Sorry.'

'And you never said.' His eyebrows lifted and his kohl-rimmed eyes widened. 'Wow.' A pause. 'And they're selling? Bloody hell — *selling*?' he asked, shaking his head as if he'd just witnessed a miracle.

Emerald smiled at his obvious shock. 'In fact, I've been invited to attend a gallery open evening in Mayfair — so that has to be a good sign, right? I will schmooze with dealers and convince them to come and visit Suzie's gallery. And they might just notice my paintings hanging there.'

Finbar patted her hand. 'I'm sure it's your ticket to fame and fortune. Just don't forget your old mates when you're hobnobbing with your betters.'

'Finbar, I have about three friends in the whole world and you're the best of the lot, so I'm hardly likely to forget you, am I?'

Finbar brightened. 'And you never know, you might meet your Prince Charming at the exhibition.'

She smiled bleakly. 'I don't think Prince Charming exists — and if he did he'd probably be gay knowing my luck.'

'You're right, of course, so make sure you give me a call, if he appears,' Finbar said. 'I'm far better at this lurve thing than you. Now come on, cheer up, it's all coming good.'

Emerald gave him another wan smile.

'Good girl. Now, let's celebrate your talent for wielding a paintbrush so splendidly. An ice cream I think.'

'Let's not forget my total inability to cope with the opposite sex — surely that's worth celebrating, too?'

Finbar nodded. 'The I Scream Parlour is the place to be, and the ice creams are on me.'

'With sprinkles on?' Emerald asked.

'Definitely. Chocolate flake and sauce too, don't you think?'

CHAPTER THIRTY

On the appointed day, Emerald arrived at the art exhibition, the invitation tucked inside her bag in case they didn't believe she was a guest. She was somewhat taken aback that there were no other guests milling around, helping themselves to the usual complimentary champagne. There was an air of subdued affluence, hinting that it was a very exclusive exhibition, and she suddenly lost her nerve and wondered if she could leave without too much trouble.

But before she had chance to do an about turn, an immaculately turned out woman wearing a grey silk trouser suit that rippled as she walked greeted her warmly, enclosing Emerald's hand in both of her own, her fingers all soft skin and glossily shining pink fingertips. 'Emerald Montrose, lovely to meet you at last. You are becoming quietly famous around these parts.'

'I am?' She gazed around at the empty room, wondering at the whereabouts of these supposed people who thought she was famous. She frowned. 'Have I mistaken the date?'

'Not at all, my dear. I'm afraid I amended your invitation. I needed you to come earlier than the rest of the guests. You see, you are exhibiting some of your exquisite paintings here today.'

Emerald narrowed her eyes. 'I am?' she repeated.

The woman's laugh echoed throughout the room, bouncing off the blond-wood herringbone flooring and the flock wallpaper, the embossed birds of paradise and exotic flowers fairly vibrating with colour. 'Your cousin Suzie arranged it.' She passed her mobile phone over to Emerald. 'My name is Anna Greenfield-Howes. Call her if you are concerned.'

Emerald took the phone from the stranger to see her cousin's number already programmed in, showing up brightly on the display. She passed the phone back. 'It's fine. I'm sure she has my best interests at heart . . . but I am surprised she didn't tell me — or want to come with me.'

The woman ignored Emerald's query as she flipped open her bag and took out an engraved business card which she held out to Emerald with a flourish. 'Here's my card.' *Art Consultant* with long telephone numbers was printed underneath her name.

Emerald studied it. It seemed Anna Greenfield-Howes had offices in Milan, New York and London and had all sorts of letters after her name, denoting qualifications that Emerald had no clue about, though she presumed they were relevant in the world of art.

'Okay then. What happens next?' she asked, slightly confused but happy to go along with it.

The woman's smile reappeared as she passed Emerald an elegant folder, her manicured nails tapping on the front of it.

'Here's your itinerary. Your sponsors will shadow you and your potential customers will show their interest, so be prepared to answer questions about where you get your inspiration, your artistic style — that kind of thing.'

Emerald tried not to let her jaw drop. 'I have sponsors? How come? What on earth is going on here? It sounds like some kind of weird auction.'

'It's simply a way of maximising your sales. Your work will be exhibited alongside some of the finest new artists in the world. This has taken a lot of preparation, but as long as you let me take care of everything, tonight you will be acknowledged for the exceptional artist that you are.'

Emerald was sceptical. 'But I only knew about this last week. Who is behind the exhibition?' She knew that a huge injection of funds were necessary for any exhibition, let alone one that was on the scale that this one was shaping up to be. She watched as works of art were carried through the door, many pictures already adorning the gallery, she could see just through the corridor.

The woman's eyes levelled with hers. 'Yes, that's true.' She looked at her watch. '*Bene.*'

Emerald's stomach flipped at the single Italian word. 'This is to do with Marco Cavarelli, isn't it?'

The beautiful head of Anna Greenfield-Howes tilted to one side, her elaborate coiffure barely moving. She looked at Emerald as if the odds of her actually knowing anyone of worth would be slight. Emerald detected the implication, from the angle of her head, that if any crumbs of interest came from a sponsor she should be extremely grateful.

Emerald bristled, her sense of unease deepening. 'I don't want to go anywhere near that man.'

'I don't know the sponsor personally, but I would suggest you consider very carefully whether or not to take this opportunity. You might never have this chance again, and believe me, if you are serious about your art you will regret such a decision.' Her demeanour had changed and her eyes raked over Emerald as if she was now unworthy of such a proffered gift.

Emerald had debated at length whether wearing her Doc Martens with a dress was a good move, but was determined to be true to herself these days and the Docs had stayed. She now looked down at the beautifully polished wooden floor and felt a twinge of worry that she might leave indents.

She stepped inside the main hall to hear a female voice firing off a volley of orders in unmistakable Italian. She shot a quizzical glance back towards the Greenfield-Howes woman, who seemed — Emerald wasn't sure why — to be acting as some kind of agent, and she, in response, inclined her head. 'There's our host. I'll introduce you in a minute.'

Emerald, confused by these people supposedly in charge of the exhibition, nevertheless breathed out a sigh of relief as her initial fear that Marco was involved began to fade. She watched an older lady gesticulating in a typical Italian style, as young men did her bidding, the former's keen eyes missing nothing as the men hoisted paintings on and off walls. Her importance in the exhibition was clear and everyone danced to her attendance as she fired out rapid sentences in a mixture of accented English and Italian.

Emerald turned around, slowly, and in awe, forgetting about Marco for a moment, as she caught a glimpse of a world of mystique she hadn't known existed. She smiled wryly: Italian people, Italian design and the Italian language — and not a Marco in sight. She would have to get used to hearing Italian without automatically assuming he would be lurking somewhere.

'Ah, Mrs G. How lovely to see you again.' Anna Greenfield-Howes greeted the elegantly dressed lady as she came towards them, her black lace dress and string of glossy pearls at her throat shouted Italian sophistication. 'Please, may I introduce Emerald Montrose?' She turned to Emerald. 'Emerald, Signora Giovanelli is from one of the great houses of Florence. Her family have a long history of art academia, which, combined with great investments, has made her one of the most influential art dealers in the world.'

The host inclined her head towards Emerald. 'So, this is the talented young lady we have been so looking forward to meeting.' She smiled elegantly at Emerald. 'Welcome, Emerald. Maria will show you to a room where you can change.' She gestured to a young woman waiting behind her.

'Change?'

'An outfit has, I believe, been laid out for you.'

Emerald's brow creased in bewilderment. Surely that wasn't normal? She looked down at her slightly outlandish outfit and back up at Signora Giovanelli, who was indeed dressed as if attending a cocktail party. But Emerald liked her own style and was loath to change just to accommodate visitors to an art gallery. It was also bloody weird.

As Emerald dithered, Maria inclined her head and directed Emerald up the stairs.

She huffed out a breath in annoyance. 'Okay, fine, show me the way,' she said, allowing herself to be led up a winding staircase.

Maria pushed open a door leading off the landing, instructing Emerald to return to the downstairs lobby as soon as she was ready. She led her into an opulent room with washed silk ivory festoon blinds and muted gold lamps. *What was this?* Something wasn't right and Emerald's heart thudded with anxiety as Maria retreated silently, closing the door behind her.

A fitted red dress made from gossamer-like silk, with a thin silver belt, was hooked over the wardrobe door on a hanger, and a pair of silver high-heeled sandals sat snugly in a box surrounded by tissue paper. Once again, thoughts of Marco returned. It was similar to the dress she'd bought in Edinburgh to show him she was not a woman to be ignored. Her heart did a sad little flip at the memory.

She pushed away her thoughts. It was all in the past and she had to think of the future now. She ventured closer, puzzled, as she touched the beautiful dress and allowed the fluid fabric to slide through her fingers, appreciating the fine silk. She knew it would fit her without needing to hold it up against her body and wondering who cared enough to make sure of it. It was most odd. Why hadn't Suzie mentioned anything about this?

She decided to phone her and find out but as she reached for her phone an unmistakeable voice said, 'It's so that you stand out from the crowd — not that a dress would make any difference. All very standard for a sophisticated gallery opening.' The deep, unmistakable voice resounded in the room and Emerald whipped her head around to find the source of the voice, her heart racing.

Marco, sitting casually in a leather chair, his legs crossed at the ankles, smiled as if it was only yesterday that they'd last spoken.

Emerald gasped with shock as a mixture of anger and reluctant joy flooded through her body. 'I bloody knew it.'

'Lovely to see you too, Emerald. I've missed you.'

'You've kidnapped me!'

He laughed, the deep rumble she remembered so well. 'Always the drama queen.'

'Well, what else do you call this, then — manoeuvring me into a risky situation, making me dress up for you?'

'Dress up for *me*? Good grief, you make me sound like something out of a Liam Neeson thriller. You should be an actress, not an artist.' He spoke quietly and she, almost involuntarily, stepped closer to him, noticing that his face was strained, if not downright unhappy, the grooves around his eyes etched deeper into his skin.

'The exhibition starts in one hour. Half a dozen or so of the finest new artists, including you, will be presenting and discussing their art. You have the talent to succeed, so we — your cousin Suzie, and myself — have procured the services of the renowned Baroness Greenfield-Howes from start to finish, to ensure everything runs as smoothly as it should for you.'

She stared at him, speechless. 'I thought you'd given up on me.'

'Our relationship maybe, but I will not give up on your talent.'

She nodded slowly, taking his words in.

'I'm trying to make amends, Emerald.'

'You did all of *this*?' She waved a hand towards the door indicating the exhibition on the other side of it, and the dress. 'I didn't ask for your help and I don't need it.'

'Emerald you have an extraordinary talent and I would like to see it nurtured.'

'Then it's a shame you didn't make more of an effort at nurturing it when you had the chance.' She bit her lip as the pain she'd tried so hard to conquer rushed back, knocking the fight out of her. All she'd wanted was his love and loyalty.

Suddenly it all flooded out. 'You knew about my struggles in life, you knew how hard it was for me to trust anyone — and still you let me fall in love with you. I could have survived on your love alone. Instead you threw everything I offered right back at me. You betrayed me.' She could hear that she sounded pitifully like a child wailing, but she couldn't help it.

'I waited for you to call me when you'd cooled down, so I could explain, but you never did,' he shot back. 'And I found you — but you tried to kill me. Death by bronze — not a heroic way to go.'

'Now who's being a drama queen?' She couldn't resist saying it.

Marco's smile was half-hearted though, as if he struggled to rise to the occasion. Maybe he had struggled, Emerald thought, melting slightly.

'Honestly . . .' He paused. 'Too much rides on this exhibition for you to become upset right now. I just want to help.'

'Like you helped me in my last career? No thank you.'

'That was a misunderstanding.'

'How on earth is it possible to misunderstand the text you sent me? You made my position quite clear.'

He breathed out heavily. 'Okay, I got things wrong, but this is not the time or the place. Stay for the exhibition, chat to the guests and let them put a face to the amazing artist that you are.'

Glowering at Marco, she tried to clear her jumbled brain. It was alarming to find herself face to face with him again, and her instinct was to run — but her art was all she had left now, and it *was* tempting to talk to the experts. He certainly owed her for ending her flying career. She paused. 'Very well, but then I'm going home and I'll have no need to see you again.'

He stood up, and if she didn't know how ruthless he was, she would swear she saw sorrow in his eyes. 'Don't do this to us.'

'There is no *us*.'

He took a step towards her. 'You say that, but I know my face haunts your dreams. Deny it if you can.'

Emerald took a step backwards to keep her distance. 'How would you know such a thing?'

'Because *your* face haunts my dreams.'

She paused, took a breath. 'Don't flatter yourself, Mr Cavarelli.' She fairly spat out his name. 'It was only ever a fling.'

'No, it was not.' His half smile was knowing, as if he could read her thoughts. He took a step closer — was just inches away from her. She yearned to lean in to him, to remind herself of the warmth of his skin, his singular masculine smell, feel his lips on hers — just one more time. No, she would not allow her desire to betray her. 'I've moved on, Mr Cavarelli. I don't need you in my life.'

Marco closed his eyes briefly and when he opened them Emerald was gratified to see raw pain in them, but her triumph was short-lived when he nodded curtly.

'So be it.' He took a step away from her, spinning on his heel.

She faltered. She didn't want him to leave but he'd already reached the door. 'Marco?' she called.

He turned around, his face cold and devoid of emotion as he stared straight at her, waiting, his hand resting on the door-knob.

But no words would come out. She'd spent so long trying to hate him that she didn't know how to be nice.

The silence lengthened until Marco, with a tight smile, said, 'You're welcome.' He closed the door behind him, leaving Emerald, once again, wrong-footed for being ungrateful and not being able to speak her mind.

CHAPTER THIRTY-ONE

Emerald had never been the centre of attention before, apart from when she was thrown from Star and woke up to find herself flat on her back in the sand with a sea of worried faces looking down at her. It was disconcerting that she appeared to have gone from a nobody to a minor celebrity in a matter of minutes. It was also very strenuous work pretending to be what everyone expected her to be, when she wasn't sure herself who that person was.

She felt tight as a drum, highly strung and worn out from the adrenaline high. Most of her anxiety was because of Marco's proximity rather than the fact that she was being flattered, interrogated and even pawed at, by a variety of men with foreign accents, and presumably, huge bank balances.

She was exhausted and tense, having spotted Marco at various points of the exhibition — surrounded, it seemed, by women. They all gravitated towards him: willowy beauties, dark-haired sex sirens, sophisticated women with laughs that matched their tinkling gold bracelets. They were everywhere, and she acknowledged that his world was light years away from hers.

She was out of her depth with Marco — always had been. She had pretended, hoped, that the imbalance between their lives would be surmountable, but deep down she knew she was destined to be the one standing at the edge of the playground hoping someone would ask her to join in. She was grateful that Marco had arranged this for her, but she would slip away as soon as she could and resume the life she could handle.

Eventually the exhibition died down and she allowed herself to be congratulated by Anna Greenfield-Howes and Signora Giovanelli as she sipped at a glass of pink champagne. The whole day had been surreal from start to finish and she was still struggling to believe that art experts considered her to be so talented that they were prepared to pay out thousands of pounds for her work, or to sponsor her to exhibit at up-and-coming exhibitions around the world.

She'd stopped looking for Marco, who, having earlier been everywhere her gaze rested, was now nowhere in sight. She was glad of it really, she decided, as she snuck back up the stairs to retrieve her clothes.

When she opened the door, Marco was once again sitting in the chair he had vacated earlier. He stood up. 'You were wonderful, Emerald. I am very proud of you.'

She nodded. 'Not wishing to be rude, but really it's not your place to be proud of me.' *He'd given that right away*, she thought churlishly.

'It seems that you are already richer than you were this morning, and your name will soon be on most of the art world's lips. Would you like to celebrate? Just say the word and I will arrange it. Anything. The whole universe is yours. I have a helicopter standing by and within half an hour we can be up in the air.'

'I just want to go home, Marco,' she said. 'Don't do this to me. I can't think straight.'

Marco's face fell at her bald statement. 'But you look so beautiful in that dress that you deserve to go somewhere wonderful. I'll take you to Venice, Paris — you name it.'

'No, thank you. I'd like to get out of this dress and get a cab home.' She plucked at the fabric of the dress as if it burned her, impatient now to return to her own world.

Marco inclined his head, his facial expressions once again blank. 'As you wish.' He walked towards her, stopping inches away. 'Allow me to help you.' He raised his hand to her shoulder as he took another step forward. He looked her in the eye. 'Yes?'

Their eyes met and slowly, very slowly she turned around for him to unzip her dress. She stood as still as a statue. She wouldn't let him see that his touch bothered her.

He hooked one finger around the strap of the dress and slid it past her shoulder.

Her lips trembled. She wanted to protest, but she was mesmerised. He slid the other strap down over her shoulder, the slight touch of his fingertips setting her skin alight. He dropped the lightest of kisses on her bare shoulder and she shuddered.

She couldn't move. It was as if Marco's touch had frozen her to the spot even as her skin burned up.

He drew the zip all the way down to her lower back. The sliding sensation of the cold zip and the air chilling her skin made her shiver, but not as much as Marco's breath, cooling on her neck.

If she didn't clutch the dress to her chest it would fall away from her body. She was so tempted to let it pool to her feet — to prove that whatever Marco did, it wouldn't move her.

Dear God, she wanted him, but she would not let him control her in this way. The craving that rippled through her core was becoming unbearable as Marco trailed his fingers across her shoulders.

It was time to call a halt. She would be lost if she permitted him to take one more liberty with her. Goosebumps peppered her arms and she tried to stop the shiver that ran down her spine.

Did he really think she was going to allow him to take off her dress? But she yearned to feel his touch and her breath quickened as she struggled to remain composed.

As if her thoughts had transferred to him, his fingers traced down her spine, trailing indecisively, but temptingly, down to her bottom. Her nipples ached, waiting for his caress, her breasts straining as heat suffused her body.

He moved yet closer and whispered into her ear, finally bringing her to her senses. '*Cara mia*, I think we both know we were more than just a fling.'

She clutched at the bodice of the dress, pressing it to her breasts to stop it from sliding to the floor in a sheath of slithering satin, and then decided, yes, she would let it fall, to remind Marco of what he had lost. She prepared herself.

'I can undress myself, Mr Cavarelli,' she breathed. She took a step away from him, turned around and fixed her eyes on his, as she let go of the dress. His eyes widened and she stared back defiantly. The dress slid slowly, seductively, to her feet, a scarlet testimony of gravity, leaving her naked apart from her white lacy briefs and silver high heels. 'See?'

Hunger burned in Marco's eyes as he took in her curves and she stood motionless and proud, inviting him to look. Her eyes, grave but rebellious, refused to release their hold on his. *Look what you lost*, they said. At least that was what she hoped they said. Physically, she craved his touch, her skin ached with a desperate longing.

Marco's gaze travelled over her body and stopped at the softness of her breasts. His fingers twitched but he held his arms stiffly by his sides. She silently commended him on his restraint, even though she saw him swallow hard a couple of times.

It was enough to bring her out of her trance. She wasn't the trusting young woman who would fall for an easy line and a soft touch anymore. She stepped out of the dress and slipped off the shoes, leaving them neatly inside the circle of satin. Unspoken words hovered in the air and Marco took a step forward, his eyes questioning.

Electricity crackled between them and she almost met him halfway. It would be so easy. Her every sense was liquefied with molten heat and she was grateful for the slight breeze that fanned her skin, unable to believe that she could be so aroused without even being touched. Marco did that to her. It was enough of a reminder that she needed to move before she lost the self-control to refuse him.

He raised his hand to touch her, to claim her, a soft smile playing around his mouth. She sidestepped away from his reach, stopping him in his tracks. 'Think again, Mr Cavarelli.' Her words sounded husky and sexy, giving away her state of mind, but she didn't care. She would not waver now.

Confusion clouded Marco's eyes, although he covered it quickly. *Good*, Emerald thought. Maybe he would finally understand what he had given up. She was gratified to see a flash of hurt in his eyes too, as she turned her back on him to retrieve her own clothes.

She allowed herself a brief moment of regret, closing her eyes against the pleasure she had just lost, but she knew it would be transient, and she had no room for such an indulgence if she wanted to keep her pride.

Marco, ever the one in command, had already recovered from their hypnotic stand-off. 'Keep the dress — and the shoes. They are Manolo Blahniks — I had them especially made for you.'

The click of a door catch told her that he had left. She spun around but all that was left in the room, apart from a tumble of scarlet satin and a pair of silver sandals, was an empty leather chair, alone in the middle of the floor.

CHAPTER THIRTY-TWO

The months since her official launch as an artist had been good to Emerald and she easily earned enough to move back to her apartment. She was financially secure and upbeat again, although acute loneliness tugged at her in the evenings. She had spent her life looking after herself and was used to her own company, but since rebuffing Marco, a different kind of loneliness emptied out her reserves of composure, even though she was busy most evenings, sorting out gallery pictures and interviews.

Marco had, as she had anticipated, returned to Italy — according to Finbar — and she endeavoured to forget all about him. She mostly failed, especially when she met up with Finbar, who talked non-stop about how loved up he was with one of the stewards he'd recruited specifically because he had "eyes you could drown in". Finbar appeared to be running the new airline splendidly, and Marco had shown his face and then upped and left almost as soon as the first flight had become airborne, as if his sole purpose had now been completed and he'd lost interest.

Emerald felt incomplete — suspended in time, as if the present was transient and she was waiting for her real life to start again. It kept her on the wrong side of happiness and she was tired of being unhappy. She simply played out the role that was expected of her, listening to Anna's sage advice and entering into the world of promotion and marketing with as much enthusiasm as she could muster.

She appeared to have been allowed into an inner sanctum of eclectic artists who were in Anna's care, and was more often than not ferried to her destinations in a private aircraft or helicopter as if it were no more than an Uber cab.

To this end, one sunny day in July, she boarded an aeroplane to Florence, her thoughts turning inevitably to Marco as she took her seat. It was a private business aircraft and there were four other passengers, accompanied by Anna, attending the opening of a large gallery that was going to display their work. All were Italian and their native tongue was music to her ears, although it brought a kind of sadness with it too. She was looking forward to visiting Italy once more and it made her wonder if she was perhaps cured of Marco, since she was feeling overall so positive about the trip.

The aircraft landed with barely a quiver of silver wings as rubber met tarmac, and the procedure she was becoming used to started all over again: handing their passports to a waiting representative who took them to customs, settling into a black Mercedes and sitting back enjoying the view from the window until they arrived at their swanky hotel. She supposed Marco had lived like this for all of his adult life. It certainly made life a lot easier. Money talks, they said. It certainly did.

She climbed out of the car at their hotel destination then froze, her senses on overdrive. She'd been to this particular hotel before — it was where she'd had the disastrous meeting with Rick, her almost then-boyfriend, as she thought of him now. That meant that Marco's hotel was only minutes away, she realized with a pang. Although she knew that the odds on him being there were slight, she couldn't shake it from her mind.

She showered and changed, flicked the television channels over, checked her notes and marked off in her iPad the pictures that were up for sale. But still she couldn't settle. In the end she picked up her key card and popped it in her handbag. She knew where she was heading, even though she didn't know why.

The hotel was no more than a short stroll away and she took in the surroundings that she remembered so well. She half expected a feeling of remorse and shame to consume her as she thought of the fateful night that she had met Marco, but her memories were surprisingly comforting.

She paused outside Marco's hotel, unsure if she wanted to go inside, but she took a deep breath. *Just for old times' sake*, she told herself striding determinedly into the *Crepuscolo* bar. She gazed up at the magnificent ceiling, wishing she could see the replica that he had created in the refurbished hotel in the Isles of Scilly.

She sat down on one of the bar stools, her movements mimicking those of that fateful day, except, of course, for the glaring absence of the lead male role. Ordering a sparkling water, she glanced at the bartender, but it wasn't the same man as before.

As she sipped at her drink, annoyed at herself for dwelling on past events, the bartender pushed a bowl of olives towards her. She noticed with a jolt the plastic daggers spearing their tender hearts and felt as if she was on some kind of a time loop. Olives were one of those foods she wasn't sure if she loved or hated, but she picked one up and toyed with it, anyway. She decided to try one and raised it to her mouth, when she was stopped by a voice behind her.

'Careful, they're tricky little buggers, if I remember rightly.'

She spun around, almost toppling off her seat. Marco stood there, eyes narrowed as his gaze skimmed over her drink. He looked away immediately, but not before Emerald had seen the movement.

'Sorry, old habits and all that,' he said.

Emerald's heart was pounding. She had thought she wanted to put an end to the memories, but now that Marco was standing in front of her, she realized that wasn't why she had come at all.

'Why are you here? I thought we'd said all we had to say.' His tone wasn't aggressive, but neither was it the *welcome home, darling*, greeting she might have preferred.

'I was thirsty.' She took a hefty swig of her drink to prove the point, offended by his bitter tone.

He picked up an olive and popped it into his mouth. 'And I'm quite hungry.' He looked at her. 'Why don't we go for something to eat?'

She hunched over her drink in the possessive way she had done the last time she was in this bar. 'I'm fine right here,' she mumbled into her drink, the hairs prickling on her neck as she felt his eyes on her back.

'Fine. May I sit here?'

'Your bar — sit where you like.' She cursed her words. *Why was she being like this?*

Marco ran his fingers through his hair, clicked his tongue in annoyance and shook his head. 'I'm so pleased to see you have matured since the last time I saw you.'

She couldn't help but laugh. She was being childish but he brought out the worst in her sometimes. He was so bloody proper. She straightened her spine. 'Hello, Mr Cavarelli. No, I don't know why I came here tonight, either, except that I was passing and I thought I'd take a walk down memory lane, since I have such fond memories of our time together.' She waved to the barman. 'A white wine, please, a large one.'

Marco fired off some Italian at the bartender and he reached under the counter.

Something snapped in Emerald. 'Don't tell me I'm getting water again! I am a bloody grown up and if I want a glass of wine, I'll have a bloody glass of wine.'

'*Si, Signore.*' The bartender brought out a chilled bottle and two glasses. He kissed his fingertips. 'One of the best in the house.'

She looked at him suspiciously. 'Oh,' she said, disconcerted.

Marco said, 'I just thought that if you were determined to do this again, you might as well have a good vintage. Less of a hangover the next day, too.'

'Oh, okay. Sorry.' She huddled back over her drink. She should leave right now, but she felt an invisible thread pulling her towards Marco. Her mind told her she needed to break the thread and walk, but her body was egging her on to weave it tighter still.

Marco poured the pale liquid into each of the glasses and lifted one up towards her. 'Cheers.' He took a sip and put the glass back on its little mat. 'That is a very good wine, try it.'

She looked at him, puzzled. What was he trying to do, pretend that nothing had changed, or act as if they were on a date? She lifted the wine to her lips and the aroma hit her before the taste. A heady mix of honey and vanilla assailed her and she closed her eyes, savouring the taste before the liquid slid gloriously down her throat.

Marco looked at her closely, a small smile playing around his lips. '*Sì*. That is how you should drink wine.'

She nodded, almost speechless as the flavours teased her palette. She gazed into her glass, aware that Marco continued to stare at her, his eyes gentle. He reached out a hand and although she recoiled at his immediate touch, he didn't draw it away, but started trailing circles on the skin of her wrist until she felt obliged to look at him.

'Emerald.' His voice was gentle and he sounded weary. 'Can we please move on from this?'

'I gave myself to you and I trusted you — and you repaid me by sacking my colleagues — and me.' She'd been through this before, told him this before, and yet she hadn't been aware how deep her hurt ran as her eyes pooled with tears, even though she was boiling with anger. She dashed the tears away savagely and glared at him.

'Emerald, I needed to get rid of dishonest staff, you must see that.'

Emerald was open-mouthed at such logic. 'But not me!' She picked up her wine glass and took a huge slug.

'No, not you, that was never part of the plan, if you'd let me explain. And can I just mention — that is really not the best way to appreciate that particular wine.' He pointed a finger at the bottle, but hastily withdrew it when Emerald shot him a withering look and drained her glass in a single gulp. 'Quit telling me what to do, will you? I didn't mind when I was in love — when I knew no better — but you have no rights over me now.'

'Okay, you can drink it that way, if you wish.'

He winced as she slammed the glass down.

'Emerald,' his voice held a note of urgency. 'Please take the time to listen to me, if nothing else.'

She sighed and thrust out her chin, looking at him mutinously. 'Okay. Go on.'

'Can we at least retire to my rooms to talk this through?' He picked up the bottle of wine and his glass, indicating for her to follow.

She pulled a face behind his back and regretted it, feeling as if she'd betrayed Marco when she caught the eye of the bartender who sniggered conspiratorially. She snagged her glass and caught up with Marco. 'You have rooms here?'

'Yes, on the top floor. My family and I use them when we are on business, but I find that recently, I have been staying here more often.' This was the first Emerald had heard about it — but then, she knew little about Marco's private life. They walked to the top floor, Emerald puffing a little. 'Haven't you heard of lifts?'

He threw her a smile. 'It would be sacrilege to change this beautiful building, would it not?'

She gazed around at the intricate panelling and the large entrance hall that could be seen from the first-floor gallery and had to agree with him. Stone statues and formidable portraits brought back uncomfortable memories, and she turned away from the imposing figures, lest they remembered the drunken girl of earlier and looked down their aristocratic noses once more.

Marco unlocked a large oak door at the very top of the building with an old-fashioned brass key and kicked it open with his foot, holding the wine bottle and his glass in the other hand. Light flooded in through slatted blinds and Emerald blinked as her eyes adjusted to the bright sunshine. She looked around as she waited by the doorway for Marco to invite her in, noticing a decidedly feminine touch in the Italian decor. She wondered if his wife had chosen the furnishings.

As if reading her mind, Marco said, 'My mother collects the Royal Copenhagen figurines. She comes here in the winter when it's cold in the mountains.' He studied Emerald, apparently wondering what to do with her now she was in front of him. 'Let's sit on the balcony. The sun isn't so fierce now.' He opened the large French windows and stepped outside inviting Emerald to join him.

She followed him outside and sat on a rattan sofa with big squashy cushions. Marco sat down next to her, closer than was comfortable and she shifted over a few inches.

He breathed in, pressed the bridge of his nose with his thumb and forefinger, and took a long breath out as he studied her and considered his words. 'Emerald.' He reached out a hand and touched her hair, running a rogue tendril through his fingers. 'Emms.' He smiled weakly, testing her, and she smiled back, suddenly shy. It was such an insignificant moment but it seemed to melt away all of the hostility that had backed up, festering in her mind and stopping her from living.

She looked at the man she'd missed so much, and wanted, right then, to turn the clock back. 'I'm so sorry about how it's all been, Marco.' Tears pricked her eyes and she wondered when she had become such a baby. She was always blubbing these days. 'It's just . . . I'm so lonely without you.'

But if she thought Marco would fall at her feet at her apology then she had read him all wrong.

'I understand that you were hurt by my actions, but you misunderstood them. As you know, I take the security of my business very seriously and let me assure you that none of my actions came from anything you told me in the Scilly Isles. I needed people I could trust. It was purely business and there was no room for emotion.'

Emerald nodded, taking in his proud face, his jaw with just a hint of stubble, his impeccable business suit, and the tie — undone just slightly, adding to the overall package of a successful man in control of his life. She wanted him to kiss away her own unhappiness. She wanted him to love her in return, and if he didn't react soon she thought she might throw her arms around him and beg him to make love to her there and then.

'I am sorry that we can't be together but I realize we are too different, yet too similar in our determination and our principles.' Marco looked down at his hands, unhappily.

What the . . . ? 'Sorry, I wasn't concentrating. What did you say?' She was convinced she'd misheard him, but her fingers started to tremble.

'I said I'm sorry that we could not make it work, and I understand. I just wanted to explain why I acted the way I did.'

'That's all?'

He nodded. 'Thank you for giving me this opportunity.'

Emerald had to remind herself to close her mouth. 'So, when I saw you at the exhibition and . . . I, err, became undressed.' She swallowed hard. 'Is that what you were going to tell me?'

'Became undressed?' He smiled at her words but nodded in acquiescence. 'In essence, yes.'

Heat flashed across her cheeks at the memory of what she'd done — enticing him to stare at her in an almost naked state. She closed her eyes. *Dear God, would it never end?* 'Okay, thanks for putting the record straight.' She picked up her bag. 'I'm glad we've sorted that out. I'd better get going now.'

'No, please . . . Finish your drink first.' Marco tried to grasp her hand but she was too quick for him.

'Gotta go, bye. Thanks again,' she added for no discernible reason other than inherent good manners, and was out of the door before he could stop her.

She didn't stop until she had fled down the stairs and out of the hotel, where she leaned against the outside wall, gasping for breath, screwing up her eyes against the pain. It hurt too much. Everything to do with Marco hurt too much. It had to stop. This was the end of it.

She pushed herself away from the wall, resolutely. She would finish her tour at the end of the week and start afresh. She would not dream of what might have been, or look over her shoulder every time she heard an Italian accent.

Her old life was finally done.

CHAPTER THIRTY-THREE

By the time the exhibition tour started, Emerald had regained her equilibrium and was more positive in her mind about her career. Now that Marco was definitely out of the equation, she could embrace the art world and focus on herself.

She zipped herself into a cream linen dress with short sleeves and a sweetheart neckline and slipped on some navy wedges. The dress was modest but suited her hair colouring and emphasized the deepening tan she'd acquired while sitting in the traffic-free piazzas, sketching the street vendors and the locals.

She glanced in the mirror and was surprised, as she often was these days, to see the reflection of a tall, willowy woman with high cheekbones and full lips. She liked what she saw and hoped that another corner had been turned as a new assertive Emerald emerged. Slicking on some pink lip gloss, she set off for the exhibition, tucking her invitation to *Retrospection and Introversion* into her bag even though she was now well known enough not to need to show an invitation.

The exhibition she was visiting that day was a relaxed affair, giving Emerald time to stroll around to look at the other paintings when there was a quiet moment. She turned in to an alcove by a large door, which she'd missed earlier, to find a cluster of pictures lining the walls. She guessed this was the "introversion" part of the exhibition where serene pastels, watercolours and gentle charcoal portraits were intended to calm the mind.

One wall was full of charcoals and she moved towards it to get a better look at the style of the artist. They were tastefully framed charcoals, quite small but perfectly executed. As she grew closer, her eyes widened in disbelief. Her hand flew to her mouth as she stifled a cry. *Where the hell had they come from?*

She reached out and touched one, tracing the contours of the face she knew so well, shaking her head, unable to believe that her love for this man had been laid bare for everyone to see. Each portrait showed Marco Cavarelli at his most vulnerable: a close-up of him asleep on a sofa, his eyelashes fanning his cheek, his jaw jutting pleasingly as the light hit it from the window of an aeroplane. His expression was serious as he worked over his laptop.

There was even the very first one she'd drawn of him, with steam coming out of his ears and horns on his head. That was framed in red and drew the eye straight to it.

'These are excellent, aren't they?' Anna sidled up to Emerald and studied the pictures. 'It was fortunate that we could include them in the exhibition. They lend just the right tone, promoting what we are trying to achieve — not just trying to sell art for profit, you know?'

'Where . . . where did you get them?' Emerald stammered, thrown by the images on display when she'd thought they were safely tucked away somewhere.

'Why, Marco Cavarelli loaned them to us. He is the patron of the exhibition and it was wonderful that he could add these.' Anna peered at them. 'They're not signed, but the artist must be someone who knows him well. The medium of art is a wonderful way to express one's emotions, and these positively vibrate with love, don't you think?' Anna smiled gently. Emerald looked at her and knew that Anna knew.

'They're not for sale,' she exclaimed as angry tears blurred her vision.

Anna patted Emerald on the shoulder. 'Oh, no, I don't believe Mr Cavarelli would sell anything as precious as these.'

Emerald unclenched her fists, determined to regain control. It wasn't her fault that her soul had been exposed for all to see. Blinking back tears, she gave Anna a watery smile, trying her utmost to pretend nothing had changed, but inside she was seething. How dare Marco do this to her? How dare he steal her work and bare her emotions to the art world while simultaneously rejecting her? It was too much.

She walked quickly out of the exhibition, flagged down a cab and instructed the driver to go straight to Marco's hotel. She didn't care if he was there or not — she would bloody well wait all night if she had to.

She marched across the marble floor and up the staircase, her anger driving her on, until she stopped outside Marco's door. She took a deep, steadying breath which made no difference whatsoever and rapped on the door, almost crying with fury.

Marco opened the door and she launched herself through it, stumbling in her haste. 'Emerald, what a lovely surprise!' He tried to kiss her cheek but she lashed out at him.

'Get away from me. I don't want you to touch me!' Her eyes blazed.

'So it seems.' He raised his hands and stepped away from her.

She squared her shoulders and glared at him. 'You.' She stabbed a finger in the air. 'You do nothing but betray me.' She pushed his shoulder as he stepped forward, swiping at her eyes. 'I hate you.'

'Then why are you here?'

'To tell you how much I hate you.'

He inclined his head as if it was a satisfactory explanation. 'Please calm down.' He planted himself in front of her and tried to pull her into his arms. He reached out to stroke her hair, making soothing noises, but she pushed his chest as hard as she could, to free herself from his grip.

'Get off me.'

'Emerald, what is going on?'

'You stole my portraits, my pictures, my *soul*.'

Marco sighed, his shoulders sagging perceptibly. 'It's not all about you, you know, I was helping out the organizers of the exhibition.'

His blasé attitude incensed Emerald, who stood with clenched fists, breathing so heavily she could barely speak, her jaw aching with the tension.

Marco simply glanced at her, inclined his head and said, 'Come through.' He led her into the sitting room, leaned against a table, folded his arms and studied her.

'Please don't think I want to be here. I had no intention of ever seeing you again,' she said through gritted teeth, taking in the open laptop with a mug of coffee cooling next to it.

'And yet . . .' He motioned with his hand, pointing out the obvious.

'I know, here I am again, but . . .' The white-hot anger that had carried her through the streets of Florence as she railed against him, dissipated as she finally took in his face, his body, his everything — every single thing that she loved. She felt her lips tremble and bit her lower lip determined not to cry as she stared at him, loving him, wanting him. He looked cool and composed in a perfectly fitting crisp, blue linen shirt rolled up to the elbows, his dark eyes confused as he listened to her ranting at him. She hated him for it.

Yes, she hated him so much. How could he treat her in such a way? 'Do you know what? I'm done here with you. Take my pictures, take my mind, my heart . . .'

'Emerald. All I did was display your very fine charcoals at the exhibition—'

'You showed everyone!' She fell into a chair, uninvited, as her legs gave way.

'I showed everyone what?'

'You bared my soul and it was not yours to show. How dare you?' She rubbed at her eyes, smearing mascara across her cheeks.

'But there was nothing to tell — you told me that. You assured me, if I remember rightly, that there was nothing between us — that it was just a fling.'

Emerald clenched and unclenched her fists. She really thought she might break down into full-on sobbing, if she stayed much longer. 'I hate you.'

'So you said.'

She glared at him, wanting him, just for once, to shout back, or admit that he was in the wrong. Was he even capable of emotion? 'Bloody man,' she hissed.

Marco lifted an eyebrow but made no comment.

She shook her head and ran a hand across her forehead, utterly deflated. There was nothing left that he could do to her, now. She gathered herself, intending at least to leave with a shred of dignity. 'If you could make sure my drawings come back to me, please.'

He studied her. 'Why did you draw my face so many times?'

'What?'

'If you hate me so much, why did you draw me so many times?'

'Because . . .'

'I'll tell you what, why don't we have a glass of champagne, while you think about the answer? I was just about to open a bottle.'

'I don't want a glass of champagne.'

But Marco ignored her and she heard the quiet pop as the cork was pulled. He nudged a glass into her hand and she held it awkwardly, grudgingly, but she could hardly drop it on the floor, much as she was tempted.

'Let's sit on the balcony, shall we?' Again, he didn't wait for her answer but picked up the bottle and his glass and took them outside. She followed, watching him surreptitiously. His own jaw was clenched and his back was rigid. He wasn't quite as relaxed as he was trying to appear, and was probably keeping hold of his own temper, she decided. She wished he would fight back — she needed him to fight back, so she could feel vindicated.

'Bloody man,' she hissed under her breath again, reluctantly joining him on the rattan sofa, once more. She sipped her champagne, the bubbles making her tongue tingle. She didn't even notice the taste of it, although she imagined it was a great vintage. She set her still-full glass down. He wasn't going to appease her that easily.

Marco turned his head towards Emerald, watching her with measured eyes, taking his time to evaluate her, and it annoyed her. She picked up her glass again under his intense scrutiny and drained it in one go.

He drew in a breath. '*Bene*! Let's talk, now you have calmed down a little.'

She narrowed her eyes. Was there no way to fluster him?

He continued. 'I was prepared to believe that you didn't want to see me again, but—'

'Just tell me why you sent me a text asking me to clear my desk,' she interrupted him. 'I think the answer to that will pretty much sum up your true character. What you did to me was . . .' She choked out the words, the remembered pain hitting her with a thump, straight to her heart. She met his eyes. 'It was unforgiveable, Marco.'

'Drink more champagne, Emms,' Marco instructed, pressing his forefinger and thumb to the bridge of his nose, an action she'd noticed he did when under duress.

She glared at him for calling her Emms as he refilled her glass.

'I want to show you something.' Marco stood up and pointed into the distance. 'Look over the hills to where the sky meets the greenery. Just there, you can see the glint of a lake if you look really hard.'

She squinted at the horizon and found a long flat roof amid a field of green, beside a lake that looked like a drop of rain it was so far away.

'What about it?'

'Next to the lake is my house. I started building it five years ago. It was to be my family home, but my wife left me for a flashier version of myself, before it was completed. She took off in my E-Type Jag — which, incidentally, I never saw again. I, unsurprisingly, didn't have the enthusiasm to finish the interior of the house and pretty much moved in here.' He leaned over the balcony railings as he gazed over the hills, his mind seemingly elsewhere. Finally, he turned around to face her.

She gulped at her champagne and stared at him. 'And?'

'Until I met you.' His statement was flat, without emotion and Emerald was once again left confused.

'When I left you in England, it was to instruct the builders to restart my *home*.' He emphasised the word *home* but he sounded weary.

Emerald was puzzled as to the relevance of his story. 'Good for you.'

Marco's voice became wistful. 'My house in the mountains is wonderful. You can see for miles on a clear day and night time, well, all the stars in the universe gather to show off.

'But, back to our conversation . . .'

'I asked you to clear your desk so that you would find the tickets for you and I to visit Florence. I had removed the barrier stopping me from declaring my intentions, as it were,' he said, talking over the top of her. 'Unfortunately, things didn't go quite to plan. As bad luck would have it, Charlotte went into labour before printing off the tickets and putting them in the envelope on your desk for you to find. I returned to England not even a week later by which time you'd already disappeared — and blocked my number.' He put his hand over his heart.

'So, your turn. Back to your drawings and why you chose to draw someone you hated so much, so *very* many times, and why you thought I had taken your soul when I borrowed your portraits.' He sat back down next to her and his eyes levelled with hers.

289

His nearness was intoxicating and she felt slightly dizzy. She really shouldn't have knocked back that glass of champagne.

'Well . . . you just shouldn't have taken them and used them without my permission.'

'The folder was in your drawer at work.'

'You had no right to look through my private things.'

'You left them behind and they were on my property.' Marco raised his hands in appeal. 'I'm sorry, that's a weak excuse, okay? But I would like to know why you are so upset about me showing them to the art world.'

Emerald took another slug of her champagne. 'It doesn't matter now.'

'It mattered fifteen minutes ago — why not now?'

She looked for an answer in her wine glass and when it wasn't forthcoming she looked at Marco instead, her eyes no longer full of hostility.

He stared her out with eyes that sparked humour and interest, mixed with a flash of exasperation. In return she brazened it out, glaring right back at him until their eyes locked.

A heartbeat passed and she waited for Marco to speak as a small smile flickered on his face and his eyes softened. 'Might it be because your love for me shone out of those drawings? I might be wrong, of course.' He raised his glass to his lips and gazed at her from over the rim.

She stared back, remembering the lips that she had sketched on paper so many times and how much she enjoyed being kissed by them, while snuggled in their owner's arms. She slid her gaze away. As if she'd confess to loving him after he'd said it was all over.

But unexpectedly he took the glass from out of her hand and trailed his fingers along her arm and upward to caress her neck, a whisper of his skin touching hers.

She shivered involuntarily. This wasn't how it was supposed to be. She was supposed to be angry with him. 'Marco, why are you touching me?'

'Because I like the softness of your skin and it's been too long since I held you.'

'Oh.' She swallowed and tried not to lean in to his caress as he drew closer. His lips hovered near her shoulder, his breath warm and inviting.

'You were about to leave, weren't you? Finish your drink first,' he whispered into her skin, which sizzled at his touch, her body heating with longing.

'I would, but it's kind of hard to pick up my glass right now . . .'

He was definitely far too close to ignore. She hovered between indecision and action, feeling confused and awkward. Should she tell him to back off or draw him closer?

He smoothed her cheek with his palm and turned her face towards his. 'I left England so that we could do this thing the right way. I did not want you to be just another rumour on the society circuit and when that journalist published the photos of us, in St Martin's, for the first time ever I felt violated — for you as well as me. Normally I just smile and shrug it off.' He shrugged now. 'And, being the old-school type, I also wanted to tell my father of my plans.'

'Oh!' The breath left her body in a rush at his words. 'I didn't know. Your plans?'

'I had thought we could marry eventually and you could live over here, in my beautiful house that is now complete, but I realize now that it was presumptuous of me to make such a huge decision on your behalf. I was taught to look after my women, but I guess it's far too outdated an idea nowadays to be considered chivalrous.'

Emerald could only stare wide-eyed at him as he continued. 'When I left you behind in England, it was to finalize my divorce. I had a newfound sense of urgency that in hindsight was probably misplaced, but it felt real at the time.' He glanced at Emerald and she thought his expression was one of someone who didn't much like what he saw.

'When we travelled to Florence together — using the tickets that never materialised — I was going to show you my house, and then we were to travel to a lovely hotel in Bora Bora for a proper holiday — where you categorically would not have needed your welly boots or a hat — and privacy is taken very seriously. That was why I asked you to clear your desk — in the disastrous text message I sent you.'

Emerald pulled away from Marco's touch. This conversation was too important for distraction. She thought for a minute before speaking. 'I spent half of my life being told what to do, before realising that no one actually cared what I did as long as it didn't interfere with their plans.' She clasped his hand in both of hers and went on. 'I'm sorry that it's made me what I am, but I don't think I'm past redemption, if — you know — you wanted to take another chance on me.'

'You don't have the monopoly on betrayal, you know. I've been hurt too,' Marco said. 'Not many people end their days unscathed by love. But to be loved you need to give love. The same with trust. I am prepared to trust you and it's a given that I love you.'

'A given, is it?' She smiled. 'Not the most romantic way for someone to say *I love you.*' A flicker of a smile crossed her face. She finally understood how hard it was for him to lay his feelings out, but everyone has a story that shapes their emotions. Nodding in understanding, she said, 'I would like there to be an *us* again.'

'So, we will work at our relationship.'

'Are you asking me, or telling me?'

'I'm hoping that you'll say what I want to hear.'

'I love you?'

He smiled. 'That's the one.' He took her hand. 'So, can we work through this, together, given your — err change in circumstances?' Marco was silent for a moment, before saying, 'By that, I mean that I'm hoping the art studio I've set up for you will be enough to entice you to my villa in the mountains. Or maybe the paddock for your horse, or maybe the infinity pool will swing it — whatever floats your boat.'

'That sounds like the purest form of bribery.' Emerald laughed, crinkling her nose as if she was thinking about his offer.

'It works for me.' Marco shrugged, grinning. Another beat passed before he leaned towards her and cupped her cheek with his hand. 'I love you and want to do right by you, just tell me what that is.' He lowered his lips to hers, delivering the softest kiss, holding infinite tenderness and love. Emerald sighed with relief. He drew away, saying, 'You have no idea how much I've missed your kiss. Stay with me, Emms, tonight.'

'And we are in it for real, this time?'

'I always was.'

Emerald smiled, forgiving him instantly. 'I'll have to phone Anna to say I won't be returning with the team.'

'I already did.'

'What? When?'

'When she called to tell me you were on your way to see me. I wasn't going to let you go this time.'

Emerald shook her head. 'And you said you'd changed!'

'Do you want me to change more?'

'No.' She smiled. 'I love you just the way you are.'

'*Bene.*' He stood and held out his hand and angled his head towards the bedroom.

She narrowed her eyes. 'Are you suggesting that we go to bed, Mr Cav.'

'We could—' he raised an eyebrow '—*reacquaint* ourselves with each other.'

'Not the subtlest offer I've received, but—'

'Let's just run with it, eh?' He grinned as she took his hand.

Emerald looked out into the distance at the sun, sending orange shards of light through the clouds, burnishing the sky and lighting up the horizon. It reminded her of a picture that hung over the chapel at St Teresa's convent. *God coming down to Earth in all His Glory*, she seemed to recall. She sucked in a breath, her gaze switching to Marco and back to the incredible sunset behind his head. Her fingers twitched in her urge to paint it.

Marco swivelled around, taking in the view. He turned back to face Emerald, his eyes wide with incredulity. 'Really?'

Her expression was rueful. 'Sorry, but . . .'

Marco's face fell.

She grinned, took his outstretched hand and said, 'There will always be another sunset,' and followed him into the bedroom.

THE END

THE CHOC LIT STORY

Established in 2009, Choc Lit is an independent, award-winning publisher dedicated to creating a delicious selection of quality women's fiction.

We have won 18 awards, including Publisher of the Year and the Romantic Novel of the Year, and have been shortlisted for countless others. In 2023, we were shortlisted for Publisher of the Year by the Romantic Novelists' Association.

All our novels are selected by genuine readers. We are proud to publish talented first-time authors, as well as established writers whose books we love introducing to a new generation of readers.

In 2023, we became a Joffe Books company. Best known for publishing a wide range of commercial fiction, Joffe Books has its roots in women's fiction. Today it is one of the largest independent publishers in the UK.

We love to hear from you, so please email us about absolutely anything bookish at choc-lit@joffebooks.com

If you want to hear about all our bargain new releases, join our mailing list: www.choc-lit.com/contact

ALSO BY JACKIE LADBURY

LOVE IS IN THE AIR
Book 1: LOVE IS IN THE AIR
Book 2: ANYONE BUT YOU
Book 3: THE TAKEOVER

STANDALONE
HAPPY CHRISTMAS EVE
THE POTTER'S DAUGHTER

Milton Keynes UK
Ingram Content Group UK Ltd.
UKHW031108280724
446129UK00004B/172